Stars Collide

by

H.P. Munro

D1713388

About the Book

It's tough growing up in the spotlight and Freya Easter has had to do just that. Being part of the Conor family, who are Hollywood acting royalty, has meant that every aspect of her family's life has been played out in the spotlight. Despite her own fame, Freya has managed to keep one aspect of her life out of the public eye. However, a new job on the hit show Front Line, and a storyline that pairs her with the gorgeous Jordan Ellis, may mean that Freya's secret is about to come out.

In a world of glitz and glamor, Jordan Ellis has come to the conclusion that all that glitters is not gold. She has become disillusioned with relationships and, longing for a deeper connection, she is surprised when it comes in the form of a most unexpected package.

Whilst their on-screen counterparts begin a romantic journey, Freya and Jordan also find themselves on a pathway towards each other.

Stars Collide is a Red Besom book

www.red-besom-books.com

eBooks are non-transferable.

Please respect the rights of the author and do not file share.

Copyright@2014, H.P. Munro

ISBN-13: 978-1499357776

All characters within this work are fictitious. Any resemblance to real persons, living or dead, is purely coincidental.

Acknowledgements

I love to write about strong, funny women and I'm fortunate that in my life I am surrounded by a plethora of them, who have provided support, laughter and unwittingly one-liners, situations, characteristics or names to my writing. So thanks goes to them.

Special thanks goes to my mum and sisters, Jackie and Lorraine, who never in their wildest imaginations ever thought they'd be avidly reading lesbian fiction. It's a family hobby now!

Thanks also to Karin for ideas, Soricha for the fruit inspiration, Cathy for the final read and Marshall for being a demon with the highlight function.

As ever a huge thank you to my wife for reading countless versions, and trying to fix the numerous errors I make while writing.

For Jane

Contents

May 2011

"What time is Daniel getting here?"

It was a struggle but Freya Easter managed not to roll her eyes at her grandmother's query.

"He should be here soon."

She was pleasantly surprised that she managed to make her tone even and not laced with the frustration that was bubbling under the surface of her wooden smile. She could predict the route this conversation was about to take, as her grandmother was nothing if not predictable when it came to her life. She waited for the inevitable 'I don't understand why you couldn't just stay together.'

"You know I've never understood why you two couldn't just stay together."

Freya turned to watch her grandmother drain her second, or was it her third, martini. Freya did a mental count, it was her second. The third usually moved the critique of Freya's life onto her career choices. Specifically, how her acting career was yet to reach the family's standard level of success. She couldn't be sure, but Freya thought that she spotted a mischievous glint in her grandmother's eye when she spoke – or it could just be the gin she'd imbibed?

"Anna, you know perfectly well why Dan and I aren't still married."

It never struck Freya as odd that when growing up she called her grandmother by her first name; but when you grow up as part of Hollywood royalty, normal is subjective. Freya had been eight before she realized that it wasn't that her parents and grandparents knew a lot of people, it was that a lot of people knew them and that not every child spent their days playing on movie sets.

"I know, it's just that in my day all of that sort of stuff was done behind closed doors," Anna huffed. She waved her martini in Freya's direction as she continued, "Rock Hudson did it, all those women in the sewing circle too."

Thankfully, her mother calling her name avoided any response from Freya. Despite not being out publically, Freya had always been honest with her family about her sexuality. Her marriage to Dan ten years ago had been a favor for her best friend to allow him to move to America. However, it had only served to confuse her grandmother.

"Dan's here sweetheart."

Freya said a quiet prayer to any deity that deemed to listen and stood to leave her grandmother sitting under the shade by the pool.

"Be a sweetie Freya and get me another," Anna called out, holding her martini glass up in the air like a small hand bell. "And while you're up at the house do something with your hair, ponytails are for children and women who sweat and you're neither."

Taking the glass, Freya made her way back towards the house deliberately swishing her ponytail as she walked to irk Anna further. She paused beside her father to swat his ass as she passed. Turning from his task of peppering steaks and heating the outside grill, he noticed the martini glass. "For you or for Anna?" he asked smiling.

Freya looked over her shoulder as she climbed the stairs towards the house, "Who do you think?"

The rich tone of her father's laugh followed her ascent. As she reached the French doors, leading into the kitchen, she could hear Dan's English accent inside.

"You are looking more fabulous each day Mrs Conor," Dan gushed, holding Freya's mother at arm's length. Dressed impeccably as ever, Dan looked tanned and relaxed in blue jeans and a white linen shirt, his dark hair tousled carelessly. However, Freya knew that despite appearances it would have taken a full hour of preening to get it to look as effortless. "If only Freya had one ounce of your grace and style."

"I know that you know I'm here, you dirt bag," Freya laughed as she stepped in.

Dan turned at the sound of her voice, his blue eyes sparkled with mischief as the look of mock horror on his face quickly dissolved into a wide grin.

"It would be no fun if you weren't listening, little Easter Egg," he replied. Walking towards her, with his arms held wide for a welcoming hug, he soon engulfed her in his arms and easily lifted her off the ground in a tight bear hug. "Are you putting on weight?" he asked as he dropped her heavily.

"You cheeky-"

"You two are impossible," Freya's mother interrupted what was no doubt about to be a colorful insult from her daughter to her best friend and ex-husband, "Make yourselves useful. Dan, mix Anna one of your martinis. Freya, come help with the potato salad."

Dan dutifully took the martini glass from Freya and held up four fingers, he raised his eyebrows in surprise when she responded with three. "So we've not made it onto your woeful career yet?" he grinned.

"Not yet, we're still on if Rock managed to marry and be gay why can't you? So if you can make it a really strong one we can skip the career chats and go straight to how much she misses Grandpa."

"Freya," her mother said in a warning tone, "be nice, please don't upset your grandmother. You know how maudlin she gets near your grandpa's birthday."

Dan acknowledged her request behind her mother's back, pouring a large measure of gin into the mixing glass with a wink.

"I know Mom, I'll behave," Freya said with resignation as she pulled ingredients from the large fridge. She smiled as her mother placed a kiss on her shoulder as she passed.

Small in height compared to her daughter, Francesca Conor was still a stunning looking woman. As a result she had managed to do something that was a rarity these days in Hollywood; her career had never faltered as she aged and she was still able to attract movie roles which younger actresses would give their capped teeth for. She was also something of an oddity, still happily married after thirty-five years to her leading man from her Oscar-winning breakout film.

Despite Dan's assertions about her grace and elegance, Freya had inherited her mother's high cheekbones, dimples and dark hair. Her height, lean athletic frame and striking green eyes were all Conor traits, passed from her grandfather to her father. Whilst she was the only one of their clan without an Oscar, TONY, BAFTA or any other type of award – although tempted, she didn't count the cup she won playing Ping-Pong at summer camp – she was undeniably a Conor. Regardless of her using Easter as her surname, one look at her beside her parents and her heritage was obvious.

"So Dan, how're things with you? I haven't seen you since New Year's," Francesca remarked, as she seemed to glide around the large kitchen, performing an intricate dance with their cook who was enduring the family's intrusion of the kitchen with thinly veiled tolerance. "I'm assuming that your absence was due to a boyfriend?"

Smoothly straining the cocktail into the glass Dan winced, "It was but, alas I find myself yet again on the shelf."

Freya turned around, her mouth open in surprise, "Oh Dan, I'm sorry. When did that happen?"

"Yesterday," Dan shrugged as he popped an olive into the glass and tossed another into the air, catching it deftly between his teeth. "It's okay, what's for you does not go by you," he said lifting the glass. "Now if you'll excuse me I am off to spend time with my favorite Hollywood legend and spirit animal."

Both mother and daughter watched his exit with thoughtful expressions.

"I don't want either of you any other way," Francesca mused. "But sometimes I do wish that your marriage had been real for both your sakes."

"Mom," Freya replied in a warning tone.

Francesca held her hands up defensively, "Only because you're both lousy at love."

"Harsh, Mom."

"True, Freya."

Freya huffed as she mixed the mayonnaise into the potatoes, jumping as her mother's arms wound around her stomach.

"She's out there just waiting for my baby to come along and sweep her off her feet," Francesca said softly, squeezing Freya gently.

"Who is?"

"The one Freya, your one."

***

"So has Freya told you her good news?"

Shooting her best friend daggers, Freya looked around at her family gathered around the outside dining table.

"It was a phase and she's not really gay?" Anna asked with a hopeful look on her face.

"Mom," Dylan Conor placed a hand on his mother's arm, "stop that."

"What? I was kidding," Anna shrugged theatrically.

"What's your news sweetheart?" Francesca asked after glowering towards her mother-in-law. Anna had the good grace to look sheepish as she sipped her drink.

"I've got a job," Freya shook her head while mentally breaking several bones in Dan's body. "They've picked up my option on *Front Line*."

The celebratory noises and barrage of questions coming from her parents and grandmother drowned out the last part of her announcement, and she shot another glare at Dan.

"Mom, Dad, Anna, please, it's really not a big thing."

Dylan rose from the table, "Of course it is honey, we must celebrate." He disappeared back towards the house to locate some champagne.

"So tell us all about it," Anna said, beckoning Freya with her hand. "Who's directing?"

Dan gave her an apologetic smile as she ground her teeth. The conversation they were about to have was exactly why she had no intention of making an announcement today. From experience, this sort of thing was better proclaimed over the phone, preferably whilst in another state, if not country.

"It's not a movie Anna, it's a TV show. I was on as a guest at the end of last season, and I'm going to be a regular next season."

Anyone watching would have thought that Freya had announced that she was planning to shave her head and ride a goat down Santa Monica Boulevard, or proclaim her membership of the Republican Party. Anna's mouth gaped open and she clutched her chest as if she had been shot. It was the exact pose that she had used in no less than twelve of her movies over the years, the only difference was that now an ill-advised face lift twenty years earlier had lessened her expression range.

"Not a movie!" Anna rasped.

Dylan reappeared with a bottle of champagne and tray of glasses.

"Put it away, don't waste it," his mother waved her hands above her head as if trying to ward off evil spirits. "She's doing the devil's work."

Putting down his load, Dylan pulled his daughter into a hug, "I think it's great. Mom, don't be such a snob."

"Your grandfather will be turning in his grave," Anna sniffed, quaffing an almost half-full martini glass.

"We cremated him Anna," Francesca said dryly towards her mother-in-law. "And Finn would be happy that Freya had got work."

Freya appreciated the effort, but her mother was blowing smoke up her ass and they both knew it. In the Conor family there was a pecking order. For her grandfather, theatre came first. He had shared billing with most of the greatest thespians to have graced a stage, and performed some of the biggest roles. His Hamlet was still regarded as amongst the best ever. Lured from the UK to Hollywood by the promise of financial gain, the highly regarded Shakespearean actor was dedicated to his craft on stage, but the canny Irishman in him also wanted to earn a bob or two. His intention was always to do a couple of films, bleed as much cash as he could out of the experience, then return to his beloved stage. However, he had not reckoned on Anna Murphy.

Anna came out of the womb tap dancing. Both her parents had been vaudevillian performers, and as soon as she could walk and talk, she'd joined the family act before being picked up by a film studio and turned into a child star – all before the age of six. Her career carried on like a relentless juggernaut and she grew into a box office banker with her musical hits. She was twenty-one when Finn Conor came to America and she had him whisked up the aisle practically before the ink was dry on his passport stamp. To Anna, the movie was god. Theatre was okay – as long as it was musical theatre – but she had never shared her husband's love of the Bard.

Two more vastly different characters you could not have imagined, and yet it worked. They drove each other insane right up until Finn's death almost ten years previous, but they had one thing in common.

They both hated TV.

Freya's parents had a more balanced view towards roles, although neither had 'slummed' it on TV as Anna was often heard to remark when a former movie star appeared on the small screen. They both knew that it was tough out there, and that Freya was determined to carve out her own career, without interference or assistance from them.

It had been a surprise to the family that she had turned to acting at all. Growing up, she had always maintained that she did not intend to join the family business. In fact, she had fought kicking and screaming against all aspects of her family's legacy in Hollywood, deciding to study overseas in England to distance herself. This was to be her undoing as while studying at Cambridge, and under the allure of a girl, she agreed to join the drama society. Whilst her passion for the girl waned after a few months, the love of acting grew and before she knew it, after completing her degree, she had applied and was accepted to The Royal Academy of Dramatic Arts. That her grandfather got to see her graduate from the prestigious school was still a source of pride for Freya.

Had it not been for a health scare with Anna, she would not have packed up her life in New York a year ago. She left behind theatres and plays to return to the city that she had professed to hate while growing up, to move into her grandmother's guesthouse to keep an eye on her. She didn't like to point out to her grandmother that, albeit inadvertently, she had sown the seeds of her granddaughter's eternal damnation, since the theatre scene in LA was not as vibrant as New York. However, if there was one more comment she might forget her reticence.

Dan, determined to clean up the mess that he had created, chipped back into the conversation. "I think it's fabulous, it's only the biggest show on network primetime," he said proudly, lifting the glass of champagne that Dylan had poured him.

She flashed Dan a grateful smile.

"At least it's network, which means she'll keep her clothes on this time," Anna muttered into her glass. "I'm still recovering from seeing something no grandmother should see when she appeared on that cable show."

While peeved at her grandmother's comment, there was also a small sense of pleasure that at least Anna had made the effort to watch her in something. Which was news to Freya.

"So what part of the show will you be on this time?" her mother enquired as she poured more champagne in Anna's glass, hoping the alcohol would keep her occupied or the effects would eventually shut her up completely.

The show was set in part in an US Army Hospital in Germany, the other half of the show featured a Combat Support Hospital in Afghanistan. During Freya's initial appearance she had been in the Combat Support Hospital, which required a lot of location work out in the deserts surrounding Los Angeles.

"I think I'm going to be based on the German set, but I'm meeting with the producer next month to find out more. Like I said, it's no big deal," she shrugged.

"And she gets to work with the delectable Jordan Ellis," Dan said, sipping his champagne, his eyes wide with innocence.

"Why do I know that name?" Anna asked, staring off towards the swimming pool as her still sharp mind, which belied her years, rattled through her mental 'who's who' list. A look of recognition flooded her features. "I know, blonde girl, big brown eyes like a deer, won the TONY award the year they gave me the 'good Lord she's still alive, we'd better give her something before she buys it' award. We saw her show Freya, she has a good set of pipes on her," Anna continued, nodding to Dan as he held the champagne bottle at her glass.

"Oh, Freya's all about the pipes," Dan smiled, managing to move his arm in time to take the impact out of Freya's punch as he poured Anna a fresh glass.

"Well congratulations, I'm proud of you," Dylan said holding his glass up. "A toast. To the hope that you have a stunning season and that it takes you where you want to go."

Freya was fairly sure her grandmother muttered something about 'going to Hell in a hand basket' under her breath. However, she ignored it as she was happy to bask in the tiny bit of pride that securing the role had given her.

"So she's on the show, Jordan Ellis?" Anna asked.

"Yes, she plays another doctor," Freya answered, wondering if the raised eyebrow of her grandmother meant that the show had gone up in her estimation or Jordan had gone down.

**

Jordan carefully balanced the holder with two cardboard coffee cups and the bag of bagels in one hand before pressing the doorbell and hearing the two-tone sound resonate through the modern open plan home as it bounced off the tiled floors. A moment later she heard the sound of dogs barking and muffled swearing. Locks clunked, and eventually the door opened to display a frazzled looking Sabrina Morales. The body that had graced the covers of many magazines was currently wrapped in a silk dressing gown. Her dark brown hair, usually so perfectly styled, had been pulled into a messy knot at the back of her head and her skin, the color of which matched the latte held in Jordan's hand, was annoyingly as perfect without make-up as it was with.

"I knew I should have bought something with a gate to keep the riff raff away," Sabrina huffed, before breaking into a wide smile. "Welcome home, you're looking well, despite the fact that you have the audacity to show up on my doorstep all jetlaggy."

Jordan followed Sabrina into the house, stepping carefully to avoid the two chihuahuas who seemed determined to destroy her sofar successful attempt to keep the coffee in the cups.

"What makes you think I'm all jetlaggy?"

"It's eight a.m. on a Sunday morning, I'm guessing you're still on New York time."

"I bring gifts," Jordan said smiling, lifting the cup holder up.

"Whatcha brought me?" Sabrina asked, wafting into the kitchen and pulling down two large mugs from a cupboard.

"Coffee the way you like it and bagels."

"There goes my no carb, coffee or dairy diet," Sabrina sighed, then held her hands out flexing her fingers like a small child begging for candy. "Gimme."

Laughing Jordan handed over the coffee cups and opened the bag.

"So, how was New York, New York?" Sabrina asked, concentrating on pouring the coffee from their cardboard cups into the oversized mugs.

"Busy, noisy and utterly wonderful."

"I asked you about New York, not me," Sabrina joked, raising a sculpted eyebrow as she sniffed the contents of the mugs and handed Jordan hers. "Latte for you."

"It was great to be back there, and the play was a brilliant experience," Jordan took her latte and breathed in its scent before sipping.

"So are you ready to pack it all in here and head back east?"

A hint of worry appeared in Sabrina's tone as she considered that the return to New York could spark a need in her friend to return to the city where she first tasted success.

"Weirdly, this time it felt like I was coming home getting on the plane to come back. I think buying my house last year has made me start to put roots down here."

"Well hallelujah, I'm so glad 'cause I'm terrible at long distance things."

"Thanks to, 'he who shall remain nameless', I've never had to go down that route."

Sabrina snarled at the non-mention of Jordan's ex-boyfriend who, when she received the offer to move to LA and appear on *Front Line,* had promptly ended their relationship, stating that he didn't want to move and didn't believe in long distance relationships.

"Did you see him while you were there?" Sabrina asked cautiously.

"God no."

"Did you see anyone while you were there?" her tone turning from caution into outright teasing.

"I had a couple of dates, but I was so busy, and you know what? I'm so over the bullshit," Jordan stood up on the stool to reach over and grab a bagel from the bag, which somehow during the conversation had gravitated towards Sabrina.

Sabrina swallowed a mouthful of bagel, washing it down with a noisy slurp of coffee, "Bullshit how?"

"Don't you wish you could meet someone and it felt real? That you have a connection with them. That the conversations you have with them are adult and not full of pretentious crap?"

"You've been reading too many romance novels again, Jordan," Sabrina tutted, opening the sliding doors and stepping out to observe her view across the city and down to the ocean.

Jordan got up to follow her, "I'm fed up of a relationship being like a power play and never feeling like I'm the one with any of the power."

Sabrina tilted her head, "Oh honey, with that body, believe me you have *all* the power." She let out a loud chuckle.

"That's just it, we keep looking at the surface, and wondering why after a while there's nothing else there," Jordan sighed, trying desperately to form the words that would describe her current state of malaise about her previous approach to relationships. "You keep saying that you being bisexual means that it's the person that you're attracted to, and not the wrapping. Maybe that's where I've been going wrong."

Sabrina nodded thoughtfully, "You also remember me saying that it has to be hot wrapping!"

Jordan ignored her, lost in her musings, "I want a partnership with someone, and if that means worrying less about the package it comes in, then so be it."

"Really, you have no preference?" Sabrina's tone failed to mask her incredulity. While she didn't think for one moment that Jordan was questioning her sexuality, it was progress that she was querying her appalling taste in men.

"Nope."

Narrowing her eyes, Sabrina studied her friend closely, "Eyes, hair?"

"Would be good if he had them, but personality counts."

"So, penis or vagina?"

Jordan spluttered her coffee. Coughing, she scowled at Sabrina who was taking great joy in shocking her. Deciding that two could play that game, she smiled sweetly, "Just the one, preferably, but which one doesn't really matter."

Sabrina guffawed loudly, "Touché, and nice try straight girl."

"How'd you know?" Jordan teased.

Sabrina motioned to her body, "'cause sweetie, if you were a switch hitter, there is no way on this earth you would not have tapped this already." She managed to keep her face neutral for all of two seconds before they both burst into peals of laughter.

"I don't know whether to be offended by your laughter," Sabrina said haughtily when their giggling died down.

"I love you, but I can assure you there will be no tapping," Jordan giggled, still amused by Sabrina's fake vanity.

They stood together in companionable silence, each lost in their thoughts as they looked over the rooftops of LA.

"Enough of depressing relationship talk. What's happening with you and work? Did they like the pilot?" Jordan asked.

"Did they like the pilot?" Sabrina replied incredulously. "They did not just like the pilot, they loved the pilot, and we have a twentytwo episode season that starts shooting next month. I'm coming after your time slot girl, you better watch out."

"Bring it, bitch," Jordan grinned swatting the back of her hand against Sabrina's ass.

"Oh for that I am so having that last bagel," she pushed Jordan lightly and ran giggling back into the house, yelping as the disgruntled blonde chased after her.

June 2011

Jordan straightened her top and exhaled nervously as she knocked on the door. She heard a muffled 'come in' from the other side. She opened the door and peeked round towards the occupant of the office.

Sitting behind a large desk, with her red frizzy hair sticking out at odd angles from where she had recently run her hands through it, Eleanor French's face broke out into a wide welcoming smile, "Jordan, good to see you. Did you have a good summer break? Take a seat." The diminutive woman indicated towards one of the large soft seats to the side of the office.

Regardless that this was now her third season on the award winning army hospital drama *Front Line,* Jordan was always nervous when she had her meeting with the series' producer. She was still under her original seven-year contract with the network, but this was the meeting when Eleanor would map out the season's arc for her character Captain Georgia Van Hausen, the feisty trauma surgeon. With the recent influx of new actors, Jordan was unsure whether this conversation would have her dying tragically this season. With her newfound realization that LA was starting to feel more like home, she did not want anything to jeopardize that feeling of security. In relation, she was not ready to put herself back into the world of pilot pimping and face the potential rejection that that particular joy could bring.

"Yeah, I did a play off Broadway," Jordan replied, proud of her work in New York during the summer hiatus. While she had done plenty of stage work before, it had tended to be in musical theatre. The opportunity to perform in a serious play had given her the chance to flex her acting abilities away from the character that had made her a household name.

"I saw your reviews, they were really good," Eleanor commented as she sat down on the soft seat beside Jordan. "I guess you're wondering what we've got in store for you this season?" she smiled.

Jordan returned the smile, hoping that her boss wouldn't notice her nerves and that she was managing to disguise that her stomach was churning.

"As always, Eleanor."

"We talked last December, when the 'don't ask, don't tell' repeal legislation went through, about exploring a character's sexuality and I know you put your hand up to say that you would be willing to portray that," Eleanor started carefully. Jordan nodded slowly, recalling the conversation. "Well, we at ELFREN Productions feel that now is the time to bring that storyline to life, and I wondered how you felt about us taking Georgia down that journey?"

Jordan's brain fired off into a myriad of directions. She wasn't going to be thrown on an IED, and she gave silent thanks that she'd managed to avoid the grim reaper story of the season. This meant a meaty storyline, some good drama to get her teeth into and the potential to help a community that, thanks to her theatre work and circle of friends, she was intrinsically linked to. Unexpectedly, her mind also fleetingly passed over the conversation she'd had with Sabrina about relationships the month before.

"I'd love to," she smiled broadly. "It's great that we get to tell this type of story and help with visibility."

"Excellent," Eleanor clapped her hands. "I hoped that you would feel that way." The small woman stood, circled over to her desk and picked up the phone, "Sammy, can you send Freya in please?"

Jordan raised an eyebrow. Freya Easter had joined the cast at the end of the previous season as Captain Emily Dollar. She was introduced as a foil for the ex-boyband member, turned actor, Blake Devon's character Damien Holt, while he was on the combat set. Emily had immediately fitted in with the quirky nature of the show's characters, even gaining her own fan section on the show's messageboards. When the network announced that they were looking to promote Freya to a series regular after they had extended her initial three-episode appearance to the end of the season, Jordan and her closest friends on the show, Greg and Dianne, had taken bets that by the end of the season Freya and Blake's characters would be hooking up. They had even created a portmanteau for the couple, as was the tradition for couples on the show. However, the season ended without the hook up, and it now appeared that the bets on Hollar were premature.

Freya entered the room, her smile bright even though she was biting her bottom lip almost to the point of drawing blood.

"So Freya, grab a seat," Eleanor pointed to the seat she had vacated beside Jordan. "It would appear that you're both keen to take the storyline on."

Freya gave Jordan an encouraging smile.

"So, this season we'd like to take it slowly to let the viewers get used to the connection with the characters before we explore the…physical aspect of the relationship," Eleanor coughed. "We want to make sure we do this responsibly. The network has received criticism from GLAAD about their portrayal of gays and lesbians, so we want to make sure that this gets done right."

The two actors nodded as they listened to the formidable woman before them lay out her ideas for the development of their character's relationship. At the end of the meeting, Eleanor gave each of them a brisk hug.

"We're going to do good work here, ladies. I've arranged for a meeting with GLAAD for you so you can ask questions about what your characters might be going through. Particularly the difference between a…" she hesitated as she searched for the correct phrase, "I believe the term is a 'Gold Star' lesbian entering a relationship with a woman whose previous relationships have all been with men."

They allowed themselves to be guided from the office, both exhaling slowly as Eleanor closed the door behind them.

"So..." Freya grinned.

Jordan turned to face her, "So indeed."

"Have you ever -"

"Been gay for pay?" Jordan interrupted laughing. "Yeah, I played a lesbian killer on *LA Blues* a couple of years before I got the role here. So have you played gay?"

Freya nodded, smiling at the irony that in her public life, she was used to playing straight, "Yeah I had a small role in *Velvet Girls* when it was on."

"So, did you...?" Jordan trailed off, chewing the side of her mouth. A slight blush appeared on her cheeks.

Freya immediately realized where Jordan was going with her question and saved her the embarrassment of clarifying, "Yup, had to get hot and heavy in a nightclub bathroom. You?"

Jordan shook her head. "No, I just killed my lover with an ice pick," she laughed, scuffing her shoe against the floor.

"Well let's hope history doesn't repeat itself. It's actually easier than doing it with a man," Freya smiled, her smile however quickly turned to a frown. "The scenes, I mean," she clarified, hoping that her neck had not started to redden with embarrassment.

Jordan laughed, "I'll hold you to that." She checked her watch. "I've got to go," she said reluctantly. She hadn't had the opportunity to chat one on one with Freya before and was surprised when she realized that she had been smiling throughout their conversation.

"I'll see you on Wednesday at the table read?" Freya asked hopefully.

"I will be there."

Freya gave her a final smile before turning and walking off, her long legs covering the ground with ease and soon putting distance between them.

Jordan turned to leave, and then hesitating, she turned back around. "Freya," she called after the retreating actress.

Smiling, Freya turned and jogged back, her dark curls bobbing around her shoulders, "Yeah?"

"Are you free on Saturday?"

Mentally going through her diary in her head, Freya could not think of anything that would trump spending time with Jordan; a woman whose blonde hair fell in smooth waves, the silky locks just begging to have Freya's fingers trail through them. Her brown eyes seemed perpetually to send out 'take me to bed' signals to anyone they captured in their gaze, or at least that was Freya's interpretation of Jordan's look. Although she reluctantly acknowledged that her grandmother's doe-eyed description could also apply. Her body was lithe but curved in all of the right areas, and the absolute cherry on the top of the exquisite cake, as far as Freya was concerned, was that she was actually an inch taller than Freya – something that was a rarity in her life. Realizing that she had not answered the question and was possibly even drooling a little, Freya gave a little shake and tried to appear nonchalant, "I think I am. Why, what do you have in mind?"

"I have a charity thing. It's a music workshop for kids that have been victims of bullying. We introduce them to music as a way to boost their confidence. I was wondering whether you wanted to come along."

To be fair, Freya had been sold at 'Are you free?' but she gave a look as if she was seriously considering the request, before smiling broadly, "I'd love to."

"Great, if you give me your number I'll text you the directions to the school where we're meeting."

Embarrassed, Freya pulled out her phone, "Two seconds, I can never remember my number." She located the entry that Dan had put in her phone with her own number and held the phone out to Jordan.

"What's a numpty?" Jordan asked, looking at the name of the entry on Freya's phone.

"British for idiot, my friend thought he was being funny."

"Ahhh," Jordan smiled. "Now smile for me." She held up her camera phone to take a snapshot of Freya to add to her contact info. She laughed loudly at the image captured; Freya's green eyes were crossed and she had stuck her tongue out.

"Are my eyes shut? 'cause my eyes are always shut in photos," she grinned as Jordan held the phone so she could see the photo.

"Nope, they're open and it's a beauty," Jordan grinned. "If I'm ever in need of cash I may sell it to the media. So I'll text you the info and see you on Saturday."

"Great, I'm looking forward to it and to working with you," Freya said, as Jordan turned to go.

"Me too."

As she watched Jordan leave the office, Freya's shoulders slumped slightly. *Being firmly in the closet sucked*, she thought, as she contemplated the potential scrutiny she was exposing her personal life to by saying yes to the storyline. As if that wasn't enough, now she was worrying about how she was ever going to get through a day in Jordan's company without making a fool of herself, never mind an entire season, pretending to be in love with her.

***

"Are you listening to me at all, Egg?"

Dan's voice filled the car as Freya navigated through the streets of a part of LA she was not familiar with, and she checked her satnav for the hundredth time to make sure she was heading the right way.

"Yes, I'm listening," she replied distractedly as she checked the street names while she drove.

"What did I say, then?"

"Rule one. Do not ogle hot co-star."

"Okay, you were listening, so that's rule one. Rule two, do not call her your hot co-star, her name is Jordan. Say it with me, Jordan."

"Her name is Jordan, got it."

"You need to not think with your hooha, Egg, and think with your head. What are you wearing? "

"Now is not the time to try and have a dirty phone call with me Dan."

Hearing a loud snort down the phone line, Freya laughed, "I'm wearing my green sweater."

"The V-neck? You sneaky little bugger, that's the one that makes your eyes go pop and your boobs go boo!"

Putting the car into park, Freya gripped the steering wheel. Standing in the shadows of the building was Jordan, looking amazing in black jeans and a white Henley T-shirt. Both items clung to her body so tightly that they looked as though they'd been painted on. She had pulled her hair into a messy ponytail and pushed sunglasses onto the top of her head. Freya watched her unobserved as she greeted people warmly, directing them into the building.

"Are you there? You've gone quiet."

"Sorry Dan, I'm here. I've just pulled into the school parking lot."

"What are you doing? You sound all breathlessy."

"Breaking rule number one," Freya stated, ending the call before Dan could shout at her. Grabbing her phone and keys, Freya got out of the car.

Jordan checked her watch, wondering whether the directions she had given Freya had been adequate. Her decision to ask Freya to the event probably surprised her more than Freya. Despite questioning her motives several times, she was yet to come up with an adequate response for the impromptu invitation. She smiled and greeted some more attendees to the workshop, providing them with guidance on how to find the gym hall where they would start the session before breaking out into smaller groups. She turned and looked out across the parking lot, her face breaking into a smile as she spotted Freya getting out of her car. She had asked Freya to come dressed casually, and it was a relief to see her dressed in faded blue jeans and a green V-neck sweater. Jordan had once invited Sabrina along to a workshop and, despite the same instruction, she had stepped up looking every inch the Hollywood star, putting everyone on guard for the first hour of the day until the sheer force of her personality won everyone over.

As Freya approached, she pushed her sunglasses up onto her head. "So I found it okay," she grinned, stepping into the hug offered by Jordan.

"I'm so pleased. I was worried that I had sent you in the wrong direction."

Jordan stepped back. Struck by how green Freya's eyes looked, words fell unbidden from her mouth, "Wow, your eyes are amazing."

"Thanks, I grew them myself," Freya laughed. "It's the sweater. Apparently it makes my eyes pop." She silently added *and my boobs go boo*, as Jordan's gaze swept down to her sweater.

"Well, they're definitely popping today. So are you ready for this?" Jordan asked, as she led them towards the entrance.

"Absolutely, just tell me what I need to do."

"Well, we all start out in the main hall and then we break out into smaller groups. We have musicians, singers, actors and dancers here and all are hosting small workshops. I thought you could stay with me, I'm taking the singing."

They moved into the hall and Freya was surprised to see over a hundred kids of all ages sitting patiently waiting on the day beginning. The hall echoed with excited chatter.

"Grab a seat, I have to go up front for a bit," Jordan said, pointing over to a plastic chair set against the wall.

Freya wandered over, smiling at the other adults lining the walls.

"Hi," Jordan called. The noise continued for a moment before she spoke again and silenced the room, "Hi, it's great to see you all here today. My name is Jordan Ellis and I'm one of the founders of the Future Arts Foundation. I know many of you will have heard how our foundation came about but there are some newbies here today, so suck it up 'cause you're gonna hear it again."

Jordan let the laughter wash over her before starting to speak again, "I was always the tall kid in class, I tried to make myself smaller, tried to hide so no one would notice me, tried anything to be just like everyone else. I was called all sorts of names and had all manner of comments made about my height. I lost confidence and I became so painfully shy that even putting my hand up in class to answer a question would make me break out in a sweat."

Jordan paused, letting her gaze sweep around the room and disconcertingly finding two green eyes easily within the sea of faces looking at her; two eyes that seemed to be taking in the very essence of her. She coughed and regained her composure, "I used to sing when I was alone and then, when I was twelve, I had a music teacher who encouraged me to sing publicly. Through her, and through music, I found my confidence. I found my voice and I started to walk tall. We are all different, we are all special, and you are safe here today to express who you are, to walk tall, and to be whoever you want to be. You will be respected and you will treat others in that same way. So please have fun today and make some loud, joyful noise."

The hall filled with the noise of chairs scraping on the floor as children stood and headed off to their relevant stations that were based on the sticker color they had been given on arrival.

Jordan walked back towards a solemn looking Freya.

"You didn't mention that it was your charity," Freya said quietly. "This is amazing, I'm in awe."

"You may not feel quite so in awe after a couple of hours. Notice I said joyful noise, not tuneful," Jordan joked, trying to deflect Freya's compliments. She had not yet reconciled the feeling she'd had when their eyes had met during her speech, the feeling that somehow Freya was able to effortlessly move beyond the façade that she presented to the world at large.

***

Three hours later and Freya realized what Jordan meant. She had listened to several groups start off murdering songs that previously she had liked, then through gentle coaching from Jordan and the other singing teachers, herself included, end with respectable renditions.

As the newest group finished their first attempt, Jordan stepped forward to give them the same instruction their predecessors had received.

"That was a great first attempt. Now can anyone tell me what a clarinet needs to make music?"

Several arms thrust into the air, and Jordan selected a small girl at the front.

"Air, you need to blow into it," the girl said shyly.

"Yes you do, and your voice is the same. The more air you get to your voice, the better it will be. It protects your vocal cords and gives more power to your voice. So the first thing we're going to do it learn how to breathe."

"Pretty sure I've been doing that my whole life."

Jordan's eyes scanned the group, looking for whoever had spoken. Unable to work out whom exactly had the smart mouth, she carried on, "You may have been. However, what we're going to do is learn how to breathe properly." Feeling the need for some moral support up front, she turned to her group of coaches who were standing to the side, "Freya, can you come help me?"

Freya propelled herself off the wall she had been slouching against and joined Jordan, "What do you need me to do?"

"Can you sing an A and breathe up into your chest?"

What appeared to be a simple request had Freya flummoxed for a moment. When you grow up with Anna Conor as your grandmother, there is no such thing as breathing up into your chest.

Freya concentrated as she took a breath in, feeling relief as her chest and shoulders rose. She opened her mouth and let out a steady note, which quickly lost steam.

"Okay, how was that?" Jordan asked the group, who gave murmurs of approval.

"Don't knock yourselves out too much, guys," Freya said, frowning comically.

"Did you notice what happened when Freya took a breath?"

"Her boobs got bigger," the same voice from the earlier smart comment replied.

Jordan flushed at the comment, her brain seemed stuck on pause, as whoever had added that little nugget to the conversation had spoken the truth; Freya's already ample cleavage had increased impressively. She threw Freya an apologetic glance.

"Apart from my fabulous décolletage, and thank you by the way, did anyone notice anything else?" Freya asked.

"Your shoulders lifted," another voice interjected.

Relieved that they were back on subject Jordan took over again, "Yes, they did. This time Freya, can you breathe properly?"

Freya took a breath. Feeling her diaphragm expand fully, this time when she sang the note came out with more power and she was able to hold it for longer.

"So what was different this time?" Jordan asked, smiling as she received the answers from the group. "Okay, so let's look at how Freya did it." She moved to stand beside Freya. "Could you turn side on?" she whispered.

Moving as instructed, Freya found herself holding her breath as Jordan stood closely beside her. She could feel Jordan's breath fanning her hair as she spoke to the group about posture. She realized that she had not been listening when a warm hand rested on her abdomen and she twitched in surprise at the contact.

"You should feel your breath push your stomach out. If you're doing it correctly your chest shouldn't move at all," Jordan smiled to the group, her hand still placed on Freya's stomach. Idle thoughts of how soft the cashmere felt in comparison to the taut muscle she could feel beneath the surface, and how many crunches Freya must do, was replaced by the realization that Freya's stomach wasn't moving. She leaned closer to whisper in her ear, her nose filled with the subtle scent of coconut from Freya's hair, "Are you holding your breath?"

Freya jumped slightly. "Sorry," she gulped and took a deep inhalation, pushing Jordan's hand out in demonstration.

Stepping back, Jordan clasped her hands together to hide the fact that they were trembling slightly. She forced a smile onto her face then clapped her hands loudly, "So, everyone have a practice at breathing, and then we'll have another go at the song."

July 2011

As Freya walked into the large room, the day had a 'first day of school' feel to it as she heard the laughter and banter of the actors as they grabbed bagels and coffee from the Craft Services table before taking their place at the table read. She smiled an acknowledgement at a few of the regulars that she'd had scenes with before the show's hiatus. The male lead on the show was goofing around with Greg Burnett who played the show's lothario, Major James Love.

"So I hear you and Ellis are going to be the hospital's Ellen and Portia?"

When Freya turned towards Dianne Cruz, who played Anthea Waters, one of the commanding officers on the show, the actress's eyes twinkled with humor as she sipped her coffee.

"Erm, yeah I guess," Freya mumbled, turning her attention to the plate of pastries.

"You get fans for life, you know," Dianne grinned. "The gay ladies are nothing if not loyal. I played gay years ago and I still get voted onto sexy lists and sent mail."

Freya made a non-committal noise as she poured her coffee into the paper cup and lifted it to her lips to take a careful sip.

"So have you done the vagina monologues before, Jordan?" Dianne asked as the tall blonde appeared, causing Freya to spurt coffee.

Jordan opened her mouth to answer but stopped as Eleanor clapped her hands, calling them around the table.

Freya smiled to herself as she watched the cast slip into the same seats as they had been in when she had first joined the cast. The most predictable thing about working on this show was the cast's seating habits at table reads. She sat down in her seat listening as Eleanor gave the cast a pep talk on creating a legacy on TV. Finally, they opened their scripts and waited to see what life they would breathe into their characters in the season premiere.

Jordan quickly scanned the script for any Georgia dialogue. Comfortable that she had a couple of pages before she would have to speak, she took her time listening to her colleagues' voices as they spoke their characters' words for the first time, before allowing her mind to drift towards Freya who was sitting following the script intently as she always did.

Jordan had noticed, during the previous season, that Freya would twirl her hair as she concentrated. She had found herself thinking about the green-eyed woman several times over the two weeks since the charity workshop. She had been impressed with how natural Freya had been with the children, patiently working with them and always ready with a smile and praise. She shook herself as her mind wandered back to the breathing exercises and the feel of Freya's firm stomach, which seemed completely at odds with the soft curves of her breasts. Recognizing a line said by Greg, Jordan looked at her script frantically, casting aside all thoughts in order to find the exchange between their characters in time to read her line out.

Freya raised her head out of her script at the sound of Jordan's voice, and she joined the laughter around the table as Jordan nailed the comic timing of her line at the first read. There was no doubt in anyone's mind how good Jordan was at her job. She had a real talent for comedy, but with the same breath could have you tearing up at the depth of sadness she could bring. Even at the table reads, where most were just marking their lines out and getting used to the feel of the words in their mouths before exploring their character's motivations and feelings, Jordan was already imprinting aspects of her final performance into the scenes. Freya snapped out of her reverie as she heard her cue. Reading her line, she was pleased when her delivery elicited laughter around the table. She had spotted Jordan's distinctive chuckle amongst the laughter, and the thought that she had made Jordan laugh made her smile.

At the end of the read Freya was disappointed that she and Jordan still didn't have any dialogue together, but at least they would be in a couple of ensemble scenes. *Eleanor was not lying when she said that they were taking it slow,* Freya thought to herself as she gathered her script together, not noticing her co-star standing directly behind her.

"I guess at this rate we might be speaking by episode three, in love by episode four, broken up in episode five and back together in episode six," Jordan leaned forward and whispered.

Freya bit her top lip to stop herself from laughing.

Eleanor's voice gave them pause as she reminded everyone about her annual Fourth of July party on Monday. There was a collective response before everyone returned to his, or her, conversations.

"I was just thinking it might even be next season before we speak," Freya whispered back as they walked towards the exit.

Jordan snorted, "Eleanor's idea of taking it slow usually lines up with sweeps week, so you should probably get ready to pucker up soon. I have a wardrobe call in five, where are you off to?"

"Wardrobe," Freya grinned. "I love this part of the job."

Jordan looked at her quizzically.

"The scrubs and BDU pants. I have a friend in London who's shooting a period drama, she says the costumes are torture; corsets and a million layers."

"I'd love to do something like that," Jordan mused as they walked amicably together. "I mean corsets are hot."

Freya cleared her throat trying to rid her brain of the thought of Jordan in a corset, "My friend says they're more uncomfortable than hot. She got pissed at me when I sent her pictures of me in scrubs. She says it's unfair that she's trussed up and I'm working in what she calls PJ's and sneakers."

"Actors, we're never happy," Jordan sang as she opened the door to wardrobe and motioned for Freya to enter.

Freya's clothing range had grown since last season. As she looked along the rack of clothing identified for Emily, she noticed some civilian wear amongst her costumes. For the first time she would get to see more of her character's personality out of work being exposed – and exposed was exactly the right word for it – as she pulled the short 'Daisy Dukes' and tank top that Emily would wear in her own time off the rack.

"Well hotdamn," Jordan said softly. "Emily's got game," she added, nodding at the clothing in Freya's hand.

"Emily's going to have her ass hanging out is what Emily's going to have," Freya mused, frowning at the denim shorts.

"Well, I'm sure that you have a lovely ass," Jordan's eyes widened in horror as she realized what she had said. "And on that note, I'm going to leave you to get on."

Freya smiled at the blush that was now gracing Jordan's cheeks. "Me and my ass thank you," she grinned, waving her shorts in goodbye.

After an hour of trying on the outfits that would appear during the season, Freya was back in her own clothes when Jordan reappeared beside her after her own costume fitting.

"So I'll see you on Monday?" Jordan asked, referring to Eleanor's Fourth of July soiree.

Freya hesitated, "I was probably not going to go. I'm not really big on parties."

Jordan looked at her aghast, "You're kidding, right?"

Looking confused, Freya shook her head slowly, "No…why? Is there something that I should know?"

Pulling her to the side to make sure they couldn't be overheard, Jordan lowered her voice, "Eleanor is kinda big on us being one big happy family. Not to go to the party at her house on Monday would be a mistake."

"How big of a mistake?"

"Well the last person not to go to a party of Eleanor's was Spencer Harris."

Nodding slowly, Freya started to see where this was going, "Her character was blown up by a grenade launcher."

"Exactly. Now I'm not saying the two things were related, but…" Jordan shrugged. "Do you want to be the one to test the theory out?"

"Ask me again."

Jordan grinned, "So, I'll see you on Monday at the party?"

"Absofrigginglutely," Freya replied, mirroring Jordan's grin.

They walked along the corridor together in silence until Freya laughed softly, "Thank you for looking out for me."

"Well what kind of fictional girlfriend-to-be would I be if I let you fend for yourself, and make the social faux pas of the century?"

"Indeed! You have started strongly in the fictional girlfriend stakes, so far you're number one on the list."

"There's a list? How big is this list?" Jordan asked, throwing open a set of double doors and squinting as bright sunlight hit them. She held her hand to her chest in mock horror as Freya held her hands a foot apart and shrugged nonchalantly.

"I'm not sure I'm comfortable with my fictional girlfriend being such a slut," Jordan huffed, as they paused, before giving Freya a prod in the side as she turned to walk away. "You can ponder on how to make that up to me later…first on the list indeed," Jordan tossed over her shoulder.

"Poke me like that again and you'll drop to second," Freya shouted, her eyes widening as she considered how a sentence like that could be misconstrued. "What a filthy mind you have there, Freya Easter," she said to herself in a fair impression of her grandfather's Irish brogue.

**

The party appeared to be in full swing by the time Freya arrived fashionably, although not deliberately, late. Her tardiness was due to Anna insisting on showing her the newly digitally enhanced version of *Monday Girl;* the film that had resulted in her first Oscar for Best Actress. Freya had to admit her grandmother could act, and her distinctive voice sounded better than ever on the re-mastered edition. Freya had grown up not just with the recordings of her grandmother's voice – almost weekly she would hear one of the many songs her grandmother had recorded on the TV or radio – but also with the songs that she would sing to Freya as they played together. Anna always made time for Freya during her childhood, and Freya knew that, somewhere beyond the gin-soaked diva she portrayed to the world at large, Anna was also still the woman who had sat for hours teaching her granddaughter to play piano and rummy. Her relationship with her grandmother was as complicated as Anna herself.

She grabbed the one glass of champagne she would allow herself from a passing waiter and walked out onto the large patio area. It seemed most of the cast and crew had gathered out there in the pleasant LA evening. Her remark to Jordan about not coming to the event had been an honest one. Freya didn't like the 'see and be seen' aspect of her job. She usually avoided these types of engagements, and if she did come to one, she certainly didn't lose control of what people saw of her. Too many times when she had been younger her life had ended up in gossip columns, and she was careful not to provide any fodder for the vultures that waited on the sidelines for any such opportunity.

She nodded hellos to anyone who caught her eye as she subconsciously scanned the crowd for Jordan. As she spotted her deep in conversation with Sabrina Morales, she recalled that Sabrina had been in relationships with women before, and an irrational sense of jealousy sparked in her. They made a striking couple, Sabrina's dark Mediterranean looks contrasting starkly with Jordan's girl-next-door appearance. Caught in a dilemma about where to go, she turned to scan the crowd again. Arriving alone meant that she had to infiltrate conversations already flowing. She had spotted a likely possibility when she heard a familiar voice shout her name. Turning, she waved across to Jordan who was beckoning her over.

"Hi, you made it then?" Jordan said, giving her a quick hug. "I was worried that maybe you had opted for the brave but foolish option."

"I'm afraid I'm not brave but can be foolish, but on this occasion I'm just tardy," Freya smiled. "I'm hoping that Eleanor hasn't noticed."

"Eleanor sees all," Sabrina interjected. "It's nice to meet you Freya, Jordan has spoken about you a lot."

"It's nice to finally meet you too, Sabrina. I saw you in that indie film *Grosvenor Square* last year, really lovely performance."

Sabrina glowed. "I like her, she can stay," she whispered conspiratorially to Jordan.

The sound of someone tinkling a glass to get everyone's attention halted any attempt at conversation. Looking across the patio, Eleanor stood on a table, her husband hovering anxiously as she waited for the noise to die down.

"Thank you all for coming, I appreciate it. I like to celebrate occasions like this with my family, and I consider each and every one of you a member of that family. I am blessed to have here not only old and beloved members of my *Front Line* family, but also new additions to the family. In particular I'd like to welcome the cast and crew of *Agents*; the newest colt in the *ELFREN* Production Company's stable."

Placing a hand on Jordan's forearm, Sabrina leaned in and whispered in Jordan's ear, "That's me, I *am* an FBI Agent."

Jordan stifled a laugh.

Freya watched Sabrina lean in to whisper in Jordan's ear and felt her jealousy rack up a notch. They seemed completely relaxed in each other's company, with their small touches and private smiles. She sighed resignedly and refocused as Eleanor wound up her welcome speech with a light hearted but equally ominous, 'Eat, drink, just don't throw up in the pool.'

"Has that happened?" Freya asked.

"Two years ago," Sabrina answered. Switching her empty glass for a full one as a waiter passed.

"Should I ask what happened to the guilty party?"

Jordan leaned towards Freya and said in a dramatic voice, "Never seen again."

"You'll make a cute couple," Sabrina said, looking critically at them both.

Freya looked surprised at Sabrina's comment, then smiled, "It's going to be great."

Jordan nodded in agreement.

"Have you worked out your couple name yet?" Sabrina asked, spotting someone across the patio and waving.

"No, I hadn't…" Jordan stopped as her brain worked out the possible permutations. "Oh no, you have to be kidding me."

"What?" Freya asked, looking in confusion between Jordan, who was rolling her eyes, and Sabrina who had a smug smile on her face.

"Dollhausen, we're going to get called Dollhausen," Jordan sighed.

"I've heard worse," Sabrina laughed. "Now if you two fake lady lovahs will excuse me, I'm going to go try to build some rapport with my leading man, 'cause I'm going to need all the help I can get to fake being in love with him."

They watched as Sabrina sashayed across the patio towards a tall blonde man.

"So what's the deal tonight?" Freya asked, sipping her glass of champagne. As she was only having one, she had to make it last.

Jordan shrugged, "No idea, I've never been to one before." She laughed at the look of shock on Freya's face, "I'm kidding, although I did cut out early last year as my sister was visiting, and despite her being a corporate lawyer and incredibly intelligent, I have to restrict her access to people from work. She spent the entire night calling everyone by their character names. She's actually never forgiven me for joining *Front Line,* she said me being on it made it less real for her."

Freya frowned, "The possible plague outbreak she could believe, but you being on the show made it less real?"

Jordan guffawed loudly, "I know, go figure! Do you have any brothers or sisters?"

Surprised by the question, Freya took a moment before answering. Normally people asked her questions about her parents or grandparents, never just normal questions you would ask when trying to get to know someone. Usually people knew too much about her and her family to start with.

"Erm, no, just me. I saw you on Broadway you know, before *Front Line*," she grinned, eager to change the subject.

Jordan's eyes widened in surprise, "You did?"

Freya swallowed her mouthful of champagne and nodded, "You were…" She struggled to find the words that summed up what she had thought. "Breathtaking," she finished, her tone full of genuine awe.

Jordan blushed, "That's sweet of you to say."

"Nope, not sweet, honest. So what made you want to become an actress?"

"The film *Monday Girl*, I was six when I saw it and I knew that I wanted to be Anna Conor. I met her when I won my TONY and wanted to tell her that she was the reason that I became an actress, but I was so awestruck that I could barely say hello."

Before Freya could respond, Jordan slapped her hand against her forehead, "Oh my god, I'm such an idiot. I was asking you whether you had brothers or sisters, and then I start to prattle on about your grandmother. I'm so sorry, I totally forgot."

Almost since birth, Freya had developed a sixth sense that told her when someone was being genuine or whether they were simply trying to get close to her in order to gain access to her family. The look on Jordan's face told Freya that she had genuinely forgotten.

"Don't apologize, it made me feel normal," Freya said smiling.

Jordan reached out and held her arm. "You are normal, you're about the most normal person I think I've met," she said softly.

"Are you calling me dull?" Freya joked.

Swatting her gently, Jordan laughed, "Okay have it your way, you're weird."

"Growing up in my family, weird is all a matter of opinion." Unusually, Freya felt comfortable enough in Jordan's company to talk freely about her family. "When I was growing up while others were learning their ABC's, I was being taught mine by Anna. A stood for 'always show up on time on set'. B was 'be prepared and know your lines'," she paused, enjoying the sound of Jordan's laughter, "and C stood for courteous, although studios and producers pay your wage, the fans are your boss, so be nice. Finally, D was 'don't admit you can't do something'. If a director asks you say yes, then figure it out afterwards."

Jordan gave her an empathetic smile, "All of my family are lawyers, and while you were learning your ABC's, I was learning the constitution. As you can probably gather, I'm the black sheep."

"I know that feeling well." She saw Jordan's puzzled look, "TV is, and I quote from Anna, 'The devil's work'. Your family must be proud of you now."

"Yeah, but it all still feels like a completely different world to them, and they worry about me."

"Well, if it's any consolation, I think you're doing marvelously well," Freya said, nudging Jordan with her shoulder.

"Right back atcha fake girlfriend-to-be."

Eleanor's voice rang out as she instructed everyone to get into a good position. It was only then that Jordan realized how much time had passed. Talking with Freya had been easy and fun, and her attention had been so consumed by the dark-haired woman that she had barely registered it getting dark.

Everyone moved to get a better view of the fireworks that Eleanor had arranged. Already they could hear the soft pops of other displays nearby. Freya could feel the warmth from Jordan's arm pressed against hers. As they stood ready to watch the spectacle, the touch of Jordan's skin on her own was all that Freya could concentrate on. It felt as though a fire was sweeping through her body from that single ignition point.

The first firework exploded into the sky, flooding the dark canvas with colors. As is required with fireworks, the assembled crowd ahh'd at the spectacle. The pyrotechnic display was reaching a crescendo when Freya noticed a waiter moving towards her, attempting to thread his way through the throng of people. She stepped back to clear a space, only to find nothing beneath her foot. The action knocked her off balance and she lurched backwards. She whirled her arms around frantically in an attempt to restore her equilibrium, but she could feel that the action was simply delaying the inevitable. She saw Jordan's eyes widen in horror as she realized her fate.

The splash was embarrassingly big, the sort of splash that makes you wonder the size of the person that caused it. If it had not been for the lungful of water that she had ingested, Freya was tempted to stay at the bottom of the pool to drown in embarrassment. *There are worse ways to go* she thought, before survival instinct kicked in and she pushed towards the surface. She emerged from the water spluttering and wiping water from her face. Pushing her soaked hair out of the way, she kicked her legs to keep afloat.

The fireworks were forgotten as the partygoers turned their attention to the woman treading water in the pool, several doubled over in mirth.

Jordan was standing with her hands over her mouth, which was wide in shock but starting to tug into a smile as she swallowed down the laughter that threatened to escape.

Sabrina edged up to Jordan, "This is the point where you should stop gawking and help the poor woman out of the pool."

Jordan leant over to the edge of the pool and offered Freya her hand.

"Here, let me help you out," she said, sucking at her top lip to stem the laughter.

"It's okay, you can laugh," Freya grinned as she took Jordan's hand and pulled herself out of the pool. "So technically, I didn't throw up in the pool," she whispered, earning a load guffaw from Jordan.

Jordan's laugh died in her throat as she gulped. The loose white linen shirt Freya had been wearing was now transparent, as was the material of her lace bra. Jordan licked her lips subconsciously as her eyes traced the outline of Freya's now erect nipples. "We should get you covered up," she responded, her tone obviously distracted.

Eleanor rushed over. "Oh my god, are you okay? Let's go get you dried up. I'm not sure I have any clothes that will fit you though, we're not exactly the same size," she said, looking up at the actress, who was more than a foot taller.

"I have gym clothes in my car, I'll go get them," Jordan offered, glad of the excuse to get away from her sopping co-star and their boss. She stepped out into Eleanor's drive and puffed out a long breath of air.

What the hell was that about, Ellis? she mentally chided herself. *You're straight, just because you're going to be playing a lesbian doesn't mean you become one. That is taking the Stanislavski method a step too far. Get a grip.*

She shook her head. She had seen naked women before, including Sabrina whose body was known to have caused traffic jams when she had appeared semi-naked on a billboard. However, Jordan had never before experienced anything resembling arousal in relation to another woman, and yet her body was positively thrumming as she thought about Freya and how her shirt had clung to her.

"Get a grip," Jordan repeated aloud as she popped the trunk of her car and pulled out her gym bag. Feeling more composed, she turned to head back towards the house.

***

"Good morning, good morning."

Freya buried herself lower under her duvet as her grandmother sang her way through the guesthouse looking for her.

"There you are! It's almost noon, why are you in bed? Are you sick?" Anna asked, opening the shutters in Freya's bedroom, letting the light flood in.

"No, I'm hiding."

"What did you do?" Anna sat down on the bed and smiled as Freya edged towards her until her head rested on her lap. She started to stroke the dark curls, waiting for Freya to open up.

"I made a fool of myself at the producer's party last night." Freya still couldn't believe what had happened – she was usually so careful to avoid bringing attention to herself. One minute she had been standing reveling in the touch of Jordan's arm on hers, and the next she was falling completely out of control. She had no doubt that Hollywood blogs and gossip sites would be full of the incident, and she was mortified at the thought.

"What did you do? Did you get drunk and make a pass at her?" Anna asked, her hand pausing mid stroke as Freya lifted her head and glared at her.

"No, I didn't," she replied angrily. She gave a small humph, "I fell in her pool."

"That's it?" Anna laughed. "Honestly Freya, that's nothing. I was once at the studio exec's house for a big fancy party when my knicker elastic broke, and down they came."

Despite herself, Freya started to giggle at the picture her mind conjured up of the incident, "What did you do?"

"Stepped out of them and moved to the other side of the room and started to speak to whoever was there. Your grandfather bent down, picked them up, and stuffed them in his pocket," Anna laughed loudly at the memory. "You worry too much about what everyone thinks about you. When you're done moping I was going to take a drive out to the warehouse and, since you lot think I'm about to keel over and die at any moment, I thought you might want to come too."

"Give me five minutes and I'll be right with you."

Looking at her granddaughter's appearance Anna frowned, then leaned down, and placed a kiss on Freya's head, "Take twenty, you need it, and I'm not in a hurry."

Freya's eyes fluttered with annoyance, but she was well practiced at ignoring her grandmother's veiled barbs. "Give me twenty then," she ground out as she flung the covers back and swung her legs out of her bed with determination.

***

"So, not that I don't love coming here, but why are we here today, exactly?" Freya asked, moving between the rows of movie memorabilia that her grandmother had collected over the years.

"I'm selling the collection, Freya," Anna said with regret as her wrinkled hand reached out to straighten a prop on the tall shelving that lined the walls of the warehouse.

Freya stopped walking, "What? Why?"

Anna gave her an indulgent smile then reached out to cup her cheek, "Because I'm not getting any younger and your father has no interest in it all. The only one that loves this stuff as much as me is you, and I'm not about to burden you with the cost of storing it and preserving it."

"Who are you selling it to?"

"The rat company is looking to split the collection up and put it in their theme parks," Anna sighed. "So today, we're going to take the items that we'd like to keep before their assessors come in to itemize it all. Don't want that oversized rodent getting all the good stuff, do we?" Freya grinned, heading off towards the shelf where the items she knew she wanted to keep were stored.

***

"You fell in the pool!" Dan snorted.

"Shush now, you're not making me feel any better," Freya groaned as her head thumped onto the table in the bar.

"Way to impress your hot co-star, Egg," her friend laughed, taking a sip of his beer.

"Dan, don't, just don't, and we're not calling her that, remember?" Freya thumped her head rhythmically against the table. "This is such a mistake."

"What? You agreeing to be the lesbian lover of the woman you lusted after before you joined the show, while remaining so far in the closet that Aslan is licking your butt cheek? Noooo, what could go wrong with that?!"

Freya sat up. "I did not lust after her," she said indignantly.

"Of course you didn't," Dan frowned and shook his head. "Remind me again. Was it because you were or weren't attracted to her that you had the screen cap of her in a white tank top and fatigues as a screensaver?" Dan smiled, dodging the peanuts being thrown in his direction.

"Okay, so I had a crush," Freya conceded. "But that was then, and now –"

"And now you're going to be kissing her," Dan laughed, tossing a peanut in the air and catching it in his mouth.

"Oh God," Freya groaned throwing herself sideways on the booth's seat. She sprung back up and reached over, grabbing Dan's wrists.

"What am I doing agreeing to this story arc? It's just asking for trouble Dan, and I'm not sure I'm ready to come out publicly."

Her friend placed his hand on top of hers, squeezing gently, "We all have to at some point, my little Easter Egg."

"Seriously, Dan, it's okay for you, you're in fashion – it's practically a pre-requisite. But in Hollywood, it's almost like it has its own 'don't ask, don't tell' policy. And besides, there is already so much about me and my family out in the public domain, that I prefer my privacy."

"Sweetie, it's time to step out of the glass closet. It will come out eventually. Hell, you've been lucky so far, thanks to that weird lesbian thing of staying friends with your exes." He pointed the neck of his bottle of beer in Freya's direction for emphasis, "You need to decide if you want to control the message, or let it control you. It might be time to put on your big girl pants and come out."

Freya placed her head in her hands. "Aslan licking my butt cheeks...really!" she grinned, grabbing Dan's beer and taking a drink from it.

August 2011

Five weeks later, the season premier was complete. Episode two was in post-production, filming was almost complete on the third episode and they were gathered for the read through of the fourth episode's script. The read through was in full swing when Freya and Jordan exchanged a quick glance as they reached the page in the script where their characters would interact for the first time.

"Crap," Freya read out.

"Dollar, stop wiggling. I can't tell if it's broken or not if you wriggle," Jordan replied.

"It hurts," Freya whined, gaining a small chuckle from Jordan at her childish pout.

"Of course it hurts, that was a pretty nasty spill you took," Jordan read from the script, contorting her face into an exaggerated frown as she shook her head towards Freya.

"Yeah, well, you should have been looking where you were going."

Jordan pursed her lips and placed her script onto the table and looked towards Freya, waggling her finger as she started to bob her head back and forth, "I was looking where I was going, you came hurtling out of nowhere at sixty miles an hour."

Freya glanced at the script. "I was not hurtling anywhere, I was on my way to the ER," she corrected petulantly. "Now, Van Hausen, will you just fix my damn ankle." she scowled over at Jordan, her eyes twinkling with amusement.

"Only if you stop wiggling," Jordan retorted, "and let me get a damn x-ray to fix your damn ankle." She flipped over the page, "Damn woman."

"Who?" Greg asked.

"Captain Dollar. She barrels into me on the stairs, falls down them, and then shouts at me as if it's my fault, when I'm trying to help her."

Greg rubbed his chin, his fingers creating a noise against the bristle of his stubble as he read his line out, "But she is hot, maybe I should go in there and show her some of the old Major Love charm to cheer her up."

"I think she'd prefer Georgia's bedside manner to yours, Love," Dianne chipped in.

"What?" Jordan and Greg said in unison, high-fiving each other at their timing.

"I mean that while you're a lady's man, Love…Emily is a lady's lady," Dianne read, flipping her script over quickly.

The rest of the episode focused on the ongoing saga of the show's main relationship, and Freya quickly switched off and spent most of her time surreptitiously watching Jordan as she and Greg sat nudging and poking each other as if they were kids in kindergarten.

As the table read came to an end, the group dispersed to either the trailers or the set to record the final scenes for the third episode.

"Jordan, Freya," Eleanor shouted after them. "There's a couple of reps from GLAAD in my office to speak to us. Can you two head up now and I'll be there in a minute."

On arriving at the small *Front Line* office, Jordan and Freya greeted Eleanor's assistant and entered her office. They smiled towards the two women who were standing and admiring the show's awards displayed in Eleanor's office alongside other memorabilia.

"Impressive collection," one of the women commented as she came across to shake their hands. "Samantha Hale and this is my colleague, Victoria Foster."

"I always thought one displayed awards in the loo," Victoria remarked, her clipped English accent contrasted against the soft lazy tones of Samantha's Texan drawl.

"That's where I keep mine," Jordan grinned, indicating towards the soft seats. The four women sat down and looked at each other expectantly, no one sure who should be leading the conversation.

Jordan looked at Freya who was shifting nervously in her seat and playing with the tie of her scrub pants. Jordan decided to take control, as her co-star was looking anywhere but at the women seated around the small coffee table.

"Sooo, our characters are going to…" Jordan's expressive face scrunched up as she selected her words. "Become involved."

"Eleanor said you were interested in exploring the relationship dynamic between a Gold Star lesbian and a newly realized bisexual?" Samantha asked, looking directly at Freya for a response.

"Um, yeah," she replied nervously.

As soon as Freya had entered the room, she had recognized Samantha from a party she had attended with Dan. A party where Freya's sexual orientation would have been in no doubt, if her closedancing with her female date was any indication. Freya was terrified that Samantha would say something either directly, or indirectly, about her sexuality.

"So what do you think might be the issues that a relationship with that particular dynamic would throw up?" Samantha probed gently.

Jordan chewed thoughtfully on her nail, thinking back to when

Freya stood dripping pool water onto Eleanor's guest room carpet, "I suppose from Georgia's perspective there is dealing with new and confusing thoughts about being attracted to a woman for the first time, and then I guess there could be insecurity around on both parts. Am I enough?" She stopped as Eleanor slipped into the room and sat down before indicating for her to continue. "Yeah, am I enough? Would she want to be with someone more experienced with gay relationships? I mean with this being Georgia's first time in this position."

"Freya, what do you think?" Victoria asked.

Freya nodded as if considering her response. She had only halflistened to Jordan speaking, as for the most part her brain was in blind panic. Aware that so far her responses made her appear as articulate as a truculent teenager, she sighed, "I suppose for Emily, the 'am I enough?' factor could be concerns that Jordan's character will want to go back to a male-female relationship."

"Absolutely, all are common issues. One thing we are keen to make sure of is that the bisexual aspect isn't portrayed as promiscuity. It's not a *'can't decide'* option," Victoria nodded enthusiastically as she spoke.

Jordan nodded, "I was speaking to a friend who is bisexual and she said that, for her, it's the person not the wrapping that's important. Although she also said that she likes the wrapping to be hot." She grinned apologetically.

Eleanor clapped her hands, "Absolutely, we want to show Georgia's journey of self-discovery, and we want it to be an organic growth of realization which maintains authenticity, rather than anything done for titivation."

There were murmurs of agreement.

"I want to show Emily as someone who is comfortable and confident about her sexuality, but who is completely at sixes and sevens and undone about her feelings for Georgia," Eleanor explained, as Freya continued to examine the ties of her scrub pants.

Samantha smiled, "That's great. We need positive visibility in terms of a successful woman who is open and out there with her sexuality, and for it to be treated as normal by her employer and coworkers. It's a really important and interesting time for LGBT rights at the moment, what with the end of 'don't ask, don't tell' in sight. So for this to be set in the background of a military hospital, well, that's even better. We'll really get a chance to see how this institution is adapting."

Freya could feel herself shrinking as Samantha continued to speak.

"It's important that adults, but even more importantly that teenagers out there, see a positive role model. Preferably real, but fictional is the next best thing. So they understand that there's life after high school," Samantha smiled warmly. "What you're doing here is important."

"Exactly," Eleanor slapped the arm of the chair. The sudden noise made Freya's head jerk up; she was almost down to the last strand of her extremely frayed nerve.

Jordan had been watching Freya throughout the meeting, and concern around her feelings towards the storyline had started to grow. She was afraid that her co-star was starting to have second thoughts. She kept glancing over as the women continued to discuss common misconceptions and the pitfalls that other shows had fallen victim to. Freya participated in the conversation, but appeared distracted and jumpy throughout.

"Well, thank you for your time ladies," Eleanor smiled, shaking the hands of both Samantha and Victoria. "I'd appreciate your feedback when we've filmed a bit more of the relationship, just to make sure we're representing responsibly."

Samantha passed Jordan and Freya her card, "Just in case you want to speak at any point during the process." She flashed Freya a quick look of understanding, "Call anytime."

Freya returned her look with a grateful smile, her anxiety finally starting to wane as she realized that Samantha was not about to out her to her boss.

As they walked towards their trailers, Jordan chewed nervously on her bottom lip. "Are you having second thoughts about this?" she blurted.

Freya's head snapped round, "No, no, I'm not. It's just it's a big responsibility, and," she looked up towards the blue sky, "don't you worry about the exposure this could create for us, you know, in the media?"

Jordan's eyes widened. She had not considered this angle before, and had only thought about the storyline and the positive aspect it would bring, not about the potential for a backlash of any sort.

Freya watched Jordan's reaction. Realizing that the taller actress had not thought anything about the potential consequences, she backtracked, eager to put Jordan's mind at rest again, "I mean, it's probably just me catastrophizing," she smiled. "It's a bit presumptuous that people would want to read anything about us." Her mind went back momentarily to the conversation she'd had with Dianne about gay fans and their fervor, "I'm probably just thinking the worst." She gave a quick smile, for once eager to end her time with Jordan so she could berate herself again in private for agreeing to the story arc, "I'll see you tomorrow." She waved and headed quickly towards her trailer without looking back.

Jordan watched Freya leave, mulling over what she had said. Shrugging, she turned, "We've nothing to worry about." A frown appeared on her forehead as she remembered her arousal when looking at Freya after the pool incident. "Nope, nothing to worry about at all," she muttered as she walked towards her trailer.

"Sabrina, what's it like?" Jordan asked, turning onto her front to give her back some sun.

They were lying by Sabrina's pool enjoying a relaxing Sunday which, following the weeks of mad activity as both settled back into their grueling working patterns, was a welcome relief.

"Do you have cream on? 'cause I do not want to have to listen to you moaning that you've burned your lily white skin," Sabrina looked over the top of her sunglasses at Jordan. Her oversized sunhat flopped down and she pushed it up irritably.

"Yes mom, I have cream on," Jordan replied like a petulant teenager. "So, what's it like?"

"What's what like?" Sabrina asked, sipping water through a straw.

Jordan groaned, "Kissing another woman."

"Are we talking for a role or for fun?"

"Either."

"Well," Sabrina said grinning. "For a role it's work, so it's like work! For fun, it depends on who you are kissing, and what you feel for them and how compatible you are. So have you locked one on with Freya yet?"

Spinning around on the lounger, Jordan spluttered, "What? No! Why would you say that?"

"Because you're lady lovahs on the show," Sabrina replied, frowning at her friend's reaction. "You have had your first kiss, haven't you?"

Jordan relaxed as she realized that Sabrina was referring to the show, "We're only about to have the read through for the fifth episode."

"And still no kiss! My, how restrained, it's almost like a Brontë novel," Sabrina smirked at Jordan's eye roll. "Wait. Are you worried about kissing her?" Sabrina pushed her sunhat off completely so she could see her friend.

"Why would I be worried?" Jordan blustered, knowing full well that if there was a scale of worry, she was off of it.

"You tell me. You have kissed a woman before, haven't you?"

Jordan slunk down on the lounger, a sheepish look on her face as she shook her head.

"What, not even for work?" Seeing Jordan shake her head again, she smiled, "Well, I imagine that Miss Easter is a good kisser. For a first you could do worse."

Jordan felt her skin blush at the comment. The confusion Jordan felt around Freya had progressed steadily since the charity workshop and, as if to compound it further, ever since the Fourth of July 'poolwatergate', as she had started to refer to it in her head, she had found her eyes lingering on Freya. The thoughts swarming her brain were rapidly becoming less of a friend and co-star slant and more potential lover. Knowing that they would be kissing at some point for the show, she had started to watch Freya's lips anytime they had a conversation, wondering whether they were as soft as they looked and how they would feel on her skin.

Sabrina watched over the top of her sunglasses as her friend obviously worked through something in her head, a dark flush spreading up her throat to her cheeks, "You sure you have cream on? You're looking red over there."

Shaking her head as if to clear her brain, Jordan stood up, "I might just head inside; it's got a bit warm out here."

Watching her go, Sabrina chuckled to herself. "Sure it has," she muttered, pushing her glasses back fully on her nose.

**

"I am amazing," Jordan announced as she flopped down onto the sofa beside Freya, allowing her arms to stretch along the arm and back of the seat as her head tipped back to rest on the sofa.

When she did not get a response from the brunette sitting at the other end, she lifted her head up.

"Emily, I said I. Am. A-May-Zing," she twirled her hands to encourage a reply. "Which is when you say, why are you amazing? What have you done Georgia?" sitting forward she could see tears flowing down Freya's face. "Emily, are you okay?" Jordan asked, moving towards Freya, her tone full of concern. Before she could say anything further, Freya spun on the seat and launched herself across the sofa in her direction. Her arms wound tightly around Jordan's waist as she buried her face under Jordan's chin.

"Cut," the director shouted. "Excellent, guys. We've got Freya's shots, we just need to switch the camera angle for Jordan's close up at the end of the scene, so if you can stay in position."

It was the end of August, and they were filming their first scenes for episode five of the season, which had seen their characters' friendship develop during the episodes following Emily's accident. For the past two hours they had been shooting what would prove to be a pivotal moment in the relationship between their characters; Emily's vulnerability and depth of character would be shown as she grieved for a lost patient, receiving support from Georgia.

Jordan rested her chin on the top of Freya's head as they waited while the crew measured the light and distance for the shots. "How you doing down there?" she could feel Freya's shoulders shift quickly as she laughed.

"I'm good, thanks. How's junket week going for you?" Freya asked, trying to spark up any conversation that would help her ignore that fact that she was nestled against Jordan's breasts.

"My favorite time," Jordan laughed in response to Freya's question.

As the show's airing date neared, the actors found their busy work bubble pierced by the reality of having to promote the show. Their call sheets were steadily filling up with a variety of press activities. This week was set aside for on-set interviews for the extras section of the show's season DVD, as well as interviews in the press suite with a number of presenters from the countries around the world where *Front Line* aired.

"So, what's your entry for the dumbest question competition?" Jordan asked, trying not to move her head while the crew bustled around them measuring and setting up the cameras.

"Apart from the veiled attempts to find out about my mom's new film, you mean?" Freya laughed. "It would have to be what would Emily be if she wasn't a surgeon or in the army?"

"What was your answer?"

"To which question?"

"Both."

"That as far as I was aware, my mom's film had nothing to do with *Front Line.*"

Freya could feel Jordan chuckle as she held her head in place, listening to the steady rhythm of Jordan's heart.

"For the other, that's a really good question, although probably one for the writers, not me. But if I had a say, then she'd probably still want to help people, maybe be a teacher or something? What about you?"

She felt Jordan stiffen slightly at her question. The arms holding Freya in place tightened, momentarily pulling her closer, "They asked how my family reacted to me playing a gay woman."

Freya sucked a breath in. Trying to control her reaction, she released the breath slowly and wet her lips, giving herself time to respond, "What did you say?"

"That if they wanted to apply a label, then Georgia is technically bi-sexual. However, I'm not big on labels, and I think Georgia is attracted to Emily the person, and her gender is almost of no consequence. That my family is incredibly supportive of my career and of this storyline as it's an important one, and that so far in my career, amongst other roles, they have seen me play a murderer, a drug addict, a prostitute, and an alien, and have so far been able to tell the difference between me and the characters I play."

"Ouch, wish I'd been there to see that."

"Okay, thanks Jordan. Freya, you can move, we're set up," the director shouted over.

Freya straightened up and gave a sheepish smile as Jordan stretched her back slightly, causing her top to ride up a little.

"Can we take it from Georgia's line of 'You did everything you could'," the director smiled, checking his copy of the script as the actresses moved back into position.

Freya lowered her head and wound her arms back round Jordan's waist, gulping slightly as her fingers encountered the smooth skin of Jordan's back instead of the soft cotton of her scrub top.

She composed herself as the scene marker snapped closed in front of the camera.

"You did everything you could," Jordan said, stroking Freya's soft curls. "We can't save everyone."

Freya allowed a now familiar sob to escape. Her entire body felt drained from spending the majority of the morning crying, "Did I?" She pulled herself out of Jordan's embrace, "I'm not so sure." She placed a trembling hand to cover her mouth as she pushed herself off the sofa and ran towards her exit mark, stopping once she was clear of the cameras and line of crew.

Jordan rose with Freya as if their bodies were pulled together magnetically. She had done this action instinctively the first time that Freya had broken from her embrace during their rehearsal. When Freya moved away she felt a void that surprised her, and had automatically risen to follow her. The director had loved her reaction and it had stayed as part of the scene. Counting to three in her head, she allowed herself to drop back down onto the sofa and sighed, making sure that her face delivered the nonverbal dialogue of the scene.

Forty minutes later, Jordan and Freya were finished and walking back across the lot. Freya yawned loudly, stretching her arms behind her head as she walked. The effort of spending the morning in a perpetual state of distress had tired her out, and she was desperate for a shower and a nap.

"So, are you still okay for Saturday?" Jordan asked, smiling acknowledgements to the crew as they walked. "I know you're not big on parties."

Freya dropped her arms down and rolled her shoulders, "I'm not, but it's not every night that your fictional about-to-be-girlfriend has a birthday party."

"Excellent," Jordan grinned, jumping in front of Freya and shimmying as she walked backwards. "Remember, the theme is musicals."

"I remember, don't worry," Freya smiled. "You sure it's okay if I bring someone?"

"Absolutely," Jordan fell back into step beside Freya. "However, I'm not sure what the etiquette is on bringing a date to your future fictional girlfriend's birthday bash."

Freya laughed as they reached the point where they would separate to go to their trailers, "Try saying that again five times, fast." She grinned as Jordan stuck her tongue out playfully, "Anyway this is not a date, it's a friend." She lowered her voice and used a flirty tone, "Could it be that my future fictional girlfriend is jealous?"

"Jealous! Moi?" Jordan laughed clutching her chest. "I'm perfectly secure in our fictional about-to-be relationship, it's you that has the jealousy issues, remember?"

Freya giggled and shook her head, "Well, me and my fictional insecurities will see you on Saturday, birthday girl. Really good work today, thank you." She smiled and skipped off towards her trailer, her mood suddenly lighter following her brief conversation with Jordan.

Jordan chewed her lip watching Freya skip, waving her arms wildly as she went. "Jealous," she mused, recalling the tight feeling in her chest when Freya initially asked whether she could bring someone to the party, she laughed at herself and shook her head. She walked towards her trailer still speaking to herself, "What the hell do you have to get jealous about Jordan?"

***

"Will you just calm down Freya, we've got plenty of time," Dan rolled his eyes as his friend continued to fidget in the back seat of the cab. "We'll be arriving fashionably on time, since you made us leave so bloody early," he sighed.

"I thought you British are all about manners and such like," Freya grumbled leaning forward to check the line of traffic in front of them.

"We British, as you so delightfully put it, are all about pretending that things are okay when we really want to punch someone," Dan replied. "Slight difference. Oh, and cups of tea. We're *all* about the tea."

Freya laughed, feeling herself relax slightly as her fingers grasped around her small purse and the flat box that contained Jordan's gift.

"So what did you get her?" Dan asked, indicating towards the box.

"Just a picture," Freya replied nonchalantly, and switched her attention out of the window hoping that Dan wouldn't press further.

Dan narrowed his eyes, realizing there was more to the gift than Freya was letting on. He knew better though than to try to pry it from her now, he would simply wait until she'd had a few drinks and then interrogate her. "So, am I coming as your friend or beard tonight? Just so I know if I have to man up, so to speak," Dan smirked, nudging Freya with his elbow.

She glared at him while jerking her head towards the cab driver, then through gritted teeth Freya hissed, "Friend."

Picking a cream thread from his letterman sweater that had dropped onto his tight black jeans, he realized that Freya was wound tighter than he'd originally thought. "Seriously, sweetie you need to relax," he smoothed. "It's just a party."

Freya's glare softened as she recognized that she had been taking her nerves out on Dan pretty much from his arrival at her home. "Sorry," she smiled sheepishly and sighed.

Watching streets pass by, she reasoned with herself that she was just nervous because this was the first time she'd socialized with anyone from work after the pool incident, and not because it was Jordan's party that she was going to. However, she was very aware that Jordan was the woman who before joining the cast of *Front Line* had been her celebrity crush, and that getting to know the woman behind the character she played just meant that the crush was in danger of becoming something more if she didn't keep a tight check on herself.

"I do think it's rather delicious that you chose these outfits for us," Dan mused.

"Why's that?" Freya asked, knowing that she would probably regret asking the question.

"Well, think about the lesson that *Grease* tells you. In order to get the '*one that you want*', you have to either take up running or dress like a slut and start smoking."

Freya smacked his arm in mock outrage, "Are you calling me a slut?"

Dan rubbed his arm absently, "Oh get down off your high heels. No, I'm not calling you a slut." He shook his head, then turned to look out of the window. Waiting the perfect amount of time, he added, "Dressed like a slut, maybe. An actual slut, no."

"Sometimes I don't know why I put up with you."

The cab pulled up outside Jordan's modest Spanish-styled cottage in West Hollywood. Freya took a breath, opened the car door and, wobbling slightly on her over ambitious heels, stepped out onto the sidewalk.

She stood waiting at the stairs leading up to Jordan's front door while Dan paid the cab driver. She bent over with laughter as he turned and walked to her, imitating John Travolta's strut from *Grease*. "So Danny, how do I look?" she asked in an Australian accent, giving a slight twirl and fluffing up the blonde wig covering her own hair.

"For the fourteenth time since I came to pick you up, you look…" Dan scanned his eyes up taking in Freya's red stiletto sandals and her long legs encased in tight, shiny black leggings that looked like they had been painted directly onto her skin. Moving his head up, he came to where Freya's trim waist looked even smaller from the belt encircling it. Finally, he nodded his head as he studied the tight black top that stretched across her torso, pushing her breasts up and leaving her shoulders exposed, "Like a very expensive prostitute, dahling."

"Dan!" Freya wailed.

"Egg!" he mimicked back. Then, taking pity, he gave her a smile, "You look perfect as Sandy sweetie, seriously," he kissed her forehead and took her hand, then led her up the stairs and pressed the doorbell. "I swear Olivia didn't look as hot as you look. Although to be fair, she wasn't rocking the cameltoe look," Dan said absently, as he checked his quiff in the window of the door.

Freya looked down at her crotch, horrified. "Cameltoe!" she shrieked. As the door opened to reveal Jordan, she looked up, her face frozen in horror. "Mazel tov," she yelled excitedly, pulling the gift she held tight against her thighs, hoping that Jordan hadn't heard her previous exclamation.

Dan snorted loudly at his friend, "Hi, I'm Dan. Thank you for allowing me to come to your party." He held out his hand, which Jordan shook, smiling warmly. "I have to say, you look exquisite," Dan remarked, holding Jordan's hand up to examine her costume. "Doesn't she, Freya?"

Freya found that her mouth had suddenly become extremely dry and her tongue appeared welded to the roof of her mouth, as she drank in the sight of Jordan dressed in a crimson corset. Fine black lace detailed the garment's panels, which led down to a short ruffled skirt. The outfit was an updated and more risqué version of the outfit that Anna had worn in *Monday Girl*. Freya had just got to Jordan's legs, which were decorated by fishnet tights, when Dan's query reached her ears.

"Amazing," she managed to choke out, feeling her cheeks burn. "Slightly more revealing than my grandmother's corset," she paused, her face pulling into a grimace. "Now that's not a phrase I ever expected to say."

Jordan laughed, "Well thank you, and welcome." She moved from the doorway to let them enter.

Dan motioned to Freya to pass first and, as she walked past him glaring, he whispered in her ear, "You're okay on the camel front, I was teasing."

She elbowed him in the ribs as she entered Jordan's home.

"This is for you," Freya smiled, handing Jordan the box that contained her gift. "You have to keep it until tomorrow to open," she said, frowning and not releasing the box.

Jordan laughed, "I promise. I will open it on my birthday and not before."

Freya narrowed her eyes, sizing up whether she believed Jordan or not.

Jordan gave her a wide-eyed nod and Freya grinned, letting go of the box, "All right then, I believe you."

"You look…" Jordan raised her shoulders as she tried to find the right word to describe how Freya looked in her costume, before allowing her shoulders to drop as she finally settled on the word. "Fantastic," she smiled broadly.

Dan watched with interest as the two women looked at each other smiling, their eyes saying what their mouths were unwilling to. Finally, feeling like a third wheel, he coughed, "Are we the first to arrive? Freya has a habit of making me early for things."

"No," Jordan shook her head, startled that she had appeared to lose herself momentarily when Freya smiled at her. "There are others here, come on through."

Jordan placed Freya's gift carefully on the table in her hallway and led the way towards her living room.

Entering the room, Freya nodded hello to a couple of people from work. She smiled as she spotted Dianne and Belinda deep in conversation. On the show their characters were adversaries, but in real life, they were close friends. Dianne was dressed in black as Elphaba from *Wicked*, her face and hands painted green, while Belinda was dressed as Glinda and was looking resplendent in her white skirt, jacket and tammy.

Handing Freya and Dan flutes of champagne, Jordan nudged Dan's arm, "So Dan, Freya hasn't told me how you two know each other."

Dan accepted the champagne and tipped it forward slightly in acknowledgement. "Cheers to your birthday," he smiled, raising the glass to his lips and taking a small sip. "Oh, she keeps me very much out of the limelight," he smirked. "It's almost as if she's ashamed of me as her husband."

"Husband?" Jordan spluttered. "I didn't realize that you were married."

She looked between Freya and Dan in surprise. The tight feeling that had occurred in her chest when Freya mentioned bringing someone had returned, but this time it had a vice like grip on her and it was taking all of her effort not to clutch the area.

"Were married," Freya clarified, glaring at Dan. "We were married, a loooooong time ago," she smiled apologetically at Jordan.

"Jordan," a disembodied voice shouted from somewhere in the house. "Where're the napkins?"

Torn between going before Sabrina wreaked havoc in her beloved kitchen and continuing the conversation, Jordan dodged back and forth on her three-inch heels. She finally decided that a Sabrina tornado whipping through her cupboards demanded her attention more. She turned reluctantly to Freya and Dan, "I should go, Sabrina and my kitchen are not a good mix, excuse me."

Freya spun quickly, smacking Dan as she turned. "What the hell are you doing, Dan?" she hissed. "I said friend. Not beard. Friend!" she emphasized with another smack to Dan's arm as she spoke.

"Did you see her face?" Dan whispered back.

Freya's eyes widened, "I saw her look shocked, which is not unusual considering I've never mentioned being married. Seriously Dan, I could kill you sometimes."

Dan shrugged, "Must have been mistaken, because I could swear that Miss Thing there has a soft spot for you."

Rolling her eyes she gave Dan one last thump, "Don't try and meddle Dan, I'm warning you."

"So what did you get her?" Dan asked cautiously, deciding that his curiosity outweighed the commonsense approach of ensuring that she had imbibed sufficient alcohol to get a direct answer.

"I told you, I got her a picture."

Dan watched Freya's face with narrowed eyes. "Oh, good Lord Freya, you got her a *'wouldn't I be a wonderful girlfriend and you should leave the world of penis and run to me gift'*, didn't you?"

"Is there a shop for that sort of gift? Hallmark should make a card with that, they're missing out on a niche market," Freya replied lightly, hoping that Dan would let it go.

"Tell me you didn't get her something thoughtful and meaningful and adorable," Dan sighed.

"Okay I didn't get her something thoughtful and meaningful and adorable," Freya parroted back, knowing that her gift could easily fit any of those categories.

Dan rolled his eyes and looked over towards where Jordan was now standing with Sabrina, "She keeps looking over, you know."

"Who?" Freya replied nonchalantly.

"What do you mean who?" Dan scoffed. "Your soon to be getting a restraining order against you co-star, that's who."

Freya laughed.

"In fact, I think she might be talking about you."

Freya looked up at Dan, desperate to turn around and look but not daring to, "What's she saying?"

Dan rolled his eyes and gave Freya one of his condescending looks, "Wait a minute until I move this lock of hair behind my ear so my bionic hearing can pick out what she's saying. Who the hell am I, Jaime Sommers?"

Freya scowled at her friend. "I never got that. What was her hair made from...lead?" she mused.

"Whose hair?" Dianne asked as she joined Dan and Freya.

"The bionic woman," Dan smiled directing the conversation away from Jordan and her possible feelings. "Freya is about to go into one of her rants about the lazy interpretation of super powers on TV in the seventies. Make sure your glass is full, it's a good one. I'm Dan, by the way."

***

Jordan stood chatting with Sabrina while taking any opportunity she could to look over to where Freya stood laughing with Dan and Dianne. She could not seem to help herself. Freya captivated her, she felt her spirits lift whenever she was in her company, and it was becoming more and more difficult not to be around her.

"So who's the hottie with your lesbian lovah?" Sabrina smirked.

Jordan choked on her drink, "What?"

"The hot guy that's with Freya, the one you can't stop looking over at?" Sabrina indicated with her eyes, arching an eyebrow.

"That's Dan, Freya's ex-husband, and I'm not looking over at him," Jordan snorted, taking a swig of her champagne.

"So who are you looking at while practically salivating?" Sabrina furrowed her forehead, looking over towards Dan and Freya. "Wait, I knew it, you 'like her, like her' don't you? Is that why you were stressing about kissing her? I know we joked about not worrying about the wrapping before, but I didn't think you were serious about it," Sabrina almost hopped on the spot at her realization. Always ready to tease her friend, she started singing softly, "She's the one that you want, ooh, ooh ooh."

"Sabrina, seriously I –" Jordan was cut short when a roar went up across the room as the music was turned off.

Greg was standing over beside Jordan's piano, his *Phantom of the Opera* mask now pushed up and resting on his head. "Ellis, time for a song," Greg shouted. "We need a piano player. Can anybody play?"

Dan stood waiting on Freya saying that she could. Sighing at his friend's reticence, he grabbed her elbow and thrust her arm into the air, waving it back and forth until Greg caught sight of her.

"Dan, I haven't played in ages, put my arm down," Freya growled.

"Excellent, the Golden Child can play," Greg shouted, using Freya's much hated press nickname, given to her as her birth coincided with both parents receiving their first Best Actor Oscars and her grandfather's lifetime achievement award.

Greg waved his arm over towards where he was standing, "Get over here Easter and tinkle Jordan's ivories."

Freya shot one last look of anger at Dan as she walked over to Greg and sat nervously at the piano. She could feel her hands get moist at the thought of playing in front of people. Suddenly she felt as though she was nine years old again and about to play at her piano recital. She felt two hands rest on her shoulders, and instantly relaxed as she caught sight of Jordan's red nail polish in her peripheral vision.

"Do you want sheet music?" Jordan asked, leaning forwards to grab a book from the top of the piano.

Freya gulped slightly at having Jordan's cleavage beside her head. "Yes please," she squeaked.

Jordan flipped the book open and positioned the music on the piano's stand.

"This one okay?" she whispered as she pointed to a song, not wanting to make Freya feel uncomfortable if she was not able to play it.

Freya quickly scanned the sheet music and nodded. Jordan gave her shoulders an encouraging rub, and then turned to face her friends gathered around the piano. "Well, I suppose since Greg here insists that I sing," she chuckled as her comment elicited a range of groans and laughs from her friends and colleagues. "Okay, I know, like anyone could stop me singing. Okay, Freya?"

Flexing her fingers, Freya started to play the introduction to the song. Her confidence growing as she played, she felt the hairs on her neck start to tingle as Jordan's voice joined her.

Swaying gently, Freya played the instrumental piece. Completely lost in the music, her fingers danced across the keys as she poured passion into her playing in a way she had never experienced before. She was as one with the music. No longer reading from the score, she closed her eyes and slowed, waiting for Jordan's voice to become enmeshed with her again.

Playing the final chord, Freya sat dazed. She had always enjoyed playing the piano, but hearing her playing supporting Jordan's beautiful voice had taken her enjoyment to a level previously undiscovered. She had never felt so connected to someone through music, and was struggling to remember if she'd ever had such a connection, period.

The partygoers stood silent, stunned by the beauty of what they had just heard, until a few smatterings of applause started what became a cacophony of noise. Freya turned shyly in her seat, watching as Jordan gave over exaggerated curtseys then took her by the hand to encourage her out from the behind the piano.

Freya joined Jordan with her own bows. She took a deep breath to center herself as the music from the stereo started up again and the crowd dispersed back around the room. She looked down at her fingers, still entwined with Jordan's, as her co-star hugged a couple of people who were paying her compliments.

When they were standing alone Jordan turned to her. "Thank you," she smiled, gathering Freya into a tight hug.

Freya felt her stomach flip as she returned the embrace. Then, suddenly overwhelmed by the emotion that she had felt during the song and from being in Jordan's arms, Freya pulled away.

"You're welcome," she smiled. Unable to say more for fear of turning into a bubbling wreck, she turned and walked away leaving Jordan standing beside the piano.

Freya made her way through the house before finding a door that led to the backyard, where the soft lights shimmering in the pool were the only illumination. She breathed a sigh of relief that the party had somehow not spilled out to the back, and was still contained within the comforts of Jordan's home. She needed space and time on her own to gather her thoughts, and piece together her resolve to stop herself from making the error of falling for a co-star who was either straight or involved with Sabrina Morales. Either way, in her experience, neither would come to any good.

"You okay?"

The voice startled her and she spun round so quickly that she almost toppled over in her heels.

"Careful, can't have you diving into the pool at every party," Jordan said smiling. She held out one of the bottles of beer that she had in her hand.

"Thanks," Freya said, accepting the bottle.

"God, my feet hurt," Jordan grumbled, lifting up one foot. "In fact, I'm going to liberate them now, damn the consequences. It's my party!" She held onto Freya for support as she flipped the back of her shoes. Stepping down, she groaned in pleasure at the sensation of the cool tiles under her feet. She turned slightly, the height difference between the two women now shifted in Freya's favor.

"Are you okay? You kind of left me hanging in there," Jordan asked cautiously, making her way over towards the stone bench at the side of her garden.

Freya sighed and followed. Sitting down beside Jordan, she took the opportunity to kick her own shoes off, "I'm sorry. I just needed some fresh air."

"So, Miss Easter, you do seem full of surprises tonight," Jordan smiled, tucking her hands and her bottle between her knees. "A wonderful piano player," she nudged her shoulder gently against Freya's, "and married?"

Freya allowed her head to fall back against the wall behind them. "The piano playing you can thank my grandmother for. The marriage, well, I met Dan while I was studying in England. I was rooming with him and his then boyfriend," she glanced over at Jordan to see her reaction. Not sensing one she continued, "Dan is an amazing photographer and he wanted to move here, but couldn't get a visa. I figured since marriage was unlikely for me, I could do him a favor. So we got hitched and lived together in New York for a couple of years, until we could divorce and make it look authentic." She took a long swig of her beer, "Then, when Anna got sick I moved here, and Dan decided to come with me so that I wasn't alone in dealing with the circus that surrounds my family – and he stayed. I'm surprised that you didn't read about my marriage or divorce, it was in all the gossip rags."

"I'm not big on gossip. So how come you didn't think you'd ever marry?"

Freya mentally chastised herself for that comment. However, before she had a chance to respond, Sabrina opened the door to the garden and stepped out. Spotting Jordan, she waved, "There you are, it's almost midnight. We're working up to the biggest rendition of Happy Birthday for you. But only if you get your ass back in here." "Aw crap," Freya muttered as she lifted her shoes up. "I don't think there's any hope of me getting my feet back into those."

"I'll go commando, if you do," Jordan smiled, lifting her own shoes.

"Deal."

They walked towards Sabrina, who was holding the door open. As they reached the door, Sabrina touched Freya's arm gently, "Sweetie, I'm not sure that I should be the one to say this, but you do realize that your ex-husband is gay, don't you?"

Freya looked shocked and rocked back on her heels, her face then morphing into a bemused smirk, "You know, that would explain all the anal sex."

She shook her head and walked past a gasping Sabrina.

"She's messing with you, Sabrina," Jordan smiled, entering her home and using the tip of her finger to close Sabrina's mouth.

***

Jordan stretched out across her bed, opening her eyes slowly to test whether her alcohol consumption from the previous night had caused any damage. Relieved that her head appeared to be clear, she lay thinking about the previous evening. Almost immediately, her mind drifted to Freya. When she had left the room after their duet, Jordan had had only one thought, to follow Freya to check that she was okay. As she pictured Freya in her outfit, she remembered the gift she had brought. Jordan sat up suddenly, and sprang out of bed to retrieve the box from the hallway where she had placed it the previous evening.

She picked up the box and carried it back to her room. Sitting cross-legged on her bed, she opened the lid. On top of the tissue paper was a handwritten note.

Something for your toilet

Happy Birthday, love Freya x

Smiling, Jordan lifted the note, placed it beside her, and pushed the tissue paper to the side, revealing a simple silver frame. What was behind the glass made her gasp. She was looking at a photograph of herself on the night she won her TONY, meeting Anna Conor. Jordan didn't even know that anyone had taken a picture of the meeting, but what surprised her more was the letter in the frame beside the photo.

Dearest Jordan,

I was humbled and honored to find out that I played even the smallest part in your desire to pursue a career in acting. I watched you perform on Broadway in awe and with admiration and was pleased you were so rightfully recognized by our industry for that role.

I wish you continued success in the future.

Yours,

Anna Conor

Jordan allowed her fingers to trace the outline of the letter, still unable to believe what she was looking at. She brought her top lip into her mouth as she felt tears well up and start to spill down her cheeks. Sniffing, she swiped her hand across her cheek and reached across to her nightstand to pick up her cell phone. Blowing out her cheeks and releasing the air slowly, she selected Freya's name from her contact list. She laughed as the photo that she had taken of Freya appeared on her screen.

***

Freya sprinted along the trail, and reaching a pile of rocks, she threw her arms in the air in triumph and jumped on the spot, spinning back around as Dan reached her.

"I beat your ass!" she shouted, punching her friend on the shoulder as he leaned over trying to catch his breath.

Dan hacked a cough as he tried to catch his breath, "God, I have got to stop smoking."

"Yes you do, loser," Freya pummeled her fists on his shoulder, slowing and stopping as Dan looked up glaring at her. "Sorry, I got carried away," she shrugged.

"You're annoyingly perky today," Dan said, placing his hands on his hips and stretching his back. "I mean, you're usually annoying, but the perky is a new addition."

Freya stood on one leg, pulling her other leg up behind her and stretching out her thigh.

"I had a good time last night, what can I say?"

Placing his hands against the rocks, Dan stretched his calf. "I gathered," he replied in a withering tone. "You need a new agent."

Freya rolled her eyes, "We're not having this conversation again, Dan."

"We're going to keep having this conversation until you see sense, Egg," Dan sighed.

"Can we leave it please?" Freya pleaded. "Can't we just run?"

They started to run back down the track.

"Are you going to tell her that you're gay?" Dan huffed as they jogged together.

"You know that I can't," Freya shook her head, knowing immediately that Dan was talking about Jordan.

"Won't," Dan corrected. "I know that you won't. I still don't get it, Freya. I know this isn't just about you being worried about your privacy. You've been out to your family since you were eighteen. You were out and happy when I met you, and then your mum's agent takes you on and you believe him when he tells you that your career will get ruined. It won't, Freya."

Freya stopped running, "How many out men or women do you know with regular spots on primetime TV?" she asked as Dan kept running.

Stopping, Dan turned and walked back to Freya. He frowned as he thought. "Four, no five," he looked unconvinced as he answered.

"Now, how many in the closet actors do you know appearing on TV?"

Dan closed his eyes, "More than that."

"And there's a reason for that, Dan. It might not be right, but it's what happens. I was out of work for eighteen months when I arrived back here. I didn't like it, Dan. I'm thirty-four and I don't want to be supported by my family. It is hard enough being the Golden Child and being compared to my parents! I don't want to give anyone a reason for not giving me a job, and I like this gig," Freya started to jog away.

Dan quickly puffed his way back alongside her shoulder, "Can't you at least come out at work, keep it low key?"

Feeling her phone buzz on her arm, Freya stopped running and looked at Dan as she reached up to press her Bluetooth earpiece to answer the call.

"The less people who know, the tighter control I have."

"Control freak," Dan snarked, as she answered her call.

"Jordan, Hi," Freya's eyes widened, and she started to flap her hands at Dan as he made swooning faces.

Jordan rested her fingers on the picture now sitting on her lap, "Hi, I hope you don't mind me calling?"

"No, not at all."

Freya turned her back on Dan, who was batting his eyelids and fluttering his hand at his chest.

"How are you? Oh, and happy birthday again."

"I'm…" Jordan took in a deep breath, "I'm so touched, I can't believe you remembered."

Freya pulled her lips into her mouth, her smile still obvious thanks to her dimples and twinkling eyes.

"Weeeell, I *was* at your party and it was only last night. I know my memory can be a bit hazy but I think I'd remember." *Especially when you were dressed that way,* she added silently.

Jordan smiled at the playful tone in Freya's voice, "I meant my present."

Freya swallowed hard, lowering her voice and in a serious tone, she smiled as she answered, "I knew what you meant, and you're more than welcome."

Jordan picked up the picture and studied the image and letter behind the glass for the umpteenth time since she opened the gift, "I have no idea. I mean, how did you?"

Freya kicked her shoe into the dirt and put on her best Humphrey Bogart voice, "Let's just leave it that I know people that know people."

Jordan chuckled, "Well I know that it's your grandmother and all but I meant the photo. I know I was having a fangirl moment when I met her, but I don't remember any press around taking photos."

"There weren't," Freya said quietly. "I was there with Anna that night. I took the photo."

Embarrassed that she had not remembered seeing Freya, Jordan's brain almost exploded at the thought that she had been in Freya's company before without realizing it. This fact was almost inconceivable to her now, especially in light of her experience the previous evening when she was conscious of being zoned in on Freya's every movement.

"I am…I can't tell you what I am. I'm overawed. Thank you."

"Did you like the other part of the gift?" Freya asked, suddenly nervous that she had gone too far.

"There's another part?"

Jordan turned the frame over to study the back. Seeing nothing, she pulled the box across her mattress and burrowed under the tissue paper until she found another smaller flat box. Opening it she gulped loudly, as inside was a script from *Monday Girl*.

"Oh my," she said breathlessly. She flipped open the script, pausing as she saw handwritten notes in the margin, "Oh my god, this was your grandmother's actual script from the movie?"

Freya smiled at Jordan's reaction, "It is. I hope you like it."

"Like it? I love it! Oh Freya, this is too much."

"Nonsense, she'd prefer it go to you than being sold off. So what're your plans for the rest of the day?" Freya asked as Dan tapped her on the shoulder and indicated with his head that they should start back. She rolled her eyes, but jogged lightly alongside him.

Jordan flopped back against her pillows and studied her ceiling, "Nothing much, I was going to be doing something with Sabrina, but she's got some promo work to do for some make-up company she's working with. What are you doing? It sounds like you're on the move."

"I'm out at Griffith Park with Dan, we've just been running. Listen, we're just heading back to the car now, if you give me a couple of hours I'll be free, if you want to go grab lunch or something?" Freya winced as she finished speaking. *Way to sound desperate,* she thought, as she waited for Jordan's reply.

Jordan chewed on her top lip, her mind picturing Freya in running gear, beads of sweat running down... *woah*! She sat up abruptly on her bed, stopping her brain from continuing the trajectory it was on.

"Jordan, are you still there?" Freya asked, turning her arm to see the screen of her phone in case she had lost signal, while mentally kicking herself for putting Jordan into the position of having to turn her down.

"Sorry. Yeah, I'm here, that would be great. I'll see you in a couple of hours," she replied mechanically. Her mind still reeling from the image she had conjured up, she dumbly hit the end button on the call.

"So, still not going to come out at work, hey?" Dan asked as he noted Freya's expression as she pressed her earpiece.

"To use a British vernacular, Dan, naff off," Freya stuck her tongue out and sprinted off at full speed down the trail.

"I give you three weeks, Egg," Dan shouted as he picked up his pace and gave chase.

***

"The Yard?" Freya stopped and pushed her sunglasses up onto her forehead, as she looked at the open gates leading into the courtyard of the best-known gay bar in West Hollywood. "This is where you want to get lunch?"

"Have you had their all-day breakfast quesadilla?" Jordan replied, as if her response fully justified her choice of restaurant. She entered the bar, walked across to an empty table in the courtyard, and sat down.

Freya scrunched her eyes closed and pulled her sunglasses back onto her nose as she shook her head. She followed Jordan into the bar and sat down, quickly scanning the bar's other patrons. She picked up her menu and started to read the content intently. Jordan frowned at Freya, who had buried her face in the menu as she played with her hair nervously as if trying to bring it down in front of her face.

"Are you embarrassed to be seen in a gay bar?"

Freya's head shot up, her green eyes wide as, from behind the safety of her sunglasses, they raked back and forth as she scanned the courtyard quickly again, "No, no. I've been here loads, with Dan."

"Okay then," Jordan's face relaxed and she smiled broadly at Freya, then dropped her gaze to study her own menu.

After they had ordered, Freya relaxed and finally removed her sunglasses in the shaded courtyard. They were chatting animatedly when Jordan suddenly leaned forward and whispered, "Incoming, eight o'clock."

Before Freya had a chance to turn, she heard a voice behind her shoulder.

"I'm so sorry to bother you."

Freya felt a hand placed on her shoulder, "But we're from Chicago and we're big fans of yours and the show, and I wondered if…"

Freya turned round to look at the owner of the hand, who was looking at Jordan in awe. She smiled at the small balding man who was now standing stooped over, clutching his hands between his thighs. He glanced at Freya, then did a double-take that Hanna Barbera would have been proud of.

"Oh my god, you're Freya Conor, I mean Easter," he exclaimed, turning back to his partner who was standing looking embarrassed, and mouthing a '*sorry*' in their direction. "Look, Jerry, it's Georgia and Emily," the bald man stage-whispered.

Freya laughed. "Hi, what's your name?" she held out her hand.

The man's look of surprise turned into one of absolute devotion as he took her hand and shook it.

"I'm Mike."

"Well Mike, I'd like to introduce you to my friend Jordan," Freya smiled, indicating over towards Jordan, who was watching the exchange with an amused expression on her face.

"Hi Mike, lovely to meet you," she smiled broadly, holding her hand out.

Mike looked down at Jordan's hand in disbelief, before placing his own shaky hand into hers.

"And you too, Jerry," Jordan smiled, tilting her head and acknowledging the taller man, who looked like he wanted the ground to open and swallow him whole.

"Oh my god," Mike muttered to himself as he looked back and forth between the two women. "My friends back home will never believe this when I tell them."

Freya grinned and turned in her seat, "Jerry, do you have a camera or a phone camera?"

Mike's partner shot her a grateful look as he nodded and pulled out a silver camera.

"Excellent," Freya stood up, placing her napkin on the table. She grabbed Mike's hand and steered him across towards Jordan. Slipping in behind Jordan's chair, she casually let one hand drop onto Jordan's shoulders as she loosely put her arm around Mike's waist. "Ready?" she asked Jerry, who nodded as he took the picture.

Before moving, she looked over expectantly at Jerry, "Did it take? Did I have my eyes shut? 'cause I usually have my eyes shut in photos."

Mike practically skipped over to Jerry to look at the picture, "It's perfect, thank you."

He hesitated as he looked to be experiencing an internal battle raging in his mind, but finally he sighed. "Could I maybe have a picture of just the two of you?" he asked, his eyes pleading with the two actresses.

At some point, without realizing, Freya had placed her other hand onto Jordan's shoulder. She looked down, trying to gauge Jordan's response.

"Sure," Jordan smiled. Reaching her hands up, she lifted Freya's hands from her shoulders and pulled them down, bringing her closer by wrapping her arms around her neck. "How's that?" she asked, leaning her head towards Freya's until their cheeks were almost touching.

"Oh, you two are going to make just the cutest couple on the show," Mike smiled as he examined the photo he had taken.

"Well, be sure to watch September thirteen when we're back on," Jordan smiled, reluctantly releasing Freya's hands and allowing her to stand up.

Freya moved back to her seat, waving a goodbye to Mike and Jerry. Sitting back down, she laughed to herself as she placed her napkin back on her lap.

"You're amazing," Jordan mused, as she took a sip of her water.

Freya froze, keeping her head still and her face neutral, she raised her eyes to look towards Jordan. Straightening up in her seat, she gave Jordan a small smile, "I am? And why would that be?"

"Well, you practically commando crawl in here so that you're not seen, and then you go and do something like that."

"Remember, I went to the Anna Conor boot camp of how to treat those that pay your wage. Plus, when I was eight, I really liked The Pom Poms."

Jordan frowned, "The cheerleading singers? ...Seriously?"

Freya scowled, "Do not mock my awesome taste in music as a child. Besides, looking back, I think it was the cheerleading outfits." The last part came out before Freya was thinking, and immediately she realized her mistake.

"You wanted to be a cheerleader?" Jordan asked surprised.

"Noooyes, yes I did," Freya corrected, hoping that Jordan hadn't picked up on her original answer. "Anyway, I was a big fan and I saw them and tried to get an autograph, and they snubbed me," she waved her hand to indicate it wasn't a big deal. Looking up at the patio heater above them, she finished her story, "I cried for days afterwards, so I promised myself that I wouldn't ever do that to anyone. We do what we do for Mike, and people like him."

Jordan tilted her head and studied the woman sitting opposite her. She was an enigma, and every new piece of information that Jordan got her hands on made her desperate for more. She smiled and nodded, "We are so going to make a cute couple."

Freya gave Jordan a strained smiled, "Yeah, we are."

"What, you don't think we'll look cute together?" Jordan asked, noticing the strange expression on Freya's face.

"Yeah, I mean no, we'll look amazing together," Freya blurted out, just as the waiter placed her macaroni and cheese in front of her. "Thank you," she smiled at the waiter.

"I can't believe you ordered macaroni and cheese," Jordan shook her head, eyeing up her own plate of food.

"What, I like to order things I can't make when I come to restaurants," Freya shrugged as she took a mouthful of her lunch and practically groaned with pleasure.

Jordan put her fork down and looked incredulously at Freya, "You can't make macaroni and cheese? You are kidding, right?!"

"Nope," Freya grinned, popping another mouthful in. "Mmmm." She waved her fork in the air and gave Jordan a cute smile, "But I've been able to make martinis to die for since I was seven."

Jordan chuckled and then started to eat her quesadilla.

"I mean, our characters are like fire and ice," Jordan continued as she ate her lunch. "Georgia's all heart on the sleeve and everything out there."

Freya couldn't help but smile at the animation in Jordan's face as she spoke about her character.

"And Emily..." Jordan frowned. "Emily is all happy façade while holding everything close and hiding her vulnerability."

Freya narrowed her eyes, studying her co-star. "You think it's a façade?" she asked carefully.

"I think that she gives the impression that everything is up for discussion and cards on the table, but I think that it's all on her terms," Jordan responded, shrugging. "She hides her vulnerability. Whether it's because she feels the responsibility as a soldier or a doctor I'm not sure, but she strikes me as a bit of a control freak."

Feeling suddenly exposed, as if Jordan was speaking about her instead of her character, Freya muttered, "Twice in one day. Really?!"

Jordan looked up from her plate, "Sorry?"

"Dan," she shook her head as she spoke. "He called me a control freak earlier, and now my character is a control freak too."

"You're a control freak?" Jordan smiled, about to laugh, but instead assuming a serious expression when she saw Freya's face. "Nothing wrong with that, but you do realize there are things that you can't control."

"I know that," Freya shook her head irritably. "And I'm not a control freak, really, I just like…" Freya sucked on her cheek and let her shoulder fall as she placed her fork down, "being in control."

Jordan smiled as two men greeted each other affectionately at the bar, "But you can't control what others do, or who you're attracted to or fall in love with." She returned her attention to Freya and chuckled, shaking her head, "At this moment, you can't even control macaroni and cheese."

She reached over and wiped a piece of pasta sauce from the side of Freya's mouth using her thumb.

Freya's mind went blank at the contact. She cleared her throat and picked up her fork again.

"Thanks," she blushed as she focused her attention on the remainder of her food, trying to quell the jumble of thoughts and feelings coursing around her mind and body.

Jordan pulled her hand back and closed her eyes, giving her head a small shake. Her action had been without conscious thought, and now Freya was looking anywhere but at her. She pushed her plate back slightly, "Excuse me, I just need to go use the ladies."

Jordan stood up and walked through the bar towards the restroom. Once inside she paused, resting her hands against the sink. She'd had to get away from Freya, the awkwardness that had suddenly descended upon their table had been intense. Looking up at herself in the mirror, comprehension appeared all over her face. *Oh my god, she probably thinks I'm coming onto her.* Jordan's eyes widened and she ran her hands through her hair. *I bring her to a gay bar and then I invade her personal space and now she's all looking at her food and not at me. She thinks I'm coming onto her.*

Jordan turned to leave the restroom, but stopped and turned. Looking at herself in the mirror, her panicked expression dropped from her face, "I was coming onto her."

She breathed slowly as she processed her actions and feelings from not just the previous evening and through the day, but practically from the moment she had started working closely with Freya. She recalled the thoughts she'd had earlier, and how she'd struggled to pick the right outfit for their lunch at The Yard.

"I'm coming onto her, oh good Lord."

Jordan threw her hands up in the air, bringing them down hard against her thighs. Focusing intently at her reflection in the mirror, she gave herself a talking to. "Stop it, stop it now. Go act normal, Jordan Samantha Ellis."

If ever she felt the need for a reality check, using her full name usually gave her the reminder she needed about the person she was. It reminded her that she was still the girl from Orlando that joined the choir to help her confidence and was shocked to find a voice that knocked her choirmaster on her ass.

She slapped her hand against the restroom door and strode purposefully back towards their table. She hesitated as she was about to re-enter the courtyard, upon hearing Freya laugh as she signed an autograph for a woman.

"Act normal," she chanted to herself, waiting for the woman to leave before continuing her journey to her seat.

"You okay?" Freya asked. "I wasn't sure if you were done," she indicated over towards Jordan's plate.

"Yeah, I'm done," Jordan nodded, looking up and catching the waiter's eye she nodded her head for the check, and then dropped her gaze back to the table as she fidgeted nervously.

Freya was not sure what had happened, but Jordan had practically sprinted away from the table, and now she was barely speaking and spending an inordinate amount of time adjusting the cutlery on the table. She was about to speak when the waiter set a saucer down with the bill. Both of them reached for the check at the same time.

Freya's hand rested on Jordan's, "Please, let me, it's your birthday."

Jordan looked down at their hands, her eyes trailed slowly up Freya's arm until she reached her smiling face; her green eyes were still piercing even in the dull courtyard.

"Thank you," she rubbed her thumb gently against Freya's hand before slipping her hand out and placing it on her lap.

As they collected their belongings and headed out of the bar, neither noticed the man sitting alone in the corner slip his camera back into a bag.

***

Freya flopped down onto her sofa with her bowl of popcorn. Picking up the TV remote, she started to flip through the channels, looking for something to watch. Her cell phone buzzed from the table behind her. Reaching her hand behind her head, she picked it up and looked at the display. Her stomach flipped as she saw it was a text from Jordan. It had been eight hours since their lunch at The Yard, and Freya had given up trying to fathom why it had ended on such an awkward note. When they had reached their cars, she had pulled Jordan into a friendly goodbye hug, and couldn't help but notice her tense.

"Oh seriously Freya, it's a text," she shook her head as she opened the message.

I'm watching you

Still holding her phone, Freya looked nervously around her living room, frowning. She jumped when the handset started to vibrate in her hand. Looking down, she saw it was Jordan calling. Pressing the receive button, she brought the phone slowly to her ear.

"Hellooo," she said cautiously.

"I pressed send too soon, and realized that it probably sounded kinda creepy," Jordan laughed. "I'm watching you on cable, *Velvet Girls* is on."

Freya laughed as she balanced her phone under her chin and picked up the remote, flicking through the channels until she came across the same episode. "Oh God," she muttered, embarrassed as she watched herself on TV. "I can't believe you're watching this. I thought you were going out to celebrate your actual birthday?"

Jordan shifted on her sofa, plumping up the cushions behind her, "Yeah, I couldn't be bothered. I'm getting old, it takes me two days to recover from a late night now. What about you?"

Freya looked down at her hoodie and thick cotton pajama bottoms, "You know, the LA glam lifestyle."

"Sorry, are you going out?"

"Jordan, I'm in my PJs eating popcorn, and now watching myself on TV, thanks to you," Freya laughed, ignoring the beep of her cellphone indicating another call. "Oh," Freya recognized the scene. "Jordan, stop watching, turn it off."

"What? Why? ...Oh!"

Jordan's eyes widened as she watched one of the main characters in the show place her hand inside Freya's bra. "Hot and heavy in a club bathroom indeed," Jordan chuckled, sitting up to watch the scene.

Freya watched the scene through her fingers, "Yeah...I'm blushing right now."

They both watched in silence as the scene progressed and there were shots of a hand slipping beneath the waistband of Freya's trousers.

Despite knowing it was work, Jordan had an irrational surge of jealousy as she watched the scene. "So, we've got our first kiss scene rehearsal tomorrow," she slapped her palm to her forehead, taking the phone away from her ear and glaring at it as if it was the phone's fault that she had just said that.

"We do," Freya replied as her house phone started to ring. She swung her legs off the sofa, stood up and walked over towards her phone, "You nervous?"

"Nooo," Jordan blustered, hoping that Freya didn't detect any hint of nerves in her voice.

"Good, 'cause I'm an awesome kisser." Frowning at the name on the caller display on her landline, Freya ran her fingers through her hair, "Jordan, can I call you back? My agent is calling me."

"On a Sunday night?"

"Yeah, and on the landline so it must be something important. I'll call you right back."

"Sure, speak soon."

Jordan hung the phone up and turned her attention back to the TV, scowling and muttering *bitch* anytime the main character that had made out with Freya came on screen.

Freya picked up her landline, "Hey, Dominick."

"Is there a reason why I'm looking at photographs of you and Jordan Ellis right now?"

"Are you bored? 'cause if you are my episode of *Velvet Girls* is on," Freya walked towards her kitchen. "Residuals, Dominick," she sang.

"Open your email Freya."

Her agent's voice sounded unimpressed despite the mention of money, which meant he was pissed at something.

Freya changed direction and headed back towards the sofa, grabbing her iPad as she went. She hit the envelope icon and waited for her emails to load.

"What am I looking for, Dominick?"

"An email from me."

Freya went to the folder called *Ten Percent* where her agent's emails automatically redirected, located the email from Dominick, and opened it. She clicked on the link that he had inserted into the email, and gasped as photos of her with her arms around Jordan's neck appeared on the screen. She scrolled down the website. The next photo had Jordan reaching out to wipe the sauce from her face. She groaned as she saw that her eyes were shut, making her look like she'd melted into Jordan's caress. The last image was of them as their hands met, when they'd reached for the bill.

"Always with the eyes closed," Freya rolled her eyes.

"That's all you've got to say?" Dominick roared. "Did you see the story that went with the pictures?"

Freya scrolled over. "Shiiiiiiit," she breathed, as she read the headline beside the pictures.

Has the new Front Line on screen romance spilled over to off screen?

Spotted out in one of West Hollywood's hottest gay bars having an intimate lunch were co-stars Jordan Ellis and Freya Easter. These two hot actresses will be embarking on a torrid affair when Front Line hits our screens in September and it looks like the ladies have been getting a little extra rehearsal time in.

Tune in for the hot Army Doc drama starting back September 13th at 9pm on ETWC.

"Torrid affair!" Freya ranted. "We're half way through shooting episode five and we haven't even kissed, for Christ's sake!"

"Missing the point, Freya," Dominick interrupted. "I'm going to put out a rebuttal saying you are not gay."

"What?" Freya started to pace the floor. "No. No you're not!"

"We have to do something."

Freya took a couple of deep breaths and counted to five, "No. We don't. I'm telling you I don't want you to do that."

"In that case, get out of your sloppy house clothes and put some make-up on. I'll get one of my young unknowns to take you out on the town and get you seen around with a man," Dominick started to scroll through his client directory.

"No. Dominick, listen to me!" Freya raised her voice. "I am not Rock Hudson. I am not going out on a set-up."

"What the hell has Rock Hudson got to do with anything? You will do what I tell you to do," Dominick answered calmly. "I have your best interests at heart Freya."

Freya felt her anger swell inside of her, "See, Dominick, you think you do, but you do not have my best interests at heart. Thanks to you, I'm back to where I was at seventeen, hiding who I am for fear of recrimination. I have enough hang-ups with my family, without adding my sexual orientation back onto the pile. I'm tired of hiding, Dominick."

"We are not having this conversation again Freya. I will have trouble getting you roles if you come out."

"You will have no trouble getting me anything, Dominick," Freya swallowed back the tears that were threatening to fall. "You're fired."

"You can't fire me Freya, we have a contract."

Biting her lip to stop it trembling, Freya pulled the phone away from her ear and stared at it.

"That's why God invented lawyers," she yelled into the mouthpiece, then punched the end call button and hurled the phone across the room. Picking up a cushion, she clutched it to her chest and sank back onto the sofa.

***

"You not working?" Anna asked, as she sat down on the lounger next to Freya and held her hands over her brow to shield her eyes from the sun.

"They don't need me 'til later."

"So, are you going to mope around here all morning?" Anna asked, picking at imaginary lint on her linen trousers. "It's not good for you sitting out in the sun you know, you'll get skin like leather."

"Please Anna, not today," Freya pleaded.

Anna held her hands up in supplication, "I just came out to check that you were okay and see if you wanted to have breakfast with me in the main house."

Opening one eye, Freya looked at her grandmother suspiciously, "Really, that's all you wanted?"

"That, and to see whether you're finally out of the cupboard."

"Closet, Anna. The term is closet, and no, I'm not officially out. Why are you asking?"

"Your mom called from Poland asking if you were okay. Dominick called her ranting about you being on a date with Jordan Ellis."

"I wasn't on a date with Jordan Ellis," Freya said petulantly.

Anna stood, huffing at the effort it took, "I know I give you a hard time about being gay." She ignored the snort from Freya at her remark, "You wanna know the reason why? I want to see you get passionate about something…anything. You are so like your grandfather. He used to keep everything inside, never letting emotions show unless he was acting them, and I am telling you Freya, it's not healthy. It seems the only thing that gets a rise out of you is me baiting you about being a lesbian. I honestly don't give a damn who you rub genitals with. It bothers me more that you're wallowing on TV instead of in film or stage where you should be, but I'm happy as long as you're happy." She made a derisory sound, "Here's what I'm struggling to understand. Anytime I do bait you, you tell me you're not ashamed of who you are, but anytime you talk about the public knowing, all I seem to see in you is shame." She let her words sink in before cupping Freya's cheek, "Breakfast in ten, if you feel like company."

Freya's shoulders sagged as she watched her grandmother walk slowly back towards her home.

***

Dumping her jacket and purse on the chair, Freya stood surveying the inside of her exceptionally tidy trailer.

"Home from home," she mused, as she checked her watch and saw that she had an hour before she needed to be in rehearsals. Letting out a loud exhale, she dug her phone and iPad out of her bag, and scowled at the number of missed calls from Dominick.

After their fight, she had unplugged her landline, switched off her cell and sat in the dark in her living room contemplating what to do. The best approach to it all seemed like avoidance of everyone, and she had managed this up to a point. Moving her 'pity party for one' out to the pool that morning had compounded the issue when Anna had made her feel even worse.

She lay down on the sofa and opened up Dan's latest 'amuse Freya' ploy, and started to read. She had to admit that his latest find had managed to take her mind off her fight with Dominick and had kept her occupied into the small hours, which was why she was now feeling slightly frazzled.

She had been reading for about ten minutes and had just reached a really good part, when there was a soft knock at the door. Lifting her head slightly from the pillows that she'd surrounded herself with, she yelled, "Come in."

The door opened and the top of Jordan's head appeared as she climbed the steep steps up into Freya's trailer.

"Hi," she smiled shyly hovering in the doorway.

Freya felt a hotness rise in her cheeks as she sprang up and clutched her iPad close to her chest, "Hi."

"Do you want me to leave it open?" Jordan pointed to the door. "In case people think we're in here…" she leaned forward and lowered her voice to a whisper, "doing it."

Freya couldn't help but laugh as Jordan waggled her eyebrows suggestively, "No, it's okay, you can close it."

Jordan closed the door. Keeping her hand pressed against the handle, she hesitated slightly before turning and walking into the body of the trailer. She had rehearsed this conversation in her head several times, but now the words seemed jumbled in her mind.

"You didn't call back," she blurted.

The look of surprise on Freya's face mirrored her own, as that had never been her opening gambit in any of her practice runs.

"Yeah, I'm sorry. I got into a big fight with my agent and I fired him, and then my brain melted," Freya rested her chin on her iPad, still hugging the screen to her body.

Jordan sat down on the sofa beside Freya and placed a hand on her knee, "It's okay. I tried to call you, but your phone was switched off. I just wanted to know you were okay."

Freya felt the blush that had started when Jordan had entered the trailer get worse at the contact, "Sorry, I was so pissed off with Dominick, my agent. I'm good though. How about you?"

Jordan shrugged, "Yeah, I'm good too." She shifted in her seat so that she was facing Freya, "My sister called to ask if she should be thinking about buying a hat, and my grandma called saying that she was happy that I had finally found someone and that she is fine with my apparent gayness. I didn't even know she could access the internet, but apparently she's on twitter…with twelve followers." She noted that Freya's normal easy smile was missing, and she looked tired. Deciding to change the subject away from the gossip currently circling them, she noticed that Freya was hanging onto her iPad as if her life depended on it, "Sorry, were you in the middle of something?"

Freya looked down at the device then back at Jordan. Aware that she looked like she had been caught with her hand in the cookie jar, she decided to come clean, "Dan has got me into something." She stopped, not sure how to approach the explanation. She played a couple of options through her brain, her head bobbing back and forth as she silently sang 'eeny meeny' in order to choose which to take. Deciding to go full throttle, she took a deep breath, "Have you ever heard of fanfic?"

Jordan's eyes narrowed. "Fanfic," she thought for a moment, then started to shake her head. "Nope, should I?"

"Well, it's where fans of a show, or a relationship on a show, create their own stories using the characters."

"Ooookay," Jordan pursed her lips, not quite comprehending where Freya was going with this. Suddenly, her eyes widened and her eyebrows shot up. "Oh, do we have fanfic? Is that what you're reading?"

Freya coughed slightly, "Yeah, yeah we do, and yes it is what I was reading."

Jordan clapped her hands, "How cool! Excellent, let me see." She held out her hands for the tablet, waiting for Freya to hand it over. She scowled slightly when there was hesitation in passing it over, "What? Let me see!"

Reluctantly, Freya passed the iPad over and sat back, closing her eyes as Jordan cleared her throat and started to read aloud.

"*Staring deep into brown eyes, Emily stroked Georgia in a steady rhythm,*" pausing, Jordan looked up at Freya, who had opened one eye and was smiling sheepishly. She looked back down at the screen and continued to read aloud, "*She increased the pace when she felt the blonde's breath quicken and body tense. Georgia bit her bottom lip to stop from crying out...*Freya!" Jordan's jaw was wide open. "This is…" Jordan pointed at the screen. Her mouth was moving, but no words were coming out.

"I know, they go where the show doesn't," Freya opened her eyes and shrugged. "Most are set in the show, but this one is an AU, that's Alternate Universe. So it's the 1600's, and I'm a duchess and you're my servant. Here," she took the tablet and tapped the screen until she found the paragraph she was looking for, "Aha, read this." She passed it back to Jordan who was still looking at Freya, her face unreadable.

"How come I'm the servant?" Jordan grumbled, then shook her head slightly, trying to rid the image created in her head of Freya touching her. She could feel a dull throb start to beat a tattoo between her thighs as the image refused to go. Licking her lips, she took the iPad back from Freya and looked at the paragraph that she was pointing to. This time, she opted not to read aloud for fear of the arousal that she was feeling becoming apparent in her voice.

"You look flushed, are you ill?" Georgia asked, concerned as the flush on Emily's skin increased, creating a pink dapple on the white skin of her bosom.

Emily pressed the back of her hand to her forehead, "I'm fine, just a little dizzy. Perhaps I should sit."

In truth, the cause of her lightheadedness was Georgia herself. It seemed the closer the proximity the more Emily's heart would beat faster. She felt as though her blood was boiling in her body and at any moment she would combust.

Despite being waved away Georgia took Emily's arm and guided her to a stone seat in the orange grove. She looked around frustrated at the lack of water in the grove then, deciding it would be better than nothing, she reached up and pulled an orange from a nearby tree. She peeled it quickly and held out a slice to Emily, "Here, eat this it will help."

"I'm fine Georgia, don't fuss."

Unperturbed Georgia knelt down in front of her, so close that Emily could feel her breath on her face, "Please do not fight me on this, you will take the orange." She held the slice up in front of Emily's mouth.

Feeling her heart beat even faster, Emily leaned forward, her green eyes never wavered from the concerned brown eyes watching her carefully as she took the slice of orange between her lips. She wondered what it would be like to feel Georgia's skin on her lips instead of the skin encasing the segment of fruit. She bit down and a rush of juice filled her mouth and moistened her lips. She held her breath as Georgia pulled the remainder of the fruit away and carefully used her pinky to swipe across her bottom lip, before placing the other half of the slice into her own mouth.

Okay, Jordan thought, *so not helping with the horny thoughts.*

She passed the iPad back and cleared her throat, "It's good, really good." Wiping her hands nervously on her jeans, she started to ramble, "Wow, who knew that we had such creative fans. Look at the time, I should go get ready for rehearsal." Aware of her coursing emotions, she sprang up from the sofa and walked quickly to the door. "See you in a bit," she threw over her shoulder as she yanked the door open and left the trailer, allowing the door to bang closed behind her.

Freya watched Jordan fluster her way out of the trailer, and was about to follow to make sure that she was okay when her phone rang. Looking down expecting to see Dominick's name, she smiled when she saw who was calling, "Hey, Dan."

"Hey, sweetie. You still reading about yours and Jordan's nubs?"

She snorted with laughter, "I've just shown Jordan one of them and I think I may have scared, or scarred, her for life."

"Well if she's anything like you, she'll be walking around in a permanent state of horn after reading about the blessed release as she swept her finger across the brunette's engorged bundle of nerves," Dan recited in a melodramatic voice.

"Was there a purpose to this call?" Freya smiled.

"Just checking you're okay after last night, and to see if you're ready to get hot and heavy with your blonde lady lover."

Freya's smile faltered as she remembered what scene they were rehearsing, "Um, yeah, all is well, gotta go." She hung up the call and flopped back on the sofa, "Crap."

Jordan stood outside Freya's trailer and let a long breath leave her body. She started to walk slowly back to her trailer, her mind racing a thousand times faster than the pace she was walking. *So now I'm really turned on and have the next two hours rehearsing our first kiss scene.* She practically growled at the thought. "Excellent," she laughed, shaking her head, "Just excellent."

***

Standing outside the door to the rehearsal room, Jordan twisted her script in her hands. *It's just a job, same as any other job, just a job,* she chanted in her head, her hand hesitating on the door handle for the fifth time.

"Hey, Jordan, you going in?"

As if burned, Jordan pulled her hand back, and turned and smiled at the suited studio executive who, as it was the show's first same-sex kiss, was going to be joining them at the rehearsal.

"Hey, Lesley. Yeah, was just about to."

Jordan followed Lesley in and smiled a greeting towards the usual suspects dotted around the room. She spotted Steve the Director of Photography sitting with his back to the door, and grinned as she flung her arms around his neck.

"Make sure you make me look pretty, Steve," she whispered in his ear.

Steve laughed at what had become their running greeting over the past three seasons, "Don't I always?!"

As she looked up, she noticed Freya standing beside the Craft Services table.

"Yeah you do, that's why you're my favorite," Jordan sang, straightening up.

Freya turned and smiled over towards her, tucking her hair behind her ear. She figured that if Jordan was feeling awkward about what she had shown her, then it might be easier if she made light of it somehow.

"Hey Jordan, they've got fruit. Do you want an orange?" Freya shouted, holding up the fruit so Jordan could see.

Immediately, Jordan felt a flush start to creep into her cheeks as she recalled the paragraph that she had read earlier with Freya. Unable to formulate a suitable response, she dumbly shook her head. She was still trying to work out if Freya was deliberately teasing her, when she shouted again.

"Oranges aren't the only fruit, that we have I mean. There are apples, if you want an apple?"

Looking over, she could see the wide grin on Freya's face, dimples appearing deep in her cheeks. Jordan flashed a quick scowl over towards her, now certain that her co-star knew exactly what she was doing.

Jordan walked over to join Sarah-Jayne, the writer, and Toby, the director for the episode, who was a fellow cast member taking the helm. Having Toby in charge made the process easier in some respects, because he knew the show, and in others harder, because he *knew* the show.

Finally, with everyone assembled, Sarah-Jayne started flipping open the script to the scene. She brushed her long chestnut hair from her face as she scanned down the page.

"This scene follows on from the ensemble one you're rehearsing tomorrow," she looked up at the two actors. "We've known Georgia has started to have feelings for Emily, and you're oblivious to this, Freya. Although we've shown through all the hangdog looks over the past couple of episodes, that the feeling is mutual." They all laughed at the writer's comment, "So, we've had the night scene playing baseball on the base and Jordan, you've stormed off after Emily has given you a hug to keep you warm. The confusion has become too much for you, so you lash out."

Toby smiled, "You both know what you're doing. I really want this scene to pop. All the tension, all the unrequited feelings, the desire, the passion are all bubbling under the surface, and I want an explosion."

Jordan gulped slightly. *Shouldn't take too much to conjure up the feelings for this scene,* she thought. "Okay," she said, marveling at her ability to mask the emotional maelstrom currently fizzing around in her head.

They read over their lines a couple of times, working out the timing of their responses and trying to get the flow and rhythm right. Happy that they had that nailed, they started to talk about the physical direction.

"I'd like to physically show the push and pull of Georgia's attraction," Jordan mused. "Like she's trying to get away but keeps getting pulled back in."

Toby nodded. Leaning forward, he rested his elbows on his knees. "Reminiscent of the funeral fight?" he asked, referring to a scene Jordan had shot in a previous season, narrowing his eyes as he pictured the scene in his mind.

"Sort of, yes," Jordan nodded, rising and moving over to the space that they used for rehearsal.

"Okay Freya, are you happy with what you need to do?" Toby asked.

Freya nodded and, giving her thighs a quick nervous rub, stood up and walked over to stand opposite Jordan, placing her script on the floor beside her.

"So, do you want to do the kiss this time, or leave it?" Freya asked, feeling her heart race at the mention of kissing Jordan, even if it was only a work kiss. She chewed on her bottom lip nervously.

Jordan saw the nervous look on Freya's face, and decided that they both could do with the get out, "Later, I think, let's just concentrate on the dialogue."

Freya nodded, giving Jordan a small smile to try to mask her disappointment, "Okay."

They smiled at each other, and then Jordan turned and took a step to put some distance between them. Freya watched as Jordan rolled her shoulders and let her head fall back before rocking it back and forth, her long blonde tresses dancing down between her shoulder blades at the action.

"Okay," Toby shouted. "Action."

Jordan started to walk away purposefully.

"Georgia," Freya shouted after her, starting to follow in Jordan's wake. "What the hell happened back there?" Freya picked up her pace, and had almost caught up with Jordan when the taller woman spun around so quickly that it caused Freya to pull up short.

"Stay away from me," Jordan hissed, emphasizing each word, her lips so tense that she was almost snarling. She turned away again, but stopped when she felt Freya's hand on her forearm. She turned again, and this time tears were starting to form in her eyes. "Please," she pleaded, her voice starting to crack.

"No, you don't get to treat me like crap and then storm off," Freya raged. "I don't deserve that. All I did was offer you a hug to warm you up."

Jordan yanked her arm from Freya's grip. "Please, Emily, go back," she turned, and started to walk away again, swiping her hand angrily at the tears falling down her face.

Freya tensed her entire body, trying to show the frustration practically oozing from her, "No! Tell me what I've done to offend you." She moved quickly, positioning herself in front of Jordan, "I don't get it. Is this because I'm gay? Because I…I thought we were friends."

Jordan felt her breathing increase – this was the point in the script that they were meant to kiss. She looked at Freya, whose green eyes were scanning her face looking for the answer to her question, while knowing from the script what that answer would be.

Without forethought, Jordan felt her hands start to rise. She placed them quickly on Freya's cheeks and pulled the smaller woman towards her, clashing their lips together. She allowed all the frustration that she had been feeling towards the woman to pour into the kiss.

Freya was stunned. Their conversation had been that they were not going to do this, but here she was.

Jordan was kissing her.

The tension that she'd built up in her body during the scene drained from her muscles as she felt Jordan's soft lips on hers. She closed her eyes, relaxing into the moment as the frantic nature of the kiss slowed and became tender. Then, as suddenly as it started, Jordan pulled away. Freya's head moved forward slightly, as if her body understood her need to continue without her brain telling it.

Opening her eyes, she looked into Jordan's brown eyes, which were still glistening from crying.

"I don't want to be friends with you," Jordan murmured softly. She exhaled and turned, leaving Freya standing with a look of confusion on her face that was only in part an act.

Jordan let out a slow breath before turning and walking back towards Freya, "I'm sorry, I know we agreed, I just got caught up in the scene." She hoped that Freya didn't see through her lie.

"No, no, it's okay, it was…good…definitely explosive," Freya answered, still a little dumfounded from the kiss. She glanced over to where Toby was talking with Steve and Lesley, his hands motioning around as he spoke, "I think it may have been a bit too cable for Lesley."

"What?" Jordan turned to look over towards the small gathering assembled around the chairs. "Too much?"

She berated herself for getting carried away. The moment that their lips had met, she had become only partially aware of the others in the room. If it hadn't been for a noise from one of the crew snapping her brain back into professional mode, she probably would still be kissing Freya now.

Freya shrugged as she shifted from foot to foot, needing desperately to take her mind off her libido, which had been raging after she'd gorged herself into the early hours of the morning reading fiction describing them together. Jordan reading it aloud had almost tipped her over the edge. But the kiss…the kiss was the end for her.

Toby walked over to where they were standing, "That's what I had in mind. We may need to downplay the kiss a little for the network though, and Steve has asked could you put your head the other way for the shot?"

Jordan nodded, and watched as Toby walked back to join the others.

"Downplay how?" she whispered.

"Guess he means no tongues," Freya whispered back.

"I did not!" Jordan hissed loudly, her eyes wide in horror.

Freya scrunched her nose. "Yeah you did," she smiled. "But just a little."

"Ready to go?" Toby asked.

They both looked over towards him, back to each other, and then took their places to repeat the scene.

Two hours later and they had rehearsed the scene numerous times. After kiss number one was described as 'too hot for primetime' by Lesley, kiss number four as 'I've kissed my gran with more passion' from Toby, which caused some stunned looks around the room, they finally agreed on kiss number eight as the winner for the scene. With that decided, the two actors agreed to skip the kiss until they came back for blocking and dress rehearsal.

"Okay let's call it there and have a break," Toby said. "Good work Jordan, Freya," he nodded in their direction.

As they collected their scripts, Sarah-Jayne called Jordan over to discuss something in a later scene. Reluctantly, Freya watched as Jordan and the writer poured over the script. Realizing they could be some time, she left and headed back to her trailer alone.

She pushed the door to her trailer open and climbed the steps. She was almost inside when she gasped in surprise, as sitting on her sofa studying his Blackberry, was Dominick. He looked up at the sound of Freya entering.

"Why the hell does your trailer have a cooker in it? You don't cook at home, never mind at work."

Freya looked over towards the cooker which, to be fair, she had also wondered about, "The cooker is meant to be in the trailer, unlike you, Dominick." She held the door open, waiting for her former agent to leave, "I fired you, remember?"

"Please hear me out, you've been ignoring my phone calls and I've been trying to speak to you." Dominick sat forward on the sofa, placed his phone down on the table, and clasped his hands in front of him, "I'm sorry Freya, I was wrong. I will do whatever you want me to do."

Freya looked at her agent's apologetic expression and knew that it was genuine. For all his bluster, Dominick was a good guy at heart. She also suspected that either her mother, or grandmother, may have given him a flea in his ear. She closed the door and walked over towards him. "Saying that was bound to have hurt," she joked. Then, fixing him with a serious stare, she continued, "I don't want to hide anymore, Dominick."

"I will go all out, I promise. We can do it properly, announcements, interviews. You could write a book," Dominick said, hopeful that Freya was going to forgive him.

"I don't want to make a big deal out of it, Dominick, I just want to be me," Freya sighed. "I don't want it to look like I'm ashamed anymore."

"Absolutely, anything you want," Dominick replied.

"Anything?" Freya asked, raising an eyebrow.

"Anything."

"Cupcakes delivered to me for a week," Freya frowned as she calculated how much she was pissed at him, "and ten thousand dollars donation to a local LGBT charity." The fact that Dominick was also her mother's agent gave Freya unusual advantage over him, which she used only sporadically and usually for altruistic reasons.

Dominick nodded, relieved, as he had expected twenty thousand. The last time they had fought to this degree, and Freya had fired him, it had cost him ten thousand dollars to a children's charity. "Aaaaand ten thousand for Jordan's Future Arts Foundation."

Dominick groaned.

"Dominick! It's tax deductible, quit bitching."

Dominick smiled as he stood up and held his arms out, "Done."

Freya grinned and walked over to hug her agent. Despite their differences over her being out publicly, they had always had a good relationship, and sometimes Freya thought that Dominick knew her better than she knew herself. She was relieved that this meant that she would not be looking for new representation, never mind the cost of trying to get out of the contract they had.

"That's why God invented lawyers!" Dominick murmured as he hugged Freya. "I'm so stealing that line."

***

Jordan walked over towards Freya's trailer. She had wanted to speak to her after the rehearsal, but the episode's writer had caught her to go over notes. She bit on her thumbnail nervously as she walked. They really had to talk, because Jordan was fairly positive that Freya wasn't acting during their kiss either. As she raised her hand to knock on the door, she heard a man's voice on the other side and hesitated.

"So, now that you love me again, dinner later?"

Jordan tried to place the voice, but could not work out to whom it belonged.

She heard Freya laugh, "Okay, but you're paying."

"Of course I am, only the best for my girl."

She heard the voice get louder and realized that the owner was coming to the door. Panicked that she would be caught eavesdropping, Jordan leapt from the steps and hid round in the shade of Freya's trailer.

The door opened and Dominick turned to place a kiss on Freya's cheek as he left, "I knew you'd take me back, you love me too much."

Jordan poked her head around the trailer in time to see a handsome older man turn and smile broadly towards the door of the trailer, where she assumed Freya was standing. She slumped back against the metal side of the trailer as she heard Freya laugh and close the door. She clutched at her chest where a dull ache had settled, as she realized that what had happened in the rehearsal room had been just work for Freya.

***

Returning to her trailer, Jordan pulled out her phone and selected Sabrina's name from her contacts.

Sabrina sat patiently, waiting for the make-up artist to finish applying her eye shadow before retrieving her phone. She smiled as she answered the call.

"Jordan. Guess what, oh, you'll never guess…I got to fire my gun today," she said excitedly. When she didn't get the response she was expecting, she scowled, "What's up doc?" She waved thanks to the make-up woman, as she stepped out of the chair and walked to a quiet spot to get some privacy.

"Hey," Jordan responded. "You working tonight?"

Sabrina arched an eyebrow, watching the crew setting up the next scene. "No, we're on the martini shot," she said, referring to the final shot set-up of the day, "so I should be done in a couple of hours. Why, what's happened?"

Jordan scowled, "What do you mean, what's happened? I just thought that maybe you could come over and I'll cook."

Sabrina stepped out of the shade and onto the street where they were filming scenes for her show, "I'm an FBI agent, I'm trained in these things."

Jordan rolled her eyes, "You do know that when you say stuff like that, I never know whether you are joking or have become delusional."

Scowling, Sabrina sighed, "Okay, women's intuition then. Is that better? Regardless, spill."

Jordan gave a small laugh and took a breath, "Have you ever fallen for a co-star?"

"Oh, honey, please," Sabrina looked down the busy street. Shielding her eyes from the sun, she waved to the crowds hemmed in behind barriers to keep them out of shot. "That's happened to all of us at some point," Sabrina dropped her hand. "Please tell me it's not Greg."

Jordan chuckled and shook her head, "It's not Greg, you can relax."

"So who? Wait." Sabrina pulled the phone closer to her mouth and whispered, "Is it your lesbian lovah?"

"No making fun Sabrina, I'm being serious. I don't know what's going on with me," Jordan lay down on her sofa. "I lost the plot today rehearsing our first kiss scene. I think the studio exec almost had a heart attack."

"I knew it, you like her!" Sabrina said gleefully. "Do you think it's mutual?"

Jordan sighed and rested the back of her hand on her forehead, "I don't know. I thought so…maybe."

Closing her eyes, she thought about the conversation she'd just overheard, "But I just went back to her trailer to talk to her and she was with this older guy, and he's talking about how she loves him and he's taking her out to dinner tonight, and now I don't know what to think."

Hearing someone call her name, Sabrina turned back towards the set, "Jordan, I've got to go, I'll be at yours at eight-thirty. Dress nice, we're going out." She hung up the call, then, before heading back to work, typed a quick text message and hit send.

***

Jordan checked her hair one more time in the mirror as she waited on Sabrina picking her up. As she put her shoe on, she heard her home phone ringing. Still only wearing one shoe, she hobbled to grab the handset. "If you're running late, Sabrina," she said menacingly.

"Eh? Jordan, hi, it's Becky," a wary voice came down the line. "From the Foundation."

"Oh God, Becky, I'm so sorry," Jordan grimaced. "I'm waiting on someone and I thought you were her, sorry. What's up?" she asked, hobbling back to the bedroom to grab her other shoe.

"You wanted to be notified of donations over five thousand dollars, so you could thank them personally," Becky smiled as she looked down at the details on her pad. "We just received a donation this afternoon of ten thousand dollars from a Dominick Spence, on behalf of Freya Easter." Becky winced and pulled the receiver away from her ear as a loud bang came through the phone.

Jordan retrieved the phone from the floor, where she had dropped it on Becky's announcement. "Sorry Becky, the phone slipped. That's great, thanks, I'll be sure to thank them, her, them. Thanks," Jordan flustered, and hung up the call.

"But you…" Becky looked at the phone now playing a dial tone in her ear, "haven't got their details," she finished, shrugging as she put the receiver back in the cradle.

The doorbell rang, and Jordan picked up her purse as she hurried towards the door. Placing her phone back on the stand as she passed by, she grabbed her jacket and flung open the door. Standing in front of her was Sabrina.

Jordan's eyebrows rose as she took in her appearance. She had pulled her dark hair into a low ponytail tucked in at the nape of her neck, and her eyes were hidden behind the oversized black sunglasses perched on her nose. Looking down, Jordan tilted her head to the side as she surveyed the black turtleneck, tight black leggings and knee length black boots that her friend was wearing.

"Um, Sabrina, are we going on a jewel heist or something? 'cause I'm not really dressed for it," Jordan indicated, pointing at her own black wrap dress.

Sabrina pulled her sunglasses down her nose and peered over the top of them, "We're going on a recon mission."

Jordan stepped out of her door and pulled it closed behind her, "Recon mission? We have got to get you off of that show before you do some damage."

"Shush, we're going to check out your lesbian lovah and her man." Sabrina started to walk down Jordan's stairs, gesticulating as she walked, "I had a friend contact a friend who knows a paparazzi photographer, and they said that Freya was heading towards DeLucca's. So, that's where we're going."

"Please tell me that you don't have a balaclava in your purse," Jordan said wearily, as Sabrina slipped her arm through hers.

"What, with this hair, are you kidding?" she laughed as she opened the car door for Jordan to get in. "Oooo, but I did go to Radio Shack and get us these," she grinned as she got into the car and removed two small walkie-talkies from her oversized purse.

"Can't we just use our phones if we have to?" Jordan asked skeptically as she took one of the handsets.

"You're no fun, Jordan," Sabrina scowled as she leaned forward to speak to the driver. "To DeLucca's, we're on a mission." She sat back in her seat and started to rummage in her purse. "Dammit," she cried.

"What, you forgot the pepper spray?" Jordan asked sarcastically.

Sabrina looked up, "No, that I've got, but I left the binoculars on my bed."

"Couldn't just go out for a nice meal," Jordan muttered to herself, shaking her head and looking out of the window as they drove towards downtown.

***

"Sabrina, I've changed my mind," Jordan pulled at Sabrina's sleeve as they walked towards the entrance of the restaurant. "Can't we go somewhere else and forget about this?"

"Do you want to know if she's seeing this mystery man or not?"

"I could just ask her," Jordan shrugged

"Where the hell is the fun in that?" Sabrina replied, grabbing Jordan by the front of her jacket, and pulling her through the restaurant doors towards a bald tuxedoed man standing behind the welcome podium.

"Miss Morales, it's lovely to see you," the maître d' welcomed them into the restaurant. Jordan hovered behind Sabrina, trying to peer through the thick plants separating the entrance from the main body of the restaurant to see if she could spot Freya. "Do you have a reservation for this evening?" he asked politely, trying frantically to scan the restaurant's book to spot her name.

"If she doesn't, I have several," Jordan muttered.

Sabrina elbowed her in the ribs as she gave the maître d' a warm smile, "I do, thank you, it's wonderful that you've managed to squeeze us in. I've been hearing wonderful things about the food here."

"Why thank you, I hope that we live up to what you've heard." He looked down at the table planner in relief at finding her name, "We have your table ready, if you'd like to follow me."

Sabrina walked into the restaurant scanning for Freya. She spotted her sitting with her back to the entrance. Her hair's dark waves had been calmed into a smooth sheen, and she sat bobbing her head animatedly as she spoke with the attractive man sitting opposite her. Sabrina grabbed the maître d's arm with both hands, hauling him back towards her, "Where exactly is our table?"

The bald man looked at her confused, "We have the best table in the house reserved for you over there."

Sabrina followed where his finger was pointing, towards the table beside Freya and Dominick.

"No, sorry, that won't be acceptable," Sabrina spun around, looking for a table that would keep them out of the eye-line of both Freya and her date whilst providing them with a perfect vantage point for observing. She spotted a table where a couple were sitting, clinking their glasses in a toast. "We'd like that table over there," she pointed towards the table.

Used to the whims and demands of the Hollywood set, the maître d adopted his most sickly sweet tone, "Miss Morales, I'm very sorry, but we already have diners at that particular table."

Jordan watched the exchange while inwardly dying of embarrassment. However, she was grudgingly impressed as Sabrina seamlessly palmed a fifty-dollar note into the maître d's hand.

Sabrina picked at the man's suit collar and batted her eyelids, "How about you provide them with a bottle of champagne by way of apology, and we'll pick up the cost."

Rolling her eyes at the exchange, Jordan leaned forward, "We'll pick up their check for dinner as well."

Sabrina turned, and forgetting that she was still wearing her dark glasses, glared at Jordan who simply glared back. Eventually realizing she was going to lose the staring contest, Sabrina reluctantly turned back. "And we'll pick up their check," she murmured.

"One moment please," the man smiled and headed towards the couple sitting in Sabrina's desired spot.

Grabbing Jordan, Sabrina spun round and moved them behind another section of potted plants. She watched Freya's table for any physical interaction between her and the mystery man sitting with her.

Ignoring the stake-out for the time being, Jordan looked at the thin-stalked plant she was standing behind and raised an eyebrow. "Okay, not even a size zero could hide behind that," she chuckled.

Sabrina turned her head and looked over the top of her sunglasses. "Fine, get behind me," she growled.

Jordan moved so that she was peering over Sabrina's shoulder, as the slightly taller actress started to bob her head back and forth mimicking Jordan's voice, "We'll pay for their dinner."

Sabrina turned to face Jordan and drawled, "She'd better be worth it, that's all I'm saying." She smiled politely at a middle-aged woman walking towards them alongside an elderly woman.

"Shhh," Jordan whispered, as she tried to see past. She leaned to the left, shifting her weight so she could get a better view, when she felt herself start to topple as she overbalanced on her heels.

"Woah," Sabrina breathed, as she reached out and grabbed Jordan. Placing her arms around her waist and pulling her back onto her feet, she held onto her friend until she was certain that she was steady again. The elderly woman looked the two women up and down and gave them a dirty look before turning away and following the younger woman into the restaurant. "Did you see that?" Sabrina asked, her mouth gaping open.

"See what? My head was practically buried in your cleavage," Jordan responded, straightening her dress.

"That old woman just gave us the stink-eye," Sabrina pointed towards where the woman had gone.

"Probably another one not happy with the change of direction of Georgia. I've had a few letters saying they'll never watch again," Jordan replied shrugging, still trying to watch Freya's table.

"Ladies, your table is ready," the maître d' held his arm out to usher them into the restaurant. Both women scurried through the restaurant to reach the safety of their table, and immediately hid their faces behind their menus.

"Lose the glasses Sabrina," Jordan hissed.

"No, they make me look mysterious."

"They make you look like Bono. Now lose them," Jordan growled as she reached out, removed the glasses, closed them and put them down on the table beside them.

"Totally ruined my look now!" Sabrina grumbled, as she read the menu while keeping an eye over towards Freya. "So, do you know who he is?"

Jordan shook her head, "Never seen him before."

"So, do you want to talk about what's going on with you? 'cause enquiring minds would like to know what's so special about Freya that has you skipping along the Kinsey Scale."

"I honestly have no idea, I've never been attracted to women in that way before. I just get this sense of happiness, and peace, when I'm around her. She's funny and kind and, despite her family, she's really got very little ego," she sighed. "And then there're the other thoughts." She leaned closer to Sabrina, "Sexy thoughts."

"So, when did you start to feel these unfriendly thoughts?"

Laughing, Jordan's mind brought back an image that had the same effect on her now as when she first saw it, "I knew for sure after she fell in the pool at Eleanor's, when she climbed out and her shirt was wet and see through. It was like a shot of pure adrenalin to my libido. I have *never* had that happen before with a woman or a man. I've never even thought about women in that way. I mean, I can appreciate a fantastic body like we all can, but, this…obsession that I have, is unnerving. I really want to do things to her. I have no idea what things, but things!"

"Has she given you any indication that she's interested…or even gay?"

"I don't know. Maybe I'm just reading the signals wrong. Maybe she's just a really friendly person. I mean, first there was the birthday gift, which was amazing." She placed her elbow on the table and rested her chin in her hand, "And then that kiss. I swear that she wasn't working during that kiss. And then the donation to the foundation."

"Hmmm," Sabrina responded distractedly, as she had become engrossed in the menu. "The food here looks amazing." She looked up as she processed Jordan's words, "Wait, what donation?"

Jordan looked down through the menu, and had to agree with Sabrina as there were at least three things that she was desperate to try, "She made a donation to my charity today of ten thousand dollars, paid in by her agent Dominick Spence."

Sabrina lifted her purse from the floor and pulled out her phone, selecting the internet application. She typed Dominick Spence into the search field and hit the search button.

"Dammit, no signal. Wait here, I'll be back in a minute."

Sabrina reached for her sunglasses but was beaten to them by Jordan.

Jordan shook her head, "Nuhuh. Not happening."

"Spoilsport," Sabrina pulled her purse to her chest and left the table, returning momentarily to whisper menacingly in Jordan's ear that she was not to order without her.

She walked across the restaurant towards the restrooms, keeping a careful watch on their targets as she went. Sweeping through the doors, she checked her phone and smiled when the 3G-signal symbol appeared. She waited patiently for the page to load.

"Gotcha," she remarked, as a photo image of Dominick was amongst the results. She reached into her purse and pulled out her small walkie-talkie.

Jordan looked over towards Freya, she could see her head moving as she spoke. Every now and again she would throw back her head, and Jordan could hear her laughter.

What am I doing? Jordan thought as she observed her co-star. *This is madness.*

She was about to go over and say hello and put an end to the whole debacle, when she heard a crackle coming from her feet. Frowning, she leaned down to see where the noise was coming from.

"Sabrina," she sighed as she realized that the noise was emanating from her purse. She opened the zip and clasped her hands around the walkie-talkie that Sabrina had given her earlier.

"Major Disaster, do you read me?"

Jordan couldn't help but give a small laugh at the nickname Sabrina had given her while she'd worked on *Front Line*. She pressed the speaker button and spoke into the handset, "Agent Provocateur, I can hear you. Now where the hell are you?"

"Restroom. Come here, I have something to show you but I'll lose my signal if I come back in."

Jordan rolled her eyes, tore her napkin from her lap and thumped it down onto the table, "I'm coming."

Sabrina looked up as the restroom door opened, expecting to see Jordan. Her smile froze when she saw it was the elderly woman from before. Remembering the earlier look the woman had given her, she scowled before returning her attention to her phone. She heard a cubicle door close and lock as the main door opened and Jordan entered.

"Look who I found," she held her phone up for Jordan to see.

"That's him," Jordan gasped. "How did you?"

Sabrina held a finger to her lips and pointed towards the closed cubicle door. "That's Dominick Spence!" she whispered.

Jordan slapped her hand to her forehead, "Her agent. They had a fight at the weekend, she must have forgiven him."

Sabrina put her phone and the two-way radio back into her purse, "Well, that's that sorted, then. Can we go say hello and stop you moping around like a love-sick teenager?"

"Thank you," Jordan reached up and pulled Sabrina into a hug as the cubicle door opened and the elderly woman moved to the sink to wash her hands.

The two actresses pulled apart and went to return to the restaurant. As Jordan reached for the door handle, the old woman muttered under her breath, "Ought to be ashamed of themselves."

Jordan spun back round, "I'm sorry? Is there a problem?"

The woman finished drying her hands and crumpled up the towel throwing it into the waste. "Her I could expect it from, she slept with anything that moved in that hospital," she said pointing in Sabrina's direction.

Sabrina's mouth dropped open and her eyes widened in shock.

"But you, you I expected better from. What that boy did to you was terrible, and I would have thought having been cheated on you would know better." She turned back to Sabrina, "Did you know that she's seeing that lovely Captain Dollar? 'cause she is. My daughter told me so." The woman wagged her finger in their face. Returning her glare to Jordan, she continued to rant at her, "And while that poor girl is out in Germany serving our nation, you are in LA with that, that, floozy. Shame on you, shame on you both." With that, the woman bustled past the two shocked actresses and left the room.

There was a momentary pause before both women burst into peals of laughter.

***

"They were all over each other in the ladies' room, it was disgusting."

Freya's attention diverted from Dominick telling her about an interview he had lined up for her, and zoned into what sounded like an older woman's voice behind her. From the remark, it sounded like someone had been getting hot and heavy in the ladies'. Freya couldn't help but smirk at the thought.

"So I just gave them a piece of my mind. It's a damn shame what they're doing to that poor Emily girl, and she doesn't even know. That tall one, the one that left for the FBI, she's a brazen one." Frowning at the turn of the conversation, Freya leaned back in her chair to hear the rest of what was being said.

"Mom, I told you when we saw them earlier, they're actresses on a TV show, it's not real life. Their names are Jordan Ellis and Sabrina Morales."

Freya gasped and turned around to see who was having the conversation. As she did, her eyes caught movement across the restaurant, and she looked over in time to see Jordan and Sabrina walking across clutching at each other and laughing as they walked.

Jordan's laughter died in her throat as her eyes met Freya's, her green eyes a mixture of shock and what Jordan was sure was a hint of sadness.

Freya spun back round to face her agent. Shocked that what had only been a minor suspicion regarding the nature of Jordan and Sabrina's relationship had been confirmed in an extremely public manner, she felt her composure begin to slip, "Dominick, I think we'll skip dessert. Can we leave now?"

She unhooked her purse from the back of the chair and stood to leave. As she swept through the restaurant, she paused as she passed Jordan and Sabrina. She smiled broadly, masking the riot of emotion currently coursing through her.

"Hey, Sabrina," she said brightly. "Nice outfit."

She managed a brief nod towards Jordan, not trusting her emotions to hold if she made eye contact with her. She continued her exit, not waiting on Dominick as she left, determined to get out of the restaurant before the disillusionment she was feeling spilled out. She could hear the old woman's voice carrying across the restaurant.

"I hope you two are happy now!"

Dominick caught up with her as she stood waiting on the valet bringing his car round. She was desperately gulping in air, trying not to cry while photographers were around.

"You okay?" Dominick asked, accepting his car key from the valet.

Freya nodded, not trusting her voice.

Once settled in the privacy of Dominick's car, hot tears fell freely down her cheeks.

Dominick turned his attention from the road and did a doubletake as he realized Freya was crying, "Freya, you're not okay, you're crying. I've never seen you cry before."

She sniffed and gave a mirthless laugh, "Yeah, well, Anna's going to be proud of me for finally letting my emotions out."

"Is this to do with Sabrina Morales and Jordan Ellis?"

Freya nodded again, the movement dislodging more tears from her eyelashes. "Could we not talk about it?" she asked in a small voice. "I just want to go home."

***

You have no right, no right whatsoever, Freya chanted her new mantra to herself. This had been her default position every time images of Jordan and Sabrina came into her head. *She's a colleague not your girlfriend so you have no right to be upset.* She continued to play the phrase over in her head as she opened the door to her trailer.

"Hi."

Freya looked up, surprised at the voice as she climbed the final steps and entered her trailer.

"Hi Jordan, what can I do for you?" she smiled weakly and walked over towards the sofa to dump her bag and script on the table.

"I, I wanted to come and explain about last night, about what Sabrina and I were doing at the restaurant," Jordan stammered, picking at the hem of her top.

Freya smiled brightly, "You don't owe me any explanation, Jordan." She moved around her trailer to plug her almost dead cell phone in to charge. "We work together, who you see or what you do outside of work is nothing to do with me."

"Wait, do you think I'm seeing Sabrina?" Jordan asked, surprised. "We're not, I'm not…that whole thing with the old woman, it was a misunderstanding. The woman's daughter was really apologetic after you left." Jordan's heart sank at Freya's assessment of their relationship as colleagues and nothing more. She sighed and continued to explain, even though it appeared there was no need, "She gets confused, apparently she thought we were our characters and that I was cheating on you. She even hit Sabrina with her purse." She moved her head around to try to get Freya to make eye contact, "Thank you for the donation."

Despite the work that she had done to convince herself that she didn't care if Jordan was in fact involved with Sabrina, hearing that it was a mistake had given her a sense of relief. However, the relief was short-lived when she considered Jordan's response.

It would appear that she was now back to falling in love with a straight woman.

When Jordan mentioned the donation, she looked up in surprise, finally allowing herself to make contact with Jordan's brown eyes.

"I didn't realize he'd put my name on it."

"Well, he did, so to say thank you properly, I bring you an offering. And since you missed dessert at DeLucca's, which is to die for, by the way," she moved away from the counter she was leaning against to reveal a pie sitting on the top.

"You bought me a pie?"

Jordan shook her head as she cut a slice, "Nuhuh, I made you pie." Using a fork, she pulled out a slice of the pie and put it on a paper plate she had swiped from Craft Services. "As an Orlando girl, I made you my own special recipe Key Lime Pie." Smiling, she held out the plate and fork towards Freya.

Freya narrowed her eyes suspiciously as she took the pie and fork, "You made this?"

She looked down at the pie slice that was enticing her. She could feel the saliva start to gather in her mouth at just the faint whiff of lime. Taking the fork, she pulled off a small bitesize portion and placed it into her mouth, immediately moaning in pleasure at the sensation of the pie melting against her tongue.

"Oh my god," she mumbled through her mouthful of pie. "You seriously made this?" she asked in disbelief.

Jordan smiled, "My sister calls it my 'marry me' dish." She turned and laid the rest of the pie back on the counter.

Freya cocked an eyebrow, "Your 'marry me' dish?"

Waving her hand embarrassedly, Jordan chuckled, "She said that if I made that dish specifically for someone, they'd immediately want to marry me."

Taking another bite of the pie, Freya closed her eyes, savoring the taste, "She's not wrong." She opened her eyes and pointed at the remains of the pie with her fork, "This is a dangerous dish."

Jordan ran her hands nervously over her hips, "Yeah, I only make it on special occasions, usually for parties, gatherings, that sort of thing."

"So has it ever worked its charm?" Freya asked, taking another mouthful.

"Well, since you're the first person that I've made it specifically for, I'd have to say not yet," she pushed herself off the counter and walked towards the door. Pushing it open, she stalled. She was in two minds whether to say what was on the tip of her tongue. Finally, she smiled, "But let me know when you want to propose."

Freya stood, fork in midair, grinning as the door to her trailer closed.

***

They spent the day rehearsing the softball ensemble scene and the kiss scene for blocking. Despite never having talked about it they had, by silent agreement, decided to leave the actual kissing part of the scene until they shot it the following night. They were packing up for the day when Toby had come over to thank them for their work and remind them to check their call sheets for the next day.

"God, I love my job. Don't get me wrong, but night time shootings just throw my system out of whack for about three days, especially after a sixteen hour day," Freya grumbled, as they collected their coats.

"Ah, you should try the Ellis method," Jordan smiled, bumping her with her hip. She was glad that whatever awkwardness had been between them had faded as they spent the day in each other's company, retuning them to the light banter that she enjoyed.

Freya returned the smile. "Yeah, and what might that be?" she asked, waving goodnight to the production staff.

"Stay up as long as you can the night before." She turned around and shouted back towards Toby, "The yawn collection tomorrow night is your choice, Toby."

He waved back an acknowledgement as he stood talking through details of the following evening's shoot with the members of the production crew.

"The yawn collection?" Freya asked confused.

"You've never been on a night time shoot with us have you?" Jordan scrunched her face up. "You're in for a treat."

Freya gave her a worried glance.

"Don't worry, I'll look after you. In fact, as your almost-fictional girlfriend, who in real life got assaulted by a geriatric fan of yours for something I didn't do, I am going to make sure that you are ready for tomorrow night."

Freya pulled her hair out of the loose ponytail she had tied it into for the rehearsal. "You are? And how do you plan on doing that?" she asked, threading her fingers through her hair to separate the strands.

Jordan shrugged as she headed towards her own trailer, "I'm picking you up in two hours for the Ellis method."

As she watched her co-star sashay her way through the lot, Freya couldn't help but wonder whether she'd just been asked out on a date.

***

Turning the key in the lock, Freya pushed her weight against the door and entered her home. Her mind was currently creating a checklist of all that she had to do before Jordan picked her up. She was so engrossed in her planning that she didn't notice the feet dangling over the end of her sofa.

"Hey, Egg, how's my favorite ex-wife?"

Freya leapt in the air emitting a yelp, clutching her hand to her chest. "Dan. What the hell. You scared the crap out of me. What are you doing here? Where's your car?" she half-yelled, looking back out towards her drive in case, in her planning stupor, she had managed to walk past Dan's 1968 Ford Mustang.

Growing up in Britain, one of the first things Dan had done when he moved to America was to buy himself the type of car that he had grown up watching on TV and in movies. The car he was currently driving was thanks to his recent fascination with all things Steve McQueen.

"Bunty is unwell, she's been taken into the car hospital," Dan replied, still lying prone on the sofa, his arm draped dramatically across his brow.

Freya winced, "She's in the shop?"

This could mean a lot of pouting and dramatics as, despite his love of cars, Dan had no idea how they worked. He was more interested in the aesthetics and Christening them with wildly inappropriate names. "So, you're here to mope?"

Dan sat up. "No, I'm here to borrow your car," he grinned. "Oh, and to drop your photos off."

Rolling her eyes, she tossed her car keys across to her friend as she dragged his feet off the arm of her sofa. Sitting close together, they examined the pictures that Dan had taken of her a few weeks previous. Despite having a successful career taking fashion and publicity photographs, Dan still hankered after a career as a portrait photographer.

He had been working on pulling together an exhibition for the past year called *Twelve Hours*, where he took portrait shots of subjects from different walks of life during each hour over a twelve-hour period. Freya had been only too happy to become one of Dan's subjects, and he had followed her when she was getting ready to go to an event. They flicked through the photos, which ranged from Freya's preparations before the event, having her hair and make-up done and leaning against her sofa to put on her shoe while smiling broadly into the lens of the camera, to a shot taken the following morning, from behind, of her rising from her untidy bed and stretching.

"These are amazing, Dan," Freya nudged her friend as she looked through the shots once more.

"So, did you speak to Jordan today?" Dan asked, examining his work with a critical eye.

Freya checked the clock, "Crap. Yes, I did, and she's picking me up in an hour."

"Ooooo, you and the buxom blonde bombshell are going out, and after dark as well?"

She stood up, smacking Dan on the back of the head, "Stop reading fanfiction! For a gay man, you've become obsessed with reading about our characters' fictional sex life!"

"I can't help it, it's like crack cocaine," Dan sighed. "Right, I must be off, I too have a hot date. One can only hope that my picking him up in a Prius does not dictate how the night will end." He leaned over and kissed Freya's forehead. "Love you, Egg, be good."

He walked over to the front door and opened it. Stopping, he turned back, "Call me, but only if anything interesting happens. I'm not interested in longing looks and gentle caresses. I only want details if there's been pushing up against walls and grinding."

"Get out, pervert," Freya chimed, as he threw her a backward wave and closed the door behind him. "Right, let's get this show on the road," she said to herself, heading towards her bedroom.

***

She was almost ready, with just the final touches to her makeup to apply and her dress to slip on, when the doorbell went. Looking down at her bathrobe, she rolled her eyes, "Crap. Trust her to be an early type of person." She put down her eyeliner pencil, pulled her robe tighter around her body, and skipped to the door. She opened it and peeked her head around the edge of the door.

Jordan stood looking at her car parked in Freya's drive, her hand playing absently with the zip on her leather jacket. She heard the door open behind her, and turned to see Freya's head poking around the door.

"Hi, I'm a bit early. I hope you don't mind."

As Freya opened the door wider to allow her to enter, Jordan realized that her co-star was wearing a white robe that exposed more than it covered. Becoming extremely nervous, she started to ramble, "I wasn't entirely sure where I was going and for once the traffic was quiet so it didn't take as long as I thought. So I got here early."

"It's okay, I'm almost ready. Take a seat."

Freya pointed over towards the cream leather sofas surrounding a large marble coffee table.

"I'll be five minutes tops, I promise."

Jordan watched as Freya left the room, and then walked over to where she had pointed and perched anxiously on one of the sofas. Allowing her eyes to wander around Freya's home, her eyes settled on the scattered photographs lying on the table. She turned her head to look at one of Freya smiling at someone as they applied blusher to her cheek. She then found her hand absently moving to push that photo aside, revealing another of Freya, her head tossed back in a fit of laughter.

Sitting forward, Jordan started to examine the other photos, stopping when her hand came across a black and white shot. She picked up the image and felt an intake of breath that surprised her. The image was of Freya's naked back. She was sitting on the edge of a bed, with the white sheet rumpled behind her. Her hands were raised up into her hair, pulling it up off her neck, and leaving just a couple of tendrils caressing her shoulders. Jordan was astounded not just at the beauty and intimacy of the photograph itself, but also of its subject. She traced her fingers round the outline of Freya's shoulder blades. Realizing what she was doing, she quickly pulled her fingers away as if they'd received a burn. However, unable to resist, the tips of her fingers returned to the image and lightly caressed a pathway down Freya's spine, until she reached the small crevice in her lower back.

Gulping slightly, Jordan replaced the photo guiltily and hid it beneath others on the pile. She stood, trying to distance herself physically, if not mentally, from the multiple images of Freya strewn on the table, and walked across to examine some framed photos sitting on top of an old beaten up much-loved piano. She smiled at the various snapshots of Freya and her family. These were the candid family photos that the press did not get to see, and the smiles on faces that had graced so many screens, and were so familiar, seemed different in these private family moments. She picked up a photo of Freya and her grandfather. Their intelligent green eyes twinkled with resemblance.

"Handsome old devil, wasn't he."

Jordan smiled at the photo, "I was thinking that you look a lot like him." She turned to face Freya, her smile wavering as she noticed the short black dress she was wearing.

"What? Too much?" Freya asked, her smile frozen as she worried that she had dressed inappropriately for where they were going. "'cause I can go change," she continued, turning her shoulders and pointing her thumb back towards her bedroom.

"No, God, no, you're perfect," Jordan gasped. "I mean your dress. It's perfect."

Freya's smile returned to full beam, "Excellent, erm...I...I need a little help."

She turned her back, revealing the unfastened zip of the dress.

Jordan swallowed hard. Only moments ago she had been caressing that back in a photograph, and now here she was, faced with the real thing.

"Sure," she cleared her throat. "No problem."

She closed the gap between them. Her hands made several false starts towards the zipper before she clenched her fists and knocked her knuckles together silently.

"You okay back there?" Freya asked.

"Sorry, yeah, I've got it," Jordan took a deep breath and nodded to herself. Trying to steady her hands as she reached out, she pinched the fabric of the dress and slowly pulled the zip up, pouting slightly as she did so as the glimpse of Freya's porcelain skin disappeared behind the dark fabric.

"All done."

"Thank you."

Freya turned to face Jordan. "You look great by the way," she smiled, her eyes quickly scanning appreciatively down Jordan's curves, which were encased in a black leather jacket, black dress pants and a dark blue top, which dipped dangerously low into her cleavage. Reluctantly, Freya dragged her eyes back up from Jordan's chest and turned towards the door, "Reeeeally great."

"You have a lovely home," Jordan smiled, indicating around the room.

"Oh, I can't take any credit; it's my grandmother's guest house. I moved in to keep an eye on her when she first got sick, and I've been too lazy to move out since we realized that the woman will go until she's a hundred and fifty. It suits us both. I'm close by, but we're not living in each other's pockets. You wouldn't know that it's part of the main house unless you go out back."

"The main house must be pretty impressive."

"Embarrassingly so," Freya smiled, and then motioned towards the door. "Shall we?"

Jordan pulled her top of the range Audi up into the parking lot of DeLucca's, and Freya frowned as she recognized the restaurant from the previous evening.

"Really? You want to go back there?" she asked incredulously.

Chuckling as she put the car into park, Jordan turned to look at Freya, "We're not going back to the restaurant."

Freya watched, confused, as Jordan got out of the car.

"We're not?" she opened the door and swung her legs out of the car. Never keen to end up in magazines flashing her underwear, she was practiced at deftly navigating exiting and entering cars in short dresses.

They walked towards the entrance, however, instead of going through the main entrance, Jordan walked to the side of the building. Freya smiled as she read the gold lettering on the green awning covering an entrance, "DeLucca's Jazz House? We're going to a jazz club?"

Jordan grinned as they approached the entrance, "It belongs to the owner of the restaurant. She's a big jazz fan and so decided to combine both of her passions. I was talking to the manager last night, and he suggested checking it out."

She pulled open the door and motioned for Freya to enter, "They do a mini version of the menu from the restaurant, so maybe you can get dessert after all."

"I doubt that it will be as good as your pie," Freya replied as she entered, passing deliberately close to Jordan as she did.

Jordan pursed her lips and smirked at the comment as she followed Freya into the club.

They sat down in a booth that afforded them a perfect view of the stage where the band would play, but also gave them some privacy from the rest of the patrons. They had just ordered drinks when the emcee walked up onto the stage.

"Ladies and gentlemen, please put your hands together for Titus James and his band."

Freya and Jordan joined the applause as the band got up on stage and took their places beside their instruments. The emcee shared a warm half embrace with a handsome young black man, who was carrying a saxophone in one hand. As the man reached the center of the stage, he smiled out across the club and attached his saxophone to the strap around his neck.

"Welcome to DeLucca's, we hope you enjoy the show," he smiled, his voice a warm, honeyed tone. Turning, he counted the band in and they launched into their first number.

Freya tapped her fingers along on the table to the quick beat, as they listened to the saxophone free-styling around the melody.

Jordan leaned over, and Freya gulped as she felt warm breath at her ear.

"I take it from your fingers that you like it?"

Freya glanced down at her hand then turned her head to face Jordan, their lips only millimeters from each other.

It was Jordan's turn to gulp, when Freya's mouth tugged into a smirk as she playfully responded, "When I like something, my fingers seem to have a mind of their own."

Retreating from Freya's personal space, Jordan felt her heart beat; its quick pace almost matching that of the upbeat tempo the song was maintaining. As the band ended the song, the audience burst into a round of applause.

"Thank you," Titus smiled. "Now that we've woken you up, let us soothe your ails with something a little slower." The band started to jam. Their instruments coming together in a slow and sultry melody made Jordan feel like she was soaking in a deep, warm bath. She could feel the tension leech from her body, as her head swayed gently to the music.

A half hour later they sat in comfortable silence, each absorbed by the relaxing journey the music was taking them on.

"Thank you for this, Jordan," Freya said, holding her wine glass up in a salute.

Jordan smiled as she sipped her water, "You're welcome."

Freya smiled, then turned her attention back to the stage as she sipped her wine, her contentment almost palpable.

Throughout their meal, Jordan sneaked glances over towards her co-star, trying desperately to read what was going on in her mind. She needed to know that what she was feeling wasn't just her, that it wasn't all in her head, that she wasn't the only one whose heart was racing.

"Freya, I..."

She stopped as the waiter approached their table, a folded napkin in his hand.

"I'm sorry to bother you, but Mr. James asked that I deliver this to you, Miss Ellis."

Jordan frowned and took the napkin. Opening it, she laughed as she read the content.

"Tell Mr. James I would be honored."

Freya watched the exchange with a look of confusion on her face, "What? What just happened?"

Jordan raised her eyebrows and smiled a response. Freya gave a small 'humph', then let her head fall to the side as she lost herself once again in the music.

As Jordan's gaze trailed up Freya's neck, she closed her eyes, trying to vanquish the desire to lean over and trail kisses down the exposed skin. Jordan almost growled as she tried to control her thoughts. She held Freya entirely responsible for her raging libido. Ever since they'd read that fanfiction, she'd struggled to get images of making love with Freya from her head.

"Damned oranges," Jordan groaned.

Freya turned, "Sorry?"

Horrified that she had spoken aloud, Jordan covered her faux pas by waving her hand, "Nothing, didn't say a thing."

She looked innocently over to the stage where the band had finished playing.

"Ladies and gentleman, I have the honor and pleasure of welcoming onto the stage to perform with us this evening, the wonderful Miss Jordan Ellis."

Jordan plastered a huge smile onto her face and slid from the booth. As she walked through the tables towards the stage, Freya couldn't help but think that everything that Jordan did seemed to be permeated with a sexiness that only comes naturally, and can't be recreated. She sipped her wine as Jordan spoke with the bandleader, choosing what song she was going to sing.

The bass player started to pick out the instantly recognizable riff from 'Fever', and was swiftly joined by the pianist highlighting the refrain. Jordan stepped up and gripped the microphone. Closing her eyes for a moment, she centered herself on the stage, and allowed the music to wash over her.

Opening her eyes, she started to sing.

Moving her head back and forth, Jordan slipped the microphone out of the stand and stepped down from the stage and onto the floor of the club, where she allowed her voice to have freedom with the melody as she shimmied across the floor. She moved around the tables with only one destination on her mind. Freya sat captivated by Jordan's performance, and soon realizing where Jordan was headed bit her lip nervously, watching the slow sensuous approach.

Jordan paused at a table to tease a man sitting there, and ran her fingertips around his collar as she continued to sing.

She locked eyes with Freya, her focus unwavering as she edged closer to their table. When she arrived, she placed her palm slowly onto the cool wood and lowered herself in a catlike fashion down onto the surface.

She practically purred the last line. Standing quickly, she turned and walked briskly back to the stage as she repeated the last line while performing vocal gymnastics. As she stood back on the stage she arched back, letting loose her voice on the final line.

Freya started to clap so fast that she was sure her hands were going to come clean off her wrists.

Jordan kissed the band members in thanks and gave a small, almost shy, bow and a wave before exiting from the stage, and making her way back to their table.

Freya raised an eyebrow as Jordan slipped back into their booth. "So much for a quiet meal," she grinned, taking a sip of her wine.

***

Jordan heard a dull ringing permeate her sleep-addled brain. Realizing it was her phone, she reached across the bed and grabbed her cell. She looked at the caller display and frowned as she read 'Orlando'.

She pressed the connect button and held the phone to her ear, still lying snuggled into her duvet. "Hey there, what's up?" she asked, her voice still thick with sleep.

"Did I wake you?" her mother's concerned tone filled her ear.

"No, I was awake," Jordan lied.

Mary Ellis knew her daughter and knew when she was being lied to, but smiled at her youngest child's need to please, "You're not working today?"

Jordan stifled a yawn, "I am tonight, we have a night shoot."

"Ah, so…anything exciting happening with you?" Mary asked cautiously.

"Generally, or specifically?" Jordan asked, stretching and wincing as her back cracked in several places.

Deciding to tackle the issue head on, Mary tightened her grip on the telephone, "There're more photos of you and that girl on the interweb, and a story of you serenading her."

"Inter…net Mom, internet," Jordan rolled her eyes and sat up, fluffing the pillows around her.

"Whatever it's called, your grandma was asked at her aquarobics class this morning whether you were a…" Mary lowered her voice, "a lesbian."

Feeling an anger rise in her, Jordan tensed her hand around the cover of her duvet, "And what if I am, Mom?"

"I knew we should never have let you leave Orlando," a male voice interjected.

"Dad, you're on the line?" Jordan threw her hand up in the air. "Oh good god, Dad, if I'd stayed in Florida, the closest I would have come to acting would have been dressed as Pocahontas, singing about the wind three times a day. This has nothing to do with me being in Los Angeles."

"*Is* there something going on with you and this Freya?" her father asked.

Jordan closed her eyes and thumped her head against the headboard of her bed, "No Dad, we're just friends. I like spending time with her."

"She seems nice," Mary inserted, waving a dismissive hand towards her husband as he glared at her.

"She is, Mom, really nice," Jordan couldn't help the smile that spread across her face as she thought about Freya.

"Does she make you happy?" another voice entered the conversation, "'cause you look happy in the photographs."

Jordan rolled her eyes and shook her head, "Grandma! Mom, do you have me on speaker phone or something?"

"No, sweetheart, we were going to, but with your grandma's hearing not being as good as it used to be we couldn't. She's on the extension."

Jordan looked at the ceiling, shrugging as she threw up a silent '*why me*'.

"So, Jordan, does she make you happy?" Jordan's grandmother repeated.

"Yes, Grandma, when I'm around her I'm happy."

David Ellis raised his eyebrows at his daughter's answer, "But you're definitely not with her, are you Jordan? You're not gay?!"

Jordan rubbed her eyes, wondering what evil she had done to deserve this wake-up call.

"But she could be bi," her grandmother interjected. "Don't you pay attention, David? There are more letters in LGBT than just the L or the G."

Jordan flopped sideways and lay in a fetal position as she waited for an argument to rage between her grandmother and father.

"I think I would know if my daughter was any of those letters," David huffed. "Honey, are you?" he asked hesitatingly.

"What does it matter? She's happy!" Jordan's grandmother insisted. "I'm happy for you, Jordan. I kissed a girl back in college, it wasn't my thing as it turned out, but if that's what gets the engine revving for you, then more power to your elbow." David opened and closed his mouth several times.

Deciding that she'd had enough, Jordan sat back up.

"If you're all done. Thank you, Grandma, for sharing that…unexpected part of your past." Jordan shook her head quickly, "Like I said, yes I like her, and she makes me happy. I'm happy when I'm around her, and if it was ever to go further than being friends, then…" Jordan filled her mouth with air, releasing it rapidly, "then you would just need to deal with it."

She waited expectantly for the fall out of her announcement to hit.

Across the country, Mary and David exchanged surprised looks. Although never one to shirk from an argument if provoked, their youngest daughter had always performed the role of peace-keeper in the house, and so her passionate answer to their question told them all that they needed to know about how she felt; whether she was aware of it, or not.

Watching her daughter and her husband, Jordan's grandmother smirked knowingly.

"Okay," Mary shrugged her shoulders at her husband and smiled, inwardly cursing that this meant that she owed her mother twenty dollars from a stupid bet made after the first photos of Jordan and Freya emerged. "So tell us about her."

Jordan opened her mouth in shock, "Well, let's see." She snuggled back down into her duvet and started to tell her family about Freya.

***

Freya woke to the sound of movement in her kitchen. She swung her legs out of her bed and opened her closet door as quietly as possible. She reached in and moved her hand around until she came across the handle of a tennis racquet. Pulling it from the closet, she walked to her bedroom door and pulled it open before padding silently through her house while looking for the source of the noise. The kitchen door was ajar, and she could hear her refrigerator door being opened. Deciding to act quickly she leapt into the kitchen, yelling loudly, landing with her feet planted shoulder width apart and the racquet held out in front of her.

A loud scream came from behind the refrigerator as a milk carton hit the floor and exploded.

Freya looked down at the mess on the floor, with realization dawning on her as she recognized the footwear currently covered in milk.

"Dan! Seriously, what the fuck?"

Dan half-closed the fridge door with one hand, the other hand held tightly to his chest. "You almost gave me a heart attack, Martina," he shouted accusingly.

"You're the one sneaking into my home," Freya yelled back, taking in Dan's unusually disheveled appearance.

Slamming the fridge door shut, Dan huffed, "I wasn't sneaking, I was returning your car and making breakfast. Well, brunch," he looked at the clock. "Actually, given the time, it should probably just be lunch."

"Wait, are you doing the walk of shame?"

Lifting his feet up out of the puddles of milk, Dan flashed a wide grin, "Maybe, turns out that my date was big on the environment, and your Prius was exactly the ticket."

Freya leaned the tennis racquet against the island in the center of her kitchen, "So you didn't mention to him that it wasn't your car?" "What, and pass up the possibility of sex? Nooooo!" Dan shook his head, grabbing a cloth and starting to mop his trousers and shoes down. "Talking about sex, was there any nubbing happening with you and Jordan last night?"

Snatching the cloth from him, Freya crouched down to start mopping up the floor, "No, there was no nubbing, as you so delightfully put it. We had a lovely evening."

"You tell her you're gay yet?"

"Not yet."

Freya didn't look up as she squeezed the milk-sodden cloth into the sink and returned to clear up the rest.

"Have you moved the filters for your perky copulator?" Dan muttered, searching through a cupboard. Yelling in triumph as he pulled out a pack of filters, he started to make a pot of coffee, "You planning on telling her anytime soon?"

Stalling, Freya screwed her face up and gave her head a slight shake, "Yeeeesss."

"You're lying. I watched that show about body language; you can't fool me, madam."

"I will tell her, soon," Freya finished carefully. "I was going to last night, but…"

Dan walked round and pulled Freya into a hug, "Oh, Egg, I know you're scared that it could ruin things between you, but you're fooling yourself at the moment. She's not your girlfriend, you're not dating her, my little Eponine, so tell her."

"I know, and I will."

"Where the hell did the tennis racket come from, you're rubbish with balls," Dan grinned.

Freya wrinkled her nose. "You smell like boy sex, go shower and I'll make breakfast, brunch, lunch."

She laughed as Dan waltzed out of the kitchen warbling 'On My Own'.

Twenty minutes later Dan sat wrapped in Freya's bathrobe, scraping burnt toast with his knife, "So, what's the plan today?"

"I have an interview with V magazine this afternoon, and then have to be on set at eleven tonight. What about you?"

Finally satisfied that his toast was edible, Dan smeared jam onto it, "I'm going to go see a man about exhibition space."

Freya's hand froze in midair, her slightly soggy toast drooping.

"You're finally doing it?"

Dan gave her a small nod.

"I am so proud of you. So proud in fact, that I'll even forgive you for your rendition of 'Secret Love' in the shower."

"Living the dream, petal. Living the dream," Dan smiled.

∗∗∗

Freya entered the coffee shop and scanned the room for the reporter that she was due to meet. Seeing a woman half rise out of her seat in recognition, she smiled and walked towards her.

"Stephanie?" she asked, holding out her hand.

"Yeah, hi, thank you for agreeing to do this," Stephanie responded, shaking Freya's hand.

"It's my pleasure. Do you want a coffee or something?" Freya pointed back towards the counter.

Indicating down towards her own mug, Stephanie shook her head, "Sorry, I had to order, slight caffeine addiction."

"I'll just be two seconds," Freya smiled, and walked back towards the serving area. Ordering her coffee, she could not help but feel trepidation. This was it; she had decided that in this interview she would finally come out. She accepted the coffee mug from the waitress and walked back towards the comfy seats that Stephanie had selected.

"When's this likely to be published?"

"Errr," Stephanie raised her eyes, trying to summon the information from her memory. "Should be on the stands in two weeks' time."

"Great," Freya smiled. She bit her lip as she shot Stephanie an apologetic look, "I'm assuming my agent clarified the no go areas."

"He did. I won't ask you any questions about your family."

Freya breathed a sigh. It was always difficult navigating interviews when the questions seemed to focus on her family more than her, so she was always relieved when Dominick gave the instruction to not question her about them. She would mention them when appropriate. She wasn't averse to speaking about them, but she had become wise to journalists interviewing her as an easy access route to her more famous family members.

"So," the journalist started. "Did you know when you joined the cast that Emily was going to be a lesbian?"

Freya took a small, careful sip of her coffee, "No, I came on just for a three episode arc, and sort of thought that was going to be it. I love *Front Line,* and I was a fan before I auditioned. I was very pleased to be asked to firstly stay on the rest of last season, and then to come back as a regular this season."

Stephanie laughed, "So how were you approached about the direction that they wanted to take Emily in?"

"Eleanor French asked whether I would be interested. It was a story that they wanted to pursue, and had talked about doing a couple of times, but felt that the timing wasn't right. However, with gay rights becoming more and more front and center with the ending of 'don't ask, don't tell', etcetera, they felt now would be a good time to profile a same sex relationship in the military."

"Your character is going into a relationship with Georgia this season, who previously dated men. Do you foresee this being an issue for them?"

Freya stretched her neck. This was when she hated interviews. She hated the politics of the answers she had to give, in terms of giving enough information for people to read, but not revealing too much of the plotline.

"I think that all relationships have issues, and that a lot of those issues can be formed through insecurities with both parties, regarding previous relationships. What's nice about the story, is that the writers are approaching this like any other relationship. They're not making any allowances for it being a relationship between two women."

"What's it like working with Jordan Ellis?"

Breaking out into a genuine smile, Freya visibly relaxed for the first time since sitting down, "She's a dream to work with, we get on so well and she's incredibly talented. I feel like I've progressed working with her, as you have to really raise your game when you're acting with her, to hold your own."

Stephanie gave an awkward shift in her seat as she approached the next question, "There have been rumors that the relationship isn't just on screen."

The relaxation that Freya had been feeling instantly disappeared.

"Yeah, I saw that. Jordan is a good friend, and those photographs were taken waaaay out of context," she answered emphatically, leaving Stephanie under no illusion that that particular line of questioning was over.

"Do you think it's important to have characters like Emily on TV, giving a positive portrayal of a gay woman?"

This was it. This was the question that Freya had been waiting on.

She was going to come out.

Right now.

Right here.

She took a deep breath, "I think it's vital. Emily was already receiving positive comments at the end of last season, so people got to know her, rather than her sexuality. We have a responsibility to hold a mirror up to our country. Where there is intolerance, where there is hatred, we need to show people whose sexuality isn't an issue and who are living their lives in positive and productive ways, and where their relationships are accepted by friends and co-workers as normal." Freya took another breath, "We are in a unique position where we can be the voice for a community who for so long has struggled to be heard. Judging by the letters I'm already receiving, and we're not even on air yet, there is definitely a need."

Freya barely listened to the remainder of their conversation. She provided answers to the questions, but the whole time she had only one thought in mind.

She had choked on match point.

She hadn't given the response that she wanted to give. For some reason, the passion was there but the actual words just wouldn't come out. Before she knew it, she was shaking hands goodbye with Stephanie.

She left the journalist sitting in the coffee shop writing up some notes, and stood outside on the sidewalk, the sun warm on her skin.

Looking up, she chewed on her bottom lip. She was so disappointed with herself. She clenched her fists at her side and let out a frustrated yowl, alarming people walking past. Looking embarrassed, she apologized then spun round, yanked the door open, and strode back across to Stephanie.

"I want to change an answer."

Stephanie looked up in surprise. "Okay, which question?" she flicked back through her notebook.

"The one about positive representation," Freya nodded, summoning her resolve. "I should've started that answer by saying, 'As a gay woman in real life, I think that it's vital etcetera etcetera…' thank you."

Freya gave a tight smile then turned and exited the coffee shop, throwing her arms up in celebration as she left.

September 2011

As Freya stood hopping from foot to foot, she checked her character's watch – it was five past midnight. The temperature had seemed to plummet as soon as night fell, and she was grateful again that their characters were in the military so her feet were toasty in thick socks and boots. Putting one hand deeper into the long puffa jacket she was wearing over her uniform, she walked around waiting for Dan to pick up her call.

"Who died?" a muffled voice came onto the phone.

"Huh?" Freya responded, "No one, why would you think that?"

"Phone etiquette, Freya. A call before nine is polite, after nine but before ten is verging on the rude. After ten thirty is unacceptable, and at midnight, it better arsing be because someone has bloody died!" Dan huffed loudly, turning in his bed and switching the bedside light on.

Freya grinned down at the phone, "Well if you'd answered my earlier calls or responded to the countless messages I've left, then I wouldn't be calling you now."

"I was asleep, I had rather a late one last night, remember?" Dan yawned. "How'd the interview go?"

"I did it. I told them."

Freya danced on the spot, giddy from the feeling of lightness that surrounded her following her public coming out. She had not felt this sort of relief and empowerment since she was eighteen and told her parents…Anna had been a completely different ball of wax.

Dan sat up, suddenly wide-awake, "You told the magazine, before you told Jordan? Do you think that was wise?"

"I have two weeks before it's published. They've got a scoop, they're not going to wreck that. So, I have two weeks to tell her and Eleanor, and I know how I'm going to do it. I'm going to get her to come round on Friday, and I'll tell her then."

"Eleanor?"

"Jordan, you idiot!"

Slapping a hand to his forehead, Dan frowned, "I hope that you're right, sweetie."

Freya became distracted as Jordan walked towards her, carrying two cups of coffee. It was the first time she had seen more than just a glimpse of her since getting on set, due to their conflicting wardrobe, hair and make-up schedules.

"Gotta go, love you."

Freya hung the call up and buried her cell back into her pocket.

Dan looked at his phone. "Love you too," he said as he tossed the handset down to the bottom of the bed, turned off his lamp, and flopped back down to continue sleeping.

"Hey, Jordan," Freya smiled broadly, with her dimples on full wattage as she lifted herself up onto her tiptoes in excitement at seeing Jordan.

"Hey yourself, you look hot, warm. I mean warm, in your coat, you look warm," Jordan rambled. Horrified at her reply, she turned to look across to where the grips were finishing setting up the lighting rigs for the shoot. Everyone was aware that a long busy night lay ahead, in order to capture all the scenes they were scheduled to shoot. "Sooo, I had a nice time last night." She was relieved that this time she managed to speak without putting her foot in it.

Freya grinned and allowed the subject change, despite feeling enamored by a flustered Jordan.

"So did I, thank you. The Ellis method could be made for the win, or it could just be the coffee that I'm mainlining tonight. Either way, I'm awake…just." She wrapped her coat more tightly around her, "You know I've lived in London and New York. I've wintered in both, and yet here I am wearing more technology than they used to discover the North Pole, and in a temperature that previously I probably would've worn just a sweater to go out in."

Cocking an eyebrow, Jordan turned to look at Freya, who was yawning wildly behind her hand.

"LA is making you go soft. You realize a yawn will cost you five bucks."

Clamping her mouth closed, Freya looked quizzically at Jordan, "What do you mean?"

"The yawn collection. Every yawn on night shoots costs five bucks. The money raised goes to the director's choice of charity."

"That was what you shouted over to Toby yesterday?" Freya closed her eyes, remembering Jordan's comment.

"Yup, and you owe five bucks," Jordan chuckled. "You know, the best thing isn't the money raised, it's watching people yawn with their mouths closed to avoid paying the fee," she elbowed Freya's side and pointed towards Dianne, whose face was contorting as she tried to disguise her yawn.

"Are you busy Friday?" Freya blurted.

Jordan turned and smiled, "No, did you have something in mind?"

"I thought that maybe you could come to mine, and I'll make you dinner."

Looking at her suspiciously, Jordan replied, "I thought you didn't cook."

"I can cook, I'm hurt at the insinuation," Freya said playfully.

Grinning in return, Jordan nudged her, "Just not macaroni and cheese."

Freya frowned as she remembered their conversation at The Yard, "Okay, so maybe I'm just a really good takeaway picker."

"Then I'd love to," Jordan responded, happy that she would be spending more time with Freya.

***

"Okay, we're set to go again," Toby said patiently, trying desperately to hide his growing frustration. "Freya, all you need to do is *hit* the ball."

"Seriously, Toby, never go into sports psychology," Dianne shouted from the sidelines. "It's not like you were telling her to *miss* the ball the first thirty times she swung."

Toby glared round towards Dianne.

"Bite me, Dianne," Freya yelled, as she tightened her grip on the bat.

Chastised, Dianne rolled her eyes. "We've been freezing our asses off for forty-five minutes, and she's not done it yet. What makes you think this take will be any different?" she muttered out of the side of her mouth. "This is going to take up the entire bloopers reel."

"Shush now," Jordan frowned. "She'll do it."

Dianne shot a disbelieving look, then sighed before returning her attention to Freya as she bounced up and down to get some heat into her body.

Freya swung the bat several times, and nodded that she was ready.

"Action," Toby instructed.

The ball fired towards her and she swung the bat wildly, more in hope than judgment. There was a loud crack as she finally made contact with the softball. Throwing the bat down and pumping her fists in triumph, she ran towards her mark on first base.

Watching the small monitor, Toby gave her the thumbs up before casting a quick glance over towards the Director of Photography, who raised his eyebrows. Checking his watch, Toby shouted over, "Let's not tempt fate and try another one."

Jordan walked over towards Freya, who was being handed her coat.

"I'm sorry, I think Dianne is ready to kill me," Freya shrugged as she pulled the bottom of her coat up to close the zip.

They both looked over towards Dianne, who was still looking annoyed as she warmed her hands up around a steaming cup of coffee.

"Yeah, well, she spends most of her time annoyed," Jordan grinned. "So, you ready to pummel me?"

Freya turned around, startled, "What? Oh, the next shot."

She closed her eyes and shook her head, "Yeah, I'm ready."

They returned to the mobile trailers to get some heat while the next shot was being set up. Finally, they received a call for a hair and make-up touch up, and headed back towards first base. Taking her position, Jordan waited as the scene was called.

A member of the crew threw a ball towards Jordan. She watched it carefully, and reached up above her to catch it as Freya barreled into her knocking her off her feet, both of them landing safely onto a crash mat.

"Did I hurt you? Are you okay?" Freya asked, full of concern.

"I'm fine, in the same way I was fine when we rehearsed this for an hour on Tuesday."

Frowning, Freya pulled herself up and held out her hand for Jordan.

"Okay, but you'd tell me if I hurt you," she asked.

Jordan chuckled softly, "Yes, I would tell you."

They repeated the scene until Toby was happy and called it in. Their next shot was a continuation of that scene. Jordan lay on the ground and Freya positioned herself on top, her elbows on either side of Jordan's head.

"You okay? Am I squishing you?"

Jordan swallowed as she attempted to rid her mind of the fact that she was currently lying underneath Freya in the middle of the night, on a softball field populated with the crew and cast from the show.

"I'm good."

Freya let more of her weight rest on Jordan as the scene marker was removed from shot and action was shouted from behind the cameras.

Pulling herself back up slightly, she looked down into Jordan's eyes, "I'm sorry Georgia, did I hurt you?"

Jordan gruffed back, "No, I'm good, although I think you made first base."

Freya bit her top lip before smirking. "I think given our positions, I got further than first base," she said in a flirtatious tone.

Jordan chuckled.

"You're pretty pleased with yourself, aren't you?" she responded, flashing her own flirty smile.

Freya raised her eyebrows in surprise, "Well, what can I say. But you should wait, 'cause if you think my batting is awesome, wait 'til you see me on the pitcher's mound."

"You do realize that you're still on top of me, right?"

Freya pushed herself off her elbows and onto her hands, causing her groin to press into Jordan's as she did so.

"Just enjoying the view," she smiled, as she pushed herself up and off Jordan and held out a hand to hoist her back onto her feet.

"Cut."

Both women gathered themselves together. The unintentional push of their groins into each other had not happened before, as Freya had always rehearsed from a locked arm position. However, Toby had asked them to change the angle of their position and start closer together, in order to build the tension. The sensation had, despite their location, and reason for it, caused a surge of arousal in both of them. They stood not looking at each other as they listened to Toby's shouted instructions before preparing to redo the scene.

Seeing that both actors looked perturbed, Toby walked over, "That was great, really good work. You good to go again?"

They turned to Toby and nodded.

"Yeah," they answered as one.

"Absolutely," Jordan added, and returned to her place.

They were working fast to try and get all of the scenes done before sunrise, and the production crew were soon setting up the final scene of the night. The rest of the cast had disappeared, as this shot involved just Jordan and Freya. Despite the threat of a fine, Freya yawned. By her reckoning, she probably owed close to a hundred bucks to the charity collection by now, but was past caring. She was thankful that she was as tired as she was, as it meant that she wasn't spending time stressing that she was about to kiss Jordan again.

"Guys, not to put added pressure on you, but we're running short of darkness. So, if we could get this one nailed quickly, that would be great," Toby said, flashing them a quick smile. "We're doing this with all cameras on continuous motion," he reminded them, as they walked to their marks in the parking lot beside the softball field.

'Action' was called, and they started to film the scene that they had rehearsed earlier in the week.

***

Dawn started to break as Jordan was being driven home. She laid her head against the headrest trying to gain some clarity of thought, her mind was a fuzz. Whether it was due to the hours that they had worked or the amount of caffeine that was coursing through her system, she wasn't sure. However, one thing she was sure of most of all was that her current state was not helped by the time that she had spent kissing Freya.

Kisses that meant nothing.

Kisses that were work.

Except those kisses weren't meaningless to Jordan.

Despite the circumstances, the surrounding lights, sound equipment, cameras and crew, those kisses were not awkward like the ones that Jordan had previously experienced when working. They weren't the clinical, mechanical, going-through-the-motions-of-thescene types of kisses. Each time Freya's lips pressed against hers her professional demeanor left her, and it took all her powers of concentration to pull it back.

Jordan lifted her fingers to her lips, lightly running her fingertips across her bottom lip as her mind replayed the kisses, the easy laughter between takes, and the taste of mint on Freya's breath from the gum that she had thoughtfully used to disguise the coffee that she had been drinking throughout the night.

What she desperately wanted to know was whether those kisses were meaningless for Freya or whether, on any level, she felt anything more for her than their fledgling friendship. She was startled out of her reverie by her phone buzzing in her pocket.

"Hey, early bird," she smiled as she answered Sabrina's call.

"So, how'd the kiss go? Did you accidentally slip the tongue in again?"

Jordan rolled her eyes, wishing she had never told Sabrina about the incident at the first rehearsal.

"No I didn't, we're all done. I'm just heading home now. Whatcha doin'?"

Sabrina opened the car door and climbed in, "Just got picked up for work. So are you ever going to have a conversation with her about how you're feeling?"

Thumping her head against the seat, Jordan frowned, "She's invited me to dinner tomorrow night. I think I'm going to have to say something then, 'cause this is driving me insane."

"Wake up! For the love of God, Dan, how much sleep do you need?" Freya shouted down the phone, leaving a message on Dan's machine. "She's coming on Friday, I am so doing this!"

She hung the call up and sat back, letting a deep satisfied breath leave her body.

Her phone played 'God Save the Queen' as Dan returned her call.

"Hey, what you doing not taking my calls again?" she asked, aggrieved that Dan appeared to be screening calls.

Even though it was wasted on the empty room, Dan gave a withering look as he pulled clothes out of his dresser.

"Freya, we're really going to have to chat about manners, the sun is only just coming up."

"How much sleep do you need?"

"The amount of sleep required is in direct proportion the amount of sex had," Dan responded as he threw clothes onto his bed.

"Ewww," she screwed up her nose and shook her head to rid it of that image. "Sorry, I'm all out of synch. But I have news!"

Freya felt energized, even though she'd been working through the night. The last scene that they had filmed was enough to make her feel like she was floating. Kissing Jordan, regardless of how false the situation, was still enough to make her giddy.

"She's coming round for dinner on Friday night."

"Does she know about your cooking abilities?" Dan asked, slightly concerned that Freya's evening could end with either one or both of them with their head firmly stuck down the lavatory, thus ending all possibility of a happy ending and meaning that he was still going to be involved in her drama. *The price to pay for being a hag fag,* he thought to himself.

"She's aware of my issues. However, perhaps not the exact scale of those issues," Freya admitted. "But she is aware."

Dan sighed, knowing that he would probably regret what he was about to say, "Come to mine tonight, I'll make your meal and that way you just have to heat it up tomorrow."

Clenching her fist at getting what she had hoped for when she called, Freya composed herself before answering, "Only if you're sure. I mean, I wouldn't want to impose."

"Drop the act, princess."

Freya laughed, "How 'bout we make it movie night, and I stay over?"

"It's a date," Dan laughed, as he selected a shirt from the pile he'd thrown on the bed. "Love you wifie, see you later."

Freya gripped her cell in two hands, excited at the prospect of her evening with Jordan.

***

"What on God's great earth are you wearing?" Dan looked at his friend in abject horror.

Freya looked down at her attire. "What? It's a onesie, do you like it?" she twirled, giving Dan the full effect of the white all-in-one covered in large black splodges.

Dan pulled a face as if Freya had just held month-old milk under his nose. Holding his palm out as if to ward off Freya and her fashion taste, he snorted, "You mean, you're actually wearing a giant romper suit on purpose? You bought that?"

"Yes, I bought it. It's really comfortable," Freya pouted, brushing her hands proudly down the front of her clothing.

Walking round her as if she were radioactive, Dan pulled at the material.

"Jesus, as if it's not bad enough that you look like a cow, it has a bloody hood," he said, disgusted. "How the hell do you pee in the damn thing?"

"Well, yes, that is its one design flaw," Freya conceded. "You basically have to strip off, you'd have thought they'd have put in a flap or something," she said, bending over to examine the crotch area.

"Because that would have been a redeeming feature?" Still looking as if he was going to throw up, Dan collected the bowl of popcorn and carried it through to his living room, "So what are we watching, rugrat?"

Freya shot him a withering look as she left the room to collect the DVD, "We're watching Saw."

Recoiling, Dan shouted after her, "You know, in all those fanfiction things they think you're this nice person, when really you're a horrible witch who makes me watch horrors even though you know I hate them. And they think you can play sports. How many takes was it again before you hit the ball?"

Waiting for her to return, Dan switched the TV on and started to flick through the channels.

Freya grinned, re-entering the room and cuffing the back of Dan's head as she leaned over the sofa to snag some popcorn, "Oh yeah, I'm a bitch and it wasn't that man-… hey, that's me!"

She pointed to the screen as a photograph of her as Emily appeared. She grabbed the remote from Dan, and held it out in front of her as she balanced on the back of the sofa and turned the volume up.

***

Jordan was relaxing in her sloppies on her sofa. She had a glass of wine in her hand, and for the first time in a long time she was relaxing with a book. Her peace and quiet was shattered when her phone started to ring. Frowning at the interruption, she considered leaving it, but when she saw it was Sabrina calling she opted to answer.

"Hey, what's up?"

"Turn your TV on now and go to ENT," Sabrina's frantic voice ordered her.

Picking up the remote, Jordan switched on the television and selected the channel. When the picture appeared, she was looking at a photo of Freya. She turned the sound up a couple of notches to hear what the voiceover was saying.

"Yep, that's right folks, she's gay. We've got the insider scoop that Freya Easter is about to come out of the closet in an interview with V magazine."

The photo disappeared, and footage of Freya from the season finale appeared.

"For anyone that has lived under a rock for the past thirty-four years, Freya Easter is of course the only child of double Oscar-winning couple Dylan and Francesca Conor, and the grandchild of Hollywood greats Finn and Anna Conor. An actor in her own right, she joined the cast last season of the hit army medical drama *Front Line* as Captain Emily Dollar, and quickly became a viewer's favorite."

The anchorwoman appeared, smiling brightly into the camera while perched on the edge of a desk.

"We gave you the story back in July that she was set to become a series regular when they returned to filming a couple of months ago."

Footage appeared of Freya at a red carpet event, while the presenter continued with her voiceover.

"There have been rumors circulating about the thirty-four-yearold actress and her co-star Jordan Ellis, following the show's decision to make Emily enter into a lesbian relationship with Jordan's character, series favorite Captain Georgia Van Hausen. Neither actress has commented on the rumors. Coming up next on ENT, reality show star arrested for DUI for a third time. More after the break."

Jordan sat dumbfounded. At some point while watching, she had dropped her hand holding her phone down on to the sofa beside her. In the distance, she could hear Sabrina shouting. "Jordan, you still there?"

Numbly, she picked the phone back up.

"Yeah, I'm still here."

***

"Nonononononononononno."

Freya paced back and forth, as she listened to the TV report.

"Crapcrapcrapcrapcrap."

When her phone started to ring, she spun and looked in terror at it. Dan reached out and picked it up.

"Hi, I'm sorry; she's not here at the moment. Can I help?" he asked smoothly.

Freya paced the floor, biting at her thumb and watching Dan as he listened to whoever was on the phone. He nodded occasionally, "I'll be sure to let her know." Hanging up the phone, he stood up from the sofa and walked over, taking his friend in his arms, "That was the journalist from V who did your interview, apologizing. Her girlfriend got hold of her notes from the interview and apparently said something to someone, who said something to someone." Dan rolled his wrist, "Aaaand it wound up on the telly. She's very sorry."

Freya pulled away, a resolute expression on her face, "I need to speak to her."

"The journalist? She didn't leave a number," Dan frowned, looking at the phone to see if it had registered the number.

"Jordan," Freya corrected, taking the phone from Dan and calling Jordan's cell. She crumpled as the call went straight to her messaging service.

"Voicemail?" Dan asked, taking Freya back into a hug when she nodded and her lip began to tremble.

The phone started to ring again, however, Freya looked at the caller ID and ignored it.

"I need to speak to her," Freya hauled herself out of Dan's embrace. Rushing over to the sofa, she pulled on her sneakers and grabbed Dan's zipper hoodie, pulling it on, "Can I take your car?"

Dan spun round, trying desperately to remember where he'd put his keys earlier after collecting his car from the autoshop. He ran to the kitchen and grabbed them from the counter. Turning to run back to Freya, he stopped, turned back and grabbed his cell.

"Here," he said, as he entered the room. "Take my cell too, I'll keep yours here and answer the calls that are already starting to come in."

Freya gave him a grateful smile, "You know, if I wasn't gay and you weren't gay, I'd so marry you."

Laughing, Dan gave her a hug, "You did marry me, and divorce me, and, wait…" He looked at her in mock surprise, "You're a *lesbian*? Why didn't you say before?" He let go and pushed her off towards the door, "I love you but I'm warning you, if you so much as smear Bunty's paintwork I'm going to make money while you're hot news and sell the photos from New Year's two thousand and six."

***

Jordan had been sitting in the dark ever since she had hung up the call with Sabrina. She'd turned off the ringer on her home phone and switched off her cell.

She wasn't in the mood to deal with anyone right now.

She shook her head, recalling all the time that they had spent together. It hurt enough that Freya didn't trust her enough with that piece of information, but all this time she had been confused about her growing feelings and attraction towards Freya, and it was obvious to her now that Freya didn't share those feeling or emotions. It had to be just her that felt it, or Freya would have said something. She'd have told her that she was gay.

Jordan took a deep breath, pulling her shoulders up towards her ears, and held it. Eventually she let it back out, dropping her shoulders. She walked over towards the wall where she had hung the framed photo and letter that Freya had given her for her birthday.

Deep in thought as she looked at it, a bang at her front door made her jump. She rubbed her hand over her face almost in an attempt to wipe her brain clean as she went to answer it, praying it wasn't the media harassing her for a comment.

She checked the spy hole, frowning at the figure standing with a hood up over their head. She put the chain on the door and pulled it open slightly, "Who is it?"

"It's me Jordan, I need to speak to you."

Recognizing Freya's voice, Jordan closed the door.

Freya's heart sank as the door closed. She gulped back tears and was about to hammer on the door again, when it opened fully. Jordan reached out and grabbed her by her outstretched arm, yanking her inside and quickly closing the door before locking it.

Using both hands, Freya pushed the hood down and unzipped Dan's hoodie.

"I'm so, so, deeply sorry that I didn't tell you. I was going to, tomorrow night, but then the story," she dropped her head down and stared at the floor.

"You didn't have to tell me anything you didn't want to, Freya," Jordan shrugged, masking her hurt.

"No, but I did," Freya's head shot up and she grabbed Jordan's arm. "I really did."

Jordan peeled Freya's hand from her arm. "Why did you? Why are you even here? And why are you dressed like the Ben and Jerry's cow?" she asked, as she took in Freya's garb for the first time.

In spite of herself, Freya laughed, stopping as she saw the seriousness on Jordan's face.

"Sorry…I'm," she took a deep breath as she braced herself for what could be the speech that could change her life. "I'm here because I'm going crazy, because I really, *really* like you. I have done even before I came onto the show; I used to have you in your uniform as my screensaver." Seeing Jordan's eyebrows raise, Freya gulped, "Aaand you didn't need to know that right now, but I...I *need* to know, 'cause I may have read the signals wrong, 'cause Dan says that my gaydar is wired to the moon on occasion, but I need to know if youmf-"

She stopped as Jordan placed a finger to her lips, "I thought that we were friends, and as friends, that you would have felt able to tell me this earlier."

Freya went to speak but Jordan pressed her finger firmly against her lips, stopping her.

"Because, had you told me this earlier, I would have told you that I don't want to be your friend."

Freya's shoulders sagged at Jordan's words. She felt her heart sink and large lump rise in her throat. Seeing Freya's reaction, Jordan shook her head slightly. "Freya," she whispered, moving closer. "I don't want to be your *friend*," she repeated, as she removed her finger and replaced it with her lips.

Holding Freya's face, Jordan pressed her lips gently against Freya's, and heard a small whimper come from her co-star. She smiled into the kiss as it deepened. She could feel a smile playing on Freya's lips as she continued to kiss her with the abandon that she had yearned for during their on-screen kisses.

Freya had taken a millisecond to recover from the shock that Jordan was actually kissing her, and this time is was not for work. Involuntarily, a whimper left her as she returned the kiss, unable to stop smiling that she was kissing Jordan. She raised her hands to hold Jordan's face in place in case, by some strange twist of fate, the kiss was in fact only a dream that she needed to hold onto for as long as she could.

What started as a hesitant, almost teasing kiss rapidly grew, as pent up passion started to pour out. The kisses became deeper, more frantic as their tongues started a battle for dominance, each desperate to explore the other. Freya's hands slipped from Jordan's face and tangled in her hair. Still kissing her, Jordan dropped her hands down Freya's neck and started to push at the material of her hoodie to slide it from her shoulders. Freya released her grasp and allowed the top to be stripped from her, landing in a puddle of material at their feet.

Jordan pulled reluctantly from the kiss, her breathing ragged.

"Bedroom, now."

Freya's eyebrows shot up in surprise, her eyes wide.

"Really? I mean I'm all up for bedroom but I don't want to rush youuuuu." Her words were cut off as Jordan grabbed her wrist and dragged her out of the hall towards her room.

"I have thought of nothing else but being with you, ever since those damn oranges. So yes, bedroom…Now!" Jordan growled, as she pulled a giggling Freya behind her.

Entering the room, Jordan stopped and turned, releasing her grip. Freya could see a mix of nerves and determination on Jordan's face that she found irresistible. Giving her a gentle smile, she pulled Jordan closer and placed her lips softly against the taller woman's. Pulling away, she started to trail her lips down Jordan's neck.

"There's no pressure," she murmured.

Jordan's head sagged backwards at the sensation of Freya's lips on her neck.

"I want you," Jordan managed to say, her voice thick with emotion.

Freya lifted her head to look back into Jordan's eyes. She cocked her head and smiled, "I want you too."

Jordan lifted her hands, which were trembling slightly, and pulled at the zip of Freya's ridiculous outfit. She slowly dragged it down, exposing the valley between her breasts. Her eyes followed the route of the zip as it traversed past Freya's abdomen, which was rising and falling with her rapid breathing. Lifting her hand, Jordan allowed the back of her fingertips to trace up the gap in the material until her hand cupped Freya's face and pulled her into another kiss.

As they kissed, Freya's fingers started to pull gently at the hem of Jordan's top. She felt Jordan smile at the realization of what she wanted. They separated, their eyes never losing contact as Freya tugged Jordan's top over her head. She felt her already pounding pulse increase as she took in her first look at Jordan's naked torso.

Wrapping her arms around Jordan's waist for support, she dipped her head down and started to kiss her way down towards Jordan's breasts. Briefly, she felt the taller woman's heartbeat against her cheek, before she changed position and took a hardened nipple into her mouth. She was aware of a gasp as Jordan stumbled slightly. Freya tightened her arms around Jordan to hold her in place as she swirled her tongue around, playing with the sensitive bud.

Freya lifted her head back up, desperate to kiss Jordan again.

As they gave into a searing kiss, she felt Jordan's hands slip inside her clothing at her waist and start to work their way up towards her breasts. Her breathing increased as Jordan's hands found their destination.

Jordan pulled away and watched Freya's face flush with pleasure as she held her breasts in her hands almost reverently. Freya took her bottom lip between her teeth as Jordan swept her thumbs simultaneously across sensitive nipples.

At Freya's response, Jordan became suddenly impatient. She swept her hands up towards Freya's shoulders and pushed the clothing down, releasing Freya's top half. She snaked her hands around Freya's back, touching for real that which she had stroked in a photograph only days before. Her hands slipped down the crevice at the bottom of Freya's back as her hands moved round to glide the material of Freya's clothing down over her hips.

Freya used the toes on one foot to grip the heel of her sneaker on the other, and push it off. She repeated the process and then stepped from the pool of clothes at her feet, leaving her naked. She moved and sat on the edge of the bed. Pulling Jordan towards her she kissed patterns on Jordan's stomach as her hands pulled at the tie on Jordan's pants. Releasing the knot she pulled at the cloth, smiling against Jordan's hot skin as she felt her shimmy to help with the removal.

Jordan twisted her hands through Freya's hair, enjoying the feeling of her stomach being adorned with wet kisses. She looked down and smiled as she saw Freya's green eyes looking up, watching her every response. Kicking off her pants, she pushed Freya back towards the bed. Freya moved herself further onto the bed, as Jordan lowered herself down slowly until finally she was lying on top of Freya.

"You okay? Am I squishing you?" she asked smiling, mirroring Freya's question to her the previous night during filming.

Remembering Jordan's response Freya replied, her voice husky, "I'm good." She smirked as she recalled Jordan's line from the scene they'd shot, "I think you made first base."

Jordan grinned as she tossed her blonde hair over her shoulder, "Believe me, I have plans to go *much* farther than first base."

***

Jordan propped herself up on her elbow and looked down on the sleeping form of Freya beside her, who was laying on her front with her hands tucked up under her pillow. Smiling, Jordan reached out and started to trace patterns on Freya's back. She allowed her fingers to follow the outline of Freya's shoulder blade, grazing the back of her hand down her side. She still could not believe that she was here, that last night she had been with a woman for the first time. However, it was more than that. Last night she had been with Freya for the first time.

She felt her stomach flip as she recalled the events of the previous evening, and her thoughts awakened a desire in her to feel the now sleep-warm body lying peacefully shudder against her again. She yearned to feel the exquisite pleasure of those delicate fingers, currently obscured by a pillow, slip inside her – and to hear Freya's gasps intermingle with her own as they brought each other to release.

Carefully pulling the covers up to make room, Jordan moved so her body covered Freya's. Pressing her groin against the dark-haired woman's bottom, she held herself steady on her hands as she started to pepper the exposed back beneath her with kisses. She trailed a path down Freya's spine, barely lifting her lips as she moved herself down, kissing each bump of the blonde's vertebrae as she went. She paused, smiling, at the dimples at the bottom of Freya's back, placing her lips into the indentations. She was continuing her journey when she felt Freya move.

Raising herself sleepily onto her elbows, Freya looked over her shoulder. She smiled as her eyes locked with deep brown ones, their owner currently resting her chin on her hands splayed across Freya's backside.

"You planning on taking advantage of me while I was asleep?"

Jordan cocked an eyebrow, "Maybe."

Freya turned her top half, waiting for Jordan to raise herself so that she could extricate her legs from under her. Turning to lie on her back, she reached down and pulled Jordan up onto her. She pushed back the soft blonde hair that was falling messily around Jordan's face, tucking it behind her ears. "Morning," she smiled.

"Morning," Jordan leaned down and pressed her lips against Freya's in a chaste kiss. "Do you want breakfast?"

"What have you got in mind?" Freya replied in a flirtatious tone. However, just at that moment, her stomach growled loudly.

Jordan looked down between their breasts towards Freya's stomach, "How about eggs, and then maybe what I have in mind later?" She pushed herself up and smiled down at Freya. Unable to resist, she leaned down and nipped gently on Freya's nipple, "Just so that you eat breakfast a bit quicker." She jumped from the bed and walked across the room.

Freya propped herself up onto her elbows as she watched Jordan move across the floor, dropping back down onto the pillow when she covered up under a robe and left the room. She glanced over at the clock and groaned at the display reading of five thirty. As her hand reached across the bed and she felt the warmth from where Jordan had lain, she realized that she didn't want to be around the remnants of Jordan's presence, she wanted to be beside her. She got up and found her onesie at the other side of the bed where it had been discarded the night before. She pulled it on and walked towards Jordan's kitchen, pulling up the zip as she walked. She walked through the hall and saw Dan's hoodie puddled on the floor. She picked it up and checked the pockets, finding his cell phone. She frowned as she saw twenty missed calls, apparently from herself. Dialing the message retrieval, she walked into the kitchen.

Smiling, Jordan handed her a glass of orange juice, "Not orange slices, but the next best thing."

Pulling herself onto a breakfast barstool, Freya laughed as she recalled the reference to the fanfiction paragraph that Jordan had read aloud, her smile turning to a frown as she listened to Dan's messages.

"Dan says that there are photographers camped outside my house."

Jordan narrowed her eyes. Leaving the room for a minute, she returned shaking her head, "They're here too."

"Crap. How the hell am I going to get home without them seeing me?" she took a sip of orange juice and noted the look of disappointment on Jordan's face. "Jordan, look at me please," she begged. "I'm not ashamed of anything. Hell, I'd quite happily take out a billboard announcing to the world about what happened last night between us."

As Jordan gave a soft chuckle, Freya slipped off the stool and stood in front of her.

"But I want this, I want us," she took Jordan's hands in hers. "I just don't want us to have the added pressure of everyone watching our relationship develop. We should be able to do things in our own time, and not have to worry about that sort of stuff."

Jordan nodded. "No, you're right, plus I have some conversations to have with my family. I'd rather they heard about us from me and not the media. So, we lay low for a few weeks and it will all die down, and then…" she hesitated to finish the sentence.

"And then," Freya smiled pulling Jordan into a hug.

"Besides," Jordan murmured against Freya's shoulder. "I don't want anyone to take photos of you leaving here in that ridiculous outfit."

Freya pulled away from the hug, "Hey, I will have you know that this has a one hundred percent record with the ladies. The one time that I wore it around a gorgeous woman, she practically ripped it from me and I got lucky."

Jordan placed a quick peck on her forehead, "The desperation to get you out of it was only because of how incredibly ridiculous you look in it."

"Yeah, you keep saying that 'til you believe it," Freya scoffed. "We both know the truth."

***

After a relaxed breakfast, Freya dropped her head onto the table, "So, today I need to speak to Dominick, who'll kick my ass. Then I need to speak to Eleanor, who'll kick my ass."

"But first, we have to get you out of here unseen," Jordan said, rising from the table and grabbing her phone.

Freya watched in confusion as Jordan made a call, "Hey Alice, it's Jordan. Yeah, hi. I know, I saw them, I'm sorry about that, I'll pay for any damage to your lawn. Listen, I could do with your help with something."

Thirty minutes later and banned from leaving the house in her onesie, Freya was dressed in work-out gear borrowed from Jordan, and was finely balanced on the fence in Jordan's back yard.

"You okay?" Jordan asked, concerned at the contorted look on Freya's face as she lay across the top of the boundary between her backyard and her neighbor's property.

"Yeah, I'm just peachy," Freya replied, looking down towards Jordan.

Jordan could hear Alice's voice of the other side of the fence.

"If you bring your leg over, that's it, I've got you."

Jordan watched as Freya lifted her leg over, her body rotating so only her upper torso was visible. "I'll see you at work," she blew her a small kiss as Freya disappeared rapidly, and then winced at the small audible thud from the other side.

"I'm okay," Freya yelled. "See you later."

Limping slightly, Freya followed Alice into her house. "Thank you for doing this," Freya smiled embarrassedly.

"Oh no, it's my pleasure. It's not every day I get to smuggle a TV star out in my car," Alice said, genuinely quite thrilled by the turn of the events on what otherwise would have been a dull Friday.

"My friend Dan is meeting us a couple of blocks over."

"Excellent, where we will rendezvous and do the switch," Alice said, her eyes glinting with excitement.

Freya gave the woman a wary smile, "That's the plan."

Alice grabbed her toddler and led Freya through the house and into the garage. "You have a lovely home," Freya remarked, remembering her manners despite the situation.

"Thank you," Alice replied smiling, opening the door of her MPV. She placed her child into the car seat and strapped him in. "If you lay down there, I'll cover you up with this," Alice said helpfully, holding up a large blanket.

Wondering how her life had come to this moment, Freya climbed into the car and lay down flat on the floor of the back seat, allowing herself to be covered over completely. She heard Alice enter the car and the garage door open, and then they were off.

The photographers outside Jordan's home started to click wildly as Jordan exited the house and got into her car while ignoring their calls and pleas for a smile. She started the engine and pulled out from her drive. Pausing where her drive met the road, she checked that the road was clear. As she noted her neighbor's car pulling out, she pressed the accelerator and turned the steering wheel, driving off in the opposite direction.

***

"So, I take it there was nubbing," Dan said across to his friend, who was sitting in a daze staring out of the window as he drove her towards the studio.

Freya turned and smacked his arm, "That's none of your business."

Dan pouted, "Oh please, enough of the moral outrage! Wait, listen, did you hear that?" he turned the radio off and cupped his ear.

Freya narrowed one eye as she concentrated on listening to hear what Dan had heard, "I don't hear anything?"

"Sshhhh. Yep there it is again. It's the sound of lesbians across the world as their heads explode at the thought of you two doing the nasty."

Scowling, Freya took her fist and punched his bicep hard, "Quit it, Dan, I'm not giving you details of what was the best night of my life."

Dan gave a small smile as he glanced over towards Freya, "I'm happy for you, Egg. But she does realize that your family is quite mental, and that she has to go through the friend test?"

Ignoring the reference to her family, Freya frowned. "But you've met her, you liked her," she groaned, turning in her seat to face Dan.

Dan lifted a hand from the steering wheel, gesturing as he drove, "That was before, pre the nubbing, if you will. Now, post the nubbing, I have to give her the all clear." He indicated, pulling into the security gate of the studios. Freya flashed her ID, and they were waved on.

"You're serious about this?" Freya asked, as Dan stopped the car to allow her to get out.

As she opened the door and got out of the car, Dan leaned over, placing his elbow on the passenger seat, "As serious as I get, sweetie."

She closed the door and turned. Shielding her eyes with both hands, Freya looked over towards the studio entrance and took a deep breath as she contemplated what the day would bring.

***

Jordan opened the door to Freya's trailer and poked her head in, frowning in confusion at what she was met with.

Freya was sitting on the sofa, her face covered with a surgical mask as she stared intently into a mirror.

"Um, hi, am I interrupting something?" Jordan asked warily.

Looking over, Freya smiled beneath her mask, "No, I'm just eye acting."

"Oookay," Jordan responded, entering the trailer and sitting opposite Freya. "Any particular reason?"

"People only get to see our eyes in the surgery scenes, I just want to make sure that they see the right emotion. Test me, give me an emotion."

Jordan relaxed back into the sofa.

"Surprise."

Freya opened her eyes slightly wider and raised both eyebrows. "Anger."

Dropping her eyebrows down, Freya scowled, lines appearing on her forehead as she did so.

"Lust."

"Awww, now that's an easy one," Freya laughed, no longer acting she looked across at Jordan and started to mentally undress her.

Jordan gulped slightly as she recognized the look in Freya's eyes from the previous night.

"I think you've got that one nailed," Jordan smiled, moving forward and leaning over the table. She pulled the surgical mask down, removing it from Freya's face, and kissed her softly. Replacing the mask, she pulled back and sank onto the sofa once more, "You spoke to Eleanor yet?"

Freya pulled at the mask, undoing the ties around her neck and dropping it onto the table, "I have to go see her at three. She's in meetings 'til then."

Nodding, Jordan changed the subject, aware that Freya was anxious about her meeting with the producer. She slapped her hands on her thighs and stood up.

"I came to see if you wanted to share a lot-limo to the set," she said, referring to the golf carts used to ferry cast and crew around the studio buildings.

"Perfect, I would love to share a ride with you," Freya smiled, following Jordan out of the trailer towards the waiting golf cart.

***

"Quiet on the set, we're rolling. Background."

Freya watched the movement of the extras, then, grabbing her glove, she walked into the OR.

"What have we got?" she asked as she pulled on the latex glove, stopping as the fingers on the glove refused to cooperate. "Dammit," she yelled, ripping the glove off and returning to her place to redo the start of the scene. She puffed some air into the glove to try to loosen the fingers, in the hope that it would allow her to slip her hand in and get past her first line.

"Okay, reset and…background."

"What have we got?" she snapped the glove into place, relieved to have navigated past that particular hurdle of the scene.

"Fifty-three-year-old woman, angina, she has a tight left ostial stenosis with a normal distal coronary artery tree," Dianne said, looking up from the mannequin on the table. "She deteriorated rapidly when she came in. It's Colonel Branston's wife."

Freya nodded briskly towards the center of the room. "Has the Colonel been alerted?" she asked.

Dianne nodded as she prodded the dummy with the instruments as if both their lives depended on it. "I'm going to do a pericardial patch angioplasty to the left coronary ostium, if you're interesting in staying..." Dianne asked, pausing.

"Well, all right then," Freya smiled making sure that her smile showed up in her eyes as much as possible.

Two hours later, and they were finishing another scene in the operating room.

"Okay, one more time with the dialogue and then the pan up to the gallery. You okay for one more run up there Jordan?" Toby asked.

From her position behind the viewing glass, Jordan gave him the thumbs up.

"Great, we're rolling. Action!"

"So, what's the deal with you and Van Hausen?" Dianne asked, without taking her eyes from what her hands were doing.

Freya glanced up, "What do you mean?"

Dianne gave a half shrug, "Not that I'm not a kick-ass surgeon, but I don't usually see her observing my surgeries." She looked up towards the gallery where Jordan was sitting, then back towards Freya with a look of amusement in her eyes, "So I'm guessing that she's not here to see me rock this angioplasty."

Freya looked up towards the gallery, the camera following her until it rested upon Jordan sitting behind the glass in the gallery.

"There's nothing going on, we're friends," Freya said, returning her gaze to the patient on the table.

Jordan clenched her jaw, stood up, and stormed out of the viewing gallery.

"Cut," Toby shouted.

Dropping the surgical instruments, Freya started to flex her fingers, which were starting to cramp after the length of time they'd been filming.

"God, the smell of chitlins really makes me want to throw up now," she commented on the pig guts used during the surgical scenes.

"I know what you mean, I'm this close to becoming vegetarian," Dianne held her forefinger and thumb an inch apart.

They stepped back from the OR table and started to walk out of the set, pulling off the yellow disposable aprons as they went.

"You okay? Pretty big night last night?" Dianne asked, concerned.

It took a half second for Freya to work out that Dianne was referring to her public outing, and not what happened afterwards. "Yeah, pretty big night. I'm okay. I mean, I gave the interview, so I was ready for it to become public knowledge," Freya shrugged. "I just thought that I would have a bit of time before it was published to warn people it was coming."

"Best laid plans, hey," Dianne smiled, giving Freya's arm a quick squeeze as Jordan joined them. "I'll catch you guys later," she smiled, leaving them alone.

"I thought you might want to grab some lunch before our next shoot," Jordan asked Freya hopefully.

"Your place or mine?" Freya smiled.

***

After their lunch in Jordan's trailer they returned to the set via a quick freshen up with hair and make-up, hoping that no one asked how in the space of thirty minutes they had managed to wreck both.

They had been filming for around forty minutes when Freya noticed Eleanor join the set. She stretched her shoulders, then focused back on the scene.

"I heard what you said," Jordan spat. "The intercom was on, so I heard."

Freya frowned, "What would you prefer I told her, Georgia? That we kissed? That it was amazing? That ever since it happened I've been desperate for it to happen again? What? What should I have said? 'cause I'll go find her, and I'll…I'll tell her now." Freya infused her tone with a mix of anger and confusion.

"I don't know," Jordan replied quietly. "I…you confuse me, I'm confused around you," she dropped her head down and toyed with the hem of her combat uniform jacket.

Freya took a step forward, "We kissed, and…it was great." A small smile started to form on her lips, "I'm not sure what it meant, and I don't think you're sure what it meant." Her smile broadened as she ducked down to look into Jordan's eyes, "I want to know what it meant to both of us, before I involve anyone else."

A slow smile spread across Jordan's face as she nodded at Freya.

"Cut," Toby turned, seeing the producer watching the filming, he tensed slightly. "Eleanor, nice to see you on set."

Eleanor smiled. "Finally have a bit of free time from meetings, so thought I'd pop down. I've been watching the dailies, good work Toby," she complimented.

Toby beamed with pleasure at the comment.

"If you will excuse me, I need to catch Freya," she added, nodding over towards the tall actress.

Nodding, Toby grimaced as he guessed what the conversation was going to be about.

Eleanor walked over to where Jordan and Freya were standing laughing with bottles of water in their hands. "Jordan," she nodded an acknowledgement towards the blonde actress.

Jordan gave a nervous chuckle, "Eleanor, hi."

"I watched the dailies from the night shoot, you're doing a great job. Would you mind if I stole Freya for a moment?"

Jordan gave a quick look between Eleanor and Freya, who had a stricken smile on her face.

"Yeah, sure," she gave Freya a supportive smile. "I'll speak to you later?"

Freya gave a slight nod of affirmation and Jordan made a swift exit, looking over her shoulder as she left towards where Freya stood rooted to the spot in front of the show's producer.

"Well, how 'bout we head back to my office?" Eleanor said gently, sensing the fear from Freya. "I thought I'd come over and get a chance to watch you work before we met."

Nodding dumbly, Freya followed the smaller woman as they exited the set and sound stage. The golf cart that Eleanor used to get around the studio lot was parked jauntily outside the soundstage. Freya sat down in the passenger seat as Eleanor chauffeured them back towards the production offices. The experience was similar to Mr. Toad's ride in Disneyland, and one which required an equally firm grip.

As they entered Eleanor's office she smiled, "Don't look so damned scared Freya, you're not in trouble. I just want to make sure you're okay, and talk about what we can do to support you."

"I'm sorry, I was going to tell you today that I'd done the interview. They were meant to publish in two weeks, but the journalist's girlfriend saw what I'd said and told someone who told someone and then I find myself choking on popcorn as ENT tells the world that I'm gay before I get a chance to say anything," breathless Freya quit her rambling as Eleanor held a palm up. "I'm sorry," she added.

"We're a family here, Freya, a very diverse family," she smiled. "And you're part of that family. I only wish that you had told me before the interview, that way I would have been a bit more prepared for the network, but what's done is done."

Freya shifted in her seat, feeling as if the headmistress had just told her that she was disappointed in her.

"Are you planning on any other revelations?" Eleanor asked.

Freya shook her head emphatically, her curls bouncing. "No, that's it, nothing else. No cousins locked in institutions after frontal lobotomies or anything," she smiled weakly, wishing that her brain and mouth would start to engage with each other at some point.

"Okay," Eleanor picked up some papers on her desk, indicating that their time was up. "If there is anything that I can do, you'll let me know?"

"I'll let you know," Freya rose from the seat and exited Eleanor's office. Closing the door behind her, she exhaled slowly.

October 2011

Dan opened the front door to Freya's home, "So, what's so urgent that you call me up, after the polite time I might add, and drag me over here on a Sunday?"

Freya moved between rooms, checking plug sockets as she went. "Okay, so that light is due to go off at one," she stopped and pointed towards her bedroom, her eyes looking up with an unfocused gaze as she worked out her plan in her head. "The bedroom light is due to go off at half past."

"What are we doing?" Dan asked, yawning.

"I'm breaking out, and you're helping me. But I need it to look like I'm still here, so I've put timers on the lights so they'll go off," Freya slapped Dan's shoulders as she scurried to collect her jacket and bag.

Dan closed his eyes and shook his head. When Freya re-entered the room she found him inspecting the ceiling.

"What? What is it?" she asked, looking up to where Dan's attention was focused. "Is there a crack? 'cause I told Anna that I didn't think the building had settled."

Dan rubbed his chin thoughtfully, "Nope I was just thinking that this is the perfect place to hang the paint cans that will smack them in the face when they enter, Kevin," He slapped his cheeks and opened his mouth in a fair approximation of Macaulay Culkin in '*Home Alone*'.

Narrowing her eyes as she shrugged on her jacket, "Funny. Dan, it's been almost seven weeks, and this laying low thing isn't working for me. I'm desperate, and I need your help."

"No, you're horny," Dan waved dismissively. "Can't you two resort to phone sex or something?"

Freya blushed, "We tried, I kept dropping the phone, and was too embarrassed to put her on speaker." She opened the door to her garage and stepped in to where Dan had parked his car as she had instructed him, "So now you're helping. Pop the trunk so I can get in."

Dan's eyes widened, "What?"

"Pop the trunk!"

"You're not riding in my trunk," Dan pursed his lips and shook his head.

"Dan, pop the damn trunk," Freya growled.

A look of fear spread across Dan's face as he edged towards his car and opened the trunk. Freya threw her bag in, then, using the car and Dan's shoulder for support, she lifted her legs into the trunk and lay down.

"Jordan's garage will be open when you get there, just drive in," Freya instructed as Dan lowered the trunk and pressed it closed.

Dan drove through the deserted streets cautiously; his eyes nervously flitting to his mirrors to make sure the photographers who were still hovering outside Freya's home weren't following him. Pulling up to a junction, Dan pressed the brake, slowing his car as he approached the stop sign. Checking the road was clear, he took off across the junction.

The flashing lights in his mirrors caught his attention. "Nononononono," he muttered, as he pulled over towards the sidewalk. He gave his steering wheel a thump as the police car pulled in behind him. Putting his window down, he watched in his side mirror as the officer got out and approached his car. "Evening officer," Dan said as calmly as he could, given that he was speaking to the police while there was a woman in the trunk of his car.

"Did you see the stop sign back there?" the officer asked, pointing back towards the junction with his pen.

"I did officer, and I'm sorry. I'm still not quite used to the driving etiquette here of actually coming to a stop at the stop sign," Dan pulled his British driving license from his wallet and handed it to the police officer.

Looking at the plastic card, the police officer studied the photograph and shone his torch into Dan's face to compare, "If we wanted you just to slow down, sir, the sign would say slow down."

Dan grimaced at the bright light. "Quite, I apologize. So, do I get a ticket?" he asked hopefully.

The officer frowned at Dan's apparent eagerness to get his ticket. "Where you headed?" he leaned down, resting his hand on the roof of the car.

"A friend's house," Dan answered carefully, aware that he may have aroused suspicion in the police officer and desperate not to create any more.

"Kind of late for a visit, don't you think?"

"Absolutely, but my friend needs me," Dan smiled nervously.

The police officer cocked his head to one side. As he stood up straight, Dan breathed a sigh, hoping that his ordeal was over.

"Step out of the car please, sir."

Dan's head dropped as he opened the door and stood beside his vintage car.

"Have you been drinking?"

"No sir."

"Would you mind complying with some sobriety tests?"

"No sir."

As the officer took a step back to allow Dan room, a loud sneeze came from the trunk of the car.

"Do you have something in your trunk?" the officer asked, walking towards the rear of the car.

"No," Dan squeaked.

"Pop the trunk for me please, sir."

Swallowing down a squeal, Dan walked round to the rear of his car and pressed the button to open the trunk with shaking hands. He gripped the metal and stared up towards the night sky, not daring to look down at the sight that greeted the police officer.

"Nothing in the trunk eh?" the officer said sarcastically to Dan.

"Apart from her, just the spare tire," Dan replied weakly.

"Hi," Freya said brightly from her position in the trunk.

The police officer looked between the woman in the trunk and the tall man standing with closed eyes, biting at his bottom lip.

"There's a perfectly innocent explanation for this, officer," Freya smiled, pulling herself up to a sitting position.

"I'd sure love to hear it," the officer drawled, resting his hand on the butt of his gun.

Dan noticed the action and gulped, "We're friends, and she's trying to hide from the paparazzi, so she hid in the boot." Dan's body almost wilted as he exhaled after his explanation.

"The boot?" the police officer asked.

"He means the trunk, he's British," Freya said by way of an explanation. She held out her right hand, "My name is Freya..." "Easter," the police officer took her hand and helped her from the trunk. "You're Francesca Conor's daughter."

Never before had Freya been so pleased for the fame of her family, and she beamed a smile in his direction as Dan rolled his eyes.

"We're really sorry officer for causing you trouble, but, as Dan said, I was trying to keep a low profile," Freya said as she stood beside Dan, who was now picturing his life in prison and deciding orange was just not his color.

The police officer grinned, "Well, it appears that this has, as you said, an innocent explanation." He wrote out Dan's ticket for not stopping and handed it to him, "I'll let you both carry on your journey."

He cleared his throat as Freya raised her leg about to hop back into the trunk. "How 'bout you finish the ride up front," he smiled.

Freya nodded slowly as she lowered her leg and set it back down on the concrete.

"So, any more bright ideas that are likely to land me in prison?" Dan asked, fastening his seatbelt and starting the engine.

"Nope, that was the full extent of my plan," Freya said dejectedly, as she typed a text to explain to Jordan that their plan had had to be aborted.

Taking pity on his friend, Dan sighed, "Okay, let's look at this logically. You don't want to get caught alone in each other's homes for fear the press will put two and two together and realize you're at it like rabbits." He ignored Freya's low growl and continued, "So why not just have a select few over for a party? You two can hide in a crowd. Oh!" He started to bounce in his seat with excitement, "Halloween is coming up. Why don't you have a party?"

Freya turned slowly to look at her friend, whose head was twisting back and forth between looking at her and keeping an eye on the empty road, a huge smile on his face as he waited for the praise for his ingenious idea. "I hate parties, I try and avoid going to parties. Why would I even consider throwing one?"

"Because –"

"Ah!" Freya interrupted him before he could launch into another burst of logic 101. "Not happening. Not ever. Not discussing further, just take me home."

"But –"

"I'm not having a party, end of discussion."

***

"So, I'm having a party," Freya cleared her throat and looked around her cast mates and the members of the crew gathered for the table read. "A Halloween party on Saturday, at my place. I realize that it's kinda short notice, but it was a last minute decision, so if any of you are free, I'd love for you to come." She smiled as her colleagues nodded and waved in her direction, a few shouting out that they would be there. As she gathered up her script and Post-its, she felt a soft touch at her back.

"I'd love to come," Jordan said mischievously, knowing the effect her words would have on Freya.

Freya turned, her eyes narrowing as she realized that Jordan was playing her, "Well, since I'm doing it just so I can be in the same room as you on a Saturday night, it would be bad form to refuse."

"Maybe I can come over earlier on Saturday and help you set up. Nothing unusual in that; just two friends hanging Halloween decorations."

"Three friends," Freya corrected with a wince.

"Okay, that's not the way I saw our relationship going, I'll be honest with you," Jordan whispered. "Maybe we should set out some ground rules."

"I'd like that," Freya said thoughtfully, cocking her head to the side as she considered Jordan's words.

"Really, 'cause I'm just getting my head round being with a woman, I'm not sure I'm ready, or will ever be, for a threesome."

Freya laughed, "Will you stop! Dan's coming over to help, but it would be great if you came too." She looked around the now empty room and took the opportunity to brush Jordan's lips with her own, "I meant that I liked the sound of a relationship, duffus."

"Well, when you flatter me in such a way, I can't think of anyone else I'd rather be with," Jordan replied, using her hips to press Freya against the desk.

Freya placed her hands on Jordan's shoulders and pushed her away gently, "We should probably take it down a notch, 'cause I'm likely to throw you onto the desk and forget that we're at work."

Jordan grimaced, "You realize that every time we do a table read in here, I'm going to be thinking about that now."

Placing a quick kiss on Jordan's nose, Freya collected her belongings and slipped past her pouting co-star, "Trust me, you won't be the only one."

***

"So, how many of these are we making?" Jordan asked, as she looked around Freya's kitchen. Pumpkins in various states of carving covered every available surface. Both Jordan and Freya's hands were dyed orange from carving out the innards.

"I'm not sure, I've never really done this before," Freya admitted as she pushed her hair from her brow and surveyed her kitchen. "I've gone too far with the pumpkins haven't I?"

Jordan pulled her close, "Nooo." Seeing Freya's look of disbelief, she bit on her top lip, "Okay, maybe a little. You may be eating pumpkin soup for a while. However, this is and was a good idea." She kissed Freya slowly, smiling as Freya moaned and deepened the kiss.

"Now, now, ladies, you know the rules. You should be two feet apart at all times, and lips nowhere near each other," Dan said playfully as he swept back into the room. He ignored his friend's glare as she disentangled herself from Jordan, "So, I've been going through your wardrobe to see what I could steal as my costume for tonight." "You've what?" Freya asked, her eyebrows arching dangerously.

"Oh relax, you've not got anything in there that surprised me. You forget I've helped you move too many times not to recognize the toy box that," he waggled his fingers in air quotes, "has to go in the car, mustn't go in the van, and don't let anyone in my family open it." He grinned over at Jordan, "You are going to be in for a whale of a time, sweetie, once this whole laying low charade can be forgotten about and the clam jam is over. Anyhoo, your wardrobe was a veritable desert for suitable costume ideas. Apart from this." He held up a triangular hairpiece, "I was thinking I could go as some Tolkeiness character." He placed the hairpiece against his chin and struck a thoughtful pose, "You know, 'one ring to unite them all' or whatever the hell they say. What do you think?"

"Is that a –" Jordan started to ask, but stopped when Freya placed an orange tinged hand on her forearm.

"It is, and I'm going to enjoy every second of this. Dan, do you know what a merkin is?"

"It sounds like you're trying to say American in a woeful attempt at a southern accent. Never take up acting," he grinned.

"Funny, funny man," Freya deadpanned. "A merkin, my dear friend, is a pubic wig."

Dan's mouth gaped open in shock. "Pubic," he repeated meekly, then remembering he was still holding the wig to his chin, he let out a shrill scream and threw it on the floor. "Why?" he asked, his entire body shuddering as he walked around in circles. "Why, why, why would you have one of those?"

"Remember when I was in that revival of Hair back in London? Well, when I left they gave me my merkin as a leaving gift."

Dan's horror rose further. "You've worn that?!" he screeched, pointing at the offending article on the floor. "Against your lady bits?!"

"Every night for two months," Freya grinned. "You're welcome to borrow it."

Before Dan could splutter a reply, Anna entered the house. "Ah, good, you're in. What the hell happened in here?" she asked, casually taking in the sight of close to a hundred pumpkins.

"I'm having a Halloween party tonight."

Anna looked as surprised as her tightened facial muscles would allow, "You're hosting a party?" She looked from her granddaughter to the others present in the kitchen, "Daniel, are you okay, you look like you've seen a ghost?"

"Something like that," Dan replied, with a nauseous look on his face.

"And lovely Jordan, so good to see you again," Anna said. "I don't know if you remember as you had quite the night, but we first met when you won your TONY. Of course, all of that was before you and Freya started to-"

"Shag," Dan interjected, hoping to exact some revenge for the merkin incident.

"I was going with date," Anna said dryly, shooting Dan a look. Ignoring his muttered 'that would require actually going on a date,' she returned her attention to Jordan, "I hope that you liked your birthday gift?"

Jordan nodded dumbly, still not quite able to reconcile that *The Anna Connor* knew who she was.

"So, Freya, this party. Who are you using for catering?" Seeing a pained look appear on Freya's face, she winced, "You have arranged for food, haven't you? Or are you planning on feeding your guests with these pumpkins?"

Freya shook her head furiously, "This is why I don't host parties, I'm dreadful at it."

Jordan took her into a hug, "It's okay, we can sort something out, don't start to panic."

Smiling, Anna rubbed her hands together, "You know it's been years since I threw a party, leave it to me." She turned to leave, then slowly turned back, "Freya, not that I'm overly bothered, but if you have decided to finally put your mark on the place and redecorate, you should know I haven't had anything fur in the house since the seventies." She pointed at the merkin on the floor, "But if you must have a rug, you should go for something bigger than a rodent!"

***

"Thanks for picking me up," Jordan said, as she pulled the excess material of her wedding dress costume into the car.

"Not a worry, I thought it would be good for us to have some time to chat," Dan replied, smiling and showing the fake fangs covering his own teeth.

"You know, I always thought that saying about British people and bad teeth was a crock. Now, I'm not so sure," Jordan laughed, flashing her own fangs.

"Are you dribbling like a baby with these? 'cause I swear I'm drooling more than a bachelorette party at a male strip club."

Jordan laughed, "Yep, I keep having to make this horrible noise."

Dan sucked noisily, "That the one?"

"Yep."

"So, seriously, how are you doing with all of this?"

Jordan shrugged, "It's annoying having to hide, but we both agreed that we should for the time being."

"I meant more about the whole sexuality thing than the current practicalities," Dan said gently.

"You'd think that I'd be freaking out more, but I'm really not. I mean, I always thought that sexuality was a scale and that I knew where I fell on it. But to realize something about myself, that I never really even gave a fleeting thought to before, it should be something I'm freaking out about, right?" she toyed with the lace on her dress. "I've thought about it a lot, and Sabrina has been great to speak to, and I've been using the GLAAD rep that's supporting the show to 'hypothetically' explore my feelings. She probably thinks I'm the most conscientious actor on the planet, with all the questions I've been peppering her with about what my character might be going through. I will admit I wondered whether I should be worried or have doubts, but then I think about Freya, and there's no worries and no doubts. I've never felt this way in a relationship before."

"Well, that's good, 'cause I'm honor-bound to kick the arse out of anyone that hurts Freya, so hearing you say that gives me peace of mind," Dan smiled. "How'd your family take the news?"

Jordan blushed under her make-up, "I sort of prepared them for something happening with Freya, before anything actually happened, which helped. They've been really good. My dad was a bit funny at first, but mom said it was 'cause he's always had a thing for Freya's mom, so the whole one degree of separation thing freaked him out."

"Talking about Freya's mom, since I like you, I'm going to give you some advice on surviving a Conor party."

Jordan raised her eyebrows, "A Conor party? Her parents will be there?"

"Oh yes." Dan confirmed. "So, if at any point you feel your jaw drop and you want to say 'oh my god, is that' you can insert any famous name in there by the way, just close your mouth, and presume it is, because it probably will be." He glanced round and almost laughed aloud at the look on Jordan's face. The white make-up covering her face was almost not required, as she had paled significantly. "When you meet Freya's parents, just treat them like you would any normal couple."

"So, just act normal, that's your advice?"

"Yup, just ignore the fact they happen to be gorgeous, talented, and more famous than God." He dug his fangs into his lower lip to stop laughing as Jordan fidgeted nervously, "Oh, and of course you just happen to be banging their only daughter."

Jordan gulped audibly, "You know, I think I liked you better with a merkin on your chin."

They sat in comfortable silence as Dan navigated them through the streets of Beverly Hills towards Anna's house on Bel Air Road.

"Where are we going? You've missed the turn for Freya's," Jordan frowned, as she pointed back towards the opening.

Dan flashed her a grin, and in a breathy southern accent announced, "Why darlin', we is going to a party in the big house."

November 2011

It had been nine weeks since Freya's unexpected outing. Nine weeks, during which the magazine article was published, *Front Line's* season was in full swing, their first kiss had aired and they had filmed three and a half new episodes, which had progressed their on-screen relationship.

The irony of their characters keeping their relationship hidden from colleagues wasn't lost on them as, in reality, keeping it hidden was almost killing them as it also meant that it had been nine weeks since they had been together. Aside from Halloween, they spent as much time with each other as they possibly could, without it becoming painfully obvious that there was something deeper to their relationship. Any opportunity for physical closeness during a scene was welcomed, and they were nothing if not conscientious professionals when it came to rehearsing kiss scenes. However, despite all of that and some fairly heavy make-out sessions in trailers, they were finding it hard to maintain an aura of self-control around each other.

Freya sat at her spot for the table read, waiting for her colleagues to join her. Her mind drifted from the chatter around her and her thoughts fluttered aimlessly until the noise of chairs scraping on the floor pulled her to consciousness. She smiled as the object of most of her thoughts sat down in her seat opposite.

The director of the episode started to read out from the script, "We open with the usual monologue. The first shot is Georgia in the changing rooms before entering the shower block." The director smiled across at Belinda, the actress behind the show's main character and the voice of the show and nodded for her to start.

"As doctors, we are privy to a lot of secrets."

The director interjected with the next shot, "We switch to Alice looking at a pregnancy test."

Belinda continued, "Whether it's a young girl who doesn't want her parents to know about her pregnancy, or the inner workings of a family."

"We switch to Damien reading a letter from home, scrunching it up and throwing it angrily across the room."

Blake took a piece of paper from his pad, screwed it into a ball and threw it across the room towards Belinda.

"Or something in the past that refuses to let go of its power on the present," Belinda read, adding a spooky inflection to her tone.

The director read aloud the shots again, "We move to Sam who is looking at the scars on his leg. He rolls his trouser leg down and then, wide shot, we see Sandy has been watching him."

"It could even be something as important as who you love."

"Emily in the shower, turning round and smiling as Georgia enters the shower cubicle beside her. They kiss."

"The funny thing about secrets though, is usually they don't stay secrets for very long."

"Final scene. Anthea enters the shower block and interrupts Georgia and Emily, mid…" the director blushed slightly. "Well, you get the idea."

Both Jordan and Freya's heads shot up out of their scripts as panicked looks crossed their faces. They caught each other's eye, both thinking the same thing.

Nine weeks had been a long time!

***

Freya opened her trailer and smiled as she recognized the scent of Jordan's perfume. She had barely closed the door when Jordan was upon her.

Freya smiled as they kissed, her smile fading as Jordan's hands wandered down to cup her ass. She groaned as Jordan squeezed and pulled her closer. She dropped her head back and allowed her arms to fall, pressing her palms flat against the door and trying desperately to control herself as Jordan moved her lips onto her neck.

"Oh God, Jordan, you need to stop. Right now," Freya groaned, grabbing Jordan's face. She smiled as she leaned in to press a soft kiss on Jordan's swollen lips, "Seriously, I'm ready to explode, and I'm due on set in fifteen."

"That would be two of us. Exploding, I mean. I'm not needed 'til later, when I believe I get to work with my favorite actress," Jordan grinned as, despite Freya's protests, she returned her lips to her all too tempting neck.

"Awww, thank you," Freya smiled, swallowing hard as Jordan kissed a sensitive part of her neck. Jordan chuckled mischievously against her skin.

"I was talking about Dianne and her 'No sex in the showers' speech."

"It's a good scene," Freya said seriously. "I would never admit it to her, but I actually get kinda scared when she chews us out."

"I know. I love it when she goes all commanding officer with a heart."

"I'm not sure that I could handle an actual dressing down from her."

"Hmm," Jordan hummed against her neck. "When you start talking about dressing down, it makes me think about undressing you." "Behave, you," Freya swatted her on the ass as she leaned in to kiss her again.

As they pulled apart, Jordan growled. "I'm not sure I can take much more of this abstinence thing," she groaned, pulling away from Freya and moving towards the seating area. "Tomorrow we're filming the shower scene."

Following her, Freya moaned, "Please don't remind me. Regardless of how unsexy it's going to be, being on set, I'm still going to struggle."

Jordan started to chuckle, "What, are you telling me that you don't find flesh underwear and moleskin tape-on nipples sexy?"

Freya cocked an eyebrow and smirked, "On you, everything is sexy."

Blake looked down at the mannequin as he said his line, "Who the hell texts while driving, for God's sake? He never stood a chance. Dammit, bone fragments have nicked the artery; he's losing too much blood." He looked up and yelled, "Where the hell is Van Hausen?"

Freya looked up from her place at the stomach of the mannequin, "We've still got a bit of time. I'm not going to let a soldier who came back from the front line in one piece lose a leg after going out for a jog. We can put in a shunt, get a vascular clamp in, and try to control the bleed 'til she gets here." Turning to the nurse at her side, she said quietly, "Page Captain Van Hausen again for me."

Both actors turned towards a machine that was emitting a sudden beeping. Freya exhaled, "Crap, he's losing it faster than we can put it in. Hang another bag of O-neg. Holt, I need you to do what you're doing faster, his BP is dropping." She frowned, shaking her head slightly, "Push in five of epi. Damien, I'm having a hard time locating the source of the intra-abdominal bleeding." Her hands started to move around faster, "Crap crap crap." As the noise from the monitor started again, Freya looked towards it then scanned the room. "Get Van Hausen in here, now!" she yelled.

"Cut, and we're done here," the director said, stepping out from his position.

Freya stood back and rolled her shoulders. Blake pulled off his mask and held up a gloved hand stained in fake blood. "Good work," he grinned.

Freya laughed and smacked her palm against his.

They waited on set while the next scene was set up. While Blake was off speaking to the special effects technician, Freya was loitering around inspecting the contents of the Craft Services table. She was frowning as she decided what to eat, when she heard a familiar laugh.

She looked up and smiled as Jordan arrived on set, her hands deep in the pockets of her scrub pants.

"Hey, you," she greeted Jordan as she picked up a pastry.

Jordan grinned as she came over towards Freya, "Hey yourself." Jordan bit down on her bottom lip as she looked at Freya hungrily. "You know I'm really ravenous right now," she purred, as she picked up an orange from the fruit bowl and tossed it in her hand.

Smiling, Freya grabbed the orange from midair. "You need to stop, seriously," she whispered. "Because," she leaned closer and whispered softly in Jordan's ear. "I am aching for you to touch me right now. I can feel how ready I am for you." She glanced around quickly to make sure no one was paying any attention to them, particularly as Jordan's jaw had dropped, "So you need to stop, unless you're ready to do something about that." She leaned back, placed the orange back in Jordan's hand, and smiled.

Jordan watched, stunned to silence, as Freya left the room.

***

Walking into the OR, Jordan held up her wet hands, "Sorry, I got held up in surgery. What do you need?"

Blake turned and glared at her as he picked up the prosthetic leg and handed it to an extra.

Freya looked up with anger in her eyes as she looked over towards Jordan. "Holt, I need you back here now," she barked, dropping her eyes back down towards the mannequin. "Dr Van Hausen, you're not needed now," she said coldly without looking up.

Jordan's head reeled back and she rocked on her heels, her eyebrows shooting up in surprise. "Okay," she muttered, and turned to leave.

"Cut. Thank you all for your work today." The director smiled and shook hands with the actors, "Ladies, I'll see you at seven tomorrow on the closed set."

Jordan and Freya gave each other a quick look at the mention of the following day.

"See you tomorrow," they said simultaneously.

***

Freya picked up her cell. "You should be asleep," she said, smiling as she settled back into her pillows.

"Can't," Jordan pouted. "Anytime I close my eyes, I picture sexy time with you."

Laughing, Freya snuggled under her duvet, "Really? And what are you picturing?"

"We're in the shower and we're kissing, and I'm soaping you all over," Jordan closed her eyes, bringing up the picture that had been tempting her for hours.

"Is that what they're calling it these days?" Freya teased, as Jordan snorted down the line. "We're on the set in four hours. Seriously, Jordan, sleep."

Jordan pulled a pillow over and spooned into it, "I want to sleep beside you. I want to be curled up against you right now. I'm done waiting, Freya. I'm serious. I want to date you properly and not sneak around anymore."

Freya sighed, "I know, me too. How about this weekend? We'll go on an official date."

"Promise?"

"Promise."

***

Curling her toes on the cold floor and pulling her robe tighter around her, Jordan glanced round at the small crew working the shower scene as she waited beside Dianne for Freya to come onto set. She was nervous as hell, as this was the first time that she'd actually had to get naked. Usually she was under covers so could get away with not being totally exposed, but this was her first time in the flesh-colored thong which, at present, was riding so far up her ass that she was sure her spine was going to split.

She wriggled, trying to get more comfortable as Freya arrived wrapped in her robe. "Morning everyone, isn't it a lovely morning to get naked in front of people you work with?" she joked, greeting the crew and her cast mates.

There was laughter, followed by a series of murmured greetings as she walked over and joined Jordan and Dianne, running a hand over her wet, slicked back hair.

The director came over and smiled encouragingly, "Ladies, we all know that standards and practices have been all over our ass about this scene, so, just like we rehearsed, now is not the time for artistic interpretation. So, like we talked about, we'll be outside of the door. The camera will be following Anthea's line of vision on this shot and then, Dianne, we'll come back and shoot you entering the door from the other side."

They nodded their agreement and waited for the scene to be set up fully.

Ten minutes later, Jordan and Freya were standing in the shower.

"Okay, we're ready to roll," the director's voice came from outside.

Jordan loosened off the tie of her robe and let it fall from her shoulders, watching out of her peripheral vision as Freya did the same. They handed the robes out of the shower to a crewmember, who left the set.

"Cue the water."

They jumped a little as the water hit them for the first time, grateful that at least it was warm.

"We're rolling, positions everyone."

Freya gulped as Jordan backed herself up against the cold tile and threaded their fingers. Bracing herself on the floor of the shower, Jordan lowered herself so that Freya was standing over her. Smiling, she lifted their hands above her head before resting them against the tiles. She reached up with her other hand and pulled Freya down by the neck, and not waiting for any direction, she started to kiss her. Freya dropped her shoulder, placing her free hand on the top of Jordan's thigh as close as she could dare to where she really wanted to be. They were treading a fine line with standards and practices. It had taken a multitude of conference calls, eight hours of work-shopping the scene and numerous, often heated, discussions, before it was finally agreed that Freya's hand could be there, provided she didn't move it during the shot. She could though flex her shoulder muscles as if moving.

"Quiet on set. Action!"

Dianne opened the door and entered the shower block, to be greeted with the sight of Freya pressing Jordan against the shower wall. "What the hell do you two think you're doing?" she shouted.

Freya pulled away, turning sharply towards Dianne. Jordan's eyes widened as she attempted to hide behind Freya.

"My office. Now!" Dianne yelled, retreating from the set.

"Okay, still rolling, can we reset really quickly and do a couple more takes and then we're done. Dianne, can you remember to move to the left for the camera over your right shoulder," the director shouted.

Dianne nodded as she prepared to repeat the scene.

"You okay?" Jordan asked quickly, before they started the scene again.

Freya smiled and took the opportunity while they were alone to run her free hand over the exposed flesh of Jordan's ass. "Peachy," she replied, squeezing gently, then retook her position against Jordan's lips.

***

Freya opened her front door, and before she had time to register what was happening, Jordan's hands were on her face pulling her into a deep kiss. The two women stepped back into Freya's home as Jordan kicked the door shut with her foot. Never pulling back from their kiss, Jordan tossed her purse on the floor and shrugged her way out of her jacket. Hands pushed and pulled at clothing. Discarding items as they bounced off pieces of furniture, Jordan navigated them in the general direction of Freya's bedroom.

They smacked against the doorframe, before stumbling through it and crab-walking their way towards the bed. Freya squealed as the back of her legs hit the bed, tipping her backwards. Jordan laughed as she practically pounced on top of Freya and continued with determined focus to strip them both as fast as possible.

Dan sat on Freya's sofa, his eyes wide at the scene he had witnessed. He turned back to the pile of photographs he and Freya had been reviewing for his final exhibition selection and, gathering his prints up, he tapped them delicately on the table before placing them down in a neat pile.

"I'll just be off then," he said to no one as he stood up and collected his jacket. Reaching the door, he smiled as sounds of squeals and laughter drifted from Freya's room. Waving his arms in the air like the conductor of an orchestra, he sang, "Let the nubbing commence!"

His smile faded however as he stepped out and saw Jordan's Audi parked in a deserted manner behind his Mustang. Sucking air between his teeth, he re-entered the house and picked up Jordan's discarded purse. Rummaging around, he found the key to her car and slipped it from the key chain. He pocketed the key, removed his own car key from his pocket and, picking up a pen and paper from the coffee table, scrawled a quick note.

Hey horny lady…SWAPSY!
Enjoy driving a real car for a change.
Get in touch to exchange
D x

Happy with his note, he placed his key on top of it and slipped out of Freya's home, muttering in a Gollumesque voice, "My precious, come to Dan, pretty lady."

"What was that?" Jordan asked, pulling back reluctantly from Freya's lips at the sound of the front door closing.

Freya looked momentarily confused, grimacing slightly as she realized the potential source of the sound, "That'll be Dan letting himself out."

Jordan's eyes widened, "Oh my god, that was his car in the drive, I didn't think. I'm so sorry!"

Grinning Freya flipped them over so she was on top. Resting her weight on her elbows she enjoyed feeling Jordan beneath her, with no barrier between them.

"I'm not, he's a big boy, he'll survive," she leaned down and started to kiss Jordan slowly, immediately changing the mood between them from lust-filled frantic activity to slow, and languid caresses. Pulling away, she smiled, gazing deeply into the dark brown eyes staring back at her, "Hi."

Jordan's lips parted into a broad smile, "Hi."

Freya exhaled a slow satisfied breath as she closed her eyes and returned her lips to Jordan's.

Lightly tracing patterns with her nails on the soft skin of Freya's back, Jordan trailed her hands until they settled on Freya's backside. She pressed her closer to her as their hips started to dance against each other, desperately seeking the purchase that would allow their passion to build. Impatient to explore Freya's body further, Jordan carefully flipped them back over to their original position. She started to kiss her way down Freya's neck, following the outline of her collarbone, before dropping to take a pebbled nipple into her mouth, alternating between swirling her tongue around and flicking it over the sensitive tip. Freya's hips bucked involuntarily at the attention that Jordan was paying to her breasts.

Jordan could feel a rapid beat pulsing through her as she left Freya's breasts and began to pepper the brunette's taut stomach with light kisses. She smiled as she felt the muscles in Freya's abdomen contract, as her breathing became hurried. Her chin brushed against the soft trimmed hair that plunged deep to where Jordan knew Freya wanted her. She hesitated as she inhaled the unique scent of Freya, feeling her own arousal pool. This was her first time in this position. When they had been together before, Jordan had been so overwhelmed by the sensation that Freya created in her that she had lost herself in the feel of Freya. She had been surprised by the physical differences between them. Touching Freya felt familiar, and yet so different to when she had touched herself. She had reveled in the feeling of exploring the reactions that she could produce in Freya with her touches. She felt like an eager pupil opening her eyes in wonder at the responses created in both of them with each new experience.

Freya felt her hesitate. Looking down, her eyes filled with love as she watched Jordan. She reached down and hooked a finger gently under Jordan's chin, bringing her face up. "You don't have to," she smiled, letting Jordan know that it was okay. "Not everyone likes it."

Jordan gave her a smirk, "Oh, I want to." She pushed herself further down between Freya's thighs, pushing them wider apart as she studied Freya, her smirk becoming a wide smile. "You're beautiful," she breathed, before tasting her lover for the first time.

***

Jordan woke as bright sunlight flooded the bedroom, and immediately tightened her grip around the warm body beside her.

"Jordan, you're squeezing me and I need to pee," Freya grumbled, twisting to face Jordan, who snorted softly.

"And a good morning to you too."

Freya gave her a quick grin and leaned over to peck a kiss on the end of Jordan's nose, "Morning, sunshine." She pulled herself from Jordan's almost vice-like grip and stumbled her way across the bed, hopping off the end and entering the bathroom. Jordan lay staring at the ceiling as she heard the toilet flush and the shower being switched on. The bathroom door opened and Freya's head popped through, "I know we've already filmed it, but I wondered if you fancied perfecting that shower scene?"

She had barely reached the word 'shower' when Jordan sprang from the bed to join her.

***

Lloyd Mitchell sat in his car sipping on his coffee, swearing as the hot liquid surged through the small hole on the plastic lid, scalding his top lip. He sat with unwavering eyes trained on his potential pay dirt. Everyone else had moved on to the next thing, but Lloyd had a feeling about this one that just wouldn't go away. He noted the Mustang parked in the drive. Knowing that it belonged to the British photographer, Lloyd assumed he must have stayed the night, which from Lloyd's experience over the past weeks wasn't anything unusual.

The door of the property started to open and Lloyd fumbled, trying to pick up his long lens camera while putting his coffee down on the dashboard. He watched through the lens of his camera, clicking away as a blonde woman stepped out and placed her sunglasses on her nose. She turned back, smiling as a dark-haired woman came into sight. The rapid fire of Lloyd's camera continued to shoot as the women kissed.

"Gotcha," Lloyd smiled to himself, as he continued to capture the exchange.

***

"Wait, it's going to be okay," Jordan gripped Freya's arm, turning her towards her, when a loud roar from a motorcycle going past caused her to pause.

"Dammit," the director shouted. "Okay, we're still rolling, reset and go again."

Jordan retreated towards the doors of the arts center that doubled as the exterior of *Front Line*'s German-based treatment center. She entered through the automatic door, waiting for them to close before exiting again into the LA night.

"Emily? Emily?" she jogged up behind Freya. "Okay, this is something more than me being delayed during your surgery. Is this because of what happened this morning? 'cause, it's going to be okay." Freya turned at the pressure on her arm.

"Really? We were caught having sex, in the hospital, by our commanding officer. You honestly think that it's going to be okay?"

Freya replied, her tone flat and emotionless while her face portrayed a woman keeping her emotions in check.

"I know it will," Jordan responded tenderly. "You heard her, she's not going to discipline us. We just have to be more careful."

Freya turned as if to walk away, then whipped back, "Careful? I have been careful my entire career. All through 'don't ask, don't tell', I was careful Georgia. Not once did I do anything to rouse suspicion, or get caught doing something I shouldn't. I'm a damn fine soldier as well as a doctor, Georgia."

Jordan pulled her into an embrace. "I know you are, and I'm sorry. I shouldn't have come into the shower like that," she murmured against Freya's hair.

Pulling away, tears flowing down both cheeks, Freya looked angrily at Jordan, "No, you shouldn't. Just because being gay isn't forbidden anymore doesn't mean that I want the world knowing my private life."

Jordan held her hands up in surrender. "I was wrong and I'll admit that," she narrowed her eyes. "But I wasn't alone in that shower, and I didn't hear you complain. I get that you're angry, but are you blaming me?" she asked, starting to bristle at the undercurrent of an accusation.

"Yeah, yeah, I'm blaming you," Freya raged, then shook her head, turned, and walked off down the path leaving Jordan watching her exit.

"Cut. Okay people, it's three a.m., let's call it there," the director said smiling. "Good job," he said to Jordan as she passed him walking towards Freya who was wiping the tears from her cheeks.

"God, I hope that we get some hot make up time in the next episode, crying like that plays havoc with my karma," Freya sniffed as she ran her pinkies under her eyes.

Rubbing her shoulder comfortingly, Jordan whispered, "I know a cure for karma that's out of whack."

Freya shot her a lusty look as she smirked and shook her head, "I guess we'll find out tomorrow at the read, or should I say later today!"

As they walked towards the mobile units used during location filming, Jordan started to fidget nervously. "Freya, I was wondering whether you wanted to spend Thanksgiving together?" she asked, suddenly shy.

Immediately feeling her mood brighten, Freya smiled, "I would love to. I usually spend it with my parents, but they're in Europe, or with my grandmother, but she's on some promotional tour at the moment. They've retouched her early films and are re-releasing them. Which just leaves Dan, but, being British, he doesn't really get it. So, I would love to spend Thanksgiving with you."

Jordan grinned and bumped her shoulder against Freya's as they walked, "So tell me, where are you taking me on our official first date?"

***

Thanks to her night with Freya and then their filming schedule running into the small hours of the morning, Jordan had climbed into bed when she got home and lapsed into something akin to a coma. The following morning she had, as a consequence, slept through her alarm, meaning that she had a mad dash to get ready and be at the studio for the table read of the next episode.

She had tried calling Freya on the drive in, but her calls went straight to voicemail. Standing outside Freya's trailer, Jordan rapped her knuckles on the door before pulling the door handle. She frowned at the locked door, and stepped down from the small set of stairs. Giving the trailer one last glance, she shrugged towards the lot driver and jumped on the cart for the short drive to the rehearsal rooms.

Jordan slipped into the large room just as everyone was taking their seats. She sat down quickly, and was surprised as she registered the empty spot where Freya usually sat. A cough from the production table tore her attention from the empty seat. Eleanor French stood up, her hands nervously toying with the papers on the table in front of her, "People, this week's episode is being directed by one of our favorite directors, Catherine Gilbert."

Applauding, the assembled cast and crew gave their customary welcome. Catherine looked over the top of her glasses and smiled, raising her palm in acknowledgement.

"Before we get started, I have some news," Eleanor paused, her jaw visibly tightening as she looked around her cast and crew, her eyes avoiding Jordan's direction. "Today, the network released Freya Easter from her contract. She will therefore no longer be appearing on the show, effective immediately."

There were gasps around the table at the announcement. Jordan rose slightly in her seat, turning as she felt a hand grip her thigh. Grant gave an almost imperceptible shake of his head as he squeezed her leg once before letting go. Jordan lowered herself back down and slumped in her seat, fixing her eyes firmly on her hands, which were running up and down her thighs trying to dissipate the anger she felt.

Eleanor looked up at the still shell-shocked cast and crew, "A formal statement will be released by the network later. Please, can I ask that if you are approached for a comment, you decline. Dianne, Jordan, there will be an additional scene for you both from the previous episode, scripts will be with you in a half hour."

Dianne pushed her script back on the table. "What reason did they give?" she asked, sitting forward.

Swallowing the distaste she felt at delivering the party line, Eleanor answered, "It was felt that the chemistry in the Georgia-Emily relationship wasn't working."

"Bullshit," Dianne muttered. "I'm surprised," she continued, raising her voice pointedly. "I thought that they had a huge amount of chemistry, on screen and off!"

Jordan's head shot up in surprise and she looked over towards Dianne, who was still glaring at Eleanor.

Eleanor held her hands up, "We have an episode to get done, people. I've nothing else to say on this." She sat back down and gave Catherine a curt nod.

Grant nudged Jordan's arm and slid a piece of paper over.

You were papped kissing Freya leaving her house, I'm so sorry.

Jordan gulped and looked at Grant. He smiled sadly in confirmation, before nodding his head towards Eleanor. Jordan followed his prompt and saw Eleanor bite her lip and close her eyes before giving a small sigh and returning her attention to the script.

Looking down, Jordan noticed Grant had added to his note.

Think carefully about how you want to deal with this.

Thanks to Freya's sudden departure, Jordan's scenes were lighter than originally intended. As a result, she was able to zone-out of the majority of the read only for Grant to nudge her occasionally to warn her that a line was coming up.

As they finished the reading, Jordan leapt out of her seat and started to walk quickly towards the door. Checking her phone as she walked, she opened a text from Dan.

She's at mine. The door's unlocked so come in, if you want or are able to.
"Jordan," Eleanor called. "Can you walk with me?"

Nodding, Jordan slipped her phone into her pocket and watched as her cast mates filed out of the room, a couple of them gripping her arm in a sign of support as they passed.

***

Dan stroked the head resting on his lap. The sobs had subsided, and apart from the increasing wet patch on his trousers from her tears and the occasional sniff, causing Dan to pull a fresh tissue from the box and hand it down, they had very little interaction.

Freya lay her fingers lightly on Dan's knee as she was soothed by his gentle caresses. When she had a call from Eleanor at five in the morning after finishing filming at three, she had a hunch that all was not well, and had driven to the studio with a sense of foreboding gnawing at her stomach. *Earlier that day…*

"Come in," Eleanor called, as she knocked on the door.

Freya anxiously opened the door and poked her head in, "Hi Eleanor, is something wrong?"

As she walked into the office she noticed the open laptop on Eleanor's desk. Her shoulders slumped as she realized what the image displayed was of.

Eleanor closed the laptop, a small click breaking the silence that had descended. "I asked you, I specifically asked you," the producer had said, looking down at her feet, "and you told me there were no more secrets."

"I…I…We," Freya collapsed into a seat opposite Eleanor. "I didn't know then, what we…"

Eleanor waved her hand dismissively and sighed, "I guess it doesn't matter now, we don't have much time before the suits arrive." She stood up and walked around her desk. "I need you to know that this is not me, I…" she threw her hands up in defeat. "This. Is. Not. My doing," she repeated. "I'm really sorry."

Freya's face crumpled as realization hit. "I'm being fired, aren't I?" she asked, her voice almost a whisper. "Is Jordan being —"

Eleanor cut her off with a short shake of her head, "No, I'm sorry. It's just you."

Freya swallowed hard and nodded, a numbness settling over her.

"I know you're gonna want to rant, rave and holler to anyone that'll listen. Hell, I want to rant, rave and holler about this, and you have every right to do that," Eleanor shook her head in disbelief at the thought of what she was about to say. "But I would strongly recommend that you don't. This can be a ruthless, unforgiving, incestuous ass of a town. It'll chew you up and spit you out," she exhaled, taking Freya's hands into her own. "But it's a job, and god knows getting one of those in this business is hard enough, even if you are a Conor. And it'll be even harder, having a whole network pissed at you."

"It would appear keeping the job is also difficult," Freya added sarcastically.

"Yes, it can be," Eleanor gave a sad laugh. "I promise you Freya, when all this dies down, I will have a role for you if I still have a show. I have loved working with you, and none of this…none of this…is a reflection on your talent or ability."

The door opened, and Eleanor moved away from Freya as a suited man that she had never seen before entered. "Miss Easter, my name is Steven Abbot," he held out his hand.

Freya gave a quick glance over towards Eleanor, who had an impassive expression on her face, before returning her eyes to the outstretched hand. Eventually, she raised her own and shook it.

***

Jordan drove as fast as she could. She abandoned Dan's Mustang, which she was still driving, behind her own car. She ran up the stairs and burst through the door, her heart breaking as she saw Freya laying on the sofa, her head resting on Dan's lap.

Dan gave her a small smile before carefully extricating himself from under Freya. He gently laid her head onto a pillow and walked over to Jordan. Accepting his car key, he pulled her into a hug, "Your keys are on the table, I'm going to head over to hers to make sure that the place is okay. If you want to stay with her tonight, let me know, and I'll sleep there. Make yourself at home." He hesitated before leaving, "We've had the tears, and now the shock. If I know my little Egg, the rage should be coming anytime soon. Call me if you need help." He gave one last look towards Freya, then left her in Jordan's capable hands.

"Hey," Jordan said softly, perching on the sofa beside Freya's feet.

At Jordan's voice, Freya looked up and a fresh wave of tears overwhelmed her as she flung herself into her lover's arms.

"Shhhh, it'll be okay, I promise," Jordan soothed, her hands rubbing up and down Freya's back.

Freya pulled back, hiccupping slightly. "They fired me!" she said incredulously. "The bastards actually fired me!" She looked wide-eyed at Jordan before brushing aside her tears angrily, "They took me into Eleanor's office and fired me, Jordan!" She stood up and started to pace around the large coffee table.

Crap, thought Jordan, *Dan wasn't lying when he said anytime soon.*

"I know they did, I'm so sorry," Jordan stood up to try and placate Freya, who was striding around the table.

"I got out of Eleanor's office, and the efficient bastards had packed up my trailer into a box and left it sitting for me," she stopped pacing. "You know what, I'm done!" she started to pace again throwing her arms around as she wailed. "I'm done with LA. I never wanted to come back here, but I got guilted into it with Anna's health. My family never works in TV, and now I know why. I am done working in a place only interested in ratings and revenue and market share and demographics and…and audience profiling," she continued to rant, barely pausing for breath, "and where sponsors call the shots over creativity and the story."

Freya had worked herself so far up that nothing Jordan could say or do was going to bring her back down again.

"I'm fed up with shows pulling out of stories because they could damage the network's brand and God forbid if someone doesn't want to go on a damn roller coaster or buy washing powder because two women, who kiss on primetime, also kiss each other off of it." She stopped immediately in front of Jordan, "I love you, and I'm done with a town that thinks it can dictate to me who I fall in love with and how I'm allowed to show it!" She stopped slightly out of breath, looking at Jordan, whose eyes had widened at Freya's inadvertent admission, "And I didn't plan on the first time that I told you that I love you being me shouting it in your face." She hung her head down.

Jordan hooked her finger under Freya's chin and pulled the tearladen green eyes up to meet her own, "I love you too." She leant down to kiss Freya, who hiccupped into the kiss.

"Sorry."

"I love you, shut up and kiss me," Jordan murmured as she brought Freya closer and kissed her.

***

Freya snuggled further under Jordan's arm, and absently ran her fingertips up and down the skin of Jordan's stomach, "I didn't even get a proper exit! We just had that stupid fight about shower sex." She lifted herself up so she was laying on top of Jordan, her chin resting on her hands which were splayed across Jordan's naked breasts, "And then schlooop." She smacked her lips together, "I'm gone."

Jordan looked down, her face a mixture of amusement at Freya's description, and sadness at the accuracy of it.

It was Sunday, and the two women had holed themselves in Dan's beach house since Freya's sacking, neither wishing to step out of the bubble they had created around themselves and return to reality.

"Sucked into oblivion," Freya mused.

"At least they didn't drop you down an elevator shaft," Jordan added.

"Oh, or drop a helicopter on me!" Freya laughed. However, her laughter quickly turned to a wistful sigh.

"They re-deployed Emily to Afghanistan," Jordan said carefully. This was the first time that she had admitted to Freya that she knew the fate of her character. "I had to shoot an added scene with Dianne the day they told us. They had Emily request a deployment to a combat support hospital."

Freya sighed and shook her head at the news. "I've missed pilot season. What am I going to do?" she groaned, turning her head to listen to Jordan's heartbeat.

"Something will come along," Jordan said, sounding more optimistic than she was feeling.

***

Freya lay on her sofa, having returned home from Dan's. A box of cupcakes sat open on the table. She pulled the sleeve of her onesie over her hand, freeing her fingers so she could change the channel on the TV. Despite her loathing of the outfit, Jordan had returned it the previous evening in an attempt to cheer her up. However, neither the power of the onesie or the sugar hit of the cupcakes could shake Freya from her gloom.

She sighed as she recalled earlier that day, when Jordan had returned to work. It had felt awkward, as Jordan had got ready to head into the studio and admitted that she had a light day. Neither commented on the reason for the sudden reduction in her workload.

Freya roamed through the channels before her attention spiked at the sight of her grandmother waving towards a studio audience. Unmuting the TV, Freya recalled the text from her mother that morning, reminding her that Anna was on *Opinionated Women* to publicize the re-release of her films. Anna made her way onto the set, smiling broadly towards the presenters, air-kissing them before perching on the sofa.

"Anna Conor, it is such a privilege to have you here," the show's main presenter, Pandora Paterson, smiled.

"Thank you, it's lovely to be here," Anna replied, smiling as the excited audience broke into applause once more.

Freya zoned out as the presenters asked her grandmother about the films that she was promoting, paying just enough attention to be able to tell Anna later how great she was.

"Anna, I have to ask, are the rumors true? Has your granddaughter Freya Easter been fired from *Front Line*?"

Anna nodded and shifted uncomfortably in her seat, "Sadly, those rumors are true. I haven't spoken to Freya directly yet, but I spoke to her father this morning and he said that she was no longer on the show." She gave a taut smile, her feelings on the subject plain for everyone to see, "It is a travesty that Freya is being punished because of who she loves."

Biting her bottom lip, Freya chuckled. While in private, her grandmother often lamented Freya's sexuality, in public she was like a she-wolf protecting her family when there was any sign of attack.

"I'm not sure that is the case. The rumors are that she was let go, as the network felt that the viewers didn't connect with the onscreen relationship between her and Jordan Ellis."

Freya raised an eyebrow at this nugget of information and was about to shout at the TV, when she recognized the look on her grandmother's face. "Oh God, no," she muttered, gripping a cushion against her chest in the hope it could protect her from what was about to happen.

Anna drew herself up, straightening her back and thrusting her shoulders back, "That is a complete crock."

The audience let out a loud laugh.

"Let me tell you this," she pointed her finger in the face of one of the presenters. "This is *my* granddaughter we're taking about. She has acting in her DNA, as well as training from RADA. If she was asked to have chemistry with a block of wood, she would have it." Anna turned to the audience, "I watched her on that show, and as far as I could tell, there was not only chemistry, there was physics and a whole lot of biology going on as well."

Freya hooted with laughter along with the studio audience as Anna continued her rant, "That two-bit network wouldn't know a good thing if it bit it on the ass. What we are seeing here is plain and simple. People do not like that the women who were kissing on the show are kissing off screen as well. Well, America, get over it."

Freya leapt up onto the sofa, bouncing on the cushions as she shouted at the screen, "I love you Anna."

The buzzing of her phone distracted her from catching the last of her grandmother's rant. She typed '*through my fingers*' in reply to Dan's text asking if she was watching.

"And I wouldn't put it past that show to kill her character off with an IUD," Anna finished emphatically, her face twisted in disgust.

Snorting with laughter, Freya muted the TV and answered her now ringing phone.

"This is priceless," Dan gasped between bouts of laugher. "She just blew you up with a contraceptive device."

"I know! Just when I don't think she can surprise me ever again, she does something like this. Her publicity people will be hauling ass to gloss over this."

Her doorbell rang, and Freya was in two minds whether to leave it. The persistent ringing made her mind up for her.

"Dan, gotta go, keep watching and text me if she gets more outrageous," she said as she leapt across the sofa, jumping down and walking towards the door while still keeping an eye on the TV. Looking through the spy hole, she thumped her head softly against the door before opening it, "Dominick, good morning."

***

Walking into Freya's home holding a brown square box, Jordan flipped a light on in the darkened room. As she tossed her keys on the table, she noticed the empty box of cupcakes sitting on the table beside a large pile of papers.

"Freya?" she called, walking through to the kitchen, unable to see her girlfriend anywhere.

"In here."

Jordan turned out of the kitchen towards where Freya's voice had come from. She opened the door of the bathroom, and burst out laughing at the sight of Freya sitting in the bath, her hair soaped up into a long point above her head. Jordan put down the cardboard box she had been carrying and leaned down to kiss Freya's waiting lips.

"What, you don't like it?" Freya asked sincerely, turning her head to allow Jordan to see the full effect of her hairstyle. "I thought I'd try something new, now that I don't have to ask for permission on what I do with my hair."

"It's not your best look," Jordan laughed, taking a hand and flattening down the spike.

"Pff," Freya sniffed haughtily then smiled. "What's in the box?"

Jordan looked down at the box, frowning, "Not sure, Liz in wardrobe asked me to give it to you."

Freya leaned her arms on the edge of the tub and rested her chin on her hands. "Open it," she said excitedly.

Jordan picked the box up, taking her nail to the tape securing it. As she opened it and looked inside, she gave a small chuckle. "It would appear to be contraband," she smiled, picking out Freya's stethoscope from the show and placing it on the floor beside her feet. She reached back into the box and pulled out Freya's ACU jacket. Her character's name embroidered on the chest. "What a pity Liz hasn't put the Daisy Dukes in." Jordan pouted as she examined the remainder of the box.

"Thank God!" Freya frowned, "I hated them."

Jordan flicked water at Freya's face. "I was thinking about them more for my benefit. You seem brighter than when I left you this morning," she remarked.

"Anna cheered me up," Freya smiled, lying back in the tub. "She was on *Opinionated Women* today and she was awesome."

Jordan grinned, "I heard! There was a bit of noise about it at work this afternoon. Did she really say they were going to kill you with an IUD?"

Laughing, Freya nodded, before chewing on her lip as she decided to broach a new subject, "Dominick stopped by this afternoon."

Jordan raised her eyebrows expectantly.

"He's lined up an audition, which he says is more of a meeting, and even then merely a formality."

"Excellent, that's great," Jordan leaned over, taking Freya's face in her hands to give her a congratulatory kiss. "I'm so happy for you," she smiled.

"Watch, you'll get wet," Freya murmured against her lips.

Jordan pulled back and gave her a smirk. "Way too late for that," she replied huskily.

Freya grinned, flicking a handful of bubbles onto Jordan's nose, "Saucy!"

Laughing as she pulled back, Jordan picked up a towel to dry her face, "So, what's the role?"

The easy smile that had been playing on Freya's face faded as she took a breath, "Roxie Hart."

"As in Chicago?" Jordan asked, frowning as she put the towel down, trying to think whether she had heard on the grapevine of any productions happening in Los Angeles.

"As in Chicago and all that jazz."

Jordan sat down onto the closed toilet. "Where about?" she asked, feeling her stomach tense with trepidation at what the response was going to be.

Freya watched as fear flashed across Jordan's features.

"Broadway," Freya practically whispered the reply.

Biting her bottom lip that had started to tremble, Jordan nodded slowly, "For how long?"

"Six months, with an option after three to extend."

Jordan tipped her head back to stop the tears that were threatening to spoil what should be a happy occasion for Freya.

"When?"

"Starting in Feb, but with all the rehearsals, etcetera, they want me there next week."

Jordan swallowed hard before looking back down at Freya, who was now sitting in the tub with her knees pulled tight against her chest and a look of sadness on her face.

"Hey, it's great, you will be great," Jordan smiled, forcing herself to ignore her feelings for the moment. Realizing that she only had a small amount of resolve before her emotions would boil to the surface, she stood up and blew out a deep breath. "How about you finish up and I cook us a celebration dinner?" she smiled, leaving Freya sitting in the tub fighting her own tears.

Twenty minutes later, Freya padded into the kitchen expecting to see Jordan in full chef mode. Her forehead wrinkled at the empty kitchen, before she spotted that the door leading out to the pool was slightly ajar. Pushing it open, she looked out into the dimly lit back yard. The glow from the pool uplighters provided the only illumination. Squinting into the gloom, Freya spotted a figure laying on one of the loungers, arms folded loosely across her face. Freya rested her head against the doorframe and silently watched as Jordan dealt with the news of her imminent departure. Freya gave a small shake of her head before turning and moving back into the house.

Lying on the pool lounger, Jordan was trying to talk herself down from her current state of devastation. Life was unfair. That, she was decided on. Finally, she had met someone amazing and fallen in love, and now that person was going to move to the other side of the country. She was happy for Freya, as she knew from their conversations over the weekend that she was worried about not finding work. She also knew that her recent experiences had soured her towards TV, so theatre made more sense. However, none of that lessened the sense of loss that was starting to grow in her. She loved Freya, loved spending time with her, loved the way her brain worked and the way her body felt when against her own. Life just wasn't fair.

"So, Miss Ellis, my name is Major Easter and I'm your doctor. Tell me, what are your symptoms?"

Jordan lifted her arms from her face and opened one eye, the other springing open as her brain processed what was in front of her. The light from the pool highlighted Freya from behind. She stood with her hands on her hips, her hair pulled back into a messy ponytail, her tanned bare legs appearing a shade darker in the gloom than Jordan knew them to be. Jordan trailed her eyes up the bare legs until she reached the hem of the ACU jacket, which barely reached the tops of her thighs. Draped around Freya's neck was her stethoscope. Jordan raised an eyebrow and decided to be a more than willing participant in Freya's ploy to distract them from the large elephant that had inserted itself into their lives.

"Major?"

Freya shrugged, "I thought I deserved a promotion, what with braving all those IUDs."

Jordan chuckled softly. "I'm having chest pains," she replied, laughing slightly at the truth in her words.

"Really? Well, let me examine you and see if we can't work this out," smiling, Freya reached over and placed her palm on Jordan's forehead. "Hmmm, you're hot," she remarked sincerely, before running her hands down Jordan's neck to her glands. "I'd say there are bits of you definitely swollen."

Jordan snorted at the comment.

"Your pulse is quite fast."

Freya dipped her head placing her lips against Jordan's pulse point on her neck. "Yup, definitely fast," she murmured against her girlfriend's hot skin.

"I know I only play a doctor, but I'm fairly sure that's not how you check a pulse."

"No?" Freya said in mock confusion. "The wonders of modern medicine, Miss Ellis. Your show really must keep up with the times. Now, if you could remove your top for me?" Freya instructed, keeping her face straight as she placed the stethoscope buds into her ears and breathed onto the cold metal.

Jordan looked nervously up towards the main house, "What if we're seen?"

"Anna's still on her promo tour. There's no one else here but us."

Mollified, Jordan pulled her top over her head, flushing slightly as she noticed Freya unconsciously lick her lips at the sight of her in her burgundy bra. Freya placed the stethoscope against Jordan's chest, listening to the tattoo that was beating beneath her sternum.

"We have increased chest sounds," Freya mused, removing her stethoscope and draping it back around her neck. She placed her hand above Jordan's breast, "Breathing becoming shallow and skin is hot here too."

Shifting her position, Freya lifted her leg to straddle Jordan. "Starting mouth to mouth," she smirked, capturing Jordan's lips.

Jordan groaned into Freya's mouth as she suddenly became aware of Freya's nakedness beneath the uniform jacket pressed against her stomach. She pushed Freya's shoulders gently, breaking the kiss. "I think you should show me your bedside manner. Inside. Now!" Jordan said with urgency.

***

"We need to talk about this sometime," Freya could feel Jordan's arm tighten around her waist.

"Can't we just keep making love and not talk about it?" Jordan asked hopefully, kissing Freya's shoulder.

Freya closed her eyes. "We've been doing that for four days," she turned to face Jordan who, with her eyes still shut, pouted at the movement. "We should talk about what it means."

"What it means is that you'll be in New York and I'll be here," Jordan opened her eyes slowly and moved her head back slightly to allow Freya to come into focus. "I know what it means, Freya, and that's it," she said sadly.

"I love you and I don't want to leave you," Freya stated, stopping as Jordan placed her lips on hers. After a slow, bittersweet kiss, Jordan released Freya's lips.

"I had to stop you talking, you were about to say but," Jordan's jaw tightened. "I'm not about to ask you to choose me over your career. I love you too, and you should do this. You have to do this."

Jordan brushed Freya's hair from her forehead. "We'll figure it out. Us, I mean. We'll figure us out," she added, as she felt a tear slip from her eye and trickle down the side of her face to drop onto the pillow. "Let's just enjoy the time we have now."

Freya nodded her response as Jordan smiled.

"We have less than a week to store up a lot of sex to see us through, until I get a break and come to New York."

"We should probably get a start on that," Freya said seriously, giving a small smile before she tightened her arm around Jordan, drawing her closer.

December 2011

Jordan stood sipping a glass of champagne. Admiring the double life-sized image in front of her, she recalled the first time she'd seen it. Her cheek muscles twitched as she smirked at the memory of trailing her fingers over the photo. The smirk broadened into a smile as she thought of the times she had repeated those very same actions, only beneath her fingers was warm, soft, flesh. She jumped slightly, sloshing the champagne in her glass as two arms snaked around her waist from behind, switching her glass of champagne for another before pulling her into a backwards embrace.

"Don't drink the stuff for the punters, it's nasty! You're family, you get the good stuff," Dan whispered in her ear. He pulled away slightly to drain the content of the glass he'd taken from Jordan, placing the empty glass onto a passing waitress's tray. "There, I killed it for you, I'm your shite in brighning armour," he said, resting his chin onto Jordan's shoulder. "You do know I have other photos. In fact, I have a whole exhibition full."

"I know. I like this one."

"I know you do, perv, which is why you've been gawping at it for twenty minutes," Dan joked, earning himself a slap on the arm as Jordan leaned back against him.

"I miss her."

"Me too," Dan sighed. "I have a gift for you. Ask the scarylooking woman with the headset later, and she'll give it to you."

Turning her head, Jordan placed a kiss on Dan's cheek, "Thank you. Have you spoken to her recently?"

"The scary woman with the headset? I try not to, she instantly makes my balls retract," Dan felt Jordan's body shake with quiet laughter. "If you mean Freya, I sometimes manage to grab ten minutes with her in between rehearsal time, dance practice and singing lessons.

She sounds wiped and full of crap," he murmured. "I mean, what's with the 'don't bother travelling all this way for Christmas, it's too far and I'll probably have no time' schtick that she's trying to sell us?"

"Yeah, I got that message too," Jordan sighed, taking a sip of the champagne Dan had given her. "Mmm, good stuff's good!" she sang. "I never said thank you," she added, her tone serious.

Dan frowned, shifting slightly so he could look at Jordan, "For what?"

"Taking her to the airport," Jordan pulled Dan's arms tighter around her. "I wanted to, but probably would have made a scene standing, and holding onto her leg, at the same time as yelling at her not to go."

Dan laughed. "Who said I didn't?" only half joking, as he recalled the tear-filled snot-fest that had been Freya's departure.

"Freya said you wailed."

Snorting, Dan shook his head, "I did not wail. I maybe cried a little…like a manly man, or at the very least a semi-butch lesbian."

"Thank you anyway."

Dan snuggled closer, "That's what we do, I have her back and now I have yours, quite literally at the moment." He pecked a kiss on Jordan's cheek before releasing her, "Anyway, people to do, must schmooze my tush off."

As he turned to walk away, Jordan shouted after him, "You know, I reckon you'll make someone a great husband someday."

Dan scowled before hissing back, "Great, you've found something else to make my balls retract." He grinned, and then swept off to be showered with adulation from the exhibition attendees.

Reluctantly, Jordan tore herself away from the large image of Freya and walked around the gallery space to look at the rest of Dan's work. She was hugely impressed at the images. Capturing people going about their lives, they were natural and intimate. She was proud of Dan, whose friendship had come via Freya.

He had always been part of the package, and initially Jordan had thought that she'd resent their closeness, until she realized that they both had huge hearts and never excluded her from anything. Jokes were always explained, and she grew to understand the shared language, created over years of friendship, that existed between them. Her friendship with Dan had grown particularly over the past weeks, when both were dealing with Freya's absence. They had found solace in each other, and their mutual margarita making abilities. Jordan had wondered about Dan's easy acceptance of her, but Freya had explained that she'd passed the test in his eyes; by initially having sex with her despite the cow-print onesie and then by refusing to let her wear it again, which she'd been resolute on until the firing happened.

As she moved around the gallery, Jordan spotted the woman that Dan had told her to speak to walking over to her. Jordan touched her lightly on the arm, "Hi, excuse me."

"What?" the woman snapped, turning to face Jordan.

"Woah, I'd retract mine too," Jordan spluttered, immediately horrified that she had spoken aloud. "I mean, I'm Jordan Ellis. Dan said I was to ask you about a gift."

The woman rolled her eyes before disappearing through a door. Jordan waited, wondering slightly whether the woman was coming back. Eventually she returned and thrust a box at Jordan.

"Thank you," Jordan called after the retreating woman.

She placed her glass of champagne down and lifted the lid on the box. Inside was a frame containing the original print of the photo that she had been admiring. She smiled and, before scanning the room for Dan to say thank you, noticed black lettering inside the lid of the box.

Look beneath the photo!

Jordan narrowed her eyes as she placed the box down and lifted the photo from it. Beneath was an envelope with a Post-it stuck to it. Dan's writing was scrawled over it.

She's better in the flesh, go get her, just blame me. Better yet just get straight to the nubbing and she'll forget everything else! x

As she peeled the Post-it back, Jordan grinned as an airline logo came into view. She ran her finger under the seal on the envelope and removed a first class ticket to New York.

Dan was standing speaking to a small group of people, including a gallery owner from the east coast, with whom he was turning the charm on for in the hope that his exhibition would be picked up and shown. Their conversation was interrupted as Jordan pushed in, apologizing to the other people as she grabbed Dan's cheeks and kissed him emphatically on the lips.

"I love you," she gasped, releasing him. "Thank you."

As Jordan departed, Dan took a sip of his champagne and regarded his audience. He raised an eyebrow and shrugged, "Will not take no for an answer. It's getting embarrassing!"

February 2012

Standing in her dressing room, which was filled with 'break-aleg' messages and flowers, Freya applied her make-up. As she studied her reflection, she smiled at the photo taped to her corner of the mirror that Dan had taken of her and Jordan during her hastily arranged leaving party.

The past couple of months had been physically and mentally exhausting. Freya wasn't a natural dancer, so her efforts to first learn the steps and then make them look effortless had taken countless hours of repetitive training. Twinned with the hours spent training her voice to cope with the stress, and strain, she was about to put it through with eight shows a week, she was shattered. It was probably thanks to the draining schedule and constant activity that she hadn't curled up and wept like a baby at the distance between her and Jordan more often than she had.

Freya had tried to compartmentalize her feelings and focus on work, and this had led to her demanding that Jordan and Dan not come to New York for Christmas as both had suggested. Regardless of the hurt that her request might cause, Freya had only been thinking about having to say goodbye again, and wasn't sure she could handle it. However, as was often the case, Dan knew her better then she knew herself, and had organized for Jordan to come out.

The five days they had spent over Christmas and New Year's were absolutely what Freya needed. Jordan was able to share her Broadway experience of being in a lengthy run by giving her some tips on how to maintain her energy levels and protect her voice. She wished that Jordan had been able to make it to her first night. However, she understood that it was a big ask to have her fly across the country for what would probably be just one night, thanks to her filming schedule.

She rolled her shoulders and started to stretch her face muscles, opening her mouth and eyes wide. She stood up as she heard the company's half hour call. Fixing her costume, she started her vocal warm-ups. She could hear activity on the other side of her dressing room door as crew and cast moved between the stage, green room and dressing rooms. There was a knock at her door and a stagehand stuck his head round, his headset pushed back over his ears.

"Freya, this was handed in for you," he handed over a small square box. "Have a good show."

"Thank you," Freya said to his departing head. She put the box down on her dressing table, frowning at the lack of a card. Her hand grasped at her chest when she saw what was in the box. Nestled in black tissue paper was an orange, with '*I love you, you will be great*' written on it in neat black handwriting.

***

Jordan looked at the distinctive red lettering of the show on the theatre's marquee, and smiled at the black and white image of her girlfriend sitting forward on a box, her arms resting on her thighs, her hands dangling loosely between her legs. She was wearing an impossibly short black lace dress. With her dark hair slicked back, the dark and smoky make-up around her eyes made them even more piercing. Jordan could only imagine how mesmerizing those green eyes would have been when the photo was taken. She was incredibly proud of Freya. She knew how much work she'd put in, and she knew that she would be amazing.

When she had visited at Christmas she'd been treated to a couple of the numbers that Freya had been working on, and had been surprised at how much stronger Freya's voice had become. However, as proud as she was of her girlfriend, her main thought, looking at the image, was how great her legs were and that it had now been forty-nine days since she had kissed and held her and felt those legs wrapped around her. She checked her watch, knowing from experience that Freya would be doing her warm-up exercises, and wondered idly whether her message had been delivered in time.

"There you are," Dan growled. "I said wait there," he pointed to where he had asked Jordan to stand.

Pulling her baseball cap down lower onto her head, Jordan scowled at him, "I did, but you were taking ages and I was starting to get attention, and I just want to come enjoy my girlfriend's opening night."

"Okay, Greta Garbo," Dan smiled, hooking his arm through Jordan's. "Let's go get our seats."

***

Following the performance, the dressing room filled with wellwishers. Fellow cast and guests gave Freya congratulatory hugs and kisses, and she was happily basking in the attention. She had her back to the door while she spoke with a cast member, when a familiar British accent reached her ears.

"Trust me, she'll want so see me, she owes me alimony."

Freya turned and grinned as Dan argued with a stagehand, who was fighting a losing battle in trying to control the number of people crammed into Freya's dressing room. She flung herself into Dan's waiting arms, kissing his cheek noisily as he picked her up.

"You came!" she pulled back, about to ask what he'd thought and how Jordan was when he left her, when her attention was drawn to a figure behind him, a black baseball cap pulled down low on her head.

"Jordan!" she thumped Dan's shoulders to get him to put her down, and launched herself at her girlfriend.

"You're here! Why didn't you say you were coming? What did you think? How long are you here for?"

Jordan laughed, and silenced Freya's constant questions with a kiss. She felt the taut energy emanating from Freya following the excitement of performing start to dissipate, as she relaxed into the kiss. Finally pulling apart, Jordan grinned, "I wanted to surprise you. You were amazing, and I get the red eye on Monday morning."

"I can't believe you're here," Freya sighed, instantly forgetting the room full of people at her back. "Let's go home, I reeeeeally want to say hello to you properly," she whispered.

Jordan looked over Freya's shoulder and indicated with her head. "Don't you have an after-show party to attend as guest of honor?" she whispered in response.

"Dammit, two drinks and we're going," Freya growled in her ear, then turned and re-entered her dressing room, her hand firmly gripping Jordan's.

March 2012

The morning traffic noise could just be heard over the radio playing in the corner of Freya's kitchen, as she sat enjoying breakfast. She sat at the table with one foot up on her chair. Encircled by her arms, her knee was pulled up against her as she pulled her toast apart and slipped the torn pieces into her mouth.

"Stop watching me," she smiled, looking towards Jordan who was sitting sipping her coffee.

Brown eyes widened over the brim of the mug, "I'm not!"

"You are!"

Jordan set her mug on the table. "I like watching you," she pouted.

Wiping her crumby hands on her pj bottoms, Freya stood up and planted a crumb-filled kiss on Jordan's lips, "You realize it makes you a little creepy."

"Dammit," Jordan retorted. "I was going for all the ways creepy."

She stood up and grabbed Freya by the waist, pulling her towards her. "So what do you think we should do with your one day off, and my one fun day in New York, before I have to go back to LA?" Jordan asked playfully as she sat back down and trapped Freya between her thighs.

"I have a few suggestions," Freya mused.

"Do any of them involve leaving this apartment?" Jordan asked, chuckling.

Freya pulled on Jordan's hands until she was standing. "Nope…not one of them," she smiled, kissing Jordan and leading her back to the bedroom.

April 2012

Tossing her jacket down onto a stool, Freya flipped the switch on the kettle and brought out a jar of honey from the fridge. She spooned a dollop into a mug and waited for her kettle to boil. Her hand absently went to her throat as she swallowed painfully. After two months, despite the training and the care she was taking with her voice, she was still starting to flag. She poured the boiled water into the mug, stirring it as she walked through to her living room. Placing the mug onto the table, she flopped onto her sofa and picked up the TV remote to access her recorded shows. Despite her tiredness and her aching throat, tonight was Tuesday, which meant she got to see her girlfriend. Or at least she got to watch her on TV. She started the show and pulled the woolen blanket from the back of the sofa around her, as she sipped her drink on what had become her Tuesday post-show ritual.

The one benefit of no longer working on the show was that Freya could sit back, relax, and watch it as a viewer again. However, the downside of having been on the show was that she also understood how things worked. That, and the smell of chitlins had never left her.

Jordan, as Georgia, sat alone in an office, still devastated by Emily's departure.

Yeah, you keep mourning me, Freya thought, taking a careful sip of her drink. Even when looking upset Jordan was gorgeous. She felt a pang of sadness as she thought about the length of time since she had seen her girlfriend in the flesh.

There was a knock at the door, and Georgia shouted for them to enter. Freya watched the camera pan to a red-haired woman standing in the doorway. She had joined as a new character shortly after Freya's firing. Watching as the scene unfolded, Freya started to regret not asking Jordan more about her work. They had both studiously avoided the topic of *Front Line* during their chats and emails. Freya's attention was piqued again, as the new character moved across the room and sat seductively on the edge of the desk. Freya's eyes widened as she leaned over, plucking a paper from Georgia's fingers.

"Working late? You know what they say about all work and no play," she said throatily.

"Don't you dare!" Freya whispered, not caring about protecting her voice. She edged forward on her seat, watching as the scene unfolded before her. The redhead leaned in and placed her lips against Georgia's.

"Tart," Freya husked, pulling out her phone and typing a message furiously.

Jordan was sitting waiting for the call to her next scene when she felt her phone vibrate. Opening up the message from Freya, she fought the urge to laugh.

Seriously! Can't believe you replaced me already!

Jordan quickly typed a response, chortling as she pictured Freya watching the episode.

I will never replace you!
How'd tonight go?

Freya smiled contentedly as she read Jordan's reply. She typed her response and then drained the rest of her mug.

Was good, throat killing me.
Have had hot honey, heading to bed now.

Almost immediately after she sent it, her phone beeped with a message.

Sleep well, sweet dreams, I love you. Btw hot honey better be a drink and not a girl!

A soppy grin spread across Freya's face as she replied.

Relax! You're the only hot honey in my life, that doesn't come from a jar. I love you too, try not to enjoy kissing strange women.

Jordan smiled as her name was called and typed a reply as she gestured that she was coming.

You're the only strange woman I enjoy kissing x

She switched her phone off and slipped it back into her pocket.

May 2012

From: Ellis, Jordan
Sent: May 5 2012 10:00 PST
To: Conor, Freya
Subject: Morning

Hey gorgeous,

How was your day/night?

I'm so glad that you're now at the stage where the pranks are happening. That means you've broken the back of the performance and you're rocking it! Work here…is work. We've started filming the season finale. It's a two hour job so double the fun! Dianne asked me to say hi for her, "Hi!"

I think the production office is starting to get fed up with the Dollhausen shippers. They're still receiving torn half dollar bills from them and have a huge glass box in the office where they store them now…there's a lot!

Don't tell him…but I miss Dan, at least when he was here it felt like I had some sort of physical connection with you…no not like that! How is he?

Got to go I'm typing on my phone and my fingers are starting to cramp into a claw.

I love you,

Your Jordan x

***

From: Conor, Freya
Sent: May 6 2012 09:00 PST
To: Ellis, Jordan
Subject: re: Morning

I just left a message on your phone, I'm sorry I didn't get to speak to you before you headed to work, I miss your voice *pout*

The pranks are coming in fast and furious now, last night Nici mooned me from the wings. God knows how I managed to keep it together. I'm meeting her later. She's promised to teach me to roller blade, so we're going to go skating in Central Park and terrorize the tourists.

Dan says he misses you too. I told him (sorry) BIG mistake…he's declared you his favorite and I'm his spare now apparently. He'll be emailing you soon.

So what's in store for the finale? No don't tell me, I want to watch it.

I miss you, can't wait 'til you finish up for the season and come out…just think, a whole six weeks!

Freya

X

Jordan closed the email and picked up her phone, selecting Freya from her favorites list. She rolled her eyes as Freya's voicemail service answered the call. She listened to her girlfriend's voice telling her that she couldn't come to the phone.

"Hey Freya, I got your message and email, I'm sorry I missed you. Listen, when you get this can you call me? It's kinda important." She sighed inwardly, fighting with herself before adding, "I hope you had fun with Nici today, I love you."

She ended the call, hoping that she had managed to keep any jealousy she was feeling towards Freya's co-star from her voice. "Nici mooned me," she snipped, as she flopped onto a chair in her trailer.

***

Freya placed her new skates onto the floor and started to move around her kitchen as she listened to Jordan's message. She was about to return the call when Nici entered the kitchen and sat down at the table, resting her chin on her hands.

"Thanks for the invite for a pre-show dinner. It's weird when you're on stage, you start to eat and sleep at weird times from everyone else."

"No worries," Freya smiled, putting her phone down and opening the freezer door to look in. "I'm afraid I'm not much of a cook, but I should have something in here that even I can't wreck."

Nici noticed the photograph of Freya and Jordan pinned to the fridge door, "So, is it difficult having a long distance thing going?"

Freya lifted her head, followed Nici's eye line, and smiled at the photo, "It's not ideal, I'll give you that, but she's made it out a few times since I moved here. They finish shooting soon so she'll be here during hiatus, which means we get six weeks together, although I'll still be working." Freya straightened up, "It's hard, but we work at it." She placed her hand onto the photograph as if trying to reach out and touch her girlfriend. Shaking off the feeling of loneliness, she turned with a smile that she didn't feel plastered on her face, "How's pizza?"

***

"There's nothing happening here, Freya. I'm trying, honestly I am. You should take the option," Dominick smiled as his assistant placed a coffee in front of him.

"I don't want to take the option, Dominick. I want to be in LA," Freya replied, pacing back and forth in her kitchen running her hand through her hair. The irony of her now wanting to be in the city which she spent a large chunk of her adolescence and adulthood wanting to be away from seemed to taunt her.

Dominick switched the phone into his other hand as he took a sip of his drink, "Fine, come back to LA. But you'd better get used to sitting on your ass watching daytime TV out here, 'cause you're not going to be working, unless your grandmother gets you on her show."

Freya sighed as she hung up the phone. Anna's appearance on *Opinionated Women* had reignited her relationship with America. She now had a completely new fan-base that was not just predominantly gay men, and with her newfound popularity had come a multitude of offers. Currently, Anna was wowing the ratings with a self-titled sitcom where she played an only slightly more outlandish version of herself. After listening for years to Anna's pronouncements of TV being the 'Devil's work', Freya was sure that Hell would have to freeze over before she asked her grandmother for a job on her show.

She and Dominick had been having the same conversation for the past three weeks. The time had come for her to decide whether she wanted to commit to a longer period on the show. Despite every ounce of her soul crying out to return to LA and Jordan, her desire to work was pulling at her to stay.

The phone rang again, and she pressed the button and put it to her ear, "Hi."

"Oh my god, it's you and not your answer machine," Jordan said with just a hint of sarcasm in her voice. "I left you a message."

"Sorry. Yeah, I got it," Freya sat down, still half thinking about her conversation with Dominick. "But Nici was here for a pre-theatre dinner, and then we went to the show and I was so wiped when I got back that I fell asleep on the sofa. I was going to call you this morning, but Dominick called. I'm sorry."

Jordan felt anger surge through her, "Well at least I know where I am in your order of priority."

"Jordan, please," Freya begged, not wanting to get into a fight. "I'm sorry, you're my number one priority, I promise."

Jordan swallowed, "I needed to speak to you, Freya. This phone and email tag that we're playing, I'm tired of it."

Laying her head against the back of the sofa, Freya closed her eyes, "Me too. But hey, at least during hiatus, you can play actual tag with me every day…naked!"

"About that."

Freya felt her chest constrict. She opened her eyes and sat up, "What about that?"

"I've been offered the lead in a Lifetime movie. Filming starts in Canada immediately after we wrap here."

Dropping her head, Freya stood up and resumed the pacing that she had been doing during her call with Dominick, "How long is filming?"

"Five weeks."

Freya closed her eyes and pursed her lips, "Have you said yes?"

Jordan brushed her hair behind her ear and gripped the phone tighter, "It's a great opportunity, Freya. They approached me. I-"

"No, it's great," Freya interrupted. "I'm pleased for you. Look, there's someone at the door," she lied, desperate to get off the phone. "I'll call you later, okay? It's great."

She hung up without waiting for Jordan to reply, and threw the handset towards the sofa with all her strength. She looked at the offending item, then walked over slowly, picked it up and dialed.

"Hey Debbie, tell Dominick Freya called, and that she wants to take the option, thanks."

She hung the call up and threw the phone back down.

***

Dan was bending down, his foot resting on a park bench as he stretched out his hamstring, when Freya ran up.

"No stretching, just running," she gasped as she ran past.

Startled, Dan's head swooped around and he pivoted, before taking to his heels and chasing after his friend.

"Hey Forrest, wait up!" Dan yelled as she sped after Freya. "Are you so horny now that you have to run like Flo-Jo to get over it?"

"No, I'm mad," Freya puffed.

Dan rolled his eyes, "Why, what happened?"

Freya shook her head in time with her running rhythm, "Not ready to talk yet, still processing. What gives with you?"

Raising an eyebrow and chewing on the inside of his mouth, Dan decided to allow Freya space to process whatever was up her ass, "Well since I've given up the cigarettes I feel like a new man."

Freya gave him a sideways glance, "That's good, you're feeling healthier, fitter…a new lease of life."

"Hell no, I cough up so much crap in the morning you could tar the city. I'm eating more, which means I'm having to exercise more to keep this buff body in tip-top shape," he indicated, sweeping his hands over his t-shirt which was cling-wrapped to his muscular torso. "I mean, I really need a man," he grinned, checking out a couple of men running past in the opposite direction. Turning, he ran backwards in order to view them better.

Freya laughed, "You'll break your neck, letch. Face front!"

Dan spun back around and matched Freya's pace, as they ran in silence for a lap of the reservoir.

"So, you ready to talk about it yet, or are you still processing?"

Freya stopped running without warning, leaving Dan to run ahead a few paces before he realized and stopped.

"Jordan's not coming during hiatus."

"Whaaat?!" Dan exclaimed. "But I had so many plans for us while you were working," he huffed. "Well, that sucks," he added, closing his eyes in disappointment. Freya stood with her hands on her hips, waiting for Dan to get the point. His eyes opened, "Oh, and this is not about me right now, sorry." He shrugged, "So you're pissed off?"

"I'm royally pissed," Freya sighed.

"So what happened?"

Freya stood with her feet apart and rolled her hips, stretching out her lower back, "She's been offered a lead in a Lifetime movie."

"Oh, I love those. Is she going to prison for something she didn't do? Is Cheryl Ladd in it? Sorry, digressing again," Dan apologized, seeing Freya's face.

"I don't know what it is. She called earlier this morning to tell me that she had been offered it, and that she was going to be in Canada filming during hiatus." Freya dropped her head, embarrassed by what she was about to say, "I lied to her and told her there was someone at the door, and hung up." She looked up and saw Dan's shocked expression, "I know, you don't have to say anything. I was just so…disappointed. I miss her, and I wanted us to spend time together."

"She supported you, Freya," Dan admonished lightly. "When you got the gig here she supported you, even though it tore her apart. You didn't see the gooey mess that was left behind when you went. I did," he sighed. "She wouldn't have made this decision lightly."

Freya sat down on a nearby bench and put her head in her hands, "I know that." She pulled her bottom lip between her teeth, "I've done something that may compound things."

Dan sat down beside her and gave her a gentle nudge.

"I had spoken to Dominick earlier, and he said that nothing is happening in LA for me, so I should take the option to extend my run here."

"Have you discussed this with Jordan?"

"That's just it, I did a kneejerk thing." Freya sat back on the bench, "I was so mad at her not coming, that I called Dominick back and instructed him to take the option."

Dan slumped back on the bench beside her, "So you're staying?"

Freya bit her bottom lip and nodded dumbly.

"I don't get you two. You're putting your careers in front of your relationship."

Freya stood up, "You don't get it, Dan. We've both worked hard to get to where we are, and it can all be over tomorrow. You have to keep working, you can't stop. There are thousands of people out there," Freya swung her arms wildly to emphasis her point, "that would claw our eyes out for what we have."

Dan stood up, frowning at Freya, "What you don't get, Freya, is you love her and she loves you and you're both pissing it away, and I for one would claw your eyes out for what you two share," he stated sadly before starting to run and leaving Freya to muse over his words.

***

"Hey," Jordan pinched the bridge of her nose as she held the phone, waiting for Freya to speak.

"Hi, Jordan, I'm sorry about earlier. I was being stupid and selfish. I'm really happy that you got offered the part."

A small smile tugged at Jordan's lips. "Thank you. It's a great opportunity, and I still have a week once we're done when I can come to New York," she added hopefully.

"A minute with you is better than a lifetime without," Freya smiled, settling down into her sofa. "So tell me about the part. Dan wants to know whether you're going be wearing an orange prison jump suit."

June 2012

Jordan lay in bed, tentatively flattening out the sheet currently draped over her naked body. She propped herself up against the pillows, allowing her long blonde locks to cascade down across her shoulders. She steadied her breathing, unable to place the source of the nerves that she was feeling, and checked the clock on the nightstand, which was now flashing 00:30; around a minute after she last checked it. She frowned at the sound of a door opening and closing. Voices drifted through the bedroom door. She looked towards the door, concentrating on picking out something to help her place the voices as they got louder.

"So, I thought you were going to show me a good time," the first voice slurred.

Jordan narrowed her eyes, not recognizing the accent or voice.

"I did, and we've had a great night, and then I said I was going to show you a cab," the second voice replied, the effects of alcohol also audible in it. However, this voice she recognized immediately.

"Really? Are you always such a good girl?" the first voice asked.

Jordan pulled the covers back and picked up a robe. Putting it on she walked towards the door, listening for the response.

"Not always, no," was the giggly reply.

Jordan tightened the tie on the robe and yanked the bedroom door open in time to see a short, dark-haired woman lean forward to kiss Freya. Freya immediately raised her hands and pulled away.

"Woah, Nici, you're drunk and straight, and I'm…"

"In a relationship," Jordan finished for her. "That was the line you should have lead with," she added calmly, before turning and reentering the bedroom and collecting her clothes.

"Jordan?" Freya said in surprise, looking between her girlfriend and her co-star.

"Oops," Nici giggled. "I think your wife is pissed."

Immediately sober, Freya glared at Nici, "You should leave. Now!" She grabbed Nici's purse and thrust it towards her, turning the smaller woman and propelling her through the apartment door into the hall.

"What about my cab?" Nici asked.

"Flag one down," Freya replied, closing the door. She paused, running a hand through her hair, then pushed herself off the door and went to try and straighten things out.

"Jordan?"

Jordan stopped dragging her jeans up her thighs and held out a hand, "No, I'm not interested in what you have to say."

"It's not what it looked like, we went out for a few drinks after the show and I was worried about her getting home, so suggested that she come here and call a cab. I didn't know you'd be here, or I would have never…"

Jordan pulled the zip up on her jeans, "I bet!" She tossed her hair over her shoulder as she located her backpack that she'd brought for the weekend, "So, now I know what you get up to while we're apart. Not always a good girl!"

"What?" Freya frowned watching her girlfriend's frenetic activity. "No, no that's not what I get up to at all," she reached out and grabbed Jordan. "And I was thinking about us when I answered that question. Will you stop, please?"

Stopping at her girlfriend's touch, Jordan looked up, fighting the tears that were threatening to spill from her. "Don't worry, I've stopped," Jordan whispered, shaking off Freya's grip and pushing past her.

Freya stood rooted to the spot, only shaken from her thoughts when the front door slammed.

***

Dan looked over apologetically at the dark-haired man in his bed. "Do not move one of those glorious muscles, I will go get rid of whoever the hell is knocking on the door at this ungodly hour," he sighed, slipping out of the bed and picking up his pajama bottoms, hopping as he pulled them on.

"There better be a mother of a reason for this…" he stopped as he pulled the door open and found himself ensnared by a weeping Jordan. Looking down in surprise, he circled his arms around her and pulled her into the apartment, kicking the door closed.

He walked them over towards the sofa and sat her down, "Don't move, I'll be back in two seconds."

Jordan looked up at him, her eyes red from crying, and nodded. He picked up a box of tissues and thrust it towards her before leaving her and re-entering the bedroom.

"You should run now while you have the chance. One of my gay lady wives is here in tears, which means there's roughly fifteen minutes before the other one arrives and this apartment will be filled with more estrogen than *Steel Magnolias*."

Jackson pulled himself out of the bed and smiled, "Call me once the lesbian drama dies down."

Dan watched as Jackson dressed, his lip turned into a thoughtful snarl. "Sweetie, if we wait for that, I'll be picking up my pension. I'll call you tomorrow," he smiled, opening the door and letting Jackson exit.

Watching his date leave the apartment, Dan turned to the mess of hair and tears curled up on his sofa, "So, sweetpea, what happened?"

"I…I…" Jordan held up a wadded pile of tissues. What came after seemed to be a stream of vowels.

"Jordan, I need you to enunciate for me, gorgeous, 'cause I'm not getting what you're saying. A consonant once in a while might be good."

"I've left her," she wailed.

"Left her where?" Dan asked, confused, then seeing the 'really?' look that Jordan was shooting him, his brain kicked in. "As in left her, left her? Dumped left her?" the description prompted a fresh batch of wailing. Pulling her to his chest, Dan whispered comforting noises into Jordan's hair. Once the sobbing had subsided sufficiently, he took Jordan by the shoulders and pushed her hair back, "Tell me what happened…from the start."

"We had an insurance mix up on the film, so we stopped filming for four days, and I thought I'd come surprise her," Jordan gulped visibly before continuing. "So, I got to the apartment and thought I'd wait in bed for her getting home from the theatre, but then she didn't show and I couldn't get her to pick up her phone." Jordan interrupted her story to blow her nose, handing the tissue to a horrified Dan who deposited it in the bin. "Then she came home with Nici."

Dan wracked his brain, "Ah, Nici is the floozy one we don't like?"

Jordan nodded, swiping more tissues from the box, "And she said that Freya was going to show her a good time, so I got out of bed and she was kissing her."

Dan's eyes widened, "Freya was kissing her? Really?" Unable to believe what he was hearing, "Sweetpea, are you sure you read this right? I've known Freya a long time, and she's not a cheater. She loves you."

"I know what I saw!" Jordan growled, "Nici was kissing her, and she pushed her away and said that she was drunk and straight. I knew that something like this was going to happen."

Pulling her back into a hug, Dan rested his chin on the top of Jordan's head, "Are you sure you're not letting long distance paranoia take a grip here?"

"She flashed her ass at her!" Jordan yelled, pulling away from Dan and standing. "That's not paranoia, Dan."

"That was months ago," Dan soothed, rubbing a hand over his face.

Jordan stood beside the window, gazing out to Dan's street. "Maybe," she sighed. "But it's not working, Dan. The long distance thing…it's driving me crazy. I can't wait for the next three weeks to be up and for her to come home."

"Shit," Dan said aloud, as he realized that Freya apparently hadn't told Jordan about her decision to extend.

"Sorry?" Jordan said, turning, small sobs still hitching her breath.

Dan looked wide-eyed in panic. "Nothing, didn't say a thing," he lied. "Cup of tea?" he stood up and made to walk towards his kitchen.

"Dan, what do you know?" Jordan asked in a dangerous tone.

Turning, Dan took a deep breath, which he let out in a burst of words, "Shewon'tbecominghomeinthreeweeks." He staggered slightly as he finished.

A bang on the door interrupted any response Jordan had.

"If that's her I don't want to see her," she hissed.

Dan looked between Jordan and the door and took another deep breath, ruing his predilection for lesbians. He opened the door to see a ragged version of his best friend standing there.

"Is she here?" Freya asked, trying to look past the gap between the door and Dan.

"Yes, but she doesn't want to see you," he replied sadly.

Freya took a step forward, "Let me see her Dan, please."

Shaking his head, Dan rolled his eyes at his role between them, "I'm sorry, sweetheart. Why don't you both take tonight to think things through, and speak tomorrow?"

A voice came from behind him, "I don't want to speak to her tomorrow, either."

Dan's shoulders sagged at the words, and he turned slightly to look into the apartment. The movement allowed just enough space for Freya to shoulder charge him out of the way and enter the apartment.

Rubbing his chest bone, Dan closed the door. "Freakishly strong," he commented, following his best friend into the living room.

"I don't want to see or speak to you right now," Jordan said emphatically.

Freya moved to put herself in front of Jordan. "I don't care, you're gonna. Nothing happened. I didn't cheat on you, I wouldn't do that."

"She's been trying to get into your pants for months," Jordan spat.

Running her hands through her loose curls, Freya sighed, "I never reciprocated anything, and all I offered was friendship. I love you too much." She reached out to touch Jordan's arm, "I never cheated." Jordan looked down at the hand on her forearm, "What about lying?"

Dan was standing to the side hopping slightly from foot to foot, hoping that Freya wasn't about to walk into the trap that he'd unwittingly set in motion earlier.

"I've never lied to you," Freya said sincerely.

"When are you coming home?" Jordan asked with a hint of steel in her tone.

Dan's body withered as the trap sprung.

Freya's eyes narrowed, realizing what had happened, she turned and glared at Dan. "You told her?" she accused.

Jordan pulled her arm away from Freya. "Don't blame him, *you* should have told me," she yelled.

Still glaring over at Dan, Freya said calmly, "Dan, could you leave us alone?"

Dan nodded. Relieved at an escape route, he took a step.

"No, Dan, I want you to stay," Jordan said still staring at Freya, her jaw set.

Dan stopped and brought his foot back.

"Go, Dan!"

Dan nodded and repeated his step as Freya glowered at Jordan.

"Dan. Stay!" Jordan yelled.

"No idea how to deal with this," Dan replied, frozen in midstep, watching as the two women stood glaring at each other. "Running through the possibilities, coming up blank," he grimaced. "How about

I leave, but just to the bedroom and I put my ear to door so I hear everything?" he suggested, pointing desperately towards his bedroom. Getting no response, he hotfooted it into the bedroom, closing the door behind him and resting against it. "All I wanted was sex," he moaned to himself, thumping his head against the door.

"I'm sorry, I wanted to tell you," Freya dropped her eyes to her hands.

Resuming her watch on the street below, Jordan clenched her teeth, "So why didn't you?"

Freya closed her eyes, took a breath and straightened herself up, "I was scared how you'd react."

Before Jordan could reply, she held a hand up, "I spoke to Dominick. There's no work for me in LA, and it was either go back to nothing or stay here and work."

"So I'm nothing?" Jordan gave a sarcastic laugh.

"That's not what I meant, and you know it," Freya sat down on the arm of Dan's sofa. "I took the option partly because I was mad at you not coming here during hiatus."

Jordan spun round, "I couldn't come for six weeks, so you sentenced us to another, what, three months?" She waited to see Freya's reaction. Seeing no response, she asked quietly, "Six?"

When Freya's head dropped, Jordan shook her head in disbelief.

"Really, Freya, another six months of living like this?"

Freya looked up. Her mouth opened to speak, but no words were coming to her mind to defend her actions.

"The distance is driving me insane, Freya. Any time you mention another woman I'm having sleepless nights through jealousy, and I trust you, I do," her tone softened. "I'm sorry about earlier, but that's what it's doing to me. It's turning me crazy!"

Freya nodded, understanding where Jordan was coming from, as her own demons had also been playing with her mind. "I thought that taking the film was your way of avoiding coming out here. It's doing crazy things to my mind too," she admitted.

Jordan left the window and sat down on the sofa. "I counted up the days we've spent together since we started to see each other. We've been apart more than we've been together."

"I hate that I don't get to see you, and that we have to use email and phones," Freya admitted, slipping down beside Jordan from the arm of the chair.

"We've become pen friends with occasional benefits," Jordan sighed. "I could cope knowing there was an end in sight, Freya, without that I'm not sure I can take it," Jordan confessed, a tear dropping from her face onto her hands still folded in her lap clutching a wad of tissues.

Freya felt her heart break watching Jordan cry. She edged towards her on the sofa and took her in her arms. "I couldn't cope if we end up tearing each other apart and hating each other," she said, swallowing back her own tears as she comforted Jordan.

"So what do we do?" Jordan asked, already knowing the answer.

"We love each other," Freya replied. "We love each other enough…to let it go," she allowed the tears to fall unchecked as she held Jordan.

They stayed holding each other tightly on Dan's sofa for hours, until the morning sunshine broke through and started to reflect off the wooden floors of the apartment. Freya took Jordan's face in her hands and placed one last kiss on her lips before removing Jordan's arms from around her and standing up.

Dan heard the front door close. He got out of bed and grabbed a fleece blanket. Entering the living room, he wrapped it around Jordan's shoulders before sitting down beside her and pulling her towards him, allowing her to let all of her pain leave her body.

July 2012

Jordan welcomed the interruption of someone at her front door. She gratefully placed down the script for the season's premiere, from which she was failing to learn her lines. It had been three weeks since their breakup and, despite returning to work, Jordan had not slipped easily back into her life in LA. She opened the door and gasped involuntarily at her visitor.

"Judging by your attire, the rumors are true then," Anna Conor announced as she brushed past Jordan and entered her home.

Sticking her head out of the door, Jordan looked around to see whether anyone had witnessed the fact that Anna Conor, *The Anna Conor,* was in her house. She was disappointed that for once no-one was out in their garden on a Saturday, even at this early hour. She would have to resign herself to the fact that only the driver, sitting patiently in the Rolls Royce that Anna had arrived in, would be her verification that this was actually happening. It was as she closed the door that Anna's words registered and she surmised the reason for the visit.

"That depends on what rumors you're referring to," Jordan replied carefully, tugging at the hem of her baggy T-shirt and pulling it down to cover the small shorts she was wearing.

Anna gave her a withering look, "You go make yourself presentable. There's no need to go to seed over all of this, and I'll go make us some coffee." Anna removed her coat and placed it neatly onto the sofa, and pointed towards the door leading to the kitchen. "Through there?" she asked, already marching towards the door.

"Yes," Jordan said weakly before scurrying off to change, and wondering what was the appropriate dress wear for an audience with Anna Conor, when it would seem she's about to tear a strip off you.

She opted for a blue sundress, changed quickly, and then ran to the kitchen to join Freya's grandmother for what was no doubt going to be an awkward conversation.

"I made water," Anna declared as Jordan entered the kitchen. "The tap was the only thing I recognized in this place." She waved her hand dismissively around Jordan's prized kitchen, "Even then I'm not sure that I didn't put hot water in."

Jordan hid a smile as she picked up the glass, "I can make us something if you'd like?"

Anna tipped the water into the sink and held the glass out to Jordan, "Martini and I'm with Noel Coward, pour the gin, then wave it in the general direction of Italy."

Moving around to collect the ingredients, which she was grateful she had, Jordan decided to take the proverbial bull by the horns, "What brings you to see me?"

Sniffing, Anna narrowed one eye, "Freya is ignoring my calls, Daniel's lips are tighter than a virgin's on her wedding night, and I want to find out if those odious gossip rags had one iota of fact to them. Have you two broken up?"

Jordan placed the bottles down onto the counter, "Three weeks ago."

A look of sadness passed over what expression range Anna retained, "What happened?"

"I was stupid; I thought that she was cheating." She saw Anna's face flush with anger. "I know that she wasn't and wouldn't, but the distance thing was too much for us. The relationship was too new to withstand that sort of pressure. So we both decided to be mature and not hurt each other further." She handed over the drink to Anna.

Whatever Anna was going to say regarding the situation withered from her lips when she saw the tears glistening in Jordan's eyes as she spoke. "I'm really sorry that you weren't able to make it work. You made my granddaughter very happy, and I wish that things had worked out differently." She tipped the glass back and downed the not ungenerous drink. "Did I see a piano out there?" she asked, handing Jordan the glass and motioning her to pour another before striding from the room.

Obediently, Jordan prepared another drink and then joined the already seated Anna at her piano. As the elderly woman started to play, a look of peace descended upon her face as her fingers caressed the keys.

"Take a load off," Anna nodded towards the space she'd left on the seat. "You know, I found that music is often the best salve for a broken heart." She continued to play, "That an' gin. Today it would appear we have both, so you'll be fine!"

Despite it being nine a.m., Jordan took a sip of the drink she'd prepared for Anna, "Here's hoping."

***

Freya was annoyed with herself as she strode back to her dressing room. Tonight had not been her best performance. Her voice hadn't coped well with a couple of the high notes. It would appear that crying constantly had played havoc with her vocal cords and, to top it all, she was half a beat off for two steps during one of her dance routines. She just wanted to get changed, go home for a hot shower, go to bed and have the day end. What she wasn't prepared for was her grandmother waiting for her in her dressing room.

"What is it they say about Mohammed and the mountain?" Anna asked, while watching her granddaughter carefully. "If it wasn't for the fact I'd be comparing myself to a mountain, then it would apply here."

"Why are you here?" Freya asked, dropping down into the seat in front of the mirror.

Anna's response was interrupted by Nici poking her head around the dressing room door. "We're going out…" she trailed off as she realized that Freya wasn't alone. With her mouth slightly agape she stepped into the room, "You're-"

"Yes I am," Anna interrupted.

Standing up, before Anna decided to unleash the diva, Freya ushered Nici back towards the door, "I'm not coming out tonight, thanks for asking though." She unceremoniously pushed Nici out and closed the door.

"Was that her?" Anna asked, nodding towards the door.

"Was that who?"

"Strictly chorus line there. Was that the one that Jordan thought you were unfaithful with?"

Freya's mouth opened, "How do you know that? And I wasn't unfaithful. Ever."

Anna played thoughtfully with an earring, "I know that. You look pale."

Laughing, Freya allowed her head to drop, "I'm wearing about three inches of stage make-up. How on Earth can you tell that?"

"You were flat on three occasions, and a half beat off during that dance number in the second act."

Freya's eyes widened, "Seriously, Anna, I'm not in the mood for your critique of my performance."

"I'm not critiquing, I'm just stating the facts. That's how I know you're pale. Because my granddaughter would not go out and make those mistakes unless she's not eating properly and not sleeping."

Swallowing back the lump in her throat, Freya closed her eyes, "I feel like I'm a half beat off in my life. I didn't know that I could feel this way about someone, and now I do know, I can't unknow it. I want desperately to speak to her, to see her, touch her, kiss her and I can't. So now everything I do feels a half beat off."

She felt Anna's arms encircle her and pull her into a hug. She lay her face against her grandmother's shoulder, surprised to feel the rough cotton of a towel instead of the fabric of Anna's coat. She moved to raise her head.

As if anticipating her movement Anna murmured against her hair, "Three inches of stage make-up and silk do not mix well."

A small bubble of laughter welled up in Freya, quickly becoming a sob.

Anna held her tighter, "Oh, my dear sweet girl. Did your grandfather teach you nothing about the great tragedies? This is only the fall in act three. What you do in act four is what establishes your future."

Crying against her grandmother, Freya could only hope that there was some truth to her words.

***

"I can't believe you're leaving me," Freya sighed, taping shut a box.

Dan shrugged, "You knew that my being in New York was only a temporary thing while the exhibition was being staged," he grinned. "I'm a hit on both coasts, so now I must away to the west coast to allow the LaLas to bask in my magnificent splendor again. Plus, there's a shit load of work waiting on me when I get back."

Freya laughed as she moved to another box with her tape gun, "You're so full of shit, but I will miss you."

Dan tossed the clothes he was semi-folding into his suitcase, then leaned over to kiss the top of Freya's head, "I'll miss you too, sweetie."

Sitting on Dan's bed, Freya started to fiddle with the latch of his suitcase. "You'll see her, right?" she asked, not looking up at him. "When you go back, you're going to see her?"

Freya looked up, chewing on her bottom lip, her eyes shining with the unshed tears that were never far away when they broached this subject.

Knowing who 'she' was, Dan simply nodded.

"If she asks about me, tell her I've been okay."

Frowning, Dan sat down, "But you've not been okay."

"I know, but," Freya lay down on the bed. "I want her to move on."

Dan reached over and patted her thigh.

"I'll take care of her," he smiled, standing up to resume packing.

Freya pouted and sighed before sitting up and collecting her tape gun to continue helping Dan.

"So, what about Jackson?" she asked lightly, twirling the tape gun at her shoulder.

Dan stopped packing but didn't turn around to look at his best friend, "What about him?"

"You two have gotten fairly serious fairly quickly. I was wondering what will happen."

Dan turned, tossing the sweater in his hand into the case.

"I just watched the distance between New York and LA tear two people I love into strips. I'm not about to put myself through that." Freya nodded sadly, and turned to complete taping Dan's boxes shut.

***

"Hi, I was wondering whether I could maybe buy you a drink?" the brown-haired girl asked shyly.

Freya shot Dan a quick look before giving the girl a warm smile.

"That's really sweet, but I'm here with my friend and it's his leaving party, so I…" Freya bobbed her head as if it was a tougher decision than it was. "I really should stay with him."

The girl gave her a smile and slipped a napkin over with her number on it, "Just in case you change your mind."

Freya gave her a quick smile as she accepted the napkin, and watched the girl turn and disappear back into the crowd in the club. She was still looking over when the napkin was snatched from her hand.

"Hey," she cried, turning to see Jackson inspecting the napkin with a look of disgust on his face.

"She's trying to hit so far above her weight division it's unreal," he said, folding the napkin and placing it into a half full glass of something that was on the table when they arrived.

Dan bit at his lip to stop from laughing at the expression on Freya's face. "Oh yes, I'm leaving you in capable hands," he nodded. "While I am in a different time zone, Jackson here will be your queer steer. But just so you know, he loves *Front Line* and is a hopeless romantic who wants you to get back with Jordan."

Freya's eyebrows flashed up as she shot Dan a 'who the hell doesn't want that' look.

"So, he will look out for you and keep you safe from predatory lesbians and those that can't lick your shoes."

"Never mind licking anything else," Jackson inserted, taking a sip of his beer.

Freya rolled her eyes as she took her straw into her mouth, "God save me from gay men."

August 2012

Dan reached over to his nightstand for his phone, checking the screen he groaned and accepted the call.

"You do remember there's a time difference, Freya," he grumbled.

"Sorry, it's urgent."

"Where's Jackson? Why can't he help you?"

Freya twirled the cord of the phone between her fingers, "'cause I didn't like his answer."

Rolling his eyes, Dan lay back down on his bed, "Okay, tell me what the problem is."

"Next Tuesday. Next Tuesday is the problem," Freya breathed.

Dan had been waiting for this call, but had hoped that Jackson might have been able to cut it off at the bud. "Whatever that brain of yours is cooking up, stop," Dan sighed. "She's doing better, and if you go and send her a birthday gift that is all thoughtful and gooey, then I'm going to be spending the next few weeks cleaning up the mess."

Freya frowned, "But I…"

"She bought a damn onesie, Freya, that's the level of seriousness we're talking here, a onesie," Dan sat up and ran his hand through his bed-head hair. "Leave her."

"You and Jackson talked this through didn't you?" Freya grumbled.

Dan laughed, "We love you and we care about you, but you need to be fair to both of you, Egg, and a thoughtful birthday gift is just going to open up the wounds that are barely healing."

"I love you," came the quiet response. "I love her and I miss her."

Dan smiled, sadly shaking his head, "I love you too, and she will probably always love you, in a Dolly Parton sung by Whitney kind of way."

"Okay, bye, sorry I woke you."

"No you're not, have a lovely day sweetie."

October 2012

Dan was packing away equipment following a shoot when his phone rang. Removing it from his pocket, he waved at his assistant to keep going.

"Hey, Jordan, what's...Jordan?" he frowned when all he could hear were sobs and heavy breathing. "Jordan, where are you?"

"Home."

"Stay there, I'm on my way." Dan shouted at his assistant as he grabbed his jacket from on top of a box, "You keep packing, I've got a family emergency."

Screeching into Jordan's drive, Dan slammed the door shut on his car and leapt up the stairs two and at time before bursting into Jordan's house, "Sweetie, where are you?"

Jordan came running out of the kitchen and straight into Dan's arms. He pulled her close, "What's wrong? Speak to me."

Looking up, Jordan gulped in air, a momentary look of confusion passed over her face as she stared at Dan, "What the hell did you do to your hair?"

"I bleached it."

"On purpose?"

Dan scowled at her, "One crisis at a time. What's wrong?" He allowed himself to be pulled towards Jordan's kitchen, a stunned expression soon on his face as he took in the sight in front of him. The kitchen was filled with boxes of oranges.

"What the hell? Do you have a Vitamin C deficiency or something?"

"I ordered my groceries online and I thought I was ordering weight, but it turns out I was ordering quantity," Jordan sobbed. "And now I have oranges."

Dan looked bewildered at the reaction that the citrus fruit was generating from his friend, "You called me, at work, in tears, 'cause you have two hundred oranges in your kitchen?"

Jordan nodded, fresh tears starting to fall. "Oranges were our fruit," she wailed.

Realization dawned on Dan as he rolled his eyes and sighed, taking Jordan into a hug, "So, I guess for the rest of today we're making orange juice and marmalade."

"I was doing so well," she sobbed, wiping her cheeks furiously to remove the tears that were falling freely. "It feels like for every step I take forward, I take another back."

"Oh sweetie," Dan sighed as he started to rock Jordan forward and back. "That just means that you can cha cha cha," he grinned as he plunged her backwards into a dip, then kissed her forehead and brought her back onto her feet.

Jordan clung to his T-shirt and gave a small nod. Pulling back, she looked up into Dan's gentle eyes, "Thank you." Her eyes narrowed slightly, "Seriously though, what's the deal with the hair?"

November 2012

Freya woke up, her head thumping. She could feel heat radiating from the body beside her and she closed her eyes, willing her stomach not to decide to purge itself. As she lay concentrating on breathing in time with the pulse in her brain, she tried to piece together the remnants of the previous evening. She remembered coming out of the stage door and signing some autographs. Jackson had been waiting for her, as had become his habit for making sure that she got home okay. Apparently,

Jackson took his promise to Dan to look after her seriously. But instead of going home, she had decided that they should go out. To be honest, she had simply wanted to forget. Earlier in the day she'd seen some gossip site speak about Jordan dating someone, and she'd wanted to forget…everything. So she'd drank like a woman on a mission.

Feeling like she was about to lose the battle with her stomach, she moved the arm that was loosely draped over her stomach, and heaved herself out of bed towards the bathroom. After she had lost the contents of her stomach and what she was pretty sure was one of her lungs, she sat beside the toilet resting her head against the wall tiles, enjoying their coolness. A glass of water was placed in front of her. She heard the bath taps turn and water start to fill the tub, and hands swept her hair from her face. She looked up gratefully, "Thanks." Jackson gave her a sad smile, "You're welcome."

"You stayed over," Freya said appreciatively.

"Had to make sure you were okay," Jackson said, watching the tub fill. "You snore, by the way. Do you want to talk about it?" he asked gently.

Freya shook her head, "Not right now."

Jackson leaned down and kissed her on the crown of her head, "I'll go put some coffee on."

As he entered the kitchen, he dialed Dan's number.

"Hey gorgeous," Dan smiled, shouting down the phone, one finger in his ear to block out the noise from behind him.

"Hey yourself. Where the hell are you?" Jackson asked, raising his voice.

Dan moved to where it was a bit quieter, "Las Vegas."

Jackson moved around the kitchen collecting things to make coffee, "What are you doing in Vegas?"

"My one decided that we needed a girly weekend in Vegas," Dan shouted, rolling his eyes as he took a mouthful of beer.

Laughing, Jackson stuck the phone under his chin as he opened a new pack of filters, "And what happens in Vegas?"

Dan looked over to where Jordan was dancing on a table, the skirt of her black dress in one hand as she swished it in time to the music, her other hand running through her now shorter hair.

"Hopefully stays in Vegas. What are you doing up at…" Dan checked his watch. "Half seven on a Sunday morning?"

"My one decided to drink herself into oblivion, and is now puking her guts up," Jackson replied, switching the coffee maker on.

Dan sighed and shook his head, keeping an eye on his tipsy friend who was still strutting her stuff.

"She saw something online about Jordan dating."

"She's not dating anyone, Jackson. I mean, she's tried, but the last one lasted about an hour. Turns out none of them are Freya. Who knew!"

Dan shook his head as he watched bouncers start to make their way towards where Jordan was dancing, "Bugger, gotta go save my one's arse."

Jackson shouted, "Wait, Dan, what about you?"

Dan hesitated and smiled, "I'm not dating either, Jackson, must dash."

December 2012

Walking out of the stage door, Freya smiled at those that had waited. She chatted amicably with them, signed autographs and smiled for photos. When she was done, she walked over towards the figure waiting for her.

"So what's the plan tonight, twinkle star?" Jackson asked, putting his arm protectively around her shoulders.

"It's Tuesday," Freya said by explanation.

Understanding immediately, Jackson nodded. "I know. I have prepared for you," he smiled, giving her shoulder a quick squeeze.

They entered Freya's apartment and she shrugged off her jacket. Jackson pulled her towards the sofa and sat her down. "I have a present for you," he reached behind a chair and pulled out a wrapped parcel. Freya looked at it in surprise.

"It's not Christmas yet," she said, confused.

Jackson smiled, "No, but it's *Front Line* night. So you're going to open that, I'm going to go get you hot honey, and we're both going to watch together. And, while you ogle your ex-girlfriend, I'm going to do the same with the hunky soldier doctors!"

Jackson left her with her parcel, which she started to open while smiling at the noise of her drink being made.

"You got me a slanket," she yelled, holding the material up.

Re-entering the room, Jackson put her mug of hot honey on the table before helping her into her slanket, "Just please don't tell Dan I got you this, and don't ever combine it with your godawful onesie."

Freya pulled her hands free from the cloth, grumbling as she leaned forward to grab her mug, "No one likes the onesie."

She leaned back and snuggled against Jackson as he pressed play and started her recording of *Front Line*.

"She looks amazing," Freya sighed as Jordan came on screen.

"Would you do it differently?" Jackson asked. "If you had a second chance, I mean."

Looking up at him, Freya could see that there was something else going through Jackson's mind. She pushed herself up and hit the pause button. She narrowed her eyes and titled her head, "Okay buddy, spill."

"I love him. Dan, I mean, I love him," Jackson sighed. "But he's there and I'm here."

Freya nodded, and then leaned forward and put her mug onto the table and shifted in her seat so she was facing Jackson.

"If I learned anything in the past twelve months, it's that if you have love then you hold onto it and you move mountains for it. 'cause it's precious and wonderful and when you don't have it anymore," she choked back, willing herself not to cry any more self-pitying tears, "you're left with this void that will probably take a lifetime of other experiences to fill." She took Jackson's hands in her own, "So if you love him, you go to him. Now!"

January 2013

Jordan was clanking pots around looking for her wok, which she knew was somewhere in the pot drawer. She stopped as the sound of her piano being played in the next room reached her ears. The music was shortly joined by a melodious baritone voice singing 'Somewhere' from *West Side Story*.

Stopping what she was doing, Jordan found herself drawn towards the music. In all the time that she'd known Dan, she didn't know that he could sing, never mind play the piano. She stood unnoticed by him as he continued to play and sing.

Unable to stop herself, Jordan drifted forward towards Dan, her voice joining his as the music reached a crescendo.

Smiling, Dan turned his head, "On your own."

Jordan laughed and placed her hand on his shoulder as she let the music take over.

Joining Jordan for a final chorus, Dan closed his eyes and let his head fall back, singing out with all that he had.

When he stopped playing, his fingers slipped from the piano keys to his lap, "Jackson's moving to LA."

Jordan looped her arms around Dan's neck, placing her head beside his, "That, is the best news I've heard for months." She pecked Dan's cheek and straightened up, her eyes lingering over Dan's photograph of Freya that sat as always on top of her piano, "Let's go out to celebrate."

February 2013

Pulling her rucksack strap up over her shoulder, Freya entered the theatre and started to wind her way towards her dressing room. Enroute, she smiled and greeted the crew who were moving around back stage.

"Oh, Freya," one of the stagehands called. "There's someone in your dressing room. She said she was a friend."

Freya raised her eyebrows. "Just in case it's my grandmother again, or some stalker who is here to steal a kidney or something, can you come knock on the door in five?" she asked, looking towards her dressing room wondering who was waiting on her.

"Sure," he replied.

She placed a hesitant hand on the door handle, her heart rate increasing as a huge part of her wished that sitting in her dressing room was Jordan. She swallowed, took a deep breath, and opened the door. Her eyebrows shot up in surprise as the woman turned from the dressing table at the noise of the door opening.

"Eleanor?"

March 2013

Gripping the steering wheel, Freya sat debating with herself whether to get out of the car and knock on the door. Each time her hand reached the door handle, she hesitated and brought it back to the wheel. She looked out of the window of her hire car towards the bungalow that she had been sitting across the street from for twenty minutes. She glanced at the clock on the dashboard, wondering again whether five a.m. was too early to go and knock on the love of your life's door. She squeezed the wheel in frustration, closed her eyes, and hit her head off the headrest.

"What's the worst that can happen? She slams the door in your face!" Freya mused, speaking both sides of her argument. "You've flown two and half thousand miles across the country, and now you're sitting forty feet away from her home. Suck it up, Easter."

Freya tensed her body, giving herself a shake and opening her eyes.

"This could be it, your one and only chance....wait, that's not helping." Freya shook her head, "Way to build the pressure on yourself, and you do realize that you're talking, out loud, to yourself?" Freya put her hands to her face, cursing the nerves that had frozen her to the spot, "and answering." She took a deep breath, "Now, Freya!"

She pressed the release catch on the seat belt and moved her hand to the door handle, before pausing as her eye caught movement in Jordan's home. The curtains opened and a man stood bare-chested looking out across the front of Jordan's home. Freya felt her chest constrict as Jordan came into view. Wrapped in a robe she smiled, handed the man a mug and pecked his cheek, before disappearing out of view.

Biting on her lips, Freya reached down and turned the ignition key. She put the car in drive and pulled away.

***

Entering Dan's beach house, Freya slipped her bag from her shoulder and pushed her shoes from her feet. She padded silently through to Dan's bedroom, stopping in the doorway to smile at the vision of Dan and Jackson spooning in their bed. Despite the fact that her heart felt like a hollowed-out husk from what she had seen at Jordan's, seeing how it had worked out for Dan and Jackson sparked a little warmth back in.

"You do know that's really freaky, right?" Dan murmured, without opening his eyes or moving from his comfortable position in Jackson's arms.

Freya laughed and launched herself towards the bed, laying on top of them both and planting loud kisses on their faces, "I know!"

Jackson shuffled over, creating a space between him and Dan to allow Freya to fall between them. "How was your flight?" he asked. "We expected you here a couple of hours ago."

"I…" Freya hesitated, not wanting to admit where she had been. "I got held up getting the rental car," she lied. "So what plans do you have for me for Spring break?" she asked brightly.

***

"So when my mother visited for Christmas, she didn't know I was gay…she thought that Roger and I were flatmates. You remember Roger, Freya…eyes too far apart. So anyway," Dan continued. "We moved all of my things into the guest room so it looked as if I stayed there, and when she came to stay I slept on the sofa, magnanimously giving up my bed like the true gent I am," Dan paused to take a sip of wine. "Anyway, two weeks after and Roger couldn't find the remote control for the TV anywhere, and the stupid tosser thought my sweet dear mother might've half-inched it when she visited."

Jackson and Freya grinned at each other, listening to Dan hold court as they sat on the decking area of the beach house.

"So, when I saw her next, I asked her in passing whether she'd happened to remember seeing the remote control. Well, the sneaky old madam replied that it was underneath the pillow on the guest bed, and perhaps if I actually slept in that bed then I would have noticed it, and did I honestly think that she gave two hoots where I stuck my willie. I was her son, and if I ever lied to her again she'd turn my balls into earrings. Swears like a sailor, my mother," Dan finished his story with a flourish, draining the dregs of wine from his glass.

Freya hooted with laughter as she ran her fingers through her hair and looked across Dan's deck towards the ocean. She sipped her wine and smiled over towards Dan and Jackson, who were cuddling on the love seat.

"I've missed this about LA. The space," she smiled, gazing out across the beach, listening to the reassuring sound of the waves crashing against the sand.

"Is that all you've missed about LA?" Dan asked cautiously.

Freya looked over at him and gave a small laugh, "No, definitely not all."

Jackson reached forward for the bottle of wine to top up their glasses, "Are you going to see her while you're here?"

Taking a deep breath, Freya gave a sad smile, "I saw her this morning, that's why I was late."

She noticed the quick glance between Dan and Jackson.

"You never told me she's dating."

Dan gave Jackson a quick smile of thanks as he filled his wine glass, "She asked me not to…just like you asked me not to tell her about the two-day wonder that was Tara."

"Tania," Freya corrected, "and nothing happened there."

"Whatever," Dan waved a hand. "It's been seven months, Egg, and you're both finally starting to date. So I just thought that I'd let you move on without me playing the lesbian peace-keeping force in between. I have hung up my blue helmet."

Freya was thankful for her sunglasses as she surreptitiously swiped away the tear that fell from her face.

***

Jordan stood at her piano, her fingers following their familiar route towards the black and white photo sitting on top of the jet-black instrument. "Hey, you," she whispered, as she allowed the fingertip to follow the line of Freya's spine. She felt two arms wrap around her from behind.

"Dan's a fantastic photographer," Mike said, kissing Jordan's shoulder and looking at the image she was admiring.

"Yes, he is," she smiled, taking a deep breath and pulling herself from Mike's grasp. "So, I'll see you later once you've done the parent thing," she said, forcing herself to be cheerful.

Mike grinned, "You sure you don't want to meet them?"

"Oooooh, no," Jordan grinned, pushing Mike towards the door. "Certain."

She stood on her tiptoes and pecked him lightly on the lips. Jordan stood in the doorway and waved Mike goodbye. When his car had pulled out from the drive, she closed the door and picked up the small puppy that was her birthday present from Dan. The dog pawed her arm to get the attention it craved, turning its head into the gentle rubs she was placing behind its ear.

She and Mike had been dating for just over a month. Mike was funny, handsome, kind and gentle.

And in Los Angeles.

Everything she should want.

But Jordan's heart wasn't in it. She knew that for sure last night when Mike had stayed over, probably thinking that he was going to get lucky. However, Jordan had chickened out, and he'd had to make do with a snuggle. She had tried, and for a week or two she had even fooled herself into thinking that she could be happy with someone else. And then she'd heard a rumor about Eleanor's new show.

There had been discussions floating around for months about French planning another show, focusing on a celebrity publicist in LA. When she'd first heard about it she'd idly wondered whether, had she and Freya employed someone like that, their outcome might have been different. However, despite the talk no one had been attached to the project, until last month when she had heard chat that Freya had been approached for the lead.

She'd felt almost giddy with the thought that Freya would be coming back to LA. When her phone hadn't rung and her email inbox had remained empty, save from the usual crap, Jordan had come to the conclusion that although Freya was coming back to LA...she wasn't coming back to her.

Jordan pushed open the door to Dan's beach house. She leaned down and released the puppy from its leash. "Dan? Jackson? You home? Are you decent?" Jordan called. "'cause I'm still recovering from the last time I caught you two at it. So if you're doing the nasty, then just let me know and I'll wait outside."

When she got no response, she moved further into the house, noticing that the French doors out onto Dan's deck were open slightly. Cursing that the dog might have gotten out and was now making a bid for freedom down the beach, she ran to the doors and pulled them open. Her heart lurched up into her throat as she was greeted with the sight of Freya being heartily licked by her dog.

"Hey, little guy, who do you…?" Freya stopped as she heard the French doors open. She turned her face, which was being slavered with wet, sloppy licks from the small dog, towards the noise. She gasped quietly as Jordan stepped out onto the deck.

"Jordan."

"Freya."

They both smiled shyly.

"Is this yours?" Freya asked, holding the dog up and admiring her.

Jordan was still dumbstruck that Freya was in front of her. "Yeah, she is," she breathed.

Desperate to say a thousand other things, Freya nodded and concentrated on playing with the dog who was enjoying the attention, "What's her name?"

Jordan rolled her eyes and gulped. Tearing her eyes from Freya, she glanced out towards the beach, not seeing anything, "Roxie, her name is Roxie."

Freya's head recoiled in surprise, a slow smile starting to spread on her lips. "Hey, Roxie, nice to meet you," she said, tickling the dog's stomach. "Dan and Jackson have gone for a run," she said, turning to Jordan. Her brain was racing and she was relieved that she had hold of the dog; otherwise, her hands may have disregarded the orders that she was giving them not to grab Jordan. "Do you want a coffee or something?" she asked casually, her throat thick with the words that she wanted to say, but would not give voice to.

Jordan blinked in astonishment, the woman that she loved, that she had been breaking her heart over for seven months, was standing in front of her offering her coffee as if she was her neighbor asking her round for a mid-morning gossip. She opened her mouth to say no, "Yes, thanks."

Freya smiled. Still holding onto Roxie, she brushed past Jordan to walk back into the beach house.

Jordan caught a familiar waft of perfume as Freya passed. Her body jolted as her whole being reacted to the memories that the smell evoked.

"What the hell is it with flavored coffee?" Freya mused, looking at Dan and Jackson's cupboard contents. "We have cherry, blueberry, mint or," she looked at the packed of orange coffee and gave a small laugh. "Orange?"

Jordan blushed slightly, her hands gripping the kitchen work surface behind her, "Cherry, please."

Freya set to work to make the coffee. An awkward silence descended upon them as neither knew what to say to the other, whilst both fought their inner battles over saying what they wanted to. The water seemed to take an eternity to boil.

"A watched pot and all that," Freya said, trying to lighten the tension between them.

Jordan gave her a weak smile in response.

Taking a deep breath, Jordan decided to at least attempt to start a conversation, "So, how long are you here for?"

Freya busied herself with rearranging the mugs. She was unsure how much to disclose of Eleanor's new project, so opted to go for the line Dominick had told her to use if asked, "Just a few weeks. My run finished up at the theatre, so I'm taking a break and meeting some people, to see what options might be here for me." She walked to the fridge to get milk.

Jordan nodded, "Congratulations. The talk at the factory is that you're going to be on Eleanor's new show."

Pausing as she lifted the milk from the fridge, Freya swallowed hard. *She knew I was coming back,* she thought, *she knew, and she's dating someone else.*

"Thanks," she turned, plastering on a smile. "I'm not supposed to say much, but it's going to be great, I'm looking forward to it. We're filming the pilot, and then, who knows," she shrugged.

Feeling her breathing increase, Jordan wanted to scream at Freya, *why the hell didn't you tell me you were coming back?* She wanted to yell at her to find out at exactly what point Freya had stopped loving her and how the hell she'd managed it, because, try as hard as she had, she couldn't seem to stop loving Freya.

"You know, I should probably go, I have a lot to do," she said, gathering Roxie into her arms, unable to bear the pain that being around Freya and not being with her was causing. "Tell Dan I'll call him later," she called over her shoulder as she started to almost sprint towards the door.

Freya heard the front door slam as she slinked down the kitchen cupboards towards the floor.

April 2013

Freya tentatively knocked on the door to Eleanor's office. This was her first time returning to the production offices since she had been fired and, although her visit was for entirely different circumstances, the experience was throwing up all manner of memories.

"Come in."

She gave herself a little shake then pressed firmly on the handle, plastering a broad smile on her face to mask her nerves.

"Freya, it's good to see you," Eleanor rose from behind her desk and walked quickly towards her, taking a startled Freya into an embrace. Eleanor was not known for physical affection with her employees, so Freya put this rare demonstration of fondness down to the residual guilt that she was still feeling over how Freya was treated, and the subsequent fall out. "Come sit down," she pointed over towards her sofa area.

Freya noted that the office had not changed much in the time since she had gone, save for the coffee table. In place of the table Freya remembered, there was a large Perspex rectangle filled with thousands of half-dollar bills.

Eleanor saw Freya examining the piece of furniture and gave a small sigh, "That's my Emily table. A not so subtle reminder of what happens when we get it wrong."

She gave Eleanor a wry smile. The producer shrugged as she flopped onto her sofa, "Get it wrong, and people aren't shy in telling you. Repeatedly!"

"All in the past, Eleanor," Freya said, dragging her eyes from the fans' reaction to her departure. "I'm more interested in what you've got in store for me with the new show."

Eleanor clapped her hands together, "They loved the pilot, we've got a six episode pick-up that will get a summer slot. They'll be taking it to the up fronts next month. It's gonna be great."

"So we've got a show?" Freya grinned.

Nodding, her red hair bouncing wildly around, Eleanor returned the grin, "We've got a show!"

***

Feeling energized after her meeting with Eleanor, Freya headed towards Dan and Jackson's beach house, hoping to persuade them to go out for a celebratory meal. She opened their front door to announce her arrival and was greeted by the sound of Jackson singing loudly to ABBA in the kitchen. She grinned, and was about to add her own voice to the happy noise when she was almost bowled over by a small scruffy dog pushing her legs out of the way, taking the opportunity of the open door with all four paws.

"Damn it," Freya growled as the dog sped past her onto the street. "Roxie!" she yelled, taking off in pursuit of the grey dog.

"Please don't get killed," Freya puffed in time with her footsteps. "Roxie, c'mere," she shouted. Slowing her steps, she remembered something that Dan had mentioned during her not so subtle attempts over the past weeks to question him about Jordan.

Freya stopped and put her fingers in her mouth, letting out a loud and piercing two-tone blast. The small dog stopped at the signal. "Biscuits," Freya called in her best 'I'm not terrified that I could be the cause of my ex-girlfriend's dog getting squished' voice.

The dog paused momentarily, as if assessing its options, before running towards Freya. She let out a large, relieved sigh as Roxie got close enough for her to sweep up into her arms.

Walking slowly back towards the house, she rubbed her face in the soft fur of the dog, who was wriggling in her arms trying to lick her face, "You, my furry friend, almost gave me a heart attack." She plopped Roxie back on the floor of the hall in Dan and Jackson's home, careful to position her body between the dog and the door in case it made a second bid for freedom. As she closed the front door, Jackson peeked his head round the corner of the kitchen.

"Hey, honey, why's your face all red?" he asked, disappearing before she could respond.

Freya shot Roxie an accusatory glare, as the dog sat down at her feet dropping the teddy bear it had in its mouth onto her toes.

"Too cute. Like your mom," Freya scowled at the animal and reached down for the teddy bear, throwing it for the dog to chase. It pounded off in pursuit of the toy, and Freya took the opportunity to escape to the kitchen. As soon as she walked in, she was handed a red drink in a tall glass by Jackson, who was dancing around the kitchen with his arms above his head. "Bloody Mary," he shouted over the din, pointing down at her drink.

"Is there a reason?" Freya asked, removing the celery stalk and taking a careful sip, wincing at the strength. It appeared that Jackson had been heavy-handed with the Tabasco sauce.

Jackson picked up his glass, and clinked it against Freya's. "It's Monday," he smiled, turning down the volume on his iPod docking station. "And you had your first 'I've got a job' meeting with Eleanor," he grabbed Freya's hand and led her out onto the decking area. "So now you have to tell me all about it."

"Why do you have Roxie?" Freya asked casually.

Jackson was used to both women's 'casual' questioning of either him, or Dan, on the other, "She's been in Orlando, visiting her family."

Jackson had hoped that Freya's return to LA would prompt a reconciliation, but Freya had been back for four weeks, and his two favorite women seemed to be somewhat stubbornly avoiding each other. Dan had warned him on several occasions not to meddle, however, Jackson believed that the two women would never be truly happy apart. They had broken up on the night he and Dan had got together, so Jackson had never known them as a couple. But, loving them both dearly, and wanting them to be happy, meant that Jackson wasn't about to mention to Freya that Jordan was due at any minute to collect Roxie, which was why he was making Bloody Marys.

"Sooooo, the meeting?" he asked, raising an eyebrow.

Freya shook her head slightly, rousing herself from her thoughts of Jordan. "Good, really good, actually. They've picked us up for six episodes for the summer schedule," she smiled, genuinely excited at the prospect of the new show.

"You found somewhere to live yet?" Jackson asked, huffing after spinning Freya following her news. He surreptitiously looked at his watch to check the time for Jordan's arrival.

When she had arrived back in LA, Freya decided that this time her staying in Anna's guesthouse would only be a temporary measure and she would get her own place. She wanted, finally, to put some of her own roots down in her hometown.

"Yeah, I have," Freya took a sip of her drink. "I'm going for a second look tomorrow, if you're free?"

"Sure, if it's the afternoon," Jackson replied. "Where is it?"

"Hmm?" Freya asked, sipping her drink, buying for time by pretending she didn't hear the question.

Wise to her ploy, Jackson made sure he got eye contact, "Freya, where is the house?"

"West Hollywood," Freya mumbled against the rim of her glass, ignoring Jackson's slightly raised eyebrows. Despite being desperate to, Jackson didn't get the chance to challenge Freya's real estate choice, as Roxie started to bark at the sound of the front door opening and bounded to greet whoever entered.

"Jackson?" Jordan called, walking through the house.

Avoiding Freya's horrified look, Jackson yelled back in response, "Out on the deck, sweetie."

Freya's hand sprang to her hair as she gave herself a quick glance to check her appearance before Jordan came into view.

"Hi, oh hey," Jordan stopped, her eyes trained on Freya as Roxie squirmed in her arms. She stood in the doorway frozen to the spot.

Jackson looked between the two women, "How 'bout I fetch you a drink."

"No, it's okay," Jordan started but was halted as Jackson ignored her and pushed past to scuttle off to the kitchen, intent on breaking the world record for the longest time to pour liquid into a glass.

Jordan, realizing she had no chance of escaping, sat stiffly down on the love seat opposite Freya. "So…" she started awkwardly, "how have you been?"

Freya gulped. She was talking to Jordan. Actually, she wasn't talking to Jordan, she was staring at Jordan and in fact, if one were inclined, one could apply the word ogling as the correct description of what she was doing. Somewhere in her head, a voice screamed at her 'Speak'.

"I'm good, thanks. I met with Eleanor today, we've been picked up for a summer slot," she finished, terrified of saying the wrong thing and spoiling the moment. She chewed nervously on her lip, "Jackson said you were in Florida, is everything okay?"

Jordan looked surprised, she'd obviously been a topic of conversation. She felt annoyed with herself that even that little piece of information had caused her heart to beat a little bit faster, "I just had a few days break in filming, so decided to get away for a bit."

Deciding to push the boundaries slightly, Freya nodded slowly. "Did Matt like Orlando?" she asked, deliberately getting his name wrong.

"Mike," Jordan corrected. "We broke up," she added simply.

Freya gave a little cough, hoping that she had done enough to disguise the celebratory yelp that escaped unbidden from her lips. "I'm sorry to hear that," she replied, using all of her acting ability to maintain her decorum.

Jackson stood outside the kitchen door, his weight on one foot as he leaned in an attempt to make out what was being said out on the decking. He figured that the fact that he was struggling to hear their muted voices meant at least they weren't shouting.

The front door opened and Dan stepped through the threshold, "Hey honey, I'm –"

His greeting was cut off as a strong hand thwacked against his mouth, another gripping the back of his head to silence him. He looked into his boyfriend's eyes and offered a muffled, "What?" against Jackson's palm, his eyes wide in confusion.

"They're both here," Jackson hissed. "Out there," he jerked his head towards the French windows. "DO NOT...I repeat, do not, spoil this," Jackson warned ominously.

Dan flashed him a hurt look and pulled his hand away from his mouth, "As if I would. I want it as much as you do. What are they talking about?"

Giving a quick shrug, Jackson moved to resume his position. "I can't hear," he whispered.

Joining Jackson, Dan leaned to the side and held onto him for support as he tried equally hard to hear the conversation.

"Me neither," he sighed, scrunching his face up in concentration. "Do you think they're, you know?" he asked hopefully.

"Hey Dan!"

Jordan's voice startled both men, making them fall over each other slightly in their attempt to disguise that they had been eavesdropping. Freya however was looking at both of them suspiciously from her spot behind Jordan. "I'm just going to grab Roxie's stuff and head off, if that's okay," Jordan said.

The men hesitated, then both started to scrabble together the accoutrements that had accompanied the small dog's stay. Finally, with Roxie securely on a leash and her other items stashed in her bag, Jordan stood at the front door. "Thanks again for looking after her," she said gratefully to the two men, kissing them both fondly on the cheek. She turned to Freya and paused. "It was good to see you," she finally said.

"It was good to see you too," Freya replied, her breath catching slightly as she answered.

Jordan smiled, then opened the door and headed out into the evening sun. Jackson and Dan stood at the door waving goodbye while Freya hovered in the hall, not sure whether she should join them. Finally, she opted to return to the deck. She was sitting, her legs pulled up against her chest, when Dan and Jackson came and looked at her expectantly. She gave them a small smile, "It was a start."

Jackson stood on the sidewalk with two silver travel mugs in his hand. His eyebrows raised in surprise as, instead of the Prius that Dan would tease Freya about, she pulled up in a black Audi TT roadster convertible. The roof was down as, after a New York winter, the actress was enjoying feeling the warmth of the LA sun on her skin.

"What happened to eco-car?" Jackson asked, handing her one of the mugs before hopping into the passenger seat.

"It was a momentary weakness," Freya grinned. "What's this?" she asked, lifting the silver mug up to inspect it.

"Smoothie, I've been experimenting," Jackson fastened his seatbelt, catching Freya's skeptical look. "Drink it, it's good for you."

Freya scowled but took a sip, her furrowed brow turning into a look of surprise, "Mmmm, nice." She licked her lips and handed Jackson the mug before checking the road and pulling off.

Leaning forward, Jackson switched the music off so that he could hear the engine better. "When we get back can I have a look under the hood?" he asked, his voice tinged with boyish excitement. Despite being the owner of several auto shops, Jackson still could not stop the mechanic in him from being wound up over engines, and how they looked, and sounded.

"Sure you can, grease monkey."

Switching the music back on, Jackson settled into the ride to Freya's potential new neighborhood. "So, West Hollywood?" he asked, sipping his smoothie.

Freya concentrated on the road ahead. "Mmm?" she responded absently.

"Don't mmm me, missy, you know exactly what I'm asking. You're looking to move into Jordan's neighborhood," he said, his tone a mix of teasing and accusation.

Turning her head to look at her friend, she smiled innocently, "What?" she shrugged her shoulders. "It's a good neighborhood, and big. It's a big neighborhood, huge almost."

Jackson gave her a withering look. "Eyes on the road," he waved his finger towards the windshield. "Seriously, you're going to do this?" he asked.

"Do what? I need somewhere to live. I became familiar with the area and I like it. Nothing else," she replied.

Jackson narrowed his eyes, still not believing her. They drove the rest of the way to the West Hollywood Hills area in comfortable silence, punctuated by their efforts to sing along with songs from Freya's iPod. Jackson was in the middle of a particularly impressive, and oddly accurate, impression of Cher when he started to take note of his surroundings. They were driving up Jordan's street.

"Freya Easter, really?" he asked incredulously as they drove closer to Jordan's home.

"What? It's not like it's next door to her, you just have to drive past to get to it," she replied defensively. "Seriously, Jackson, this is not a big deal."

Jackson raised a hand and gestured that he gave up. They drove past Jordan's house and continued for another few minutes before Freya pulled into a drive. Waiting at the door of the property was the realtor. As they were shown around, Freya's excitement grew as she pictured herself living in the house surrounded with her belongings.

Jackson, meanwhile, was still pondering over Freya's decision on where to live. After a half hour of walking in and out of the rooms and peppering the real estate agent with questions, they walked back to the car. Opening the door, Freya looked over the car towards Jackson. "I'm going to take it," she said decisively.

"I know you are, sweetie. I knew you would from the moment you picked me up," Jackson gave her a smug smile. "Just please promise me that you won't start hiding in trees outside her home with binoculars."

Freya rolled her eyes. "Not everything I do is related to Jordan," she huffed, flinging herself into the driver's seat.

Slipping gracefully into the passenger seat he muttered to himself, "No, not everything, just most things."

***

Freya was pleased with herself. She had found somewhere to live, so soon there would be no more living with Anna, and the first table read had been a success. Life was good, except that the one person she wanted to tell about her week was still barely speaking to her. It was late on Saturday night, and she was sitting in her bedroom in Anna's guesthouse. Wearing her onesie and slanket, ignoring Jackson's strict orders that the two items were never to share the same space at the same time. The remnants of a take-out sat on the corner of her bed as she huddled up, studying her script in a vain attempt to learn her lines. Finally, placing her thumb and index finger either side of her nose, she squeezed her eyes closed tightly.

"I give up," she said aloud to the empty room as she tossed the script onto the bed and grabbed the TV remote from the nightstand. She started absently flicking through channels, holding her thumb down on the scroll button as the images before her changed quickly. Her mind suddenly began processing one of the images that had flashed momentarily on the screen. Selecting the back button she scrolled back through the channels to find what she thought she'd seen.

The TV screen filled with Jordan.

Freya's breath caught at the image of her ex-girlfriend crying on screen. Turning up the volume, Freya let her head drop as she watched the lifetime movie that Jordan had made during hiatus. She checked the schedule. The movie had started only five minutes before and had an hour to run. Freya gave a small, ironic smile. It looked like she would be spending Saturday night with the woman she loved, after all.

As the movie finished, Freya wiped away the tears that were flowing freely down her face. She plucked a tissue from the box on the nightstand and blew her nose noisily. Jordan's performance had been flawless. Freya had forgotten just how amazing a talent Jordan had. Her expressive brown eyes could convey every nuance of emotion. Sniffing, Freya was suddenly filled with enormous pride at her girlfriend's, exgirlfriend's, she corrected mentally, work.

She shifted on the bed onto her knees, looking for her cell. Locating it under her discarded script, she brushed the back of her hand across her nose and released a short puff of air out of the side of her mouth to shift a stray lock of hair. She quickly typed a message, and pressed send before she could talk herself out of it.

Jordan was sitting at her piano, her fingers picking out the melody of the song she had been working on with a co-writer. She had always talked about recording an album, and since her split with Freya, she had started to take the steps to turn the talk into reality. She had taken Anna's advice to heart and thrown herself into every creative outlet available to her, as a way of coping with the grief at the loss of her relationship. They had laid down the tracks on two of the songs that she was going to release as a taster to see whether there was a market for her songs and voice. The third track was still giving her sleepless nights. She couldn't get the lyrics quite right, which was why she was sitting humming the melody to herself, and every now and again softly singing the lyrics that she had written. The buzz from her phone broke her from her thoughts. She stood up and crossed the room to collect her cell. Her heart stopped as she saw whom she had received a message from.

Hi, sorry to text so late, I just watched your movie on cable and had to tell you how amazing you were…are. Freya

Jordan's lips spread into a slow smile that she could not stop becoming a silly grin. Her thumbs had started to type out a reply when she stopped and dropped the phone onto the table as if it had burned her, and started to pace back and forth.

"What are you doing?" she asked herself. "You've only just gotten over her and you're going to let her waltz back into your life, back into your heart, because she sent a cute text? You are better than this," she argued with herself, as she marched back and forth behind her sofa. "Who are you kidding? You're not over her, you'll never *be* over her," she raged at herself, stopping and looking accusingly at her cell phone lying innocently on the table. "Why, Freya? Why now? Why, when I'm feeling stronger, does seeing you for twenty minutes and then getting a text from you make me melt?" she yelled at the phone. "What do you want from me?" she walked round and collapsed onto the sofa, her forearms shielding her face, when her phone buzzed again.

Your performance was incredible. I'm still crying thinking about it…just had to tell you. Sweet dreams.

Reading the message, Jordan felt her stomach flip. After all this time, the thought of Freya being upset still triggered a response to comfort her. She let her head fall back and puffed her cheeks up, letting the air leave her body slowly. She sat up and rolled her shoulders, typing a reply into her phone and pressing send, before returning to the piano to play with her song.

Freya was pacing around her bed, chewing nervously on her thumbnail, her slanket billowing behind her like a cloak as she walked. "I shouldn't have texted," she admonished herself aloud. "You're a fool, Freya, a goddammed fool who should know better than texting your ex-girlfriend in the middle of the night when you're tired and emotional and just watched her on screen for an hour."

Her phone buzzed from the center of the bed, interrupting her diatribe. She launched herself at the bed, her landing causing the takeout box to bounce off the bed and land open on the floor. Grimacing at the mess, Freya opened the message, her breath held captive in her lungs as it loaded onto the screen.

Thank you, I'm sorry I made you cry, although you are one of life's pretty criers, not like me all snot and wailing. Get some sleep, it's late...Pleasant dreams...Jordan.

Freya laughed as she read Jordan's description of how she looked when crying, which could not have been further from the truth.

She replied, that's got to mean something, Freya thought, flipping herself onto her back and allowing herself a moment to consider that there may be hope of them finding each other again and reconnecting. She kicked her legs excitedly against the mattress before getting up to tidy the mess on the floor.

May 2013

The next month was tough for both women. Freya became acutely aware of the difference of being in an ensemble cast, and being the main character. Her workload was massive in comparison to what she'd had when she worked on *Front Line*. She had also moved into her new home, although boxes still lay unpacked, piled up messily in the corners of rooms waiting until she had a break in her schedule to unpack fully. She had not spoken to Jordan since their text conversation but, as usual, she was kept up to date on events through either Dan or Jackson.

Jordan, equally, had been caught up in the maelstrom of her career. She had finally managed to write lyrics for her final song and recorded the number. She was also on a publicity merry-go-round to promote the season's finale of *Front Line*. Her character was very much front and center on the episode, and as a consequence she had been doing the lion's share of the publicity interviews. When possible, she was also taking the opportunity to sing songs from her album. She was happy to be busy though, as it meant that she spent less time in a quandary about what to do about Freya, and she got to promote her music.

***

Standing on her front step, Freya stretched out. She took a deep breath of the morning air, placed her earphone buds into her ears, then hopped down the steps and set off on her habitual morning run.

A loud beeping noise woke Jordan, and she looked up at her alarm bleary-eyed before silencing it. Her head dropped back down onto her pillow and she lay for a split second before remembering the reason why her alarm was set. She shot upright and leapt from her bed towards the window, pulling the curtain back a fraction to allow her to see out towards the sidewalk. She checked the time on the alarm clock again, before settling into what had been her morning ritual for the past week and a half.

A minute later, Freya jogged past in her tight running gear with her hair pulled back into a ponytail. Jordan watched, her memory recalling what it was like to feel that body pressed against her own. She knew from experience that she had a half hour before Freya returned up the street on her way home. Since learning about Freya's new abode from Jackson, Jordan had been keeping an eye out for her ex. It was only by chance that she had seen her running ten days earlier at this time; and Jordan told herself, that it was also just happenstance that she was up, and at her window, at the same time the following morning.

Day ten, and Jordan was done pretending.

She was enjoying the view.

Freya reached the point on her playlist when she had to turn around and head back towards home. As she started the slog back up the hill towards Jordan's, she once again told herself that it was the best route for a run. However, she wasn't kidding anyone, let alone herself. She was running past Jordan's in the hope of seeing her. However, ten days, and there had been no sign, nothing…nada. *Maybe today would be the day,* she thought, picking up her pace in anticipation. She was literally outside Jordan's when she noticed that her lace had become undone. She gave up a silent prayer of thanks to the gods of serendipity as she pulled up and bent over to tighten it.

Jordan stood at the window, watching as Freya stopped outside her home; directly outside her home. For a moment, Jordan thought that perhaps Freya was going to come up the path, and her heart started to beat frantically in her chest. However, when she saw Freya bend down to tie her lace, a wave of disappointment came over her, replaced by outright lust as she bit her bottom lip, enraptured with the vision of Freya. She was so captivated that she forgot to remain out of sight, as she parted the curtains wider and stood on her tiptoes to get a better view.

Tying her lace tightly, Freya stood up and placed her hands onto her hips, stretching out her lower back. Her gaze drifted up towards Jordan's house, and more specifically Jordan's bedroom window, as she thought about her ex-girlfriend lying sleeping in the room. Her forehead furrowed as the curtains twitched and, for a split second, Freya could have sworn that there had been a figure at the window. She hoped that Dan and Jackson had been telling her the truth and that Jordan wasn't seeing anyone, which meant that there was a distinct possibility that the figure had belonged to Jordan. She smiled to herself, and set off to complete her run with an added spring in her step.

Lying crouched beneath her window, her knees up at her chin, Jordan started to chuckle to herself at the ridiculousness of the situation. She let out a long, deep, frustrated growl, then stood and set off for a cold morning shower.

***

Freya picked up her phone, her face wet with tears after watching *Front Line's* finale. She had enjoyed a rare evening when she was home before nine, and had taken the opportunity to unpack some boxes before pouring herself a glass of wine and settling down to watch Jordan's big moment.

She never doubted Jordan's abilities. Even before she had met Jordan, she had watched her perform on stage and on *Front Line*. Freya was blown away at the sheer emotional rollercoaster she had been taken on. She knew that Georgia had moved from the base hospital in Germany to the combat support hospital on the show, which put her literally on the *Front Line* for the first time. What she was not expecting was for Georgia to become a victim of an explosive device. She watched as Georgia ignored her own injuries as she struggled to help fellow soldiers. When rescued, nothing could have prepared Freya for the experience of seeing Jordan, as Georgia, code on the table. She had ended up on the edge of her seat shouting at the TV for them to get her back. In some irrational part of her brain it was not Georgia lying injured and dying, it was Jordan. Jordan's performance of Georgia had been immaculate.

Jordan had invited a selection of friends, from the show and other areas of her life, around to watch the episode with her. However, the person that she really wanted to be there was probably still working somewhere at the studio. From what she had gathered from Dan, Freya's workload was giving her little free time for anything apart from sleeping and her morning run. She had contemplated asking Freya round, but wasn't sure how it might be interpreted. She wasn't entirely sure how she wanted it interpreted, either. So in the end, she had opted not to mention it as, if you disregarded their morning jogging dates where Jordan was still observing her ex on her morning run from behind her bedroom curtains, there had been no communication between them since their meeting at Dan's.

The phone had rung constantly since the show finished, and Jordan had not stopped grinning as her family and friends called to congratulate her. She was talking with Jackson and Dan when Sabrina thrust her house phone towards her, one hand covering the mouthpiece.

"You're gonna want to take this one," Sabrina grinned, passing the handset.

Frowning, Jordan accepted the phone and raised the hand still holding her glass of champagne in order to place her finger in her ear to block out the sound from her living room, "Hello?"

"You're alive!"

Jordan could hear the smile in Freya's voice. She gave Sabrina a quick scowl as she stood grinning cheesily towards her, making swooning motions. Kicking open the door to the kitchen, Jordan stepped into the quieter room and started to make her way towards her patio.

"Yeah I am," she said, smiling as she slipped out into her yard. "You watched then. I thought you would have been working. Dan said that you've been pulling long hours."

Freya stretched out on the sofa, "I have, but tonight we wrapped early. It sounds like you've a full house, I should let you go. I just wanted to let you know how amazing I thought you were." Jordan's breath caught as she sat down on the stone bench that she had sat on with Freya during her birthday party. She looked out across the pool, remembering how she had looked in her costume that night, "No, it's okay, I…" She paused, wanting to tell Freya that she didn't want to speak to anyone else, but settled on, "Thank you."

"You're welcome, you should be the focus point every week on the show."

Laughing, Jordan shook her head, "Oooh noo, the workload for that was immense, no thanks. Besides, I think Eleanor would have a heart attack."

"I'll speak to her, she owes me," Freya said jokingly, screwing up her face and thumping her head back against the cushion as she realized what she'd just alluded to.

Jordan swallowed hard, trying not to dwell on why Eleanor owed Freya. "She does. Both of us, actually," she added quietly.

Freya bit her top lip, her brain and heart fighting a battle. "I miss you," she whispered, her heart having won the fight. She heard Jordan take a sharp intake of breath. The moment seemed to extend for hours before Jordan spoke.

"I..."

"Hey Jordan, Sabrina is about to make cocktails and is looking for your blender," Grant's voice drifted out from the house.

Hesitantly, Jordan waved a hand towards him to let him know she was coming. "I'm sorry, I have to go, Freya. I," Jordan closed her eyes. "Thank you for calling, it really means a lot," she added, before ending the call.

She held the handset to her chest and kept her eyes closed. She was terrified, but she wasn't sure what she was more terrified of; being with Freya and opening herself up to the possibility of getting hurt again, or losing her forever. Before Freya, she'd never given anyone an 'access all areas' pass to her. She'd barely survived losing her once, and if it were to happen again, Jordan wasn't sure how she'd cope. However, what she was starting to realize was that not having Freya in her life at all was a prospect she did not want to face. She sighed and stood up, ready to go wrestle her blender from the appliance-phobe Sabrina.

Freya sat with the phone still at her ear. She had finally taken the gamble. She'd put herself out there, and…nothing. She was ready to go round there and pound on Grant's face, as she was sure it was his voice that she'd heard shouting to Jordan and interrupting whatever she was going to say.

She had tried and, in her mind, the ball was now firmly in Jordan's court.

June 2013

"DeLucca's, really?" Freya groaned as the cab pulled into the parking lot outside the jazz club entrance. The last thing she needed when attending Jackson's birthday party, where her ex-girlfriend was likely to be in attendance, was for it to be held somewhere that she had memories with said girlfriend.

"What? It's nice, and you've always raved about it," Dan said, exchanging a quick glance with Jackson in the front seat.

Freya crossed her arms, her mouth moving as she muttered curses to herself.

Dan looked at her with raised eyebrows, "Muttley, get out of the car." He pointed to the door of the cab.

Still grumbling, Freya opened the door and got out of the car, straightening her dress and thrusting her clutch purse under her arm.

"What's with all the photographers?" she asked, puzzled as they approached the door, blinking at the flashes that surrounded her. "Has Jackson done something special to have LA's paparazzi at his birthday party?"

Dan just gave her a smile in response as he gave their names to the bouncer on the door, who lifted the red cord across the entrance to allow them to move inside.

Freya started to get more and more suspicious as they entered the jazz club, "What is this…?" Her question fell from her lips, as on stage was Jordan.

Jackson nudged Dan. "I told you we were going to be late, she's started!" he huffed, walking into the club and leaving them standing at the entrance.

Jordan's voice filled the room as she sang, the acoustics complementing the power and warmth of her voice. It was absolutely her secret weapon, and one that Freya had no resolve against.

"Dan, what is this?" Freya asked carefully.

Dan pursed his lips, "It's a showcase for Jordan. She's releasing an album tomorrow. And I'm sorry that I lied to you, but it was the best way to get you here without you freaking out."

She looked back towards the stage, and smiled as Jordan commanded the audience's attention as she sang. Her smile turned to a frown, though, as she listened to the lyrics. The song was filled with angst, and anger, towards a lost love.

"Dan?" Freya said, gripping his arm. "Dan, did she write that about me?" she asked during the instrumental, her expression full of hurt.

Looking at his friend, her face crumpling as Jordan continued to sing, Dan put a comforting arm around her shoulder, "She did, but really early on after you broke up."

Freya shook her head, "I can't stay, I can't listen, I..."

Jackson returned with three drinks in his hands. "Freya Easter, just stop. You will get your pretty little tush into the body of that club and. You…Will…Listen!" he commanded, handing her one of the drinks.

Dan grinned at his boyfriend, "I do so love it when you go all masterful." He turned to Freya, who was rolling her eyes, "Now do as he says, 'cause it's the next song you need to hear."

Freya reluctantly followed them into the club. Feeling like everyone was looking at her, she attempted to hide her discomfort with a smile as she went.

Jordan finished the song and the audience clapped wildly as she gave them a wide grin, her entire body feeling as if it was vibrating with pleasure. Her gaze swept around the room, settling on a pair of green eyes that, despite their best attempt, were looking at her with hurt in them.

"Thank you," she said into the microphone, before turning and nodding to the band to indicate that she was ready for the next song. She took a deep breath to compose herself. It was now or never. She leaned forward, closed her eyes, and allowed her voice to flow.

Time heals all wounds they say, but what do they know

Don't they realize, that time means nothing at all, without you in my life

She opened her eyes and looked directly at Freya, pouring everything she could into her voice.

I've tried so hard to move on, pretending that I'm okay

But one look into your eyes and I fall all over again

Time was always against us, but I know if I could do it again I would

So I'm sitting staring at my phone, wishing that you'd call

Dan leaned in towards Freya, who had not taken her eyes off Jordan, "This one, she wrote since you came back." He planted a kiss against the side of Freya's head, stood back upright and focused his attention on the stage, where his friend was literally singing her heart out.

Jordan closed her eyes, bouncing on her tiptoes as she allowed her voice to surge, hitting a high note. When she opened them, they went straight back to capturing Freya's as she continued.

Never loved anyone the way that I love you

But I'm terrified that I'll make the wrong move

The band repeated the final chorus as Jordan's voice played with the melody of the song, tossing it around with ease before the music died out and applause replaced it.

Freya's mind reeled at the lyrics. She needed air. She turned and handed Dan her drink. He frowned, taking the glass and watching in confusion as Freya spun on her heels and walked towards the exit, her hand running through her hair. He looked back up on the stage towards Jordan, whose face had fallen as she watched Freya's departure.

Jordan felt helpless as she watched Freya thread her way through the crowd towards the exit. She had hoped that after hearing her songs Freya would understand that she wanted them to be together, and they would be able to resume their relationship. Ever since Freya's admission that she missed her, Jordan had thought about little else. Seeing the door close behind Freya, she felt as though her heart had been ripped from her all over again. She barely noticed the applause as she stepped down from the stage and started to weave through the audience, intent on finding Freya to plead her case more clearly. She smiled absently towards well-wishers as they patted her back, her eyes never wavering from the door that Freya had escaped through. She reached for her back pocket and pulled her cell phone from it.

Freya stood in the hallway. In front of her was the exit, and she could see photographers gathered outside and so, needing privacy, she pushed through a door to her left. Entering the dark room, she realized she had entered the restaurant where the elderly woman had accosted Jordan and Sabrina. Grateful that the restaurant was closed off for the evening due to the showcase, she exhaled. Her emotions started to pour from her, and she gripped one of the chairs as a sob escaped her lips. With a trembling hand, she opened her purse, pulled out her cell, and selected a number from her favorites. She licked her lips, taking her bottom lip between her teeth as the phone started to ring. She heard a cell ringing behind her, outside in the hall. She turned as the ringing grew louder and Jordan pushed open the door to the restaurant, her phone in her hand.

Looking down at the screen, Jordan accepted the call.

"Hi," Freya said quietly into the phone.

"Hi, I've been waiting on your call," Jordan replied, a small smile playing on her lips.

Freya slowly started to walk towards Jordan, still speaking into the phone, her eyes locked on the brown, tear-filled ones studying her. "I'm sorry it took so long." Her voice hitched with emotion as she spoke, "You were…I have no words." She laughed, then hesitated, "I love you Jordan, and I'm destined to live my life loving you." Her heart pounded as she got closer to Jordan, one more step and they would be inches apart. Freya paused.

"I love you too, and I'm fed up not being with you," Jordan smiled, dropping her phone from her ear and completing the distance between them. She took Freya's face in her hands and pulled her towards her. Savoring the taste of Freya's lips, she felt complete for the first time in a year.

The two women walked back into the club, their fingers interlaced. Inside, Jackson and Dan were waiting anxiously, watching the door for the return of one or both of them. Seeing their hands linked, Jackson broke out into a, wide grin. He positioned his glass between his arm and side to free up both hands, and started to applaud their reappearance. The crowd assuming that the applause was for Jordan and her performance, and not because she was holding the hand of the woman next to her, joined Jackson.

Dan stood with a look of visible relief on his face. He was grateful that finally things were going to get back to normality. With them both happy and together, it meant that he wouldn't be getting calls at ungodly hours from either one of them. He held his glass up in a toast as they approached.

"Well, thank fuck for that," he announced. "Let's get bladdered." He put his glass to his lips and drained the content dramatically, heading off to the bar for another round of drinks.

Freya and Jordan laughed at their friend. Out of the corner of her eye, Jordan caught someone motioning to her. She turned and nodded over towards her manager, "I've gotta go 'schmooze my tush off,' as Dan would say. Don't go anywhere." She looked deep into Freya's eyes, they both smiled, and Jordan lifted Freya's hand to her cheek, placing a soft kiss on the inside of Freya's wrist before disappearing into the throng of people. Freya watched her go with her head to the side and a goofy grin on her face.

"Don't think you're not going to give me details," Jackson said, nudging her with his arm. "I want to know all about what just happened. Was it romantic? Was it hot?" he waited on a response, his eyes wide.

She shot him a quick glance, quirking her eyebrows. "It was perfect," she sighed. She jumped slightly as two arms worked their way around her neck.

Dan placed a kiss on her cheek and a glass into her hand, "I'm so happy for you both, but the most important question of the evening is..." He paused.

Freya twisted in his arms so she could see his face. "Yes?" she asked cautiously.

"Can we burn the damn onesies, now?" Dan enquired with a grin.

***

The car pulled into Jordan's drive, and the two actresses climbed out and walked slowly towards the door of her home. They were both excited, and nervous about what was about to happen, as soon as they were on the other side of the door. There had been no discussion about what the plan was after the showcase. There was no requirement, as they were both on the same page about what they wanted and needed. It had felt good to leave the club together, hand in hand, no pretense, no hiding. The photographer's flashbulbs had almost blinded them as they had climbed into their waiting car.

Jordan put her key into the lock of the door, stealing a quick glance at Freya. Still not quite believing that she was there and that they were together, she let out a soft chuckle as she turned the key, her hair bobbing at the small shake of her head.

"What?" Freya asked smiling, a hint of laughter in her voice.

Jordan looked at her and swallowed. "I have dreamed about this so many times, I'm like a kid at Christmas," she laughed.

Freya pulled her bottom lip between her teeth seductively, and leaned in towards Jordan. "In that case, you should probably get us inside and start to unwrap your gift," she husked.

In one smooth action, Jordan's hand slammed down on the handle of her door. Grabbing Freya with her free hand, she pulled her into the house and kicked the door closed behind her. Freya prepared herself for the expected rush of kisses and touches. When they didn't come, she looked at Jordan in surprise and anticipation as the tall actress stood drinking in the sight of the dark-haired woman in front of her.

"The thing about unwrapping gifts," Jordan said slowly as she took a step towards Freya. "Is the anticipation. My sister would always rip the wrapping off and have all of her presents opened at once, while I..." She licked her lips and ran her eyes, hooded with desire, up and down the length of Freya's body, taking in the toned legs and flat stomach from the morning runs, the swell of her breasts perfectly encased in the black dress that she had worn for the evening. "I would take my time and I'd still be opening, enjoying and savoring my gifts well into the afternoon," she smirked, as she brought her lips to meet Freya's in a slow, languid kiss.

She withdrew her lips and started to trail kisses down Freya's exposed neck, inhaling the faint trace of her perfume. The same smell that had made her take detours in department stores so as not to pass the stall selling it, in case she caught a hint. The same fragrance that would make her heart thud in her chest when walking past someone in the street, and catching its aroma drifting in the air. Now she smelt it directly from the skin that she had craved to touch and kiss for so long. She allowed herself to become absorbed in all that was Freya.

"Mmmm, I seem to recall that," Freya moaned, her mind drifting to the one and only Christmas they had spent together, when Jordan had visited her in New York. She had giddily opened her gifts, and had sat impatiently while Jordan took her time over each gift, carefully preserving the wrapping paper as she removed it. Her explanation to an over-eager Freya, who sat scowling while sitting surrounded by balls of scrunched up wrapping paper, was that the wrapping was a part of the gift as it added to the suspense and anticipation, and should be enjoyed as part of the gift and not tossed aside. Her girlfriend's meticulous approach to unwrapping gifts had infuriated Freya then, now…

Now she was thanking every god that she could think of for it.

Jordan brought her head back up, her brown eyes trailing slowly up Freya's flushed face, finally connecting with green eyes darkened with want. She moved to pass Freya, catching her hand as she drew even with her, before gently leading the way to the bedroom.

Jordan let Freya enter the room first. Coming up behind the smaller woman, she tugged lightly on the zipper of Freya's dress. Studiously watching the path of the zip as she pulled it down, the material of the black dress draped open, exposing Freya's skin. Reaching the small of Freya's back, Jordan slipped her hands into the gap of the dress and ran the palms of her hands up to Freya's shoulders. She pushed the straps of the dress down over her lover's shoulders. The simple black dress shimmied to the floor, leaving Freya standing dressed only in her underwear. Jordan took a step closer, desperate to feel the warmth radiating from Freya's body. She brushed dark locks to the side and tracked kisses along Freya's exposed shoulder.

Feeling as though her skin was on fire with each kiss, Freya leaned back and let her head fall back to rest on Jordan's shoulder as the blonde woman continued to adorn her body with kisses. She released the catch on Freya's black lace bra, pushing the item of clothing from her body. She snaked her arms around Freya's torso, her hands cupping newly exposed breasts. A satisfied sigh left Jordan's lips at the touch. She traced her fingertips down Freya's stomach before slipping them underneath the lace material of her underwear.

Freya's breath caught as Jordan's fingertips grazed her arousal. She closed her eyes, letting her head fall to the side. She lifted her hands up behind her, her fingers burying themselves into Jordan's luscious blonde tresses. Her stomach muscles contracted in time with each caress. Her body writhing against Jordan, she lurched forwards as the rhythm of Jordan's touch increased. A strong arm pulled her back upright, pressing her back flush against the taller woman's front. She moved her hips in small circular motions to amplify the pressure of Jordan's fingers on her. Sighs became louder, cascading into long moans, and her knees threatened to give out as her body finally released the tension that had been building in her. They stood unmoving, both breathing heavily. Finally, Freya turned and looped her arms around Jordan's neck, pulling her lover closer and kissing her languorously.

"You cheated," she murmured. "You didn't unwrap me fully, I still have clothes on."

"Who says I'm done?" Jordan smiled against Freya's lips.

***

The alarm clock buzzed, disturbing the quiet of the room, and Freya scrunched her face up in protest at the noise. She brushed her hand across her face in the uncoordinated manner of someone still not fully awake. Opening one eye to look at the offending item, Jordan reached a hand out, stretching over Freya's body to shut the alarm off.

"It's early; do you have to be somewhere?" Freya asked, turning her head slightly.

"Nope, not today, I just forgot to switch it off last night. I was distracted," Jordan muttered, nestling back behind Freya.

"I'm usually out running about now," Freya said, yawning and stretching her legs out, feeling the impact of her and Jordan's reconciliation in her muscles. "In fact, I'm usually running past here at this time," she said lightly, listening for a reaction in Jordan.

Jordan wrinkled her nose and squeezed her eyes shut, "Hmmm?"

Freya bit her top lip to stop herself from laughing as she turned herself over to look at Jordan, who was feigning sleep, and pressed her nose against her lover's until Jordan finally relented and opened her eyes with a sigh. Shifting her head back, Freya raised her eyebrows and grinned widely.

"You set your alarm?" she laughed.

"People set alarms, Freya. It's how you know when to get up," Jordan replied haughtily.

Freya narrowed her eyes. She moved her hand slowly down Jordan's side, so as not to raise suspicion, then pressed her fingers into the soft flesh where she knew Jordan was ticklish. Jordan twisted to get away from Freya, who moved with impressive speed to straddle her lover.

"Admit it Jordan, you set your alarm to get up and perv at me."

"I did no such thing," Jordan huffed in between giggles. "It's a coincidence," she yelled, trying desperately to buck Freya off of her.

"Admit it!" Freya laughed, adding a second hand to the onslaught, giving Jordan no respite as each hand took turns taunting her.

"Okay, okay. I admit it, stop!"

"What do you admit to?" Freya asked teasingly, threading her fingers through Jordan's and pushing the blonde actress's hands up above her head.

"I admit to setting my alarm so that I could perv at you," Jordan smiled, looking up at her naked lover. "I have to say, this morning's view is the best yet."

"Pervert," Freya smiled, leaning down to kiss Jordan good morning.

When they eventually separated, Freya noticed a frown appearing on Jordan's features. "You okay? Are you having second thoughts?" she asked, trying not to sound too panicked at the thought.

"What? No!" Jordan said gripping Freya tighter. "It's just I'm worried about what happens if we run into a similar situation again. I'm not sure I could cope with losing you again."

Freya rolled off Jordan onto her side and rested her head on her hand, "Me neither, so I propose we don't let it happen again. My parents have been together for years, and have managed not to let their careers get in the way of their relationship. Their approach is something we could adopt. They make decisions together and agree to a limit of the time they will allow a job to keep them apart, and even then they make sure they speak to each other every day. It's even easier for them now, with video calls." She nuzzled against Jordan's neck, "I promise I won't allow us to mess this up again. I love you too much to allow that to happen, and Anna would have my hide."

Jordan slowly rolled Freya onto her back and settled comfortably on top of her, "I love you too." She lowered her head and started to nibble on Freya's ear, "Now, what was that you called me, again?"

Freya gasped as Jordan's hand cupped her between her legs, "I honestly can't remember."

December 2013

"So, when's she due back?" Dan asked as he flipped open the pizza box and pulled off a slice, dangling it into his mouth.

Freya filled his glass with wine. "Saturday," she answered, passing the glass over and snatching a slice of pizza before Dan hoovered it up. "Two days, three hours and," she craned her neck past Dan to look at the clock on the cooker, which was the only part that Freya used, "thirty seven minutes."

Dan shot her a look of pity. "Anyone would think that you've never gone without sex before," he withered. Lifting the box, and his glass, he walked through to the living room.

"It's not about sex," Freya replied, shaking her head.

Dan was about to place the take-out onto the coffee table when Freya had spoken. His hand hovered in midair as he looked at her with one eyebrow raised skeptically.

"Okay, so it's partly about the sex," Freya conceded, rolling her eyes. "I just miss her presence, though. The past six months have been amazing; I finally feel like I'm where I should be." She looked up towards the ceiling, as if trying to pluck the words that could describe the happiness that she was experiencing. "I mean, we're great, and things are going well with the show now. They're putting us into a midseason replacement slot next month, and Eleanor's confident that we'll get a full season next year. So, no job hunting stress." She took a deep breath, "I'm going to do it, Dan. I'm going to ask her."

Dan sank into the sofa, his wine in one hand and a pizza slice in the other. He took a measured sip from his wine, "Ask her what, sweetie?"

Tucking her leg behind her, Freya sat down on the sofa beside her best friend, "To move in with me."

A look of confusion descended on Dan's face. "Aren't you already living together?" he asked through a mouthful of pizza.

Leaning forward for another slice of pizza, Freya shook her head, "Not officially."

"Ahh, my mistake, what with you never being apart for the past six months and everything, it's easy to get confused with the age-old lesbian U-Haul shibboleth," Dan replied, smiling. "So you're really going to ask her? That's huge!" He caught the look of panic on Freya's face. "Not huge, small, teeny actually, hardly worth the bother," he added quickly.

"So, how am I going to do it?" she asked, sipping her wine.

Dan let his head fall back in thought. It barely hit the back of the sofa when it shot back up. "Put her house up for sale! She's away, it could be on the market before she returns in two days, thirty, whatever," he waved his hand dismissively.

"Will you be serious," Freya growled.

Scrunching his face up, Dan reached for another piece of pizza. "Who says I wasn't?" he muttered under his breath.

They sat in silence, considering what might be the best approach.

"Get her drunk," Dan mused. "Get her drunk, do the nubbing, and ask her in the throws. She'll give you anything, you could probably get a kidney from her as well."

"You're no help."

Dan reached for a yellow Post-it pad on the table and grabbed a black sharpie. His face contorted in concentration as he wrote on the pad before detaching the Post-it and passing it to Freya. Written in his neat handwriting was…

Get her drunk – tequila not wine, tequila makes her happy. Wine = morose

Get tipsy yourself – not drunk…you're a messy drunk – you'll barf

FFS Ask… just ask her!…She'll say yes

Laughing, Freya stuck the Post-it to the table, "So I have a three point plan."

"You do indeed, now entertain me, wench. What DVD did you choose for our besties night?"

Freya leapt up and grabbed the DVD box from beside the television. "The Grudge," she said, her eyes sparkling with excitement.

"Again with the horror movies," Dan sighed, pulling the cushion out from behind his back and positioning it on his lap, ready to bury his head in it during the majority of the film.

***

Jordan used her key to open Freya's front door. She pulled her suitcase in behind her and left it propped against the wall in the hallway. She was beat after being in New York on a whistle stop tour of every chat show known to man, promoting her about-to-be- released full album of songs.

"Freya, you home?" she pouted when she received no response. Slipping her feet out of her shoes, she groaned in pleasure at the sensation and padded through to the living room, flopping down onto Freya's sofa.

She closed her eyes and let out a long contented sigh at being home. She smiled at the thought that, when the cab driver had asked for her address, the first one that came out of her mouth wasn't her own. She wanted to see Freya and didn't want to wait. However, it appeared that her arrival was ill-timed, as her girlfriend was obviously out somewhere. Deciding to go make herself a drink, Jordan wandered into the kitchen. She snorted at the DVD rental sitting waiting to go back, knowing that Freya must have had Dan round and tortured the poor man with horror movies while she was away.

Grabbing a soda from the fridge, she made her way back towards the sofa, intent on welding her backside to it until Freya returned. Her eyes absently scanned the coffee table. She smiled as she spotted a magazine with her girlfriend's face looking back at her from the front cover, a white sheet draped around her naked body. Lifting the glossy, she gave a small laugh at the inset photograph of the two of them walking hand in hand down a street, looking relaxed in jeans, Tshirts and sunglasses. Her eye was then drawn to a yellow piece of paper tucked inside the cover of the publication. Pulling it out, her eyebrows raised in surprise as she read the writing on it.

Freya pulled the thin pocket out from inside the waistband of her running shorts. She snagged her key from the material and unlocked her front door, wiping a wet strand of hair from her sweat-laced face. She had put one foot over the threshold when she spotted Jordan's case, as she pulled the earphone buds from her ears and closed the door.

"Jordan!" she yelled excitedly, skipping into the living room. Her progress stalled as she was greeted by Jordan reading the threepoint-plan Post-it.

Jordan lifted up her forefinger with the note stuck to it. "Hi, is there something you want to ask? Something that requires Dan to write you a list and apparently," she looked at the note again, "also requires a lot of alcohol?"

Gulping, Freya smiled weakly. She puffed out her cheeks.

Now, Easter, she thought, *say it…do it…speak.*

"Iwantustolivetogether, here, or at yours, or somewhere else. Just together."

Smiling, Jordan looked at the note again, "I have to say, Dan knows us pretty well. One, tequila does make me happy. I might challenge morose, though. Two, you do get messy when you're drunk. Funny, but messy and, well, number three." She stood up and walked towards Freya, who was looking at her, her expressive face a mix of apprehension and anticipation, "Number three, was never in doubt."

January 2014

"Put it down over there," Jordan gestured with her head, her arms busy trying to keep hold of Roxie in an attempt to keep the small dog from getting in everyone's path. A very red looking Dan and Jackson carried the sideboard into the room and placed it down carefully where Jordan had indicated. The two men were out of breath from carrying various pieces of furniture and boxes from the rental van into Freya's house, while all the time navigating their way around Roxie, who was on hyper mode with all of her favorite people in one place and so much activity. She was continually being dragged away by either Jordan or Freya, much to the little dog's chagrin.

Finally, after much discussion, it was agreed that Jordan would move into Freya's, as it was a bigger property. There had been some last minute lobbying for the buying of somewhere completely new to both of them and beside the beach. However, both of them had ignored Dan and his pleas.

"I'll go get you both something to drink," Jordan smiled, gratefully plonking Roxie down, who immediately launched herself towards Dan and Jackson, dropping onto her back at their feet for a tummy tickle. Jordan rolled her eyes. "Tart," she muttered towards the dog as she opened the kitchen door.

Sabrina sat on a stool at the kitchen island, with an open box in front of her. She was pulling things from it and handing them to Freya, who looked wide-eyed around the kitchen trying to decide where to put them. Jordan was prepared to not find anything she needed when she next cooked, and made a mental note to reorganize the kitchen the next time Freya was out.

"What's this?" Sabrina asked, her face puckered in confusion, as she pulled out a kitchen appliance, jumping slightly as she pressed the button and it made a noise. Freya looked at it and opened her mouth, pausing as she realized that she had no idea. She looked over helplessly at Jordan, who shook her head in disbelief.

"Seriously?" she asked, looking at the two women. Then remembering who she was speaking to, she closed her eyes and gave a small headshake, "It's a blender, I know you've seen a blender before."

Scowling, Sabrina passed the appliance across to Freya. "I've seen blenders, just not like that," she added indignantly.

Freya took the blender and looked it over. "What she said," she added, before turning and crouching down to put it into a cupboard.

Jordan wasn't sure who'd put the two most clueless-in-thekitchen people in charge of unpacking her kitchen things but, whoever it was, they were not high on her Christmas card list. She turned to the fridge to grab two sodas for Dan and Jackson, turning as she heard a snigger from Sabrina. She was holding Jordan's turkey baster in her hand with a knowing smirk on her lips. Freya stood up and rolled her eyes, "Okay, even I know what that's for."

"Sure you do," Sabrina grinned. "You know, if you two lady lovahs ever decide, I was a doctor."

"You're an actress, you played a doctor," Jordan scowled, snatching the baster from Sabrina. "And that's for Thanksgiving." She put the offending item down onto the kitchen island, ignoring Sabrina's snorts.

Sabrina picked the baster back up. "So, have you thought about it?" she asked absently as she squeezed the bulb, blowing air onto the palm of her hand.

"What, about you inserting kitchen accessories up my hooha?" Freya asked. "Have to say, not something I've given a lot of thought to." She took the baster from Sabrina and stuffed it into a drawer, "If you're talking about having kids, yes we have."

Sabrina raised an eyebrow in surprise, "Aaaand?"

Freya exhaled loudly. "Aaaand, when the time is right, then we will think about it some more. First thing is to get Jordan moved in," she grinned.

"You realize she's going to reorganize the entire kitchen, don't you?" Sabrina mused, surveying the room.

"As soon as my back is turned," Freya replied with a nod.

February 2014

Jordan's back arched, her feet pressed down onto the mattress lifting her hips up, and she gripped the sheet on the bed as Freya continued to tease her, prolonging her orgasm. Her body quivering in small spasms as her girlfriend relentlessly caressed her with her tongue.

Both were so enraptured in their love-making that neither heard the front door open and close. Dan burst into their bedroom.

"He's done it!" he exclaimed, starting to pace back and forth at the bottom of their bed, his wild eyes not registering the look of horror on Jordan's face as she clutched the sheet up against her naked chest. "Honestly, the bastard's done it," he ranted.

Freya remained frozen between Jordan's thighs, receiving a blow to the back of her head when she ran her tongue over where she knew Jordan would be overly sensitive following her cataclysmic, if somewhat rudely interrupted, orgasm.

Jordan cleared her throat, "Done what?" she asked, heaving herself up slightly on the bed, her legs pulled up with her girlfriend still positioned between them under the covers.

Dan stopped pacing and turned to face her. Taking in her position for the first time, his jaw dropped. "Is she in there?" he pointed between Jordan's legs.

Feeling her face start to flush, Jordan opened her mouth. But before she could respond, a muffled voice came out from under the bedclothes, "I'm here!"

Jordan twirled her hand in the air with a look of fake nonchalance on her face. "She's there," she confirmed.

"Did you hear me? He's done it," Dan repeated.

Jordan yelped as Freya used her hip as leverage to propel herself up and out of the covers, momentarily lying on top of her girlfriend before rolling off, pulling the sheet up to cover them both as she went. "The whole damn street heard you. Did what? And this had better be bloody good, Daniel Wright."

"You full-named me," Dan said, aghast. Assessing his best friend's current arrangement, he gave a small nod of acknowledgement, "Okay, probably deserved, given that I interrupted obvious nubbing. I'm sorry, but this is big, huge, massive." He held his arms out wide.

Jordan rubbed her hip under the cover, shooting Freya a disgruntled look, "What did Jackson do, Dan?"

Dan stood with a look of disbelief on his face, "He's only bloody asked me to marry him."

***

"I mean, marriage. I never!" Dan spluttered, his pacing had relocated from the bedroom to the kitchen as Jordan made them breakfast.

Freya watched her friend's movements, as if a spectator at a tennis match, her face contorting to the relevant facial responses to each of Dan's new rants. "I never thought I'd meet someone that I loved enough to marry," he admitted.

Freya bit her bottom lip and nodded thoughtfully. "You know, as your ex-wife, I'm a little put out by that," she said, ignoring the chuckle that came from the cooker where Jordan was cooking breakfast.

Dan stopped pacing and looked at her incredulously. "No time for funnies, Freya Easter, I'm having a frigging melt-down," he wailed.

Roxie started to bark as the front door opened and slammed close.

"Good job I made extra eggs," Jordan mused, waiting on Jackson's arrival.

"Who does that?" Jackson yelled at Dan as he entered the kitchen.

"Morning, Jackson," Freya said brightly, standing up on the stool and leaning over the table to snatch the orange juice from where Jordan had put it down.

Jackson turned his head quickly towards her. "Morning, Freya," he acknowledged. "Jordan."

Jordan waved her spatula at him in response.

"Who does that?" he repeated, glaring at Dan.

"I, I…" Dan started.

"Who storms off, two seconds after he's proposed to?" Jackson seethed. "What the fuck, Dan? I love you and I want to marry you. So will you just get over whatever breakdown you're having, and say yes," he bellowed.

"I'll say yes when I'm ready to say yes," Dan roared in response.

Jordan and Freya exchanged weary glances.

"I love you and I'm scared, I've never loved someone like I love you," Dan continued to holler. "So give me an arsing minute to have a ruddy great hissy fit. I never contemplated getting married to someone I love."

Freya raised her hand in the air, "Again, taking offence." She was stopped from adding anything further as a dishcloth flew through the air and wrapped itself round her face. She pulled the material down and glared over at Jordan, whose face was a picture of innocence.

"So yes, I'm freaking out a little," Dan added quietly, ignoring Freya's comment.

Jackson walked over and took Dan into his arms. "I love you and I know you're freaked," he said gently. "I just want to spend the rest of my life with you."

Dan hugged his boyfriend tightly. "Yes," he whispered against Jackson's shoulder. "Yes, I'll marry you."

Freya leapt off her stool and wound her arms as far as she could round the two men. "Yay," she cried, squeezing them. "Although Dan, still miffed," she added, her head tucked underneath Jackson's armpit.

Jordan watched the three of them with her head tilted to the side in thought. She felt her breath catch as she came to a decision.

***

Freya hopped off the golf cart outside her trailer and thanked the driver, before walking the short distance to her sanctuary on the set. She grimaced at the pain that the shoes her character insisted on wearing caused her. It was times like these that she really missed her scrubs and uniform.

"Hi."

She looked up in surprise as she opened the door to the trailer and climbed in. "Jordan? Did I forget something? Has something happened?" she asked, panic edging on her voice as she looked at her girlfriend standing with her back pressed against the units that edged the trailer.

"Nope, you didn't and there hasn't," Jordan smiled, pulling Freya to her and kissing her. "I just wanted to see you, so I sneaked off my set and infiltrated yours."

Freya grinned widely. "I like it when you infiltrate," she hummed, pressing her lips against Jordan's. "I have about an hour before I'm due back on set," she murmured, lowering her lips onto Jordan's neck.

Jordan's hands grasped the work surface behind her as she was almost overtaken with desire. Her eyes rolled back into hooded lids, before she gathered her wits again, "I brought you dessert."

Giggling against Jordan's neck, Freya continued to kiss, nibbling beneath Jordan's earlobe. "And I'm just about to have some of that dessert," her lips grazing Jordan's skin as she spoke.

"No, actual dessert," Jordan laughed, pushing Freya away from her gently and taking a deep breath to compose herself. She moved away from the counter that she was leaning against, to reveal a pie sitting on top.

Freya laughed. "I'm pretty sure, we've had this conversation before," she chewed on her cheek in concentration. "You bought me pie?" she asked, summoning up the words that she had used on that occasion.

Jordan shook her head and smiled, remembering her response, "Nuhuh, I *made* you pie." She pulled out a fork, sliced a piece of the pie, and put it onto a plate, passing it to her girlfriend, "In fact I made you my own special recipe key lime pie."

"You made me your 'marry me' dish," Freya smiled, closing her eyes in pleasure, as she tasted the dish.

Gulping, Jordan nodded, "I did." A hesitant smile played on her face as she licked her lips, "Freya?"

The dark-haired woman was making small, appreciative noises as the pie melted against her tongue. "Hmmm," she groaned, breaking off another slice to bring to her lips.

"Marry me?"

Freya's fork stopped in midair, the pie slithered from its perch on the cutlery and dropped back onto the plate. "Say wha..?" Freya asked in a dazed tone.

"I made you my 'marry me' pie because that's exactly what I want. You to marry me," Jordan said expectantly.

Still stunned, Freya licked crumbs from her lips and placed the plate carefully down onto the counter. She looked lovingly at her girlfriend, and nodded slowly.

Jordan's hesitant look fell from her face, replaced by utter joy as she swept Freya up into her arms, "Seriously?"

"Seriously, I want to marry you. I have since the first time I had your pie," Freya grinned as Jordan lifted her feet off the ground.

"You dirty, dirty, woman," Jordan chuckled.

Freya frowned, "I was talking about your pie, not your pie." She waggled her eyes suggestively, "However…" She pulled away from Jordan and flicked the lock on her trailer door, "I do think we have a little celebrating to do."

August 2014

"You should pee before we go in," Dan instructed, playing absently with the platinum wedding band on his finger. Even after two months of marriage he still wasn't used to the band and it had become his new 'go to' nervous habit. "'cause once you're in, you're in."

Freya jiggled her leg nervously against the floor of the limo. She looked down at her hands, smiling as the light caught the diamond on her left hand.

"He's right," Jordan added. "I've regretted not going before when I've been at these things."

Freya grumbled, her level of anxiety had been steadily increasing all day as she was primped and preened for the awards show. Her desire to bolt had almost overwhelmed her as Jordan had zipped her into the dark blue dress that she had chosen for the event, her stomach only stilling as her fiancé kissed her shoulder.

"I hate these things normally, but being nominated has just put my hatred up about twenty notches," she moaned. "Usually I just sat there for my parents and watched, but now there are expectations on me."

Jackson shrugged. "I don't get what the big deal is. You practically grew up playing with Oscars like Barbie dolls, and Jordan keeps her awards in the loo," he remarked, referring to the TONY and SAG awards that decorated their bathroom at home.

Jordan scowled at him. "You are going to be great," she said, turning her attention to Freya. "I am so, so, proud of you, and I will love you no matter the outcome," she said, gripping Freya's hand as the limo pulled up outside the theatre hosting the awards. She prompted Dan with her head, frowning at him.

"Me too," he added, rolling his eyes.

The limo driver opened their door, and Jackson and Dan stepped out to shield them from the photographers as they climbed out of the car. Freya let out one last burst of air before positioning her face into a professional mask of smiles. She paused at the car before Jordan reached down and laced their fingers. "Let's go rock the red carpet together," she whispered to her fiancé.

Nodding, Freya walked with Jordan as their two best friends followed them. For the first time ever, she was almost enjoying the experience of the red carpet, as she gripped Jordan's hand tightly. The actresses smiled and posed for the cameras. Hearing shouts from the stands, for the first time since she climbed out of the car, Freya smiled genuinely across at the fans waving to her. She laughed and squeezed Jordan's hand to get her attention, pointing out a sign in the crowd saying 'Dollhausen all the way'. They both smiled broadly and waved at the fan holding the sign. They entered the theatre and paused before separating, as they were there with contingents from their respective shows, and not sitting together.

"I'll see you afterwards," Freya said, giving Jordan a hesitant smile.

Jordan smiled warmly in response. "I will see you afterwards," she repeated in response. She gave Freya's hand one last squeeze, and then turned with Jackson towards the entrance for her seat.

Freya looked at Dan, "Well, Mr. Wright, escort me."

Dan grinned and held his arm out. "You sure you don't want to pee, Egg?" he asked again.

"For the twentieth time, no, I don't need to pee," Freya growled.

"Freya!"

Freya turned around in surprise at Jordan's voice behind her. She looked across the foyer to where Jordan stood looking resplendent with her curves accentuated by the cut and flow of the striking red dress. 'I love you,' Jordan mouthed.

Nodding, a wide smile on her face, Freya mouthed, 'I love you too,' in response.

Jordan lifted her shoulders in happiness, and then swept off to take her seat.

Freya turned back to her friend and thumped his chest, "Okay, now I need to pee."

Freya hated these events. She sat fidgeting and grumbling to herself that her dress, while looking fabulous when gliding down the red carpet or posing for photographers, was too darn tight to sit in, especially when the ceremony threatened to go on until the end of time.

"Will you stop fidgeting and sit still?" Dan hissed beside her. He straightened back up, and tugged on his tux jacket as he shot her one last glare before focusing back on the stage.

Freya frowned, giving a slight wiggle of her shoulders as she attempted to get comfortable.

"Don't frown. If they pan to you, you'll look terrible," Dan muttered out of the side of his mouth.

Relaxing her face, Freya refocused her attention on the stage. She needed to pee, badly, and now that she was thinking about peeing the need to pee was even greater. She leaned over towards Dan, "I need to pee."

"But you went before we came into the hall."

"I know, and now I need to go again," she hissed in reply.

Dan rolled his eyes, "You don't need to, you just think you do. Now sit still and look pretty."

She sat up, her leg jiggling nervously as she turned and looked around her. The familiar faces of people she knew or watched on TV surrounded her, though she sighed at not being able to see the face that she was most desperate to see. She knew she was in the hall somewhere, but short of standing up and straining her neck around, Freya hadn't been able to spot her.

She looked down as she felt a hand rest on her knee to stop the movement.

"She's here, you saw her go in. Now sit still for one bloody minute."

She placed her hand on Dan's, giving it a tight squeeze. Embarrassed at being so transparent, Freya settled down. As the ceremony progressed, she clapped when prompted by Dan. She could feel the butterflies in her stomach take on albatross proportions, as her nerves increased the closer they came to the category that was their reason for attending.

"The nominations for outstanding lead actress in a drama series are…"

Freya sat up, her nerves now playing havoc with her desire to pee. She clapped as the nominees were read out, stopping as her own name was called and giving a smile and a wave to the camera.

"If you lose, just keep smiling. But just so you know, we're through, 'cause I was only with you for the fame," Dan whispered, making Freya belly laugh.

"And the Emmy goes to Freya Easter, for *The Publicist*."

Freya froze, her eyes widened as she realized that she had won. She stood up slowly and kissed Dan quickly, then started to make her way towards the stage. The sound of clapping and cheering blurred her senses as she nervously pressed at the material of her dark blue dress. She climbed the stairs, unable to stop smiling as she accepted the award and kissed the host and award's presenter, who pointed her towards the microphones in the center of the stage. She walked over, looking at the gold statue in her hand.

Looking out across the hall, Freya let out a deep breath, "Wow, just wow. I have so many people to thank. The cast and crew of *The Publicist*, you make coming in to work each day an adventure and pleasure. My agent Dominick, for putting up with me. To Eleanor French for her talent, drive, and passion. It is a joy to work with you and be part of something wonderful." She took another breath, desperate to cram her thanks in before she got the wind up sign, "To my parents, for their unwavering love and support, and Anna, I'm sure that you'll be overjoyed that, finally, I've added my contribution to the Conor haul. I love you Grandma, and yes, she will kill me for calling her that. My two best friends Dan and Jackson, I love you more than is healthy, and finally."

She stopped and put a hand above her eyes to block out the spotlights distorting her vision.

"I know you're out there somewhere," she smiled as she spotted two tear-laden brown eyes watching her, hands up at her mouth only partially hiding the wide proud smile plastered on her face.

"There you are. My soon-to-be-wife Jordan, with whom I fell in love when I first saw her in BDUs and a tank top. That woman can rock a uniform. Despite that, I had to wait an age for our paths to cross, for her to love me back, and then for our stars to collide again to make it stick. I love you more and more each day," she grinned wildly, holding up the award. "Honey, I finally have something for our bathroom!"

Other Titles by Author

SILVER WINGS

Winner - 2014 Golden Crown Literary Society - Historical Fiction

ISBN-13: 978-1482023572

When in 1943, twenty-five-year-old Lily Rivera is widowed, she finally feels able to step out of the shadows of an unhappy marriage. Her love of flying leads her to join the Women's Airforce Service Pilots, determined to regain her passion and spread her wings, not suspecting that she would experience more than just flying.

Helen Richmond, a Hollywood stunt pilot, has never experienced a love that lifted her as high as the aircraft she flew...until she meets Lily.

Both women join the W.A.S.P. program to serve their country and instead find that they are on a collision course towards each other. But can it last?

GRACE FALLS

Highest Amazon.com and Amazon.co.uk Rank

#1 Lesbian Romance

#1 Lesbian Fiction

ISBN-13: 978-1495400544

Dr Maddie Marinelli is looking for a fresh start; she's leaving behind the ghost of a failed relationship and looking forward to starting a new job and life in San Francisco...what she didn't count on was car trouble and the colorful residents of Grace Falls.

Alex Milne has spent most her adult life putting other people's needs first. She is busy raising her daughter in her hometown while running her business and the last thing she expects is to be attracted to Grace Falls' newest, albeit reluctant, resident.

Sometimes you don't know what it is you're looking for, until it comes along and finds you.

About the Author

H.P. Munro lives in Edinburgh with her wife, and a wauzer named Boo. She started writing in 2010 when a new job took her away from home a lot and she found herself in airports, on flights and in hotel rooms with room service for one. The job didn't last but the love of writing did.

Her début novel Silver Wings won the Golden Crown Literary Society Historical Fiction award in 2014. Her second novel Grace Falls was published in Feb 2014 and quickly became a lesbian romance bestseller.

She is currently working on her fourth – 'Return to Grace Falls'.

How you can connect with HP - Website

- www.red-besom-books.com

Twitter - @munrohp

Facebook - https://www.facebook.com/munrohp

Email - munrohp@gmail.com

46136804R00186

Made in the USA
Lexington, KY
24 October 2015